Praise for #1 *New York Times* bestselling author

*N*ORA
ROBERTS

"The publishing world might be hard-pressed
to find an author with a more diverse style or
fertile imagination than Roberts."
—*Publishers Weekly*

"You can't bottle wish fulfillment, but Nora Roberts
certainly knows how to put it on the page."
—*New York Times*

"A consistently entertaining writer."
—*USA TODAY*

"Roberts nails her characters and settings with
awesome precision, drawing readers into a vividly rendered
world of family-centered warmth."
—*Library Journal*

"Some estimates have [Nora Roberts]
selling 12 books an hour, 24 hours a day,
7 days a week, 52 weeks a year."
—*New York Times Magazine*

"Roberts is indeed a word artist, painting her story
and her characters with vitality and verve."
—*Los Angeles Daily News*

"Roberts has a warm feel for her characters
and an eye for the evocative detail."
—*Chicago Tribune*

Dear Reader,

Any month with a new Nora Roberts book has to be special, and this month is *extra* special because we have for you the first two books in an exciting trilogy called The Stars of Mithra. This classic miniseries by the incomparable master of romantic suspense revolves around three strong heroines and the three priceless gems that are destined to bring them love and romance.

The adventure begins in *Hidden Star* when Bailey James wakes up in a strange hotel room with no memory of how she got there—or who she is. Knowing only that she's in big trouble, she seeks out the help of coolheaded—until he sees her—private eye Cade Parris. There's nothing Cade wants more than to believe Bailey's strange story, but what is she doing with a sackful of cash and a diamond the size of a baby's fist?

In *Captive Star* cynical bounty hunter Jack Dakota goes after bail jumper M. J. O'Leary, only to discover that she's innocent—and they've both been set up. Now, handcuffed together, they must go on the run from a pair of hired killers after the giant blue diamond hidden in M.J.'s purse.

In February look for the third book in the Stars of Mithra trilogy, *Secret Star*, along with a bonus book, *Treasures Lost, Treasures Found*, in the new Nora Roberts volume *Treasures*.

Enjoy!

The Editors
Silhouette Books

NORA ROBERTS

STARS

Published by Silhouette Books

America's Publisher of Contemporary Romance

 SILHOUETTE BOOKS
®

STARS

ISBN-13: 978-0-373-28562-4
ISBN-10:   0-373-28562-0

Copyright © 2007 by Harlequin Books S.A.

The publisher acknowledges the copyright holder
of the individual works as follows:

HIDDEN STAR
Copyright © 1997 by Nora Roberts

CAPTIVE STAR
Copyright © 1997 by Nora Roberts

Visit Silhouette Books at www.eHarlequin.com

Printed in U.S.A.

CONTENTS

HIDDEN STAR   9

CAPTIVE STAR   273

HIDDEN STAR

To white knights and their damsels

Chapter 1

Cade Parris wasn't having the best of days when the woman of his dreams walked into his office. His secretary had quit the day before—not that she'd been much of a prize anyway, being more vigilant about her manicure than maintaining the phone logs. But he needed someone to keep track of things and shuffle papers into files. Even the raise he offered out of sheer desperation hadn't swayed her to give up her sudden determination to become a country-and-western singing sensation.

So his secretary was heading off to Nashville in a second-hand pickup, and his office looked like the ten miles of bad road he sincerely hoped she traveled.

She hadn't exactly had her mind on her work the past month or two. That impression had been more than confirmed when he fished a bologna sandwich out of the file drawer. At least he thought the blob in the plastic bag was bologna. And it had been filed under *L*—for Lunch?

He didn't bother to swear, nor did he bother to answer the phone that rang incessantly on the empty desk in his reception area. He had reports to type up, and as typing wasn't one of his finer skills, he just wanted to get on with it.

Parris Investigations wasn't what some would call a thriving enterprise. But it suited him, just as the cluttered two-room office squeezed into the top floor of a narrow brick building with bad plumbing in North West D.C. suited him.

He didn't need plush carpets or polished edges. He'd grown up with all that, with the pomp and pretenses, and had had his fill of it all by the time he reached the age of twenty. Now, at thirty, with one bad marriage behind him and a family who continued to be baffled by his pursuits, he was, by and large, a contented man.

He had his investigator's license, a decent reputation as a man who got the job done, and enough income to keep his agency well above water.

Though actual business income was a bit of a

problem just then. He was in what he liked to call a lull. Most of his caseload consisted of insurance and domestic work—a few steps down from the thrills he'd imagined when he set out to become a private investigator. He'd just cleaned up two cases, both of them minor insurance frauds that hadn't taken much effort or innovation to close.

He had nothing else coming in, his greedy bloodsucker of a landlord was bumping up his rent, the engine in his car had been making unsettling noises lately, his air conditioner was on the fritz. And the roof was leaking again.

He took the spindly yellow-leafed philodendron his double-crossing secretary had left behind and set it on the uncarpeted floor under the steady drip, hoping it might drown.

He could hear a voice droning into his answering machine. It was his mother's voice. Lord, he thought, did a man ever really escape his mother?

"Cade, dear, I hope you haven't forgotten the Embassy Ball. You know you're to escort Pamela Lovett. I had lunch with her aunt today, and she tells me that Pamela just looks marvelous after her little sojourn to Monaco."

"Yeah, yeah, yeah," he muttered, and narrowed his eyes at the computer. He and machines had poor and untrusting relationships.

He sat down and faced the screen as his mother continued to chatter: "Have you had your tux cleaned? Do make time to get a haircut, you looked so scraggly the last time I saw you."

And don't forget to wash behind the ears, he thought sourly, and tuned her out. She was never going to accept that the Parris life-style wasn't his life-style, that he just didn't want to lunch at the club or squire bored former debutantes around Washington and that his opinion wasn't going to change by dint of her persuasion.

He'd wanted adventure, and though struggling to type up a report on some poor slob's fake whiplash wasn't exactly Sam Spade territory, he was doing the job. Mostly he didn't feel useless or bored or out of place. He liked the sound of traffic outside his window, even though the window was only open because the building and its scum-sucking landlord didn't go in for central air-conditioning and his unit was broken. The heat was intense, and the rain was coming in, but with the window closed, the offices would have been as airless and stifling as a tomb.

Sweat rolled down his back, making him itchy and ir-ritable. He was stripped down to a T-shirt and jeans, his long fingers fumbling a bit on the computer keys. He had to shovel his hair out of his face several times, which ticked him off. His mother was right. He needed a haircut.

So when it got in the way again, he ignored it, as he

ignored the sweat, the heat, the buzz of traffic, the steady drip from the ceiling. He sat, methodically punching a key at a time, a remarkably handsome man with a scowl on his face.

He'd inherited the Parris looks—the clever green eyes that could go broken-bottle sharp or as soft as sea mist, depending on his mood. The hair that needed a trim was dark mink brown and tended to wave. Just now, it curled at his neck, over his ears, and was beginning to annoy him. His nose was straight, aristocratic and a little long, his mouth firm and quick to smile when he was amused. And to sneer when he wasn't.

Though his face had become more honed since the embarrassing cherubic period of his youth and early adolescence, it still sported dimples. He was looking forward to middle age, when, with luck, they'd become manly creases.

He'd wanted to be rugged, and instead was stuck with the slick, dreamy good looks of a *GQ* cover—for one of which he'd posed in his middle twenties, under protest and great family pressure.

The phone rang again. This time he heard his sister's voice, haranguing him about missing some lame cocktail party in honor of some big-bellied senator she was endorsing.

He thought about just ripping the damn answering machine out of the wall and heaving it, and his sister's nagging voice, out the window into the traffic on Wisconsin Avenue.

Then the rain that was only adding to the miserably thick heat began to drip on the top of his head. The computer blinked off, for no reason he could see other than sheer nastiness, and the coffee he'd forgotten he was heating boiled over with a spiteful hiss.

He leaped up, burned his hand on the pot. He swore viciously as the pot smashed, shattering glass, and spewing hot coffee in all directions. He ripped open a drawer, grabbed for a stack of napkins and sliced his thumb with the lethal edge of his former—and now thoroughly damned to perdition—secretary's nail file.

When the woman walked in, he was still cursing and bleeding and had just tripped over the philodendron set in the middle of the floor and didn't even look up.

It was hardly a wonder she simply stood there, damp from the rain, her face pale as death and her eyes wide with shock.

"Excuse me." Her voice sounded rusty, as if she hadn't used it in days. "I must have the wrong office." She inched backward, and those big, wide brown eyes shifted to the name printed on the door. She hesitated, then looked back at him. "Are you Mr. Parris?"

There was a moment, one blinding moment, when he couldn't seem to speak. He knew he was staring at her, couldn't help himself. His heart simply stood still.

His knees went weak. And the only thought that came to his mind was *There you are, finally. What the hell took you so long?*

And because that was so ridiculous, he struggled to put a bland, even cynical, investigator's expression on his face.

"Yeah." He remembered the handkerchief in his pocket, and wrapped it over his busily bleeding thumb. "Just had a little accident here."

"I see." Though she didn't appear to, the way she continued to stare at his face. "I've come at a bad time. I don't have an appointment. I thought maybe…"

"Looks like my calendar's clear."

He wanted her to come in, all the way in. Whatever that first absurd, unprecedented reaction of his, she was still a potential client. And surely no dame who ever walked through Sam Spade's hallowed door had ever been more perfect.

She was blond and beautiful and bewildered. Her hair was wet, sleek down to her shoulders and straight as the rain. Her eyes were bourbon brown, in a face that— though it could have used some color—was delicate as a fairy's. It was heart-shaped, the cheeks a gentle curve and the mouth was full, unpainted and solemn.

She'd ruined her suit and shoes in the rain. He recognized both as top-quality, that quietly exclusive look found only in designer salons. Against the wet blue silk of her suit, the canvas bag she clutched with both hands looked intriguingly out of place.

Damsel in distress, he mused, and his lips curved. Just what the doctor ordered.

"Why don't you come in, close the door, Miss…?"

Her heart bumped twice, hammer-hard, and she tightened her grip on the bag. "You're a private investigator?"

"That's what it says on the door." Cade smiled again, ruthlessly using the dimples while he watched her gnaw that lovely lower lip. Damned if he wouldn't like to gnaw on it himself.

And that response, he thought with a little relief, was a lot more like it. Lust was a feeling he could understand.

"Let's go back to my office." He surveyed the damage—broken glass, potting soil, pools of coffee. "I think I'm finished in here for now."

"All right." She took a deep breath, stepped in, then closed the door. She supposed she had to start somewhere.

Picking her way over the debris, she followed him into the adjoining room. It was furnished with little more than a desk and a couple of bargain-basement chairs. Well, she couldn't be choosy about decor, she reminded herself. She waited until he'd sat behind his desk, tipped back in his chair and smiled at her again in that quick, trust-me way.

"Do you— Could I—" She squeezed her eyes tight, centered herself again. "Do you have some credentials I could see?"

More intrigued, he took out his license, handed it to her. She wore two very lovely rings, one on each hand, he noticed. One was a square-cut citrine in an antique setting, the other a trio of colored stones. Her earrings matched the second ring, he noted when she tucked her hair behind her ear and studied his license as if weighing each printed word.

"Would you like to tell me what the problem is, Miss…?"

"I think—" She handed him back his license, then gripped the bag two-handed again. "I think I'd like to hire you." Her eyes were on his face again, as intently, as searchingly, as they had been on the license. "Do you handle missing-persons cases?"

Who did you lose, sweetheart? he wondered. He hoped, for her sake and for the sake of the nice little fantasy that was building in his head, it wasn't a husband. "Yeah, I handle missing persons."

"Your, ah, rate?"

"Two-fifty a day, plus expenses." When she nodded, he slid over a legal pad, picked up a pencil. "Who do you want me to find?"

She took a long, shuddering breath. "Me. I need you to find me."

Watching her, he tapped the pencil against the pad. "Looks like I already have. You want me to bill you, or do you want to pay now?"

"No." She could feel it cracking. She'd held on so long—or at least it seemed so long—but now she could feel that branch she'd gripped when the world dropped out from under her begin to crack. "I don't remember. Anything. I don't—" Her voice began to hitch. She took her hands off the bag in her lap to press them to her face. "I don't know who I am. I don't know who I am." And then she was weeping the words into her hands. "I don't know who I am."

Cade had a lot of experience with hysterical women. He'd grown up with females who used flowing tears and gulping sobs as the answer to anything from a broken nail to a broken marriage. So he rose from his desk, armed himself with a box of tissues and crouched in front of her.

"Here now, sweetheart. Don't worry. It's going to be just fine." With gentle expertise, he mopped at her face as he spoke. He patted her hand, stroked her hair, studied her swimming eyes.

"I'm sorry. I can't—"

"Just cry it out," he told her. "You'll feel better for it." Rising, he went into the closet-size bathroom and poured her a paper cup of water.

When she had a lapful of damp tissues and three

crushed paper cups, she let out a little jerky sigh. "I'm sorry. Thank you. I do feel better." Her cheeks pinkened a bit with embarrassment as she gathered up the tissues and mangled cups. Cade took them from her, dumped them in the wastebasket, then rested a hip on the corner of his desk.

"You want to tell me about it now?"

She nodded, then linked her fingers and began to twist them together. "I— There isn't that much to tell. I just don't remember anything. Who I am, what I do, where I'm from. Friends, family. Nothing." Her breath caught again, and she released it slowly. "Nothing," she repeated.

It was a dream come true, he thought, the beautiful woman without a past coming out of the rain and into his office. He flicked a glance at the bag she still held in her lap. They'd get to that in a minute. "Why don't you tell me the first thing you do remember?"

"I woke up in a room—a little hotel on Sixteenth Street." Letting her head rest back against the chair, she closed her eyes and tried to bring things into focus. "Even that's unclear. I was curled up on the bed, and there was a chair propped under the doorknob. It was raining. I could hear the rain. I was groggy and disoriented, but my heart was pounding so hard, as if I'd wakened from a nightmare. I still had my shoes on. I remember wondering why I'd gone to bed with my shoes on. The room was dim and stuffy. All the windows were closed. I was so tired, logy, so I went into the bathroom to splash water on my face."

Now she opened her eyes, looked into his. "I saw my face in the mirror. This ugly little mirror with black splotches where it needed to be resilvered. And it meant nothing to me. The face." She lifted a hand, ran it over her cheek, her jaw. "My face meant nothing to me. I couldn't remember the name that went with the face, or the thoughts or the plans or the past. I didn't know how I'd gotten to that horrid room. I looked through the drawers and the closet, but there was nothing. No clothes. I was afraid to stay there, but I didn't know where to go."

"The bag? Was that all you had with you?"

"Yes." Her hand clutched at the straps again. "No purse, no wallet, no keys. This was in my pocket." She reached into the pocket of her jacket and took out a small scrap of notepaper.

Cade took it from her, skimmed the quick scrawling writing.

Bailey, Sat at 7, right? MJ

"I don't know what it means. I saw a newspaper. Today's Friday."

"Mmm. Write it down," Cade said, handing her a pad and pen.

"What?"

"Write down what it says on the note."

"Oh." Gnawing her lip again, she complied.

Though he didn't have to compare the two to come to his conclusions, he took the pad from her, set it and the note side by side. "Well, you're not M.J., so I'd say you're Bailey."

She blinked, swallowed. "What?"

"From the look of M.J.'s writing, he or she's a lefty. You're right-handed. You've got neat, simple penmanship, M.J.'s got an impatient scrawl. The note was in your pocket. Odds are you're Bailey."

"Bailey." She tried to absorb the name, the hope of it, the feel and taste of identity. But it was dry and unfamiliar. "It doesn't mean anything."

"It means we have something to call you, and someplace to start. Tell me what you did next."

Distracted she blinked at him. "Oh, I... There was a phone book in the room. I looked up detective agencies."

"Why'd you pick mine?"

"The name. It sounded strong." She managed her first smile, and though it was weak, it was there. "I started to call, but then I thought I might get put off, and if I just showed up... So I waited in the room until it was office hours, then I walked for a little while, then I got a cab. And here I am."

"Why didn't you go to a hospital? Call a doctor?"

"I thought about it." She looked down at her hands. "I just didn't."

She was leaving out big chunks, he mused. Going around his desk, he opened a drawer, pulled out a candy bar. "You didn't say anything about stopping for breakfast." He watched her study the candy he offered with puzzlement and what appeared to be amusement. "This'll hold you until we can do better."

"Thank you." With neat, precise movements, she unwrapped the chocolate bar. Maybe part of the fluttering in her stomach was hunger. "Mr. Parris, I may have people worried about me. Family, friends. I may have a child. I don't know." Her eyes deepened, fixed on a point over his shoulder. "I don't think I do. I can't believe anyone could forget her own child. But people may be worried, wondering what happened to me. Why I didn't come home last night."

"You could have gone to the police."

"I didn't want to go to the police." This time, her voice was clipped, definite. "Not until… No, I don't want to involve the police." She wiped her fingers on a fresh tissue, then began to tear it into strips. "Someone may be looking for me who isn't a friend, who isn't family. Who isn't concerned with my well-being. I don't know why I feel that way, I only know I'm afraid. It's more than just not remembering. But I can't understand anything, any of it, until I know who I am."

Maybe it was those big, soft, moist eyes staring up at him, or the damsel-in-distress nerves of her restless hands. Either way, he couldn't resist showing off, just a little.

"I can tell you a few things already. You're an intelligent woman, early-to-mid-twenties. You have a good eye for color and style, and enough of a bankroll to indulge it with Italian shoes and silk suits. You're neat, probably organized. You prefer the understated to the obvious. Since you don't evade well, I'd say you're an equally poor liar. You've got a good head on your shoulders, you think things through. You don't panic easily. And you like chocolate."

She balled the empty candy wrapper in her hand. "Why do you assume all that?"

"You speak well, even when you're frightened. You thought about how you were going to handle this and went through all the steps, logically. You dress well— quality over flair. You have a good manicure, but no flashy polish. Your jewelry is unique, interesting, but not ornate. And you've been holding back information since you walked through the door because you haven't decided yet how much you're going to trust me."

"How much should I trust you?"

"You came to me."

She acknowledged that, rose and walked to his window. The rain drummed, underscoring the vague headache that hovered just behind her eyes. "I don't recognize the city," she murmured. "Yet I feel I should. I know where I am, because I saw a newspaper, the *Washington Post.* I know what the White House and the Capitol look like. I know the monuments—but I could have seen them on television, or in a book."

Though it was wet from incoming rain, she rested her hands on the sill, appreciated the coolness there. "I feel as though I dropped out of nowhere into that ugly hotel room. Still, I know how to read and write and walk and talk. The cabdriver had the radio on, and I recognized music. I recognized trees. I wasn't surprised that rain was wet. I smelled burned coffee when I came in, and it wasn't an unfamiliar odor. I know your eyes are green. And when the rain clears, I know the sky will be blue."

She sighed once. "So I didn't drop out of nowhere. There are things I know, things I'm sure of. But my own face means nothing to me, and what's behind the face is blank. I may have hurt someone, done something. I may be selfish and calculating, even cruel. I may have a husband I cheat on or neighbors I've alienated."

She turned back then, and her face was tight and set, a tough contrast to the fragility of lashes still wet from tears. "I don't know if I'm going to like who you find when you find me, Mr. Parris, but I need to know." She set the bag on his desk, hesitated briefly, then opened it. "I think I have enough to meet your fee."

He came from money, the kind that aged and increased and propagated over generations. But even with his background, he'd never seen so much in one place at one time. The canvas bag was filled with wrapped stacks of hundred-dollar bills—all crisp and clean. Fascinated, Cade took out a stack, flipped through. Yes, indeed, he mused, every one of the bills had Ben Franklin's homely and dignified face.

"I'd have to guess about a million," he murmured.

"One million, two hundred thousand." Bailey shuddered as she looked into the bag. "I counted the stacks. I don't know where I got it or why I had it with me. I may have stolen it."

Tears began to swim again as she turned away. "It could be ransom money. I could be involved in a kidnapping. There could be a child somewhere, being held, and I've taken the ransom money. I just—"

"Let's add a vivid imagination to those other qualities."

It was the cool and casual tone of his voice that had her turning back. "There's a fortune in there."

"A million two isn't much of a fortune these days." He dropped the money back in the bag. "And I'm sorry, Bailey, you just don't fit the cold, calculating kidnapper type."

"But you can check. You can find out, discreetly, if there's been an abduction."

"Sure. If the cops are involved, I can get something."

"And if there's been a murder?" Struggling to stay calm, she reached into the bag again. This time she took out a .38.

A cautious man, Cade nudged the barrel aside, took it from her. It was a Smith and Wesson, and at his quick check, he discovered it was fully loaded. "How'd this feel in your hand?"

"I don't understand."

"How'd it feel when you picked it up? The weight, the shape?"

Though she was baffled by the question, she did her best to answer thoroughly. "Not as heavy as I thought it should. It seemed that something that had that kind of power would have more weight, more substance. I suppose it felt awkward."

"The pen didn't."

This time she simply dragged her hands through her hair. "I don't know what you're talking about. I've just shown you over a million dollars and a gun. You're talking about pens."

"When I handed you a pen to write, it didn't feel awkward. You didn't have to think about it. You just took it and used it." He smiled a little and slipped the gun into his pocket, instead of the bag. "I think you're a lot more accustomed to holding a pen than a .38 special."

There was some relief in that, the simple logic of

it. But it didn't chase away all the clouds. "Maybe you're right. It doesn't mean I didn't use it."

"No, it doesn't. And since you've obviously put your hands all over it, we can't prove you didn't. I can check and see if it's registered and to whom."

Her eyes lit with hope. "It could be mine." She reached out, took his hand, squeezed it in a gesture that was thoughtless and natural. "We'd have a name then. I'd know my name then. I didn't realize it could be so simple."

"It may be simple."

"You're right." She released his hand, began to pace. Her movements were smooth, controlled. "I'm getting ahead of myself. But it helps so much you see, so much more than I imagined, just to tell someone. Someone who knows how to figure things out. I don't know if I'm very good at puzzles. Mr. Parris—"

"Cade," he said, intrigued that he could find her economical movements so sexy. "Let's keep it simple."

"Cade." She drew in a breath, let it out. "It's nice to call someone by name. You're the only person I know, the only person I remember having a conversation with. I can't tell you how odd that is, and, right now, how comforting."

"Why don't we make me the first person you remember having a meal with? One candy bar isn't much of a breakfast. You look worn out, Bailey."

It was so odd to hear him use that name when he looked at her. Because it was all she had, she struggled to respond to it. "I'm tired," she admitted. "It doesn't feel as if I've slept very much. I don't know when I've eaten last."

"How do you feel about scrambled eggs?"

The smile wisped around her mouth again. "I haven't the faintest idea."

"Well, let's find out." He started to pick up the canvas bag, but she laid a hand over his on the straps.

"There's something else." She didn't speak for a moment, but kept her eyes on his, as she had when she first walked in. Searching, measuring, deciding. But there was, she knew, really no choice. He was all she had. "Before I show you, I need to ask for a promise."

"You hire me, Bailey, I work for you."

"I don't know if what I'm going to ask is completely ethical, but I still need your word. If during the course of your investigation you discover that I've committed a crime, I need your word that you'll find out everything you can, all the circumstances, all the facts, before you turn me over to the police."

He angled his head. "You assume I'll turn you in."

"If I've broken the law, I'll expect you to turn me over to the police. But I need all the reasons before you do. I need to understand all the whys, the hows, the who. Will you give me your word on that?"

"Sure." He took the hand she held out. It was delicate as porcelain, steady as a rock. And she, he thought, whoever she was, was a fascinating combination of the fragile and the steely. "No cops until we know all of it. You can trust me, Bailey."

"You're trying to make me comfortable with the name." Again, without thinking, in a move that was as innate as the color of her eyes, she kissed his cheek. "You're very kind."

Kind enough, she thought, that he would hold her now if she asked. And she so desperately wanted to be held, soothed, to be promised that her world would snap back into focus again at any moment. But she needed to stand on her own. She could only hope she was the kind of woman who stood on her own feet and faced her own problems.

"There's one more thing." She turned to the canvas bag again, slid her hand deep inside, felt for the thick velvet pouch, the weight of what was snugged inside it. "I think it's probably the most important thing."

She drew it out and very carefully, with what he thought of as reverence, untied the pouch and slid its contents into the cup of her palm.

The money had surprised him, the gun had concerned him. But this awed him. The gleam of it, the regal glint, even in the rain-darkened room, held a stunning and sumptuous power.

The gem filled the palm of her hand, its facets clean and sharp enough to catch even the faintest flicker of light and shoot it into the air in bright, burning lances. It belonged, he thought, on the crown of a mythical queen, or lying heavily between the breasts of some ancient goddess.

"I've never seen a sapphire that big."

"It isn't a sapphire." And when she passed it to his hand, she would have sworn she felt the exchange of heat. "It's a blue diamond, somewhere around a hundred carats. Brilliant-cut, most likely from Asia Minor. There are no inclusions visible to the naked eye, and it is rare in both color and size. I'd have to guess its market worth at easily three times the amount of money in the bag."

He wasn't looking at the gem any longer, but at her. When she lifted her eyes to his, she shook her head. "I don't know how I know. But I do. Just as I know it's not all…it's not…complete."

"What do you mean?"

"I wish I knew. But it's too strong a feeling, an almost-recognition. I know the stone is only part of the whole. Just as I know it can't possibly belong to me. It doesn't really belong to anyone. Any one," she repeated, separating the word into two. "I must have stolen it."

She pressed her lips together, lifted her chin, squared her shoulders. "I might have killed for it."

Chapter 2

Cade took her home. It was the best option he could think of, tucking her away. And he wanted that canvas bag and its contents in his safe as quickly as possible. She hadn't argued when he led her out of the building, had made no comment about the sleek little Jag parked in the narrow spot on the cracked asphalt lot.

He preferred using his nondescript and well-dented sedan for his work, but until it was out of the shop, he was stuck with the streamlined, eye-catching Jaguar.

But she said nothing, not even when he drove into a lovely old neighborhood with graceful shade trees and tidy flower-trimmed lawns and into the driveway of a dignified Federal-style brick house.

He'd been prepared to explain that he'd inherited it from a great-aunt who had a soft spot for him—which was true enough. And that he lived there because he liked the quiet and convenience of the established neighborhood in the heart of Washington.

But she didn't ask.

It seemed to Cade that she'd simply run down. Whatever energy had pushed her into going out in the rain, seeking his office and telling her story had drained out, leaving her listless.

And fragile again. He had to check the urge to simply gather her up and carry her inside. He could imagine it clearly—the stalwart knight, my lady's champion, carrying her into the safety of the castle and away from any and all dragons that plagued her.

He really had to stop thinking things like that.

Instead, he hefted the canvas bag, took her unresisting hand and led her through the graceful foyer, down the hall and directly into the kitchen.

"Scrambled eggs," he said, pulling out a chair for her and nudging her down to sit at the pedestal table.

"All right. Yes. Thank you."

She felt limp, unfocused, and terribly grateful to him. He wasn't peppering her with questions, nor had he looked particularly shocked or appalled by her story.

Perhaps it was the nature of his business that made him take it all in stride, but whatever the reason, she was thankful for the time he was giving her to recoup.

Now he was moving around the kitchen in a casual, competent manner. Breaking brown eggs in a white bowl, popping bread in a toaster that sat on a granite-colored counter. She should offer to help, she thought. It seemed the right thing to do. But she was so dreadfully tired, and it was so pleasant to just sit in the big kitchen with rain drumming musically on the roof and watch him handle the simple task of making breakfast.

He was taking care of her. And she was letting him. Bailey closed her eyes and wondered if she was the kind of woman who needed to be tended to by a man, who enjoyed the role of the helpless female.

She hoped not, almost fiercely hoped not. Then wondered why such a minor, insignificant personality trait should matter so much, when she couldn't be sure she wasn't a thief or murderer.

She caught herself studying her hands, wondering about them. Short, neat, rounded nails coated in clear polish. Did that mean she was practical? The hands were soft, uncallused. It was doubtful she worked with them, pursued manual labor of any kind.

The rings… Very pretty, not bold so much as unique. At least it seemed they were. She knew the stones that winked back at her. Garnet, citrine, amethyst. How could she know the names of colored stones and not know the name of her closest friend?

Did she have any friends?

Was she a kind person or a catty one, generous or a faultfinder? Did she laugh easily and cry at sad movies? Was there a man she loved who loved her?

Had she stolen more than a million dollars and used that ugly little gun?

She jolted when Cade set her plate in front of her, then settled when he laid a hand on her shoulder.

"You need to eat." He went back to the stove, brought the cup he'd left there. "And I think tea's a better bet than coffee."

"Yes. Thank you." She picked up her fork, scooped up some eggs, tasted. "I like them." She managed a smile again, a hesitant, shy smile that touched his heart. "That's something."

He sat across from her with his mug of coffee. "I'm known throughout the civilized world for my scrambled eggs."

Her smile steadied, bloomed. "I can see why. The little dashes of dill and paprika are inspired."

"Wait till you taste my Spanish omelets."

"Master of the egg." She continued to eat, comforted by the easy warmth she felt between them. "Do you cook a lot?"

She glanced around the kitchen. Stone-colored

cabinets and warm, light wood. An uncurtained window over a double sink of white porcelain. Coffeemaker, toaster, jumbled sections of the morning paper.

The room was neat, she observed, but not obsessively so. And it was a marked contrast to the clutter and mess of his office. "I never asked if you were married."

"Divorced, and I cook when I'm tired of eating out."

"I wonder what I do—eat out or cook."

"You recognized paprika and dill when you tasted them." Leaning back, he sipped his coffee and studied her. "You're beautiful." Her gaze flicked up, startled and, he noted, instantly wary. "Just an observation, Bailey. We have to work with what we know. You are beautiful—it's quiet, understated, nothing that seems particularly contrived or enhanced. You don't go for the flashy, and you don't take a compliment on your looks casually. In fact, I've just made you very nervous."

She picked up her cup, held it in both hands. "Are you trying to?"

"No, but it's interesting and sweet—the way you blush and eye me suspiciously at the same time. You can relax, I'm not hitting on you." But it was a thought, he admitted, a fascinating and arousing thought. "I don't think you're a pushover, either," he continued. "I doubt a man would get very far with you just by telling you that you have eyes like warm brandy, and that the contrast between them and that cool, cultured voice packs a hell of a sexual impact."

She lifted her cup and, though it took an effort, kept her gaze level with his. "It sounds very much like you're hitting on me."

His dimples flashed with charm when he grinned. "See, not a pushover. But polite, very polite and well mannered. There's New England in your voice, Bailey."

Staring, she lowered the cup again. "New England?"

"Connecticut, Massachusetts—I'm not sure. But there's a whiff of Yankee society upbringing in your voice, especially when it turns cold."

"New England." She strained for a connection, some small link. "It doesn't mean anything to me."

"It gives me another piece to work with. You've got class written all over you. You were born with it, or you developed it, either way it's there." He rose, took her plate. "And so's the exhaustion. You need to sleep."

"Yes." The thought of going back to that hotel room had her forcing back a shudder. "Should I call your office, set up another appointment? I wrote down the number of the hotel and room where I'm staying. You could call me if you find anything."

"You're not going back there." He had her hand again, drew her to her feet and began to lead her out of the kitchen. "You can stay here. There's plenty of room."

"Here?"

"I think it's best if you're where I can keep an eye on you, at least for the time being." Back in the foyer, he led her up the stairs. "It's a safe, quiet neighborhood, and until we figure out how you got your hands on a million two and a diamond as big as your fist, I don't want you wandering the streets."

"You don't know me."

"Neither do you. That's something else we're going to work on."

He opened the door to a room where the dim light flickered quietly through lace curtains onto a polished oak floor. A little seating area of button-back chairs and a piecrust table was arranged in front of a fireplace where a fern thrived in the hearth. A wedding-ring quilt was spread over a graceful four poster, plumped invitingly with pillows.

"Take a nap," he advised. "There's a bath through there, and I'll dig up something for you to change into after you've rested."

She felt the tears backing up again, scoring her throat with a mixture of fear and gratitude and outrageous fatigue. "Do you invite all your clients into your home as houseguests?"

"No." He touched her cheek and, because he wanted to gather her close, feel how her head would settle on his shoulder, dropped his hand again. "Just the ones who need it. I'm going to be downstairs. I've got some things to do."

"Cade." She reached for his hand, held it a moment.

"Thank you. It looks like I picked the right name out of the phone book."

"Get some sleep. Let me do the worrying for a while."

"I will. Don't close the door," she said quickly when he stepped out into the hall.

He pushed it open again, studied her standing there in the patterned light, looking so delicate, so lost. "I'll be right downstairs."

She listened to his footsteps recede before sinking down on the padded bench at the foot of the bed. It might be foolish to trust him, to put her life in his hands as completely as she had. But she did trust him. Not only because her world consisted only of him and what she'd told him, but because every instinct inside her told her this was a man she could depend on.

Perhaps it was just blind faith and desperate hope, but at the moment she didn't think she could survive another hour without both. So her future depended on Cade Parris, on his ability to handle her present and his skill in unearthing her past.

She slipped off her shoes, took off her jacket and folded it on the bench. Almost dizzy with fatigue, she climbed into bed and lay atop the quilt, and was asleep the moment her cheek met the pillow.

Downstairs, Cade lifted Bailey's prints from her teacup. He had the connections to have them run quickly and discreetly. If she had a record or had ever worked for the government, he'd have her IDed easily.

He'd check with missing persons, see if anyone matching her description had been reported. That, too, was easy.

The money and the diamond offered another route. The theft of a gem of that size was bound to make news. He needed to verify the facts Bailey had given him on the stone, then do some research.

He needed to check the registration on the gun, too—and check his sources on recent homicides or shootings with a .38.

All those steps would be more effective if done in person. But he didn't want to leave her on her own just yet. She might panic and take off, and he wasn't going to risk losing her.

It was just as possible that she would wake up from her nap, remember who she was and go back to her own life before he had a chance to save her.

He very much wanted to save her.

While he locked the bag in his library safe, booted up his computer, scribbled his notes, he reminded himself that she might have a husband, six kids, twenty jealous lovers, or a criminal record as long as Pennsylvania Avenue. But he just didn't care.

She was his damsel in distress, and damn it, he was keeping her.

He made his calls, arranged to have the prints messengered over to his contact at the police station. The little favor was going to cost him a bottle of unblended Scotch, but Cade accepted that nothing was free.

"By the way, Mick, you got anything on a jewelry heist? A big one?"

Cade could clearly imagine Detective Mick Marshall pushing through his paperwork, phone cocked at his ear to block out the noise of the bullpen, his tie askew, his wiry red hair sticking up in spikes from a face set in a permanent scowl.

"You got something, Parris?"

"Just a rumor," Cade said easily. "If something big went down, I could use a link to the insurance company. Got to pay the rent, Mick."

"Hell, I don't know why you don't buy the building in the first place, then tear the rattrap down, rich boy."

"I'm eccentric—that's what they call rich boys who pal around with people like you. So, what do you know?"

"Haven't heard a thing."

"Okay. I've got a Smith and Wesson .38 special." Cade rattled off the serial number as he turned the gun in his hand. "Run it for me, will you?"

"Two bottles of Scotch, Parris."

"What are friends for? How's Doreen?"

"Sassy as ever. Ever since you brought her over those damn tulips, I haven't heard the end of it. Like I got time to pluck posies before I go home every night. I ought to make it three bottles of Scotch."

"You find out anything about an important gem going missing, Mick, I'll buy you a case. I'll be talking to you."

Cade hung up the phone and stared malevolently at his computer. Man and machine were simply going to have to come to terms for this next bit of research.

It took him what he estimated was three times as long as it would the average twelve-year-old to insert the CD-ROM, search, and find what he was after.

Amnesia.

Cade drank another cup of coffee and learned more about the human brain than he'd ever wanted to know. For a short, uncomfortable time, he feared Bailey had a tumor. That he might have one, as well. He experienced a deep personal concern for his brain stem, then reconfirmed why he hadn't gone into medicine as his mother hoped.

The human body, with all its tricks and ticking time bombs, was just too scary. He'd much rather face a loaded gun than the capriciousness of his own internal organs.

He finally concluded, with some relief, that it was unlikely Bailey had a tumor. All signs pointed to hysterical amnesia, which could resolve itself within hours of the trauma, or take weeks. Months. Even years.

Which put them, he thought, solidly back at square one. The handy medical CD that had come with his computer indicated that amnesia was a symptom, rather than a disease, and that treatment involved finding and removing the cause.

That was where he came in. It seemed to Cade that a detective was every bit as qualified as a doctor to deal with Bailey's problem.

Turning back to his computer, he laboriously typed up his notes, questions and conclusions to date. Satisfied, he went back upstairs to find her some clothes.

She didn't know if it was a dream or reality—or even if it was her own dream or someone else's reality. But it was familiar, so oddly familiar....

The dark room, the hard slant of the beam of light from the desk lamp. The elephant. How strange—the elephant seemed to be grinning at her, its trunk lifted high for luck, its glinting blue eyes gleaming with secret amusement.

Female laughter—again familiar, and so comforting. Friendly, intimate laughter.

It's got to be Paris, Bailey. We're not going to spend two weeks with you digging in the dirt again. What you need is romance, passion, sex. What you need is Paris.

A triangle, gold and gleaming. And a room filled with light, bright, blinding light. A man who's not a man, with a face so kind, so wise, so generous, it thrills the soul. And the golden triangle held in his open hands, the offering of it, the power of it stunning, the impact of the rich blue of the stones nestled in each angle almost palpable. And the stones shining and pulsing like heartbeats and seeming to leap into the air like stars, shooting stars that scatter light.

The beauty of them sears the eyes.

And she's holding them in her hands, and her hands are shaking. Anger, such anger swirling inside her, and fear and panic and fury. The stones shoot out from her hands, first one, then two, winging away like jeweled birds. And the third is clutched to her heart by her open, protective hand.

Silver flashing, bolts of silver flashing. And the pounding of booming drums that shake the ground. Blood. Blood everywhere, like a hideous river spilling.

My God, it's wet, so red and wet and demon-dark.

Running, stumbling, heart thudding. It's dark again. The light's gone, the stars are gone. There's a corridor, and her heels echo like the thunder that follows lightning. It's coming after her, hunting her in the dark while the walls close in tighter and tighter.

She can hear the elephant trumpeting, and the lightning flashes closer. She crawls into the cave and hides like an animal, shivering and whimpering like an animal as the lightning streaks by her....

"Come on, sweetheart. Come on, honey. It's just a bad dream."

She clawed her way out of the dark toward the calm, steady voice, burrowed her clammy face into the broad, solid shoulder.

"Blood. So much blood. Hit by lightning. It's coming. It's close."

"No, it's gone now." Cade pressed his lips to her hair, rocked her. When he slipped in to leave her a robe, she'd been crying in her sleep. Now she was clinging to him, trembling, so he shifted her into his lap as if she were a child. "You're safe now. I promise."

"The stars. Three stars." Balanced between dream and reality, she shifted restlessly in his arms. "I've got to go to Paris."

"You did. I'm right here." He tipped her head back to touch his lips to her temple. "Right here," he repeated, waiting for her eyes to clear and focus. "Relax now. I'm right here."

"Don't go." With a quick shudder, she rested her head on his shoulder, just as he'd imagined. The pull on his heart was immediate, and devastating.

He supposed love at first sight was meant to be.

"I won't. I'll take care of you."

That alone was enough to ease her trembling. She relaxed against him, let her eyes close again. "It was just a dream, but it was so confusing, so frightening. I don't understand any of it."

"Tell me."

He listened as she struggled to remember the details, put them in order. "There was so much emotion, huge waves of emotions. Anger, shock, a sense of betrayal and fear. Then terror. Just sheer mindless terror."

"That could explain the amnesia. You're not ready to cope with it, so you shut it off. It's a kind of conversion hysteria."

"Hysteria?" The term made her chin lift. "I'm hysterical?"

"In a manner of speaking." He rubbed his knuckles absently over that lifted chin. "It looks good on you."

In a firm, deliberate movement that made his brow quirk, she pushed his hand from her face. "I don't care for the term."

"I'm using it in a strictly medical sense. You didn't get bopped on the head, right?"

Her eyes were narrowed now. "Not that I recall, but then, I'm hysterical, after all."

"Cute. What I mean is, amnesia can result from a concussion." He twirled her hair around his finger as he spoke, just to feel the texture. "I always thought that was bull or Hollywood stuff, but it says so right in the medical book. One of the other causes is a functional nervous disorder, such as—you'll excuse the term—hysteria."

Her teeth were gritted now. "I am not hysterical,

though I'm sure I could be, if you'd care for a demon-
stration."

"I've had plenty of those. I have sisters. Bailey." He
cupped her face in his hands in such a disarming
gesture, her narrowed eyes widened. "You're in trouble,
that's the bottom line. And we're going to fix it."

"By holding me in your lap?"

"That's just a side benefit." When her smile fluttered
again and she started to shift away, he tightened his
grip. "I like it. A lot."

She could see more than amusement in his eyes,
something that had her pulse jumping. "I don't think
it's wise for you to flirt with a woman who doesn't
know who she is."

"Maybe not, but it's fun. And it'll give you something else to think about."

She found herself charmed, utterly, by the way his
dimples flickered, the way his mouth quirked at the
corner just enough to make the smile crooked. It would
be a good mouth for a lover, quick, clever, full of
energy. She could imagine too well just how it would
fit against hers.

Perhaps because she couldn't imagine any other,
couldn't remember another taste, another texture. And
because that would make him, somehow, the first to
kiss her, the thrill of anticipation sprinted up her spine.

He dipped her head back, slowly, his gaze sliding

from her eyes to her lips, then back again. He could imagine it perfectly, and was all but sure there would be a swell of music to accompany that first meeting of lips.

"Want to try it?"

Need, rich and full and shocking, poured through her, jittering nerves, weakening limbs. She was alone with him, this stranger she'd trusted her life to. This man she knew more of than she knew of herself.

"I can't." She put a hand on his chest, surprised that however calm his voice his heart was pounding as rapidly as hers. Because it was, she could be honest. "I'm afraid to."

"In my experience, kissing isn't a scary business, unless we're talking about kissing Grandmother Parris, and that's just plain terrifying."

It made her smile again, and this time, when she shifted, he let her go. "Better not to complicate things any more than they are." With restless hands, she scooped her hair back, looked away from him. "I'd like to take a shower, if that's all right. Clean up a little."

"Sure. I brought you a robe, and some jeans you can roll up. The best I could come up with for a belt that would fit you was some clothesline. It'll hold them up and make a unique fashion statement."

"You're very sweet, Cade."

"That's what they all say." He closed off the little pocket of lust within and rose. "Can you handle being alone for an hour? There're a couple of things I should see to."

"Yes, I'll be fine."

"I need you to promise you won't leave the house, Bailey."

She lifted her hands. "Where would I go?"

He put his hands on her shoulders, waited until her gaze lifted to his. "Promise me you won't leave the house."

"All right. I promise."

"I won't be long." He walked to the door, paused. "And, Bailey? Think about it."

She caught the gleam in his eyes before he turned that told her he didn't mean the circumstances that had brought her to him. When she walked to the window, watched him get in his car and drive away, she was already thinking about it. About him.

Someone else was thinking about her. Thinking dark, vengeful thoughts. She had slipped through his fingers, and, with her, the prize and the power he most coveted.

He'd already exacted a price for incompetence, but it was hardly enough. She would be found, and when she was, she'd pay a much higher price. Her life, certainly, but that was insignificant.

There would be pain first, and great fear. That would satisfy.

The money he had lost was nothing, almost as insignificant as the life of one foolish woman. But she had what he needed, what was meant to belong to him. And he would take back his own.

There were three. Individually they were priceless, but together their value went beyond the imaginable. Already he had taken steps to recover the two she had foolishly attempted to hide from him.

It would take a little time, naturally, but he would have them back. It was important to be careful, to be cautious, to be certain of the recovery, and that whatever violence was necessary remained distant from him.

But soon two pieces of the triangle would be his, two ancient stars, with all their beauty and light and potency.

He sat in the room he'd had built for his treasures, those acquired, stolen or taken with blood. Jewels and paintings, statuary and precious pelts, gleamed and sparkled in his Aladdin's cave of secrets.

The altarlike stand he'd designed to hold his most coveted possession was empty and waiting.

But soon...

He would have the two, and when he had the third he would be immortal.

And the woman would be dead.

Chapter 3

It was her body in the mirror, Bailey told herself, and she'd better start getting used to it. In the glass, fogged from her shower, her skin looked pale and smooth. Self-consciously she laid a hand against her breast.

Long fingers, short trimmed nails, rather small breasts. Her arms were a little thin, she noted with a frown. Maybe she should start thinking about working out to build them up.

There didn't seem to be any excess flab at the waist or hips, so perhaps she got some exercise. And there was some muscle tone in the thighs.

Her skin was pale, without tan lines.

What was she—about five-four? She wished she were taller. It seemed if a woman was going to begin her life at twenty-something, she ought to be able to pick her body type. Fuller breasts and longer legs would have been nice.

Amused at herself, she turned, twisted her head to study the rear view. And her mouth dropped open. There was a tattoo on her butt.

What in the world was she doing with a tattoo of a—was that a unicorn?—on her rear end? Was she crazy? Body decoration was one thing, but on that particular part of the anatomy it meant that she had exposed that particular part of the anatomy to some needle-wielding stranger.

Did she drink too much?

Faintly embarrassed, she pulled on a towel and quickly left the misty bathroom.

She spent some time adjusting the jeans and shirt Cade had left her to get the best fit. Hung up her suit neatly, smoothed the quilt. Then she heaved a sigh and tunneled her fingers through her damp hair.

Cade had asked her to stay in the house, but he hadn't asked her to stay in her room. She was going to be jittery again, thinking about bags of money, huge blue diamonds, murder and tattoos, if she didn't find a distraction.

She wandered out, realizing she wasn't uncomfortable in the house alone. She supposed it was a reflection of her feelings for Cade. He didn't make her uncomfortable. From almost the first minute, she'd felt as though she could talk to him, depend on him.

And she imagined that was because she hadn't talked to anyone else, and had no one else to depend on.

Nonetheless, he was a kind, considerate man. A smart, logical one, she supposed, or else he wouldn't be a private investigator. He had a wonderful smile, full of fun, and eyes that paid attention. He had strength in his arms and, she thought, in his character.

And dimples that made her fingers itch to trace along them.

His bedroom. She gnawed on her lip as she stood in the doorway. It was rude to pry. She wondered if she were rude, careless with the feelings and privacy of others. But she needed something, anything, to fill all these blank spots. And he had left his door open.

She stepped over the threshold.

It was a wonderfully large room, and full of him. Jeans tossed over a chair, socks on the floor. She caught herself before she could pick them up and look for a hamper. Loose change and a couple of shirt buttons tossed on the dresser. A gorgeous antique chest of drawers that undoubtedly held all sorts of pieces of him.

She didn't tug at the brass handles, but she wanted to.

The bed was big, unmade, and framed by the clean

lines of Federal head- and footboards. The rumpled sheets were dark blue, and she didn't quite resist running her fingers over them. They'd probably smell of him—that faintly minty scent.

When she caught herself wondering if he slept naked, heat stung her cheeks and she turned away.

There was a neat brick fireplace and a polished pine mantle. A silly brass cow stood on the hearth and made her smile. There were books messily tucked into a recessed shelf. Bailey studied the titles soberly, wondering which she might have read. He went heavy on mysteries and true crime, but there were familiar names. That made her feel better.

Without thinking, she picked up a used coffee mug and an empty beer bottle and carried them downstairs.

She hadn't paid much attention to the house when they came in. It had all been so foggy, so distorted, in her mind. But now she studied the simple and elegant lines, the long, lovely windows, with their classic trim, the gleaming antiques.

The contrast between the gracious home and the second-rate office struck her, made her frown. She rinsed the mug in the sink, found the recycling bin for the bottle, then took herself on a tour.

It took her less than ten minutes to come to her conclusion. The man was loaded.

The house was full of treasures—museum-quality.

Of that she was undeniably sure. She might not have understood the unicorn on her own rear end, but she understood the value of a Federal inlaid cherrywood slant-front desk. She couldn't have said why.

She recognized Waterford vases, Georgian silver. The Limoges china in the dining room display cabinet. And she doubted very much if the Turner landscape was a copy.

She peeked out a window. Well-tended lawn, majestic old trees, roses in full bloom. Why would a man who could live in such a style choose to work in a crumbling building in a stuffy, cramped office?

Then she smiled. It seemed Cade Parris was as much a puzzle as she was herself. And that was a tremendous comfort.

She went back to the kitchen, hoping to make herself useful by making some iced tea or putting something together for lunch. When the phone rang, she jumped like a scalded cat. The answering machine clicked on, and Cade's voice flowed out, calming her again: "You've reached 555-2396. Leave a message. I'll get back to you."

"Cade, this is becoming very irritating." The woman's voice was tight with impatience. "I've left a half a dozen messages at your office this morning, the least you can do is have the courtesy to return my calls. I sincerely doubt you're so busy with what you

loosely call your clients to speak to your own mother."
There was a sigh, long-suffering and loud. "I know
very well you haven't contacted Pamela about arrangements for this evening. You've put me in a very
awkward position. I'm leaving for Dodie's for bridge.
You can reach me there until four. Don't embarrass me,
Cade. By the way, Muffy's very annoyed with you."

There was a decisive click. Bailey found herself
clearing her throat. She felt very much as if she'd
received that cool, deliberate tongue-lashing herself.
And it made her wonder if she had a mother who nagged,
who expected obedience. Who was worried about her.

She filled the teakettle, set it on to boil, dug up a
pitcher. She was hunting up tea bags when the phone
rang again.

"Well, Cade, this is Muffy. Mother tells me she still
hasn't been able to reach you. It's obvious you're
avoiding our calls because you don't want to face your
own poor behavior. You know very well Camilla's
piano recital was last night. The least, the very least,
you could have done was put in an appearance and pretended to have some family loyalty. Not that I expected
any better from you. I certainly hope you have the
decency to call Camilla and apologize. I refuse to
speak to you again until you do."

Click.

Bailey blew out a breath, rolled her eyes. Families, she

thought, were obviously difficult and complex posses-
sions. Then again, perhaps she had a brother herself and
was just as, well…bitchy, as the wasp-tongued Muffy.

She set the tea to steep, then opened the refrigerator. There were eggs, and plenty of them. That made
her smile. There was also a deli pack of honey-baked
ham, some Swiss, and when she discovered plump
beefsteak tomatoes, she decided she was in business.

She worried over the choice of mustard or mayo for
a time and whether the tea should be sweetened or un-
sweetened. Every little detail was like a brick in the re-
building of herself. As she was carefully slicing
tomatoes, she heard the front door slam, and her mood
brightened.

But when she started to call out, the words stuck in
her throat. What if it wasn't Cade? What if they'd
found her? Come for her? Her hand tightened on the
hilt of the knife as she edged toward the rear kitchen
door. Fear, deep and uncontrollable, had sweat
popping out in clammy pearls on her skin. Her heart
flipped into her throat.

Running, running away from that sharp, hacking
lightning. In the dark, with her own breath screaming
in her head. Blood everywhere.

Her fingers tensed on the knob, turned it, as she
prepared for flight or fight.

When Cade stepped in, a sob of relief burst out of

her. The knife clattered on the floor as she launched herself into his arms. "It's you. It is you."

"Sure it is." He knew he should feel guilty that fear had catapulted her against him, but he was only human. She smelled fabulous. "I told you you're safe here, Bailey."

"I know. I felt safe. But when I heard the door, I panicked for a minute." She clung, wildly grateful to have him with her. Drawing her head back, she stared up at him. "I wanted to run, just run, when I heard the door and thought it could be someone else. I hate being such a coward, and not knowing what I should do. I can't seem…to think."

She trailed off, mesmerized. He was stroking her cheek as she babbled, his eyes intent on hers. Her arms were banded around his waist, all but fused there. The hand that had smoothed through her hair was cupped at the base of her neck now, fingers gently kneading.

He waited, saw the change in her eyes. His lips curved, just enough to have her heart quiver before he lowered his head and gently touched them to hers.

Oh, lovely… That was her first thought. It was lovely to be held so firmly, to be tasted so tenderly. This was a kiss, this sweet meeting of lips that made the blood hum lazily and the soul sigh. With a quiet murmur, she slid her hands up his back, rose on her toes to meet that patient demand.

When his tongue traced her lips, slipped between them, she shuddered with pleasure. And opened to him as naturally as a rose opens to the sun.

He'd known she would. Somehow he'd known she would be both shy and generous, that the taste of her would be fresh, the scent of her airy. It was impossible that he'd only met her hours before. It seemed the woman he held in his arms had been his forever.

And it was thrilling, hotly arousing, to know his was the first kiss she would remember. That he was the only man in her mind and heart to hold her this way, touch her this way. He was the first to make her tremble, his was the first name she murmured when needs swirled through her.

And when she murmured his name, every other woman he'd ever held vanished. She was the first for him.

He deepened the kiss gradually, aware of how easily he could bruise or frighten. But she came so suddenly alive in his arms, was so wildly responsive, her mouth hungry and hot, her body straining and pulsing against his.

She felt alive, brilliantly alive, aware of every frantic beat of her own heart. Her hands had streaked into his hair and were fisted there now, as if she could pull him inside her. He was filling all those empty places, all those frightening blanks. This was life. This was real. This mattered.

"Easy." He could barely get the word out, wished fervently he didn't feel obliged to. He was trembling as much as she, and he knew that if he didn't pull back, gain some control, he was going to take her exactly where they stood. "Easy," he said again, and pressed her head to his shoulder so that he wouldn't be tempted to devour that ripe, willing mouth.

She vibrated against him, nerves and needs tangling, the echoes of sensations thumping through her system. "I don't know if it's ever been like that. I just don't know."

That brought him back to earth a little too abruptly. She didn't know, he reminded himself. He did. It had never been like that for him. "Don't worry." He pulled away, then rubbed his hands over her shoulders, because they were tense again. "You know that wasn't ordinary, Bailey. That ought to be enough for now."

"But—" She bit her lip when he turned and wrenched open the fridge. "I made—I'm making iced tea."

"I want a beer."

She winced at the brusque tone. "You're angry."

"No." He twisted off the cap, downed three long swallows. "Yes. With myself, a little. I pushed the buttons, after all." He lowered the bottle, studied her. She was standing with her arms crossed tight at her waist. His jeans bagged at her hips, his shirt drooped at her shoulders. Her feet were bare, her hair was tangled around her shoulders.

She looked absolutely defenseless.

"Let's just get this out, okay?" He leaned back against the counter to keep his distance. "I felt the click the minute you walked into the office. Never happened to me before, just click, there she is. I figured it was because you were a looker, you were in trouble and you'd come looking for me. I've got a thing about people in trouble, especially beautiful women."

He drank again, slower this time, while she watched him soberly, with great attention. "But that's not it, Bailey, or at least not all of it. I want to help you. I want to find out everything about you as much as you do. But I also want to make love with you, slow, really slow, so that every second's like an hour. And when we've finished making love, and you're naked and limp under me, I want to start all over again."

She had her hands crossed over her breasts now, to keep her bucking heart in place. "Oh" was all she could manage.

"And that's what I'm going to do. When you're a little steadier on your feet."

"Oh," she said again. "Well." She cleared her throat. "Cade, I may be a criminal."

"Uh-huh." Calm again, he inspected the sandwich makings on the counter. "So is this lunch?"

Her eyes narrowed. What sort of response was that from a man who'd just told her he wanted to make love with her until she was limp? "I may have stolen a great deal of money, killed people, kidnapped an innocent child."

"Right." He piled some ham on bread. "Yeah, you're a real desperado, sweetheart. Anybody can see that. You've got that calculating killer gleam in the eye." Then, chuckling, he turned to her. "Bailey, for God's sake, look at yourself. You're a polite, tidy woman with a conscience as wide as Kansas. I sincerely doubt you have so much as a parking ticket to your name, or that you've done anything wilder than sing in the shower."

It stung. She couldn't have said why, but the bland and goody-goody description put her back up. "I've got a tattoo on my butt."

He set the rather sloppy sandwich he'd put together down. "Excuse me?"

"I have a tattoo on my butt," she repeated, with a combative gleam in her eye.

"Is that so?" He couldn't wait to see it. "Well, then, I'll have to turn you in. Now, if you tell me you've got something other than your ears pierced, I'll have to get my gun."

"I'm so pleased I could amuse you."

"Sweetheart, you fascinate me." He shifted to block her path before she could storm out. "Temper. That's a good sign. Bailey's not a wimp." She stepped to the right. So did he. "She likes scrambled eggs with dill and paprika, knows how to make iced tea, cuts tomatoes in very precise slices and knows how to tie a shank knot."

"What?"

"Your belt," he said with a careless gesture. "She was probably a Girl Scout, or she likes to sail. Her voice gets icy when she's annoyed, she has excellent taste in clothes, bites her bottom lip when she's nervous—which I should warn you instills wild lust in me for no sensible reason."

His dimples winked when she immediately stopped nibbling her lip and cleared her throat. "She keeps her nails at a practical length," he continued. "And she can kiss a man blind. An interesting woman, our Bailey."

He gave her hair a friendly tug. "Now, why don't we sit down, eat lunch, and I'll tell you what else I found out. Do you want mustard or mayo?"

"I don't know." Still sulking, she plopped down in a chair.

"I go for mustard myself." He brought it to the table, along with the fixings for her sandwich. "So what is it?"

She swiped mustard on bread. "What?"

"The tattoo? What is it?"

Embarrassed now, she slapped ham over mustard. "I hardly see that it's an issue."

"Come on." He grinned, leaning over to tug on her

hair again. "A butterfly? A rosebud? Or are you really a biker chick in disguise, with a skull and crossbones hiding under my jeans?"

"A unicorn," she muttered.

He bit the tip of his tongue. "Cute." He watched her cut her sandwich into tidy and precise triangles, but refrained from commenting.

Because she wanted to squirm, she changed the subject. "You were going to tell me what else you've found out."

Since it didn't seem to do his blood pressure any good for him to paint mental images of unicorns, he let her off the hook. "Right. The gun's unregistered. My source hasn't been able to trace it yet. The clip's full."

"The clip?"

"The gun was fully loaded, which means it either hadn't been fired recently, or had been reloaded."

"Hadn't been fired." She closed her eyes, grasped desperately at relief. "I might not have used it at all."

"I'd say it's unlikely you did. Using current observations, I can't picture you owning an unregistered handgun, but if we get lucky and track it down, we may have a clearer picture."

"You've learned so much already."

He would have liked to bask in that warm admiration, but he shrugged and took a hefty bite of his sandwich. "Most of it's negative information. There's been no report of a robbery that involves a gem like the one you've been carrying, or that amount of cash. No kidnapping or hostage situations that the local police are involved in, and no open homicides involving the type of weapon we're dealing with in the last week."

He took another swallow of beer. "No one has reported a woman meeting your description missing in the last week, either."

"But how can that be?" She shoved her sandwich aside. "I have the gem, I have the cash. I *am* missing."

"There are possibilities." He kept his eyes on hers. "Maybe someone doesn't want that information out. Bailey, you said you thought the diamond was only part of a whole. And when you were coming out of the nightmare you talked about three stars. Stars. Diamonds. Could be the same thing. Do you think there are three of those rocks?"

"Stars?" She pressed her fingers to her temple as it started to ache. "Did I talk about stars? I don't remember anything about stars."

Because it hurt to think about it, she tried to concentrate on the reasonable. "Three gems of that size and quality would be unbelievably rare. As a set, even if the others were inferior in clarity to the one I have, they'd be beyond price. You couldn't begin to assess—" Her breath began to hitch, to come in gasps as she fought for air. "I can't breathe."

"Okay." He was up, shifting her so that he could lower her head between her knees, rub her back. "That's enough for now. Just relax, don't force it."

He wondered, as he stroked her back, just what she'd seen that put that kind of blind terror in her eyes.

"I'm sorry," she managed. "I want to help."

"You are. You will." He eased her up again, waiting as she pushed her hair back away from her pale cheeks. "Hey, it's only day one, remember?"

"Okay." Because he didn't make her feel ashamed of the weakness, she took a deep, cleansing breath. "When I tried to think, really think about what you were asking, it was like a panic attack, with all this guilt and horror and fear mixed together. My head started to throb, and my heart beat too fast. I couldn't get air."

"Then we'll take it slow. You don't get that panicky when we talk about the stone you have?"

She closed her eyes a moment, cautiously brought its image into her mind. It was so beautiful, so extraordinary. There was concern, and worry, yes. A layer of fear, as well, but it was more focused and somehow less debilitating. "No, it's not the same kind of reaction." She shook her head, opened her eyes. "I don't know why."

"We'll work on that." He scooted her plate back in front of her. "Eat. I'm planning a long evening, and you're going to need fuel."

"What sort of plans?"

"I went by the library on my travels. I've got a stack of books on gems—technical stuff, pictures, books on rare stones, rare jewels, the history of diamonds, you name it."

"We might find it." The possibility cheered her enough to have her nibbling on her sandwich again. "If we could identify the stone, we could trace the owner, and then... Oh, but you can't."

"Can't what?"

"Work tonight. You have to go somewhere with Pamela."

"I do? Hell—" He pressed his fingers to his eyes as he remembered.

"I'm sorry, I forgot to mention it. Your mother called. I was in here, so I heard the message. She's upset that you haven't returned her calls, or contacted Pamela about the arrangements for tonight. She's going to be at Dodie's until four. You can call her there. Also, Muffy's very annoyed with you. She called shortly after your mother and she's very unhappy that you missed Camilla's piano recital. She isn't speaking to you until you apologize."

"I should be so lucky," he muttered, and dropped his hands. "That's a pretty good rundown. Want a job?" When she only smiled, he shook his head and rode on inspiration. "No, I'm serious. You're a hell of a lot more organized than my late, unlamented secretary. I could use some help around the office, and you could use the busywork."

"I don't even know if I can type."

"I know I can't, so you're already a step ahead. You can answer a phone, can't you?"

"Of course, but—"

"You'd be doing me a big favor." Calculating her weaknesses, he pressed his advantage. It was the perfect way to keep her close, keep her busy. "I'd rather not take the time to start advertising and interviewing secretaries right now. If you could help me out, a few hours a day, I'd really appreciate it."

She thought of his office, decided it didn't need a secretary so much as a bulldozer. Well, perhaps she could be of some use after all. "I'd be glad to help."

"Great. Good. Look, I picked up a few things for you while I was out."

"Things?"

"Clothes and stuff."

She stared as he rose and began to clear the plates. "You bought me clothes?"

"Nothing fancy. I had to guess at the sizes, but I've got a pretty good eye." He caught her worrying her lip again and nearly sighed. "Just a few basics, Bailey. As cute as you look in my clothes, you need your own, and you can't wear one suit day after day."

"No, I suppose I can't," she murmured, touched that he should have thought of it. "Thank you."

"No problem. It's stopped raining. You know what you could use? A little fresh air. Let's take a walk, clear your head."

"I don't have any shoes." She took the plates he'd put on the counter and loaded them into the dishwasher.

"I got you some sneakers. Six and a half?"

With a half laugh, she rewrapped the ham. "You tell me."

"Let's try them on and see."

She slid the tray into the dishwasher, closed the door. "Cade, you really have to call your mother."

His grin flashed. "Uh-uh."

"I told you she's upset with you."

"She's always upset with me. I'm the black sheep."

"Be that as it may." Bailey dampened a dishrag and methodically wiped the counters. "She's your mother, and she's waiting for your call."

"No, she's waiting so she can browbeat me into doing something I don't want to do. And when I don't do it, she'll call Muffy, my evil sister, and they'll have a grand old time ripping apart my character."

"That's no way to speak about your family—and you've hurt Camilla's feelings. I assume she's your niece."

"There are rumors."

"Your sister's child."

"No, Muffy doesn't have children, she has creatures. And Camilla is a whiny, pudgy-faced mutant."

She refused to smile, rinsed out the cloth, hung it neatly over the sink. "That's a deplorable way to speak about your niece. Even if you don't like children."

"I do like children." Enjoying himself now, he leaned on the counter and watched her tidy up. "I'm telling you, Camilla's not human. Now my other sister, Doro, she's got two, and somehow the youngest escaped the Parris curse. He's a great kid, likes baseball and bugs. Doro believes he needs therapy."

The chuckle escaped before she swallowed it. "You're making that up."

"Sweetheart, believe me, nothing I could invent about the Parris clan would come close to the horrible truth. They're selfish, self-important and self-indulgent. Are you going to mop the floor now?"

She managed to close her mouth, which had gaped at his careless condemnation of his own family. Distracted, she glanced down at the glossy ivory tiles. "Oh, all right. Where—"

"Bailey, I'm kidding." He grabbed her hand and tugged her out of the room just as the phone began to ring. "No," he said, before she could open her mouth. "I'm not answering it."

"That's shameful."

"It's self-preservation. I never agreed to this Pamela connection, and I'm not going to be pressured into it."

"Cade, I don't want you to upset your family and break a date on my account. I'll be fine."

"I said I didn't make the date. My mother did. And now, when I have to face the music, I can use you as an excuse. I'm grateful. So grateful I'm going to knock a full day off your fee. Here." He picked up one of the shopping bags he'd dropped by the front door and pulled out a shoe box. "Your glass slippers. If they fit, you get to go to the ball."

Giving up, she sat on the bottom landing and opened the box. Her brow cocked. "Red sneakers?"

"I liked them. They're sexy."

"Sexy sneakers." And she wondered as she undid the laces how she could be in such an enormous mess and find herself delighted over a silly pair of shoes. They slid on like butter, and for some reason made her want to laugh and weep at the same time. "Perfect fit."

"Told you I had a good eye." He smiled when she evened out the laces precisely, tied them into careful and neat bows. "I was right, very sexy." He reached down to draw her to her feet. "In fact, you make quite a package right now."

"I'm sure I do, when the only thing that fits are my shoes." She started to rise to her toes to kiss his cheek, then quickly changed her mind.

"Chicken," he said.

"Maybe." She held out her hand instead. "I'd really love to take a walk." She stepped through the door he opened, glanced up at him. "So is Pamela pretty?"

He considered, decided the straight truth might be to his advantage. "Gorgeous." He closed the door behind them, slipped an arm around Bailey's waist. "And she wants me."

The cool little hum of Bailey's response brought a satisfied smile to his lips.

Chapter 4

Puzzles fascinated him. Locating pieces, shuffling them around, trying new angles until they slipped into place, was a challenge that had always satisfied him. It was one of the reasons Cade had bucked family tradition and chosen his particular line of work.

There was enough rebel in him that he would have chosen almost any line of work that bucked family tradition, but opening his own investigation agency had the added benefit of allowing him to call his own shots, solve those puzzles and right a few wrongs along the way.

He had very definite opinions on right and wrong. There were good guys and there were bad guys, there was law and there was crime. Still, he wasn't naive or simplistic enough not to understand and appreciate the shades of gray. In fact, he often visited gray areas, appreciated them. But there were certain lines that didn't get crossed.

He also had a logical mind that occasionally took recreational detours into the fanciful.

Most of all, he just loved figuring things out.

He'd spent a good deal of time at the library after he left Bailey that morning, scanning reams of micro-fiche, hunting for any snippet of news on a stolen blue diamond. He hadn't had the heart to point out to her that they had no idea where she came from. She might have traveled to D.C. from anywhere over the past few days.

The fact that she, the diamond and the cash were here now didn't mean that was where they had started out. Neither of them had any idea just how long her memory had been blank.

He'd studied up further on amnesia, but he hadn't found anything particularly helpful. As far as he could tell, anything could trigger her memory, or it could remain wiped clean, with her new life beginning shortly before she'd walked into his.

He had no doubt she'd been through or witnessed something traumatic. And though it might be consid-ered one of those detours into the fanciful he was sometimes accused of having, he was certain she was innocent of any wrongdoing.

How could a woman with eyes like hers have done anything criminal?

Whatever the answers were, he was dead set on one thing—he meant to protect her. He was even ready to accept the simple fact that he'd fallen for her the moment he saw her. Whoever and whatever Bailey was, she was the woman he'd been waiting for.

So he not only meant to protect her—he meant to keep her.

He'd chosen his first wife for all the logical and tra-ditional reasons. Or, he mused, he'd been fingered—calculatingly—by his in-laws, and also by his own family. And that soulless merger had been a disaster in its very reasonableness.

Since the divorce—which had ruffled everyone's feathers except those of the two people most involved—he'd dodged and evaded commitment with a master's consummate skill at avoidance.

He believed the reason for all that was sitting cross-legged on the rug beside him, peering myopically at a book on gemstones.

"Bailey, you need glasses."

"Hmm?" She had all but pressed her nose into the page.

"It's just a wild guess, but I'd say you usually wear

reading glasses. If your face gets any closer to that book, you're going to be in it."

"Oh." She blinked, rubbed her eyes. "It's just that the print's awfully small."

"Nope. Don't worry, we'll take care of that tomorrow. We've been at this a couple hours. Want a glass of wine?"

"I suppose." Chewing on her bottom lip, she struggled to bring the text into focus. "The Star of Africa is the largest known cut diamond in existence at 530.2 carats."

"Sounds like a whopper," Cade commented as he chose the bottle of Sancerre he'd been saving for the right occasion.

"It's set in the British royal scepter. It's too big, and it's not a blue diamond. So far I haven't found anything that matches our stone. I wish I had a refractometer."

"A what?"

"A refractometer," she repeated, pushing at her hair. "It's an instrument that measures the characteristic property of a stone. The refractive index." Her hand froze as he watched her. "How do I know that?"

Carrying two glasses, he settled on the floor beside her again. "What's the refractive index?"

"It's the relative ability to refract light. Diamonds are singly refracting. Cade, I don't understand how I know that."

"How do you know it's not a sapphire?" He picked

up the stone from where it sat like a paperweight on his notes. "It sure looks like one to me."

"Sapphires are doubly refracting." She shuddered. "I'm a jewel thief. That must be how I know."

"Or you're a jeweler, a gem expert, or a really rich babe who likes to play with baubles." He handed her a glass. "Don't jump to conclusions, Bailey. That's how you miss details."

"Okay." But she had an image of herself dressed all in black, climbing in second-story windows. She drank deeply. "I just wish I could understand why I remember certain things. Refractometers, *The Maltese Falcon*—"

"The Maltese Falcon?"

"The movie—Bogart, Mary Astor. You had the book in your room, and the movie jumped right into my head. And roses, I know what they smell like, but I don't know my favorite perfume. I know what a unicorn is, but I don't know why I've got a tattoo of one."

"It's a unicorn." His lips curved up, dimples flashing. "Symbol of innocence."

She shrugged that off and drank down the rest of her wine quickly. Cade merely passed her his own glass and got up to refill. "And there was this tune playing around in my head while I was in the shower. I don't know what it is, but I couldn't get rid of it." She sipped again, frowned in concentration, then began to hum.

"Beethoven's 'Ode to Joy,'" he told her. "Beethoven, Bogart and a mythical beast. You continue to fascinate me, Bailey."

"And what kind of name is Bailey?" she demanded, gesturing expansively with her glass. "Is it my last name or my first? Who would stick a child with a first name like Bailey? I'd rather be Camilla."

He grinned again, wondered if he should take the wine out of her reach. "No, you wouldn't. Take my word for it."

She blew the hair out of her eyes and pouted.

"Tell me about diamonds."

"They're a girl's best friend." She chuckled, then beamed at him. "Did I make that up?"

"No, honey, you didn't." Gently, he took the half-empty glass from her, set it aside. Mental note, he thought—Bailey's a one-drink wonder. "Tell me what you know about diamonds."

"They sparkle and shine. They look cold, even feel cold to the touch. That's how you can easily identify glass trying to pass. Glass is warm, diamonds are cold. That's because they're excellent heat conductors. Cold fire."

She lay on her back, stretching like a cat, and had saliva pooling in his mouth. She closed her eyes.

"It's the hardest substance known, with a value of ten on Mohs' hardness scale. All good gem diamonds are white diamonds. A yellowish or brown tinge is considered an imperfection."

My, oh, my, she thought, and sighed, feeling her head spin. "Blue, green and red diamonds are very rare and highly prized. The color's caused by the presence of minor elements other than pure carbon."

"Good." He studied her face, the curved lips, closed eyes. She might have been talking of a lover. "Keep going."

"In specific gravity, diamonds range between 3.15 and 3.53, but the value for pure crystals is almost always 3.52. You need brilliancy and fire," she murmured, stretching lazily again.

Despite his good intentions, his gaze shifted, and he watched her small, firm breasts press against the material of his shirt. "Yeah, I bet."

"Uncut diamonds have a greasy luster, but when cut, oh, they shine." She rolled over on her stomach, bent her legs into the air and crossed her ankles. "This is characterized technically as adamantine. The name *diamond* is derived from the Greek word *adamas,* meaning 'invincible.' There's such beauty in strength."

She opened her eyes again, and they were heavy and clouded. She shifted, swinging her legs around until she was sitting, all but in his lap. "You're awfully strong, Cade. And so pretty. When you kissed me, it felt like you could gobble me right up, and I couldn't do a thing about it." She sighed, wiggled a bit to get comfortable, then confided, "I really liked it."

"Oh, boy." He felt the blood begin its slow, leisurely journey from head to loins and cautiously covered both the hands she had laid on his chest. "Better switch to coffee."

"You want to kiss me again."

"About as much as I'd like to take the next breath." That mouth of hers was ripe and willing and close. Her eyes were dreamy and dark.

And she was plowed.

"Let's just hold off on that."

Gently he started to ease her back, but she was busily crawling the rest of the way into his lap. In a smooth, agile movement, she wriggled down and hooked her legs around his waist.

"I don't think— Listen—" For a damsel in distress, she had some pretty clever moves. He managed to catch her industrious hands again before she pulled his shirt off. "Cut that out. I mean it."

He did mean it, he realized, and accepted the new fact that he was insane.

"Do you think I'd be good in bed?" The question nearly had his eyes crossing and his tongue tied in knots. She, meanwhile, simply sighed, settled her head on his shoulder and murmured, "I hope I'm not frigid."

"I don't think there's much chance of that." Cade's

blood pressure spiked while she nibbled delicately on his earlobe. Her hands snuck under his shirt and up his back with a light scraping of nails.

"You taste so good," she noted approvingly, her lips moving down his throat. "I'm awfully hot. Are you hot?"

With an oath, he turned his head, captured her mouth and devoured.

She was ripe with flavors, pulsing with heat. He let himself sink into her, drown in that hot, delicious mouth, while the humming purrs that rippled from her throat pounded through his system like diamonds cased in velvet.

She was pliant, almost fluid, in surrender. When she dipped her head back, offering her throat, no saint in heaven could have resisted it. He scraped his teeth over that smooth white column, listened to her moan, felt her move sinuously against him in invitation.

He could have taken her, simply laid her back on the books and papers and buried himself in her. He could almost feel that glorious slippery friction, the rhythm that would be theirs and only theirs.

And as much as he knew it would be right, it would be perfect, he knew it couldn't be either, not then, not there.

"I've never wanted anyone as much as I want you." He plunged his hand into her hair, turning her head until their eyes met. "Damn it, focus for a minute. Look at me."

She couldn't see anything else. She didn't want anything else. Her body felt light as air, her mind empty of everything but him. "Kiss me again, Cade. It's like a miracle when you do."

Praying for strength, he lowered his brow to hers until he could steady his breathing. "Next time I kiss you, you're going to know just what's going on." He rose and lifted her into his arms.

"My head's spinning." Giggling, she let it fall back on his supporting arm.

"Whose isn't?" With what he considered really heroic control, he laid her on the couch. "Take a nap."

"'Kay." Obediently, she closed her eyes. "You'll stay here. I feel safe when you're here."

"Yeah, I'll be here." He dragged his hands through his hair and watched her drift off. They were going to laugh at this someday, he thought. Maybe when they had grandchildren.

Leaving her sleeping, he went back to work.

…She was digging in the dirt. The sun was a torch in a sapphire sky. The surrounding land was rocky and baked into muted shades of browns and reds and lavenders. Strong and pungent was the scent of sage from the pale green shrubs struggling out of cracks and crevices in the earth. With spade and hammer, she went about her work happily.

Under the narrow shade of a boulder, two women sat

watching her. Her sense of contentment was strong, and stronger yet when she looked over and smiled at them.

One had a short cap of hair that glowed like copper and a sharp, foxy face. And, though her eyes were shielded by dark wraparound sunglasses, Bailey knew they were a deep, deep green.

The other had ebony hair, though it was tucked up now under a wide-brimmed straw hat with silly red flowers around the crown. Loose, the hair would fall past her shoulder blades, thick and wavy to the waist. It suited the magic of her face, the creamy complexion and impossibly blue eyes.

Bailey felt a wave of love just from looking at them, a bond of trust and a sense of shared lives. Their voices were like music, a distant song of which she could only catch snatches.

Could go for a cold beer.

A cold anything.

How long do you think she'll keep at it?

For the rest of our lives. Paris next summer. Definitely.

Get her away from rocks long enough.

And the creeps.

Definitely.

It made her smile that they were talking about her, cared enough to talk about her. She'd go to Paris with them. But for now, she chinked away at an interesting formation, hoping to find something worthwhile, something she could take back and study, then fashion into something pretty for her friends.

It took patience, and a good eye. Whatever she found today, she'd share with them.

Then, suddenly, the blue stones all but tumbled into her hand. Three perfect blue diamonds of spectacular size and luster. And it was with pleasure, rather than shock, that she examined them, turned them in her palms, then felt the jolt of power sing through her body.

The storm rolled in fast and mean, blocking the flaming sun, dark, grasping shadows shooting out and covering the landscape. Now there was panic, a great need to hurry. Hurry. Hurry. A stone for each of them, before it was too late. Before the lightning struck.

But it was already too late. Lightning stabbed the skin, sharp as a knife, and she was running, running blindly. Alone and terrified, with the walls closing in and the lightning stabbing at her heels….

She awoke with her breath heaving, shooting straight up on the sofa. What had she done? Dear God, what had she done? Rocking herself, her hands pressed to her mouth, Bailey waited for the shudders to pass.

The room was quiet. There was no thunder, no lightning, no storm chasing her. And she wasn't alone. Across the room, under the slant of light from a globe lamp, Cade dozed in a chair. He had a book open on his lap.

It calmed her just to see him there, papers scattered

at his feet, a mug on the table beside him. His legs were stretched out, crossed comfortably at the ankles.

Even in sleep, he looked strong, dependable. He hadn't left her alone. She had to block an urge to go over, crawl into his lap and slide back to sleep cuddled with him. He pulled her, tugged at her emotions so strongly. It didn't seem to matter that she'd known him less than twenty-four hours. After all, she'd hardly known herself much longer.

Pushing at her hair, she glanced at her watch. It was just after three a.m., a vulnerable time. Stretching out again, she pillowed her head on her hands and watched him. Her memory of the evening was clear enough, no breaks, no jumps. She knew she'd thrown herself at him, and it both embarrassed and amazed her.

He'd been right to stop before matters got out of hand. She knew he was right.

But, oh, she wished he'd just taken her, there on the floor. Taken her before she had all this time to think about the right and wrong of it, the consequences.

Some of this emptiness within her would be filled now, some of those undefinable needs met.

Sighing, she rolled to her back and stared up at the ceiling. But he'd been right to stop. She had to think.

She closed her eyes, not to seek sleep but to welcome memory. Who were the women she'd dreamed of? And where were they now? Despite herself she drifted off.

* * *

Cade woke the next morning stiff as a board. Bones popped as he stretched. He rubbed his hands over his face, and his palms made scratching sounds against the stubble. The moment his eyes cleared, he looked across the room. The couch was empty.

He might have thought he'd dreamed her, if not for the books and papers heaped all over the floor. The whole thing seemed like a dream—the beautiful, troubled woman with no past, walking into his life and his heart at the same time. In the morning light, he wondered how much he'd romanticized it, this connection he felt with her. Love at first sight was a romantic notion under the best of circumstances.

And these were hardly the best.

She didn't need him mooning over her, he reminded himself. She needed his mind to be clear. Daydreaming about the way she'd wrapped herself around him and asked him to make love with her simply wasn't conducive to logical thinking.

He needed coffee.

He rose and trying to roll the crick out of his neck, headed for the kitchen.

And there she was, pretty as a picture and neat as a pin. Her hair was smooth, brushed to a golden luster and pulled back with a simple rubber band. She was wearing the navy-and-white striped slacks he'd bought her, with a white camp shirt tucked into the waist. With one hand resting on the counter, the other holding a steaming mug, she was staring out the window at his backyard where a rope hammock hung between twin maples and roses bloomed.

"You're an early riser."

Her hand shook in startled reaction to his voice, and then she turned, worked up a smile. Her heart continued to thud just a little too fast when she saw him, rumpled from sleep. "I made coffee. I hope you don't mind."

"Sweetheart, I owe you my life." He said in heart-felt tones as he reached for a mug.

"It seems I know how to make it. Apparently some things just come naturally. I didn't even have to think about it. It's a little strong. I must like it strong."

He was already downing it, reveling in the way it seared his mouth and jolted his system. "Perfect."

"Good. I didn't know if I should wake you. I wasn't sure what time you leave for your office, or how much time you'd need."

"It's Saturday, and the long holiday weekend."

"Holiday?"

"Fourth of July." While the caffeine pumped through his system, he topped off his mug. "Fireworks, potato salad, marching bands."

"Oh." She had a flash of a little girl sitting on a woman's lap as lights exploded in the night sky. "Of course. You'll be taking the weekend off. You must have plans."

"Yeah, I got plans. I plan for us to toddle into the office about midmorning. I can show you the ropes. Won't be able to do much legwork today, with everything shut down, but we can start putting things in order."

"I don't want you to give up your weekend. I'd be happy to go in and straighten up your office, and you could—"

"Bailey. I'm in this with you."

She set her mug down, linked her hands. "Why?"

"Because it feels right to me. The way I see it, what you can't figure out in your head, you do on instinct." Those sea-mist eyes roamed over her face, then met hers. "I like to think there's a reason you picked me. For both of us."

"I'm surprised you can say that, after the way I acted last evening. For all we know, I go out cruising bars every night and pick up strange men."

He chuckled into his mug. Better to laugh, he'd decided, than to groan. "Bailey, the way a single glass of wine affects you, I doubt you spent much time in bars. I've never seen anyone get bombed quite that fast."

"I don't think that's anything to be proud of." Her voice had turned stiff and cool, and it made him want to grin again.

"It's nothing to be ashamed of either. And you

didn't pick a strange man, you picked me." The amusement in his eyes flicked off. "We both know it was personal, with or without the alcohol."

"Then why didn't you…take advantage?"

"Because that's just what it would have been. I don't mind having the advantage, but I'm not interested in taking it. Want breakfast?"

She shook her head, waited until he'd gotten out a box of cereal and a bowl. "I appreciate your restraint."

"Do you?"

"Not entirely."

"Good." He felt the muscles of his ego expand and flex as he got milk out of the refrigerator. He poured it on, then added enough sugar to have Bailey's eyes widening.

"That can't be healthy."

"I live for risk." He ate standing up. "Later I thought we'd drive downtown, walk around with the tourists. You may see something that jogs your memory."

"All right." She hesitated, then took a chair. "I don't know anything about your work, really, your usual clientele. But it seems to me you're taking all of this completely in stride."

"I love a mystery." Then he shrugged and shoveled in more cereal. "You're my first amnesia case, if that's what you mean. My usual is insurance fraud and domestic work. It has its moments."

"Have you been an investigator very long?"

"Four years. Five, if you count the year I trained as an operative with Guardian. They're a big security firm here in D.C. Real suit-and-tie stuff. I like working on my own better."

"Have you ever…had to shoot at someone?"

"No. Too bad, really, because I'm a damn good shot." He caught her gnawing her lip and shook his head. "Relax, Bailey. Cops and P.I.s catch the bad guys all the time without drawing their weapon. I've taken a few punches, given a few, but mostly it's just legwork, repetition and making calls. Your problem's just another puzzle. It's just a matter of finding all the pieces and fitting them together."

She hoped he was right, hoped it could be just that simple, that ordinary, that logical. "I had another dream. There were two women. I knew them, I'm sure of it." When he pulled out a chair and sat across from her, she told him what she remembered.

"It sounds like you were in the desert," he said when she fell silent. "Arizona, maybe New Mexico."

"I don't know. But I wasn't afraid. I was happy, really happy. Until the storm came."

"There were three stones, you're sure of that?"

"Yes, almost identical, but not quite. I had them, and they were so beautiful, so extraordinary. But I couldn't keep them together. That was very important." She sighed. "I don't know how much was real and how much was jumbled and symbolic, the way dreams are."

"If one stone's real, there may be two more." He took her hand. "If one woman's real, there may be two more. We just have to find them."

It was after ten when they walked into his office. The cramped and dingy work space struck her as more than odd now that she'd seen how he lived. But she listened carefully as he tried to explain how to work the computer to type up his notes, how he thought the filing should be done, how to handle the phone and intercom systems.

When he left her alone to close himself in his office, Bailey surveyed the area. The philodendron lay on its side, spilling dirt. There was broken glass, sticky splotches from old coffee, and enough dust to shovel.

Typing would just have to wait, she decided. No one could possibly concentrate in such a mess.

From behind his desk, Cade used the phone to do his initial legwork. He tracked down his travel agent and, on the pretext of planning a vacation, asked her to locate any desert area where rockhounding was permitted. He told her he was exploring a new hobby.

From his research the night before, he'd learned quite a bit about the hobby of unearthing crystals and gems. The way Bailey had described her dream, he was certain that was just what she'd been up to.

Maybe she was from out west, or maybe she'd just visited there. Either way, it was another road to explore.

He considered calling in a gem expert to examine the diamond. But on the off chance that Bailey had indeed come into its possession by illegal means, he didn't want to risk it.

He took the photographs he'd snapped the night before of the diamond and spread them out on his desk. Just how much would a gemologist be able to tell from pictures? he wondered.

It might be worth a try. Tuesday, when businesses were open again, he mused, he might take that road, as well.

But he had a couple of other ideas to pursue.

There was another road, an important one, that had to be traveled first. He picked up the phone again, began making calls. He pinned Detective Mick Marshall down at home.

"Damn it, Cade, it's Saturday. I've got twenty starving people outside and burgers burning on the grill."

"You're having a party and didn't invite me? I'm crushed."

"I don't have play cops at my barbecues."

"Now you've really hurt my feelings. Did you earn that Scotch?"

"No match on those prints you sent me. Nothing popped."

Cade felt twin tugs of relief and frustration. "Okay. Still no word on a missing rock?"

"Maybe if you told me what kind of rock."

"A big glittery one. You'd know if it had been reported."

"Nothing's been reported, and I think the rocks are in your head, Parris. Now unless you're going to share, I've got hungry mouths to feed."

"I'll get back to you on it. And the Scotch."

He hung up, and spent some time thinking.

Lightning kept coming up in Bailey's dreams. There'd been thunderstorms the night before she came into his office. It could be as simple as that—one of the last things she remembered was thunder and lightning. Maybe she had a phobia about storms.

She talked about the dark, too. There'd been some power outages downtown that night. He'd already checked on that. Maybe the dark was literal, rather than symbolic.

He guessed she'd been inside. She hadn't spoken of rain, of getting wet. Inside a house? An office building? If whatever had happened to her had happened the night before she came to him, then it almost certainly had to have occurred in the D.C. area.

But no gem had been reported missing.

Three kept cropping up in her dreams, as well. Three stones. Three stars. Three women. A triangle.

Symbolic or real?

He began to take notes again, using two columns. In one he listed her dream memories as literal memories, in the other he explored the symbolism.

And the longer he worked, the more he leaned toward the notion that it was a combination of both.

He made one last call, and prepared to grovel. His sister Muffy had married into one of the oldest and most prestigious family businesses in the East. Westlake Jewelers.

When Cade stepped back into the outer office, his ears were still ringing and his nerves were shot. Those were the usual results of a conversation with his sister. But since he'd wangled what he wanted, he tried to take things in stride.

The shock of walking into a clean, ordered room and seeing Bailey efficiently rattling the keyboard on the computer went a long way toward brightening his mood.

"You're a goddess." He grabbed her hand, kissed it lavishly. "A worker of miracles."

"This place was filthy. Disgusting."

"Yeah, it probably was."

Her brows lowered. "There was food molding in the file cabinets."

"I don't doubt it. You know how to work a computer."

She frowned at the screen. "Apparently. It was like making the coffee this morning. No thought."

"If you know how to work it, you know how to turn it off. Let's go downtown. I'll buy you an ice cream cone."

"I've just gotten started."

"It can wait." He reached down to flick the switch, and she slapped his hand away.

"No. I haven't saved it." Muttering under her breath, she hit a series of keys with such panache, his heart swelled in admiration. "I'll need several more hours to put things in order around here."

"We'll come back. We've got a couple hours to kick around, then we've got some serious work to do."

"What kind of work?" she demanded as he hauled her to her feet.

"I've got you access to a refractometer." He pulled her out the door. "What kind of ice cream do you want?"

Chapter 5

"Your brother-in-law owns Westlake Jewelers?"

"Not personally. It's a family thing."

"A family thing." Bailey's head was still spinning. Somehow she'd gone from cleaning molded sandwiches out of filing cabinets to eating strawberry ice cream on the steps of the Lincoln Memorial. That was confusing enough, but the way Cade had whipped through traffic, zipping around circles and through yellow lights, had left her dizzy and disoriented.

"Yep." He attacked his two scoops of rocky road. Since she'd stated no preference, he'd gotten her strawberry. He considered it a girl flavor. "They have branches all over the country, but the flagship store's here. Muffy met Ronald at a charity tennis tournament when she beaned him with a lob. Very romantic."

"I see." Or she was trying to. "And he agreed to let us use the equipment?"

"Muffy agreed. Ronald goes along with whatever Muffy wants."

Bailey licked her dripping cone, watched the tourists—the families, the children—clamber up and down the steps. "I thought she was angry with you."

"I talked her out of it. Well, I bribed her. Camilla also takes ballet. There's a recital next month. So I'll go watch Camilla twirl around in a tutu, which, believe me, is not a pretty sight."

Bailey choked back a chuckle. "You're so mean."

"Hey, I've seen Camilla in a tutu, you haven't. Take my word, I'm being generous." He liked seeing her smile, just strolling along with him eating strawberry ice cream and smiling. "Then there's Chip. That's Muffy's other mutant. He plays the piccolo."

"I'm sure you're making this up."

"I couldn't make it up, my imagination has limits. In a couple of weeks I have to sit front and center and listen to Chip and his piccolo at a band concert." He shuddered. "I'm buying earplugs. Let's sit down."

They settled on the smooth steps beneath the wise and melancholy president. There was a faint breeze that helped stir the close summer air. But it could do little about the moist heat that bounced, hard as damp bricks, up from the sidewalks. Bailey could see waves of it shimmer, like desert mirages, in the air.

There was something oddly familiar about all of it, the crowds of people passing, pushing strollers, clicking cameras, the mix of voices and accents, the smells of sweat, humanity and exhaust, flowers blooming in their plots, vendors hawking their wares.

"I must have been here before," she murmured. "But it's just out of sync. Like someone else's dream."

"It's going to come back to you." He tucked a stray strand of hair behind her ear. "Pieces already are. You know how to make coffee, use a computer, and you can organize an office."

"Maybe I'm a secretary."

He didn't think so. The way she rattled off information on diamonds the evening before had given him a different idea. But he wanted to weigh it awhile before sharing it. "If you are, I'll double your salary if you work for me." Keeping it light, he rose and offered her a hand. "We've got some shopping to do."

"We do?"

"You need reading glasses. Let's hit the stores."

It was another experience, the sprawling shopping center packed with people looking for bargains. The holiday sale was in full swing. Despite the heat, winter coats were displayed and discounted twenty percent, and fall fashions crowded out the picked over remains of summer wear.

Cade deposited her at a store that promised glasses within an hour and filled out the necessary forms himself while she browsed the walls of frames available.

There was a quick, warm glow that spread inside him when he listed her name as Bailey Parris and wrote his own address. It looked right to him, felt right. And when she was led into the back for the exam— free with the purchase of frames—he gave her a kiss on the cheek.

In less than two hours, she was back in his car, examining her pretty little wire-framed glasses, and the contents of a loaded shopping bag.

"How did you have time to buy all of this?" With a purely feminine flutter, she smoothed a hand over the smooth leather of a bone shoulder-strap envelope bag.

"It's all a matter of stategy and planning, knowing what you want and not being distracted."

Bailey peeked in a bag from a lingerie store and saw rich black silk. Gingerly she pulled the material out. There wasn't a great deal of it, she mused.

"You've got to sleep in something," Cade told her. "It was on sale. They were practically giving it away."

She might not have known who she was, but she was

pretty sure she knew sleepwear from seduce-me wear. She tucked the silk back in the bag. Digging deeper, she discovered a bag of crystals. "Oh, they're lovely."

"They had one of those nature stores. So I picked up some rocks." He braked at a stop sign and shifted so that he could watch her. "Picked out a few that appealed to me. The smooth ones are… What do you call it?"

"Tumbling stones," she murmured, stroking them gently with a fingertip. "Carnelian, citrine, sodalite, jasper." Flushed with pleasure, she unwrapped tissue. "Tourmaline, watermelon tourmaline—see the pinks and the greens?—and this is a lovely column of fluorite. It's one of my favorites. I…" She trailed off, pressed a hand to her temple.

He reached in himself, took out a stone at random. "What's this?"

"Alexandrite. It's a chrysoberyl, a transparent stone. Its color changes with the light. See it's blue-green now, in daylight, but in incandescent light it would be mauve or violet." She swallowed hard because the knowledge was there, just there in her mind. "It's a multipurpose stone, but scarce and expensive. It was named for Czar Alexander I."

"Okay, relax, take a deep breath." He made the turn, headed down the tree-lined street. "You know your stones, Bailey."

"Apparently I do."

"And they give you a lot of pleasure." Her face had lit up, simply glowed, when she studied his choices.

"It scares me. The more the information crowded inside my head, the more it scared me."

He pulled into his driveway, turned to her. "Are you up to doing the rest of this today?"

She could say no, she realized. He would take her inside then, inside his house, where she'd be safe. She could go up to the pretty bedroom, close herself in. She wouldn't have to face anything but her own cowardice.

"I want to be. I will be," she added, and let out a long breath. "I have to be."

"Okay." Reaching over, he gave her hand a quick squeeze. "Just sit here. I'll get the diamond."

Westlake Jewelers was housed in a magnificent old building with granite columns and long windows draped in satin. It was not the place for bargains. The only sign was a discreet and elegant brass plate beside the arched front entrance.

Cade drove around the back.

"They're getting ready to close for the day," he explained. "If I know Muffy, she'll have Ronald here waiting. He may not be too thrilled with me, so… Yeah, there's his car." Cade shot his own into a space beside a sedate gray Mercedes sedan. "You just play along with me, all right?"

"Play along?" She wrinkled her brow as he dumped stones into her new handbag. "What do you mean?"

"I had to spin a little story to talk her into this." Reaching over, he opened Bailey's door. "Just go along."

She got out, walked with him to the rear entrance. "It might help if I knew what I was going along with."

"Don't worry." He rang the buzzer. "I'll handle it."

She shifted her now heavy bag on her shoulder. "If you've lied to your family, I think I ought to—" She broke off when the heavy steel door opened.

"Cade." Ronald Westlake nodded curtly. Cade had been right, Bailey thought instantly. This was not a happy man. He was average height, trim and well presented, in a dark blue suit with a muted striped tie so ruthlessly knotted she wondered how he could draw breath. His face was tanned, his carefully styled hair dark and discreetly threaded with glinting gray.

Dignity emanated from him like light.

"Ronald, good to see you," Cade said cheerily, and as if Ronald's greeting had been filled with warmth, he pumped his hand enthusiastically. "How's the golf game? Muffy tells me you've been shaving that handicap."

As he spoke, Cade eased himself inside, much, Bailey thought, like a salesman with his foot propped in a door. Ronald continued to frown and back up.

"This is Bailey. Muffy might have told you a little

about her." In a proprietary move, Cade wrapped his arm around Bailey's shoulder and pulled her to his side.

"Yes, how do you do?"

"I've been keeping her to myself," Cade added before Bailey could speak. "I guess you can see why." Smoothly Cade tipped Bailey's face up to his and kissed her. "I appreciate you letting us play with your equipment. Bailey's thrilled. Sort of a busman's holiday for her, showing me how she works with stones." He shook her purse so that the stones inside rattled.

"You've never shown any interest in gems before," Ronald pointed out.

"I didn't know Bailey before," Cade said easily. "Now, I'm fascinated. And now that I've talked her into staying in the States, she's going to have to think about setting up her own little boutique. Right, sweetheart?"

"I—"

"England's loss is our gain," he continued. "And if one of the royals wants another bauble, they'll have to come here. I'm not letting you get away." He kissed her again, deeply, while Ronald stood huffing and tugging at his tie.

"Cade tells me you've been designing jewelry for some time. It's quite an endorsement, having the royal family select your work."

"It's sort of keeping it in the family, too," Cade said with a wink. "With Bailey's mama being one of Di's cousins. Was that third or fourth cousin, honey? Oh, well, what's the difference?"

"Third," Bailey said, amazed at herself not only for answering, but also for infusing her voice with the faintest of upper-class British accents. "They're not terribly close. Cade's making too much of it. It's simply that a few years ago a lapel pin I'd fashioned caught the eye of the Princess of Wales. She's quite a keen shopper, you know."

"Yes, yes, indeed." The tony accent had a sizable effect on a man with Ronald's social requirements. His smile spread, his voice warmed. "I'm delighted you could stop by. I do wish I could stay, show you around."

"We don't want to keep you." Cade was already thumping Ronald on the back. "Muffy told me you're entertaining."

"It's terribly presumptuous of Cade to interrupt your holiday. I would so love a tour another time."

"Of course, anytime, anytime at all. And you must try to drop by the house later this evening." Pumped up at the thought of entertaining even such a loose connection with royalty, Ronald began to usher them toward the jeweler's work area. "We're very select in our equipment, as well as our stones. The Westlake reputation has been unimpeachable for generations."

"Ah, yes." Her heart began to thud as she studied the

equipment in the glass-walled room, the worktables, the saws, the scales. "Quite top-of-the-line."

"We pride ourselves on offering our clientele only the best. We often cut and shape our own gems here, and employ our own lapidaries."

Bailey's hand shook lightly as she passed it over a wheel. A lap, she thought, used to shape the stone. She could see just how it was done—the stone cemented to the end of a wooden stick, a dop, held against the revolving lap wheel with the aid of a supporting block adjacent to the wheel.

She knew, could hear the sounds of it. Feel the vibrations.

"I enjoy lap work," Bailey said faintly. "The precision of it."

"I'm afraid I only admire the craftsmen and artists. That's a stunning ring. May I?" Ronald took her left hand, examined the trio of stones arranged in a gentle curve and set in etched gold. "Lovely. Your design?"

"Yes." It seemed the best answer. "I particularly enjoy working with colored stones."

"You must see our stock sometime soon." Ronald glanced at his watch, clucked his tongue. "I'm running quite late. The security guard will let you back out when you're done. Please take all the time you want. I'm afraid the showroom itself is locked, time-locked, and you'll need the guard to open the rear door, as it engages from inside and out." He sent Bailey a professional-to-professional smile. "You'd understand how important security is in the business."

"Of course. Thank you so much for your time, Mr. Westlake."

Ronald took Bailey's offered hand. "Ronald, please. And it's my pleasure. You mustn't let Cade be so selfish of you. Muffy is very much looking forward to meeting her future sister-in-law. Be sure to drop by later."

Bailey made a strangled sound, easily covered by Cade's quick chatter as he all but shoved Ronald out of the work area.

"Sister-in-law?" Bailey managed.

"I had to tell them something." All innocence, Cade spread his hands. "They've been campaigning to get me married off again since the ink was dry on my divorce decree. And you being royalty, so to speak, puts you several societal steps up from the women they've been pushing on me."

"Poor Cade. Having women shoved at him right and left."

"I've suffered." Because there were dangerous glints in her eyes, he tried his best smile. "You have no idea how I've suffered. Hold me."

She slapped his hand away. "Is this all a big joke to you?"

"No, but that part of it was fun." He figured his hands would be safer in his pockets. "I guarantee my sister's been burning up the phone lines since I talked to her this morning. And now that Ronald's got a load of you—"

"You lied to your family."

"Yeah. Sometimes it's fun. Sometimes it's just necessary for survival." He angled his head. "You slipped right into the stream, sweetheart. That accent was a nice touch."

"I got caught up, and I'm not proud of it."

"You might make a good operative. Let me tell you, lying quick and lying well is one of the top requirements of the job."

"And the end justifies the means?"

"Pretty much." It was starting to irritate him, the disapproving ice in her voice. He had the feeling Bailey wasn't nearly as comfortable in gray areas as he was. "We're in, aren't we? And Ronald and Muffy are going to have a rousing success with their little party. So what's the problem?"

"I don't know. I don't like it." A lie, the simple fact of a lie, made her miserably uncomfortable. "One lie just leads to another."

"And enough of them sometimes lead to the truth." He took her bag, opened it and pulled out the velvet pouch, slid the diamond into his hand. "You want the truth, Bailey? Or do you just want honesty?"

"It doesn't seem like there should be a difference." But she took the stone from him. "All right, as you said, we're here. What do you want me to do?"

"Make sure it's real."

"Of course it's real," she said impatiently. "I know it's real."

He merely arched a brow. "Prove it."

With a huffing breath, she turned and headed for a microscope. She employed the dark-field illuminator, adjusting the focus on the binocular microscope with instinctive efficiency.

"Beautiful," she said after a moment, with a tint of reverence in her voice. "Just beautiful."

"What do you see?"

"The interior of the stone. There's no doubt it's of natural origin. The inclusions are characteristic."

"Let's see." He nudged her aside, bent to the microscope himself. "Could be anything."

"No, no. There are no air bubbles. There would be if it was paste, or strass. And the inclusions."

"Doesn't mean anything to me. It's blue, and blue means sapphire."

"Oh for heaven's sake, sapphire is corundum. Do you think I can't tell the difference between carbon and corundum?" She snatched up the stone and marched to another instrument. "This is a polariscope. It tests whether a gem is singly or doubly refracting. As I've already told you, sapphires are doubly refracting, diamonds singly."

She went about her work, muttering to herself, putting her glasses on when she needed them, slipping the eyepiece into the V of her blouse when she didn't. Every move competent, habitual, precise.

Cade tucked his hands in his back pockets, rocked back on his heels and watched.

"Here, the refractometer," she mumbled. "Any idiot can see the refractive index of this stone says diamond, not sapphire." She turned, holding up the stone. "This is a blue diamond, brilliant-cut, weighing 102.6 carats."

"All you need's a lab coat," he said quietly.

"What?"

"You work with this stuff, Bailey. I thought it might be a hobby, but you're too precise, too comfortable. And too easily annoyed when questioned. So my conclusions are that you work with stones, with gems. This type of equipment is as familiar to you as a coffee maker. It's just part of your life."

She lowered her hand and eased herself back onto a stool. "You didn't do all this, go to all this trouble, so we could identify the diamond, did you?"

"Let's just say that was a secondary benefit. Now we have to figure whether you're in the gem or jewelry trade. That's how you got your hands on this." He took the diamond from her, studied it. "And this isn't the kind of thing you see for sale at Westlake or any other jeweler. It's the kind of thing you find in a private collection, or a museum. We've got a really fine museum right here in town. It's called the Smithsonian." He lowered the stone. "You may have heard of it."

"You think…I took it out of the Smithsonian?"

"I think someone there might have heard of it." He slipped the priceless gem casually into his pocket. "It'll have to wait until tomorrow. They'll be closed. No, hell, Tuesday." He hissed between his teeth. "Tomorrow's the Fourth, and Monday's a holiday."

"What should we do until Tuesday?"

"We can start with phone books. I wonder how many gemologists are in the greater metropolitan area?"

The reading glasses meant she could pore through all the books without risking a headache. And pore through them she did. It was, Bailey thought, something like rereading well-loved fairy tales. It was all familiar ground, but she enjoyed traveling over it again.

She read about the history of intaglio cutting in Mesopotamia, the gems of the Hellenistic period. Florentine engravings.

She read of famous diamonds. Of the Vargas, the Jonker, the Great Mogul, which had disappeared centuries before. Of Marie Antoinette and the diamond necklace some said had cost her her head.

She read technical explanations on gem cutting, on identification, on optical properties and formations.

They were all perfectly clear to her, and as smooth as the carnelian tumble stone she worried between her fingers.

How could it be, she wondered, that she remembered rocks and not people? She could easily identify and discuss the properties of hundreds of crystals and gems. But there was only one single person in the entire world she knew.

And even that wasn't herself.

She only knew Cade. Cade Parris, with his quick, often confusing mind. Cade, with his gentle, patient hands and gorgeous green eyes. Eyes that looked at her as though she could be the focus of his world.

Yet his world was so huge compared to hers. His was populated by people, and memories, places he'd been, things he'd done, moments he'd shared with others.

The huge blank screen that was her past taunted her.

What people did she know, whom had she loved or hated? Had anyone ever loved her? Whom had she hurt or been hurt by? And where had she been, what had she done?

Was she scientist or thief? Lover or loner?

She wanted to be a lover. Cade's lover. It was terrifying how much she wanted that. To sink into bed with him and let everything float away on that warm river of sensation. She wanted him to touch her, really touch her. To feel his hands on her, skimming over naked flesh, heating it, taking her to a place where the past meant nothing and the future was unimportant.

Where there was only now, the greedy, glorious now.

And she could touch him, feel the muscles bunch in his back and shoulders as he covered her. His heart would pound against hers, and she would arch up to meet him, to take him in. And then…

She jumped when the book slapped shut.

"Take a break," Cade ordered, shifting the book across the table where she'd settled to read. "Your eyes are going to fall out of your head."

"Oh, I…" Good God, she thought, goggling at him. She was all but trembling, brutally aroused by her own fantasy. Her pulse was skidding along like skates on bumpy ice. "I was just—"

"Look, you're all flushed."

He turned to get the pitcher of iced tea from the re-frigerator, and she rolled her eyes at his back. Flushed? She was flushed? Couldn't the man see she was a puddle just waiting to be lapped up?

He poured her a glass over ice, popped the top on a beer for himself. "We've done enough for one day. I'm thinking steaks on the grill. We'll see if you can put a salad together. Hey." He reached out to steady the glass he'd handed her. "Your hands are shaking. You've been overdoing it."

"No, I…" She could hardly tell him she'd just given serious thought to biting his neck. Carefully she removed her glasses, folded them, set them on the table. "Maybe a little. There's so much on my mind."

"I've got the perfect antidote for overthinking." He took her hand, pulled her to the door and outside, where the air was full of heat and the heady perfume of roses. "A half hour of lazy."

He took her glass, set it on the little wrought-iron table beside the rope hammock, put his beer beside it. "Come on, we'll watch the sky awhile."

He wanted her to lie down with him? Lie down cupped with him in that hammock, while her insides were screaming for release? "I don't think I should—"

"Sure you should." To settle the matter, he gave her a yank and tumbled into the hammock with her. It rocked wildly, making him laugh as she scrambled for balance. "Just relax. This is one of my favorite spots. There's been a hammock here as long as I can remember. My uncle used to nap in this red-and-white striped one when he was supposed to be puttering around the garden."

He slid his arm under her, took one of her nervous hands in his. "Nice and cozy. You can see little pieces of sky through the leaves."

It was cool there, shaded by the maples. She could

feel his heart beating steadily when he laid their joined hands on his chest.

"I used to sneak over here a lot. Did a lot of dreaming and planning in this hammock. It was always peaceful over here, and when you were swinging in a hammock in the shade, nothing seemed all that urgent."

"It's like being in a cradle, I suppose." She willed herself to relax, shocked to the core at how much she wanted to roll on top of him and dive in.

"Things are simpler in a hammock." He toyed with her fingers, charmed by their grace and the glitter of rings. He kissed them absently and made her heart turn over in her chest. "Do you trust me, Bailey?"

At that moment, she was certain that, whatever her past, she'd never trusted anyone more. "Yes."

"Let's play a game."

Her imagination whirled into several erotic corners. "Ah…a game?"

"Word association. You empty your mind, and I'll say a word. Whatever pops into your head first, you say it."

"Word association." Unsure whether to laugh or scream, she closed her eyes. "You think it'll jog my memory."

"It can't hurt, but let's just think of it as a lazy game to play in the shade. Ready?"

She nodded, kept her eyes closed and let herself be lulled by the swing of the hammock. "All right."

"City."

"Crowded."

"Desert."

"Sun."

"Work."

"Satisfaction."

"Fire."

"Blue."

When she opened her eyes, started to shift, he snuggled her closer. "No, don't stop and analyze, just let it come. Ready? Love."

"Friends." She let out a breath, found herself relaxing again. "Friends," she repeated.

"Family."

"Mother." She made a small sound, and he soothed it away.

"Happy."

"Childhood."

"Diamond."

"Power."

"Lightning."

"Murder." She let out a choked breath and turned to bury her face against his shoulder. "I can't do this. I can't look there."

"Okay, it's all right. That's enough." He stroked her hair, and though his hand was gentle, his eyes were hot as they stared up through the shady canopy of leaves.

Whoever had frightened her, made her tremble with terror, was going to pay.

While Cade held Bailey under the maple trees, another stood on a stone terrace overlooking a vast estate of rolling hills, tended gardens, jetting fountains.

He was furious.

The woman had dropped off the face of the earth with his property. And his forces were as scattered as the three stars.

It should have been simple. He'd all but had them in his hands. But the bumbling fool had panicked. Or perhaps had simply become too greedy. In either case, he'd let the woman escape, and the diamonds had gone with her.

Too much time had passed, he thought, tapping his small, beautifully manicured hand on the stone railing. One woman vanished, the other on the run, and the third unable to answer his questions.

It would have to be fixed, and fixed soon. The time-table was now destroyed. There was only one person to blame for that, he mused, and stepped back into his lofty office, picked up the phone.

"Bring him to me" was all he said. He replaced the receiver with the careless arrogance of a man used to having his orders obeyed.

Chapter 6

Saturday night. He took her dancing. She'd imagined hunkering down at the kitchen table with books and a pot of strong coffee as soon as dinner was over. Instead, he swept her out of the house, before she'd finished wiping off the counters, barely giving her enough time to run a brush through her hair.

She needed a distraction, he'd told her. She needed music. She needed to experience life.

It was certainly an experience.

She'd never seen anything like it. That she knew. The noisy, crowded club in the heart of Georgetown vibrated with life, shook from floor to ceiling with voices and busy feet. The music was so loud she couldn't hear her own thoughts, and the stingy little table Cade managed to procure for them in the middle of it all was still sticky from the last patron's pitcher of beer.

It astonished her.

Nobody seemed to know anyone else. Or they knew each other well enough to make love standing up in public. Surely the hot, wiggling moves done body against body on the tiny dance floor were nothing less than a mating ritual.

He bought her club soda, stuck to the same harmless drink himself, and watched the show. More, he watched her watch the show.

Lights flashed, voices echoed, and no one seemed to have a care in the world.

"Is this what you usually do on the weekend?" She had to shout into his ear, and she still wasn't certain he would hear her over the crash and din of guitars and drums.

"Now and again." Hardly ever, he thought, studying the ebb and flow of the tide of singles at the bar. Certainly not a great deal since his college days. The idea of bringing her here had been an impulse, even an inspiration, he thought. She could hardly brood and worry under these conditions. "It's a local group."

"I've been duped?" she repeated doubtfully.

"No, no, this band is a local group." He chuckled, scooted his chair closer to hers, slid his arm around her shoulders. "Down-and-dirty rock. No country, no soft crap, no pap. Just kick ass. What do you think?"

She struggled to think, to tune in to the hard, pulsating and repetitive rhythm. Over the driving ocean of music, the band was shouting about dirty deeds and doing them dirt-cheap.

"I don't know, but it sure isn't the 'Ode to Joy.'"

He laughed at that, long and loud, before grabbing her hand. "Come on. Dance with me."

Instant panic. Her palm went damp, her eyes grew huge. "I don't think I know how to—"

"Hell, Bailey. There's not enough room out there to do more than break a couple of Commandments. That doesn't take any practice."

"Yes, but…" He was dragging her toward the dance floor, snaking his way through tables, bumping into people. She lost count of the number of feet they must have trod on. "Cade, I'd rather just watch."

"You're here to experience." He yanked her into his arms, gripped her hips in an intimate and possessive way that had her breath locking in her throat. "See? One Commandment down." And suddenly his body was moving suggestively against hers. "The rest is easy."

"I don't think I've ever done this." The lights circling and flashing overhead made her dizzy. Giddy. "I'm sure I'd remember."

He thought she was probably right. There was

something entirely too innocent about the way she fumbled, the way the color rushed to her cheeks. He slid his hands over her bottom, up to her waist. "It's just dancing."

"I don't think so. I've probably danced before."

"Put your arms around me." He levered her arms around his neck himself. "And kiss me."

"What?"

"Never mind."

His face was close, and the music was filling her head. The heat from his body, from all the bodies pressed so close against them, was like a furnace. She couldn't breathe, she couldn't think, and when his mouth swooped down on hers, she didn't care.

Her head pounded with the backbeat. It was unmercifully hot, the air thick with smoke and body heat, scented with sweat and liquor and clashing perfumes. All of that faded away. She swayed against him while her lips parted for his and the strong, male essence of him filled her.

"If we'd stayed home, we'd be in bed." He murmured it against her lips, then skimmed his mouth to her ear. She was wearing the perfume he'd bought for her. The scent of it was unreasonably intimate. "I want you in bed, Bailey. I want to be inside you."

She closed her eyes, burrowed against him. Surely no one had said such things to her before. She couldn't have forgotten this wild thrill, this wild fear. Her fingers slipped up into the untidy hair that waved over his collar. "Before, when I was in the kitchen, I—"

"I know." He flicked his tongue over her ear, spread fire everywhere. "I could have had you. Did you think I couldn't see that?" To torment them both, he skimmed his lips along her throat. "That's why we're here instead of home. You're not ready for what I need from you."

"This doesn't make any sense." She thought she murmured it, but he heard her.

"Who the hell cares about sense? This is now." He caught her chin, brought her face to his again. We're now." And kissed her until her blood bubbled and burst in her head. "It can be hot." He bit her bottom lip until she was ready to sink to the floor. "Or sweet." Then laved it tenderly with his tongue. "It can be fun." He spun her out, then whipped her back into his arms with such casual grace that she blinked. "Whatever you want."

Her hands were braced on his shoulders, her face was close to his. Lights revolved around them, and music throbbed. "I think…I think we'd be safer with the fun. For the time being."

"Then let's have it." He whipped her out again, spun her in two fast circles. His eyes lit with amusement when she laughed.

She caught her breath as her body rammed into his again. "You've had lessons."

"Sweetheart, I may have hooked cotillion more times than I want to admit, but some things stuck."

They were moving again, somehow magically, through the thick throng of dancers. "Cotillion? Isn't that white gloves and bow ties?"

"Something like that." He skimmed his hands up her sides, just brushed her breasts. "And nothing like this."

She missed a step, rapped back solidly into what she first took for a steel beam. When she glanced back, she saw what appeared to be one massive muscle with a glossy bald head, a silver nose ring and a gleaming smile.

"I beg your pardon," she began, but found she had breath for nothing else as the muscle whirled her to the right.

She found herself jammed in the middle of a pack of dancers with enthusiastically jabbing elbows and bumping hips. They hooted at her in such a friendly manner, she tried to pick up the beat. She was giggling when she was bumped back into Cade's arms.

"It is fun." Elemental, liberating, nearly pagan. "I'm dancing."

The way her face glowed, her voice rang with delighted laughter, had a grin flashing on his face. "Looks that way."

She waved a hand in front of her face in a useless attempt to fan away the heat. "I like it."

"Then we'll do it again." The volume eased down,

the beat smoothed into a hum. "Here comes a slow one. Now all you have to do is plaster yourself all over me."

"I think I already am."

"Closer." His leg slid intimately between hers, his hands cruised low on her hips.

"Oh, God." Her stomach filled with frantic butter-flies. "That has to be another Commandment."

"One of my personal favorites."

The music was seductive, sexy and sad. Her mood changed with it, from giddiness to longing. "Cade, I don't think this is smart." But she'd risen to her toes, so their faces were close.

"Let's be reckless. Just for one dance."

"It can't last," she murmured as her cheek pressed against his.

"Shh. For as long as we want."

Forever, she thought, and held tight. "I'm not an empty slate. I've just been erased for a while. Neither of us might like what's written there when we find it."

He could smell her, feel her, taste her. "I know everything I need to know."

She shook her head. "But I don't." She drew back, looked into his eyes. "I don't," she repeated. And when she broke away and moved quickly through the crowd, he let her go.

She hurried into the rest room. She needed privacy, she needed to get her breath back. She needed to remember that, however much she might want it, her life had not begun when she walked into a cramped little office and saw Cade Parris for the first time.

The room was nearly as packed as the dance floor, with women primping at the mirrors, talking about men, complaining about other women. The room smelled thickly of hairspray, perfume and sweat.

In one of the three narrow sinks, Bailey ran the water cold, splashed it on her overheated face. She'd danced in a noisy nightclub and screamed with laughter. She'd let the man she wanted touch her intimately, without a care for who saw it.

And she knew as she lifted her face and studied the reflection in the spotty mirror that none of those things were usual for her.

This was new. Just as Cade Parris was new. And she didn't know how any of it would fit into the life that was hers.

It was happening so quickly, she thought, and dug into her purse for a brush. The purse he'd bought her, the brush he'd bought her, she thought, while emotion swamped her. Everything she had right now, she owed to him.

Was that what she felt for him? A debt, gratitude? Lust?

Not one of the women crowded into the room with her was worried about things like that, she thought. Not one of them was asking herself that kind of question about the man she'd just danced with. The man she wanted, or who wanted her.

They would all go back out and dance again. Or go home. They would make love tonight, if the mood was right. And tomorrow their lives would simply move on.

But she had to ask. And how could she know the answer when she didn't know herself? And how could she take him, or give herself to him, until she did know?

Get yourself in order, she told herself, and methodically ran the brush through her tumbled hair. Time to be sensible, practical. Calm. Satisfied her hair was tidy again, she slipped the brush back into her bag.

A redhead walked in, all legs and attitude, with short-cropped hair and wraparound shades. "Son of a bitch grabbed my butt," she said to no one in particular, and strode into a stall, slammed the door.

Bailey's vision grayed. Clammy waves of dizziness had her clutching the lip of the sink. But her knees went so weak she had to lean over the bowl and gulp for air.

"Hey, hey, you okay?"

Someone patted her on the back, and the voice was like bees buzzing in her head. "Yes, just a little dizzy. I'm all right. I'm fine." Using both hands, she cupped cold water, splashed it again and again on her face.

When she thought her legs would hold her, she snatched paper towels and dried her dripping cheeks.

As wobbly as a drunk, she staggered out of the rest room and back into the screaming cave that was the club.

She was bumped and jostled and never noticed. Someone offered to buy her a drink. Some bright soul offered boozily to buy her. She passed through without seeing anything but blinding lights and faceless bodies. When Cade reached her, she was sheet white. Asking no questions, he simply picked her up, to the cheering approval of nearby patrons, and carried her outside.

"I'm sorry. I got dizzy."

"It was a bad idea." He was cursing himself viciously for taking her to a second-rate nightclub with rowdy regulars. "I shouldn't have brought you here."

"No, it was a wonderful idea. I'm glad you brought me. I just needed some air." For the first time, she realized he was carrying her, and wavered between embarrassment and gratitude. "Put me down, Cade. I'm all right."

"I'll take you home."

"No, is there somewhere we can just sit? Just sit and get some air?"

"Sure." He set her on her feet, but watched her carefully. "There's a café just down the street. We can sit outside. Get some coffee."

"Good." She held tightly on to his hand, letting him lead the way. The bass from the band inside the club all but shook the sidewalk. The café a few doors down was nearly as crowded as the club had been, with waiters scurrying to deliver espressos and lattes and iced fruit drinks.

"I came on pretty strong," he began as he pulled out a chair for her.

"Yes, you did. I'm flattered."

Head cocked, he sat across from her. "You're flattered?"

"Yes. I may not remember anything, but I don't think I'm stupid." The air, however close and warm, felt glorious. "You're an incredibly attractive man. And I look around, right here…." Steadying herself, she did just that, scanning the little tables crammed together under a dark green awning. "Beautiful women everywhere. All over the city where we walked today, inside that club, right here in this café. But you came on to me, so I'm flattered."

"That's not exactly the reaction I was looking for, or that I expected. But I guess it'll do for now." He glanced up at the waiter who hustled to their table. "Cappuccino?" he asked Bailey.

"That would be perfect."

"Decaf or regular?" the waiter chirped.

"Real coffee," Cade told him, and leaned closer to Bailey. "Your color's coming back."

"I feel better. A woman came in the ladies' room."

"Did she hassle you?"

"No, no." Touched by his immediate instinct to defend, she laid a hand over his. "I was feeling a little shaky, and then she walked in. Sort of swaggered in." It made her lips curve. "And for a minute, I thought I knew her."

He turned his hand over, gripped hers. "You recognized her?"

"No, not her, precisely, though I thought… No, it was the type, I suppose you'd say. Arrogant, cocky, striking. A tall redhead in tight denim, with a chip on her shoulder." She closed her eyes a moment, let out a long breath, opened them again. "M.J."

"That was the name on the note in your pocket."

"It's there," Bailey murmured, massaging her temples. "It's there somewhere in my head. And it's important. It's vital, but I can't focus on it. But there's a woman, and she's part of my life. And, Cade, something's wrong."

"Do you think she's in trouble?"

"I don't know. When I start to get a picture—when I can almost see her—it's just this image of utter confidence and ability. As if nothing could possibly be wrong. But I know there is something wrong. And it's my fault. It has to be my fault."

He shook his head. Blame wouldn't help. It wasn't the angle they needed to pursue. "Tell me what you see when you start to get that picture. Just try to relax, and tell me."

"Short, dark red hair, sharp features. Green eyes. But maybe those are yours. But I think hers are green, darker than yours. I could almost draw her face. If I knew how to draw."

"Maybe you do." He took a pen and pad out of his pocket. "Give it a try."

With her lip caught between her teeth, she tried to capture a sharp, triangular face. With a sigh, she set the pen down as their coffee was served. "I think we can safely assume I'm not an artist."

"So we'll get one." He took the pad back, smiled at the pathetic sketch. "Even I could do better than this, and I scraped by with a C my one dismal semester of art. Do you think you can describe her, the features?"

"I can try. I don't see it all clearly. It's like trying to focus a camera that's not working quite right."

"Police artists are good at putting things together."

She slopped coffee over the rim of her cup. "The police? Do we have to go to the police?"

"Unofficial, don't worry. Trust me."

"I do." But the word *police* rang in her head like alarm bells. "I will."

"We've got something to go on. We know M.J.'s a woman, a tall redhead with a chip on her shoulder. Mary Jane, Martha June, Melissa Jo. You were with her in the desert."

"She was in the dream." Sun and sky and rock. Contentment. Then fear. "Three of us in the dream, but it won't come clear."

"Well, we'll see if we can put a likeness together, then we'll have somewhere to start."

She stared down into her foamy coffee, thinking her life was just that, a cloud concealing the center. "You make it sound easy."

"It's just steps, Bailey. You take the next step, and see where that goes."

She nodded, stared hard into her coffee. "Why did you marry someone you didn't love?"

Surprised, he leaned back, blew out a breath. "Well, that's quite a change in topic."

"I'm sorry. I don't know why I asked that. It's none of my business."

"I don't know. Under the circumstances, it seems a fair enough question." He drummed his fingers restlessly on the table. "You could say I got tired, worn down by family pressure, but that's a cop-out. Nobody held a gun to my head, and I was over twenty-one."

It annoyed him to admit that, he realized. To be honest with Bailey was to face the truth without excuses. "We liked each other well enough, or at least we did until we got married. A couple of months of marriage fixed that friendship."

"I'm sorry, Cade." It was easy to see the discomfort on his face, his unhappiness with the memory. And though she envied him even that unhappiness, she hated knowing she'd helped put it there. "There's no need to go into it."

"We were good in bed," he went on, ignoring her. And kept his eyes on hers when she shrank back, drew in and away from him. "Right up until the end, the sex was good. The trouble was, toward the end, which was a little under two years from the beginning, it was all heat and no heart. We just didn't give a damn."

Couldn't have cared less, he remembered. Just two bored people stuck in the same house. "That's what it came down to. There wasn't another man, or another woman. No passionate fights over money, careers, children, dirty dishes. We just didn't care. And when we stopped caring altogether, we got nasty. Then the lawyers came in, and it got nastier. Then it was done."

"Did she love you?"

"No." He answered immediately, then frowned, looked hard at nothing and again tried to be honest. And the answer was sad and bruising. "No, she didn't, any more than I loved her. And neither one of us worried about working too hard on that part of it."

He took money from his wallet, dropped it on the table and rose. "Let's go home."

"Cade." She touched his arm. "You deserved better."

"Yeah." He looked at the hand on his arm, the delicate fingers, the pretty rings. "So did she. But it's a little late for that." He lifted her hand so that the ring gleamed between them. "You can forget a lot of things, Bailey, but can you forget love?"

"Don't."

He'd be damned if he'd back off. Suddenly his entire miserable failure of a marriage was slapped into his face. He'd be damned. "If a man put this on your finger, a man you loved, would you forget? Could you?"

"I don't know." She wrenched away, rushed down the sidewalk toward his car. When he whirled her around, her eyes were bright with anger and fears. "I don't *know.*"

"You wouldn't forget. You couldn't, if it mattered. This matters."

He crushed his mouth to hers, pressing her back against the car and battering them both with his frustration and needs. Gone was the patience, the clever heat of seduction. What was left was all the raw demand that had bubbled beneath it. And he wanted her weak and clinging and as desperate as he. For just that moment.

For just the now.

The panic came first, a choke hold that snagged the air from her throat. She couldn't answer this vivid, violent need. Simply wasn't prepared or equipped to meet it and survive.

So she surrendered, abruptly, completely, thoughtlessly, part of her trusting that he wouldn't hurt her. Another praying that he couldn't. She yielded to the flash of staggering heat, the stunning power of untethered lust, rode high on it for one quivering moment.

And knew she might not survive even surrender.

She trembled, infuriating him. Shaming him. He was hurting her. He almost wanted to, for wouldn't she remember if he did? Wasn't pain easier to remember than kindness?

He knew if she forgot him it would kill him.

And if he hurt her, he would have killed everything worthwhile inside him.

He let her go, stepped back. Instantly she hugged her arms over her chest in a defensive move that slashed at him. Music and voices lifted in excitement and laughter flowed down the sidewalk behind him as he stared at her, spotlighted like a deer caught in headlights.

"I'm sorry."

"Cade—"

He lifted his hands, palms out. His temper rarely flashed, but he knew better than to reach for reason until it had settled again. "I'm sorry," he repeated. "It's my problem. I'll take you home."

And when he had, when she was in her room and the lights were off, he lay out in the hammock, where he could watch her window.

It wasn't so much examining his own life, he realized, that had set him off. He knew the highs and lows of it, the missteps and foolish mistakes. It was the rings on her fingers, and finally facing that a man might have put one of them on her. A man who might be waiting for her to remember.

And it wasn't about sex. Sex was easy. She would have given herself to him that evening. He'd seen it when he walked into the kitchen while she was buried in a book. He'd known she was thinking of him. Wanting him.

Now he thought he'd been a fool for not taking what was there for him. But he hadn't taken it because he wanted more. A lot more.

He wanted love, and it wasn't reasonable to want it. She was adrift, afraid, in trouble neither of them could identify. Yet he wanted her to tumble into love with him, as quickly and completely as he'd tumbled into love with her.

It wasn't reasonable.

But he didn't give a damn about reason.

He'd slay her dragon, whatever the cost. And once he had, he'd fight whoever stood in his way to keep her. Even if it was Bailey herself who stood there.

When he slept, he dreamed. When he dreamed, he dreamed of dragons and black nights and a damsel with golden hair who was locked in a high tower and spun straw into rich blue diamonds.

* * *

And when she slept, she dreamed. When she dreamed, she dreamed of lightning and terror and of running through the dark with the power of gods clutched in her hands.

Chapter 7

Despite the fact that she'd slept poorly, Bailey was awake and out of bed by seven. She concluded that she had some internal clock that started her day at an assigned time, and couldn't decide if that made her boring or responsible. In either case, she dressed, resisted the urge to go down the hall and peek into Cade's room and went down to make coffee.

She knew he was angry with her. An icy, simmering anger that she hadn't a clue how to melt or diffuse. He hadn't said a word on the drive back from Georgetown, and the silence had been charged with temper and, she was certain, sexual frustration.

She wondered if she had ever caused sexual frustration in a man before, and wished she didn't feel this inner, wholly female, pleasure at causing it in a man like Cade.

But beyond that, his rapid shift of moods left her baffled and upset. She wondered if she knew any more about human nature than she did of her own past.

She wondered if she knew anything at all about the male of the species.

Did men behave in this inexplicable manner all the time? And if they did, how did a smart woman handle it? Should she be cool and remote until he'd explained himself? Or would it be better if she was friendly and casual, as if nothing had happened?

As if he hadn't kissed her as if he could swallow her whole. As if he hadn't touched her, moved his hands over her, as though he had a right to, as though it were the most natural thing in the world for him to turn her body into a quivering mass of needs.

Now her own mood shifted from timid to annoyed as she wrenched open the refrigerator for milk. How the hell was she supposed to know how to behave? She had no idea if she'd ever been kissed that way before, ever felt this way, wanted this way. Just because she was lost, was she supposed to meekly go in whichever direction Cade Parris pointed her?

And if he pointed her toward the bed, was she supposed to hop in?

Oh, no, she didn't think so. She was a grown woman, capable of making her own decisions. She wasn't stupid and she wasn't helpless. She'd managed to hire herself a detective, hadn't she?

Damn it.

Just because she had no precedents for her own behavior, that didn't mean she couldn't start setting some here and now.

She would not be a doormat.

She would not be a fool.

She would not be a victim.

She slapped the milk carton down on the counter, scowled out the window. It was Cade's bad luck that she happened to spot him sleeping in the hammock just as her temper peaked.

He wouldn't have dozed so peacefully if he could have seen the way her eyes kindled, the way her lips peeled back in a snarl.

Fueled for battle, Bailey slammed out of the house and marched across the lawn.

She gave the hammock one hard shove.

"Who the hell do you think you are?"

"What?" He shot rudely awake, gripping the sides of the hammock for balance, his brain musty with sleep. "What? Don't you remember?"

"Don't get smart with me." She gave the hammock another shove as he struggled to sit up. "I make my own decisions, I run my own life—such as it is. I hired you to help me find out who I am and what happened to me. I'm not paying you to sulk because I won't hop into bed with you when you have an itch."

"Okay." He rubbed his eyes, finally managed to focus on the stunning and furious face bent over him. "What the hell are you talking about? I'm not sulking, I—"

"Don't tell me you're not sulking," she shot back. "Sleeping out in the backyard like a hobo."

"It's my yard." It irritated him to have to point it out. It irritated him more to be dragged out of sleep into an argument before his mind could engage.

"Taking me dancing," she continued, stalking away and back. "Trying to seduce me on the dance floor, then having a snit because—"

"A snit." That stung. "Listen, sweetheart, I've never had a snit in my life."

"I say you did, and don't call me sweetheart in that tone of voice."

"Now you don't like my tone." His eyes narrowed dangerously, to sharp green slits that threatened retaliation. "Well, let's try a brand-new tone and see how you—" He ended with an oath when she jerked the hammock and flipped him out on his face.

Her first reaction was shock, then an immediate

urge to apologize. But as the air turned blue around her, she snapped herself back, jerked her chin up in the air and marched off.

He'd hit the ground with a thud, and he was sure he'd heard his own bones rattle. But he was on his feet again quickly enough, limping a little, but fast enough to snag her before she reached the door.

He yanked her around to face him. "What bug got up your—"

"You deserved it." The blood was roaring in her head, her heart was pounding, but she wasn't going to back down.

"What the hell for?"

"For…whatever."

"Well, that sure covers it."

"Just get out of my way. I'm going for a walk."

"No," he said precisely, "you're not."

"You can't tell me what to do."

He estimated he was close to twice her weight and had a good eight inches in height on her. His lips curved grimly. "Yes, I can. You're hysterical."

That snapped it. "I certainly am not hysterical. If I were hysterical, I'd scratch that nasty smile off your face, and poke those smug eyes out, and—"

To simplify matters, he simply picked her up and carried her inside. She wiggled, sputtered, kicked a little, but he managed to drop her into a kitchen chair.

Putting his hands on her shoulders, his face close to hers, he gave one pithy order.

"Stay."

If he didn't have coffee, immediately, he was going to die. Or kill someone.

"You're fired."

"Fine, great, whoopee." He let her fume while he poured coffee and downed it like water. "God, what a way to start the day." He grabbed a bottle of aspirin, fought with the childproof cap while the headache that was brewing insidiously burst into full-blown misery.

"I'm not going to tolerate having a woman yell at me before my eyes are open. Whatever's got you going, sweetheart, you just hold on to it until I—" He cursed again, slamming the stubborn cap on the edge of the counter, where it held firm.

His head was throbbing, his knee wept where it had hit the ground, and he could easily have chewed through the plastic to get to the aspirin.

Swearing ripely, he grabbed a butcher knife out of the wooden block on the counter and hacked at the bottle until he'd decapitated it. His face tight with fury, he turned with the bottle in one hand, the knife in the other. His teeth were clenched.

"Now you listen…" he began.

Bailey's eyes rolled back in her head, and she slid

from the chair onto the floor in a dead faint before he could move.

"Sweet God." The knife clattered on the floor, and aspirin rolled everywhere as the mangled bottle hit the tiles. He gathered her up, and for lack of anything better, laid her on the kitchen table while he dampened a cloth. "Come on, Bailey, come around, sweetheart."

He bathed her face, chafed her wrists and cursed himself. How could he have shouted at her that way, manhandled her like that, when she was so fragile? Maybe he'd go out and kick some puppies, stomp on some kittens, for his next act.

When she moaned and shifted, he pressed her limp hand to his lips. "That's the way. All the way back." Her eyes fluttered open while he stroked her hair. "It's okay, Bailey. Take it easy."

"He's going to kill me." Her eyes were open, but blind. She clutched at Cade's shirt as terror strangled her breath. "He's going to kill me."

"No one's going to hurt you. I'm right here."

"He's going to kill me. He's got a knife. If he finds me, he'll kill me."

He wanted to gather her up, soothe it all away, but she'd trusted him to help. He kept his voice very calm, uncurled her fingers from his shirt and held them. "Who's got the knife, Bailey? Who's going to kill you?"

"He…he…" She could see it, almost see it, the hand

hacking down, the knife flashing again and again. "There's blood everywhere. Blood everywhere. I have to get away from the blood. The knife. The lightning. I have to run."

He held her still, kept his voice calm. "Where are you? Tell me where you are."

"In the dark. Lights are out. He'll kill me. I have to run."

"Run where?"

"Anywhere." Her breath was coming so fast, the force of it scored her throat like nails. "Anywhere, away. Somewhere away. If he finds me—"

"He's not going to find you. I won't let him find you." He cupped her face firmly in his hands so that her eyes met his. "Slow down now. Just slow down." If she kept panting like that, she was going to hyperventilate and faint on him again. He didn't think he could handle it. "You're safe here. You're safe with me. Understand that?"

"Yes. Yes." She closed her eyes, shuddered hard. "Yes. I need air. Please, I need some air."

He picked her up again, carried her outside. He set her on the padded chaise on the patio, sat beside her. "Take it slow. Remember, you're safe here. You're safe."

"Yes, all right." With an effort, she evened out the air that seemed to want to clog and burst in her lungs. "I'm all right."

Far from it, he thought. She was sheet white, clammy and shivering. But the memory was close, and he had to try to dislodge it. "No one's going to hurt you. Nothing's going to touch you here. You hang on to that and try to tell me everything you remember."

"It comes in blips." She struggled to breathe past the pressure in her chest. "When you had the knife…" Fear clawed through her again with razored talons.

"I scared you. I'm sorry." He took her hands, held them. "I wouldn't hurt you."

"I know." She closed her eyes again, let the sun beat hot on the lids. "There was a knife. A long blade, curved. It's beautiful. The bone handle is deeply carved. I've seen it—maybe I've used it."

"Where did you see it?"

"I don't know. There were voices, shouting. I can't hear what they're saying. It's like the ocean, all sound, roaring, violent sound." She pressed her hands to her ears, as if she could block it out. "Then there's blood, everywhere there's blood. All over the floor."

"What kind of floor?"

"Carpet, gray carpet. The lightning keeps flashing, the knife keeps flashing."

"Is there a window? Do you see lightning through the window?"

"Yes, I think…" She shivered again, and the scene

fighting to form in her mind went blank. "It's dark. Everything went dark, and I have to get away. I have to hide."

"Where do you hide?"

"It's a little place, hardly room, and if he sees, I'll be trapped. He has the knife. I can see it, his hand on the hilt. It's so close, if he turns—"

"Tell me about the hand," Cade said, interrupting her gently. "What does the hand look like, Bailey?"

"It's dark, very dark, but there's a light bouncing around. It almost catches me. He's holding the knife, and his knuckles are white. There's blood on them. On his ring."

"What kind of ring, Bailey?" His eyes stayed intent on her face, but his voice remained calm and easy. "What does the ring look like?"

"It's heavy gold, thick band. Yellow gold. The center stone's a ruby cabochon. On either side there are small diamonds, brilliant-cut. Initials. *T* and *S* in a stylized sweep. The diamonds are red with blood. He's so close, so close, I can smell it. If he looks down. If he looks down and sees me. He'll kill me, slice me to pieces, if he finds me."

"He didn't." Unable to bear it any longer, Cade drew her up, held her. "You got away. How did you get away, Bailey?"

"I don't know." The relief was so huge—Cade's arms

around her, the sun warm at her back, his cheek pressed to her hair—she could have wept. "I don't remember."

"It's all right. That's enough."

"Maybe I killed him." She drew back, looked into Cade's face. "Maybe I used the gun that was in the bag and shot him."

"The gun was fully loaded, Bailey."

"I could have replaced it."

"Sweetheart, in my professional opinion, you wouldn't know how."

"But if I—"

"And if you did—" he took her shoulders now, gave her a quick shake "—it was to protect yourself. He was armed, you were terrified, and it sounds as if he'd already killed someone. Whatever you did to survive was right."

She shifted away, looked out over the yard, past the flowers, the leafy old trees, the tidy fence line. "What kind of person am I? There's a very real possibility I saw someone murdered. I did nothing to stop it, nothing to help."

"Be sensible, Bailey. What could you have done?"

"Something," she murmured. "I didn't get to a phone, call the police. I just ran."

"And if you hadn't, you'd be dead." He knew by the way she winced that his tone had been harsh. But it was what she needed. "Instead, you're alive, and bit by bit, we're putting it together."

He rose, paced away, so that he wouldn't give in to the temptation just to cuddle her. "You were in a building of some sort. In a room with gray carpet, probably a window. There was an argument, and someone had a knife. He used it. His initials could be *T.S.* He came after you, and it was dark. More than likely it was a blackout and the building had lost power. A section of North West D.C. lost power for two hours the night before you hired me, so we've got somewhere to look. You knew the building well enough to head for cover. I'd say you belonged there. You live or work there."

He turned back, noting that she was watching him, paying close attention. Her hands were steady in her lap again. "I can check if there was a knifing reported that night, but I've been watching the papers, and there hasn't been any press on it."

"But it was days ago now. Someone must have found—found a body, if there was one."

"Not if it was a private home, or an office that shut down for the long weekend. If there'd been someone else there, other people in the building when it happened, it would have been reported. Odds are you were alone."

It made his stomach crawl to think of it—Bailey alone in the dark with a killer.

"The storm didn't hit until after ten."

It was logical, and the simple movement from theory to fact calmed her. "What do we do now?"

"We'll drive around the area that lost power, starting at the hotel where you ended up."

"I don't remember getting to the hotel, whether I walked or took a cab."

"You either walked, took a bus or the metro. I've already checked on cabs. None of the companies dropped off a fare within three blocks of the hotel that night. We're going to move on the assumption that you were on foot, dazed, too shaken to think of hopping a bus, and since the metro only runs until midnight, that's too close to call."

She nodded, looked down at her hands. "I'm sorry I shouted at you before. You didn't deserve it, after everything you've done for me."

"I deserved it." He tucked his hands in his pockets. "I refuse to accept the term *snit* but I'll allow the phrase *out of sorts*." He enjoyed seeing her lips curve in one of her hesitant smiles as she lifted her head.

"I suppose we both were. Did I hurt you when I knocked you down?"

"My ego's going to be carrying a bruise for a while. Otherwise, no." He angled his head. There was a quick cockiness in the movement, and in the eyes that glinted at hers. "And I didn't try to seduce you on the dance floor, Bailey. I did seduce you on the dance floor."

Her pulse stuttered a bit. He was so outrageously gorgeous, standing there in the bright morning sun, rumpled, his dark hair thick and untidy, the dimples denting his cheeks and his mouth arrogantly curved. No woman alive, Bailey thought, could have stopped her mouth from watering.

And she was certain he knew it.

"Your ego seems to function well enough, bruised or not."

"We can always stage a reenactment."

Her stomach fluttered at the thought, but she worked up a smile. "I'm glad you're not angry with me anymore. I don't think I handle confrontations very well."

He rubbed his elbow, where he'd lost several layers of skin on impact. "You seemed to do well enough. I'm going to clean up, then we'll take ourselves a Sunday drive."

There were so many kinds of buildings, Bailey thought as Cade tooled around the city. Old ones, new ones, crumbling row houses and refurbished homes. Tall office buildings and squat storefronts.

Had she ever really noticed the city before? she wondered. The sloping stone walls, the trees rising up from the sidewalks. Belching buses with whining air brakes.

Was it always so humid in July? Was the summer sky always the color of paper? And were the flowers always so luscious in the public spaces tucked around statues and along the streets?

Had she shopped in any of these stores, eaten in any of these restaurants?

The trees took over again, tall and stately, lining both sides of the road, so that it seemed they were driving through a park, rather than the middle of a crowded city.

"It's like seeing everything for the first time," she murmured. "I'm sorry."

"Doesn't matter. Something will either click or it won't."

They passed gracious old homes, brick and granite, then another strip of shops, smart and trendy. She made a small sound, and though she was hardly aware of it herself, Cade slowed. "Something click?"

"That boutique. Marguerite's. I don't know."

"Let's take a look." He circled around, backtracked, then pulled into a narrow lot that fronted several upscale shops. "Everything's closed, but that doesn't mean we can't window shop." Leaning over, he opened her door, then climbed out his own.

"Maybe I just liked the dress in the window," she murmured.

It was very lovely, just a sweep of rose-petal silk

with thin straps of glittery rhinestones that continued down to cross under the bodice.

The display was completed by a tiny silver evening bag and impossibly high heels in matching silver.

The way it made her smile, Cade wished the shop was open, so that he could buy it for her. "It's your style."

"I don't know." She cupped her hands to the glass, peered through them for the simple delight of looking at pretty things. "That's a wonderful cocktail suit in navy linen. Oh, and that red dress is just fabulous. Bound to make you feel powerful and accomplished. I really should start wearing bolder colors, but I always wimp out with pastels."

Try this green, Bailey. It's got punch. There's nothing more tiring than a clothes coward.

How long do I have to stand around while you two play with clothes? I'm starving.

Oh, stop bitching. You're not happy unless you're feeding your face or buying new jeans. Bailey, not that tedious beige. The green. Trust me.

"She talked me into it," Bailey murmured. "I bought the green suit. She was right. She always is."

"Who's right, Bailey?" He didn't touch her, afraid that even an encouraging hand on her shoulder would jar her. "Is it M.J.?"

"No, no, not M.J. She's annoyed, impatient, hates to waste time. Shopping's such a waste of time."

Oh, her head hurt. It was going to explode any moment, simply burst off her shoulders. But the need was greater, the need to latch on to this one thing. This one answer. Her stomach rolled, threatened to heave, and her skin went clammy with the effort of holding off nausea.

"Grace." Her voice broke on the name. "Grace," she said again as her knees buckled. "Her name's Grace. Grace and M.J." Tears sprang to her eyes, rolled down her cheeks as she threw her arms around Cade's neck. "I've been here. I've been to this shop. I bought a green suit. I remember."

"Good. Good job, Bailey." He gave her a quick swing.

"No, but that's all." She pressed a hand to her forehead. The pain was screaming now. "That's all I remember. Just being in there with them, buying a suit. It's so foolish. Why should I remember buying a suit?"

"You remember the people." He smoothed his thumbs over her temples. He could all but feel the headache raging inside. "They're important to you. It was a moment, something shared, a happy time."

"But I can't remember them. Not really. Just feelings."

"You're breaking through." He pressed his lips to her brow, drew her back toward the car. "And it's happening quickly now." He eased her down on the seat, hooked her safety belt himself. "And it hurts you."

"It doesn't matter. I need to know."

"It matters to me. We'll get you something for that headache, and some food. Then we'll start again."

Arguments wouldn't sway him. Bailey had to admit that fighting Cade and a blinding headache was a battle she was doomed to lose. She let him prop her up in bed, dutifully swallowed the aspirin he gave her. Obediently she closed her eyes as he instructed, then opened them again when he brought up a bowl of chicken soup.

"It's out of a can," he told her, fussing with the pillows behind her back. "But it should do the job."

"I could eat in the kitchen, Cade. It was a headache, not a tumor. And it's almost gone."

"I'm going to work you hard later. Take the pampering while you can get it."

"All right, I will." She spooned up soup. "It's wonderful. You added thyme."

"For that little hint of France."

Her smile faded. "Paris," she murmured. "Something about Paris." The headache snuck back as she tried to concentrate.

"Let it go for now." He sat beside her. "I'd say your subconscious is letting you know you're not all the way ready yet to remember. A piece at a time will do."

"I suppose it'll have to." She smiled again. "Want some soup?"

"Now that you mention it." He leaned forward, let

her feed him, and didn't take his eyes from hers. "Not too shabby."

She took another spoonful herself, tasted him. Marvelous. "As handy as you are in the kitchen, I'm surprised your wife let you get away."

"Ex-wife, and we had a cook."

"Oh." She fed him again, slowly taking turns. "I've been trying to figure out how to ask without seeming rude."

He slipped her hair behind her ear. "Just ask."

"Well, this lovely house, the antiques, the fancy sports car… Then there's your office."

His mouth twitched. "Something wrong with my office?"

"No. Well, nothing a bulldozer and a construction crew couldn't cure. It just doesn't compute with the rest."

"I've got a thing about my business paying for itself, and that office is about all it can afford so far. My investigative work pays the bills and just a little more. On a personal level, I'm rolling in it." His eyes laughed into hers. "Money, that is. If that's what you're asking."

"I guess it was. You're rich, then."

"Depends on your definition, or if you mean me personally or the entire family. It's shopping centers, real estate, that sort of thing. A lot of doctors and lawyers and bankers down through the ages. And me, I'm—"

"The black sheep," she finished for him, thrilled

that he was just that. "You didn't want to go into the family business. You didn't want to be a doctor or a lawyer or a banker."

"Nope. I wanted to be Sam Spade."

Delighted, she chuckled. "*The Maltese Falcon.* I'm glad you didn't want to be a banker."

"Me, too." He took the hand she'd laid on his cheek, pressed his lips to it and felt her quiver of response.

"I'm glad I found your name in the phone book." Her voice thickened. "I'm glad I found you."

"So am I." He took the tray from between them, set it aside. Even if he'd been blind, he thought, he would have understood what was in her eyes just then. And his heart thrilled to it. "I could walk out of here and leave you alone now." He trailed a finger across her collarbone, then let it rest on the pulse that beat rabbit-quick at her throat. "That's not what I want to do."

It was her decision, she knew. Her choice. Her moment. "That's not what I want, either." When he cupped her face in his hands, she closed her eyes. "Cade, I may have done something horrible."

His lips paused an inch from hers. "I don't care."

"I may have— I may be—" Determined to face it, she opened her eyes again. "There may be someone else."

His fingers tightened. "I don't give a damn."

She let out a long breath, and took her moment. "Neither do I," she said, and pulled him to her.

Chapter 8

This was what it felt like to be pressed under a man's body. A man's hard, needy body. A man who wanted you above all else.

For that moment.

It was breathless and stunning, exciting and fresh. The way he combed his fingers through her hair as his lips covered hers thrilled her. The fit of mouth against mouth, as if the only thing lips and tongues were made for were to taste a lover. And it was the taste of him that filled her—strong and male and real.

Whatever had come before, whatever came after, this mattered now.

She stroked her hands over him, and it was glorious. The shape of his body, the breadth of shoulders, the length of back, the narrowing of waist, the muscles beneath so firm, so tight. And when her hands skimmed under his shirt, the smooth, warm flesh beneath fascinated.

"Oh, I've wanted to touch you." Her lips raced over his face. "I was afraid I never would."

"I've wanted you from the first moment you walked in the door." He drew back only enough to see her eyes, the deep, melting brown of them. "Before you walked in the door. Forever."

"It doesn't make any sense. We don't—"

"It doesn't matter. Only this." His lips closed over hers again, took the kiss deeper, tangling their flavors together.

He wanted to go slowly, draw out every moment. It seemed he'd waited for her all his life, so now he could take all the time in the world to touch, to taste, to explore and exploit. Each shift of her body beneath his was a gift. Each sigh a treasure.

To have her like this, with the sun streaming through the window, with her hair flowing gold over the old quilt and her body both yielding and eager, was sweeter than any dream.

They belonged. It was all he had to know.

To see her, to unfasten the simple shirt he'd picked

for her, to open it inch by inch to pale, smooth flesh was everything he wanted. He skimmed his fingertips over the curve of her breast, felt her skin quiver in response, watched her eyes flicker dark, then focus on his.

"You're perfect." He cupped her, and she was small and firm and made for his palm.

He bent his head, rubbed his lips where the lace of her bra met flesh, then moved them up, lazily up her throat, over her jaw, and back to nip at her mouth.

No one had kissed her like this before. She knew it was impossible for anyone else to have taken such care. With a soft sigh, she poured herself into the kiss, murmuring when he shifted her to slip the shirt away, trembling when he slid the lace aside and bared her breasts to his hands.

And his mouth.

She moaned, lost, gloriously lost, in a dark maze of sensations. Soft here, then rough, cool, then searing, each feeling bumped gently into the next, then merged into simple pleasure. Whichever way she turned, there was something new and thrilling. When she tugged his shirt away, there was the lovely slippery slide of his flesh against hers, the intimacy of it, heart to heart.

And her heart danced to the play of his lips, the teasing nip of teeth, the slow torture of tongue.

The air was like syrup, thick and sweet, as he slid her slacks over her hips. She struggled to gulp it in, but each breath was shallow and short. He was touching her everywhere, his hands slick and slow, but relentlessly pushing her higher and stronger until the heat was immense. It kindled inside her like a brush fire.

She moaned out his name, clutching the quilt and dragging it into tangles as her body strained to reach for something just beyond her grasp. As she arched desperately against him, he watched her. Slid up her body again until his lips were close to hers, and watched her. Watched her as, with quick, clever fingers, he tore her free.

It was his name she called when the heat reached flash point, and his body she clung to as her own shuddered.

That was what he'd wanted.

His name was still vibrating on her lips when he crushed them with his, when he rolled with her over the bed in a greedy quest to take and possess. Blind with need, he tugged at his jeans, trembling himself when she buried her mouth against his throat, strained against him in quivering invitation.

She was more generous than any fantasy. More generous than any wish. More his than any dream.

With sunlight pouring over the tangled sheets, she arched to him, opened as if she'd been waiting all her life for him. His heart pounded in his head as he slipped inside her, moved to fill her.

Shock froze him for a dazed instant, and every

muscle tensed. But she shook her head, wrapped herself around him and took him in.

"You" was all she said. "Only you."

He lay still, listening to her heart thudding, absorbing the quakes of her body with his. Only him, he thought, and closed his eyes. She'd been innocent. Untouched. A miracle. And his heart was tugged in opposing directions of guilt and pure selfish pleasure.

She'd been innocent, and he'd taken her.

She'd been untouched, until he touched.

He wanted to beg her to forgive him.

He wanted to climb out on the roof and crow.

Not certain either would suit the situation, he gently tested the waters.

"Bailey?"

"Hmm?"

"Ah, in my professional opinion as a licensed investigator, I conclude it's extremely unlikely you're married." He felt the rumble of her laughter, and lifted his head to grin down at her. "I'll put it in my report."

"You do that."

He brushed the hair from her cheek. "Did I hurt you? I'm sorry. I never considered—"

"No." She pressed her hand over his. "You didn't hurt me. I'm happy, giddy. Relieved." Her lips curved on a sigh. "I never considered, either. I'd say we were both surprised." Abruptly her stomach fluttered with nerves. "You're not…disappointed? If you—"

"I'm devastated. I really hoped you'd be married, with six kids. I really only enjoy making love with married women."

"No, I meant… Was it—was I—was everything all right?"

"Bailey." On a half laugh, he rolled over so that she could settle on his chest. "You're perfect. Absolutely, completely perfect. I love you." She went very still, and her cheek stayed pressed to his heart. "You know I do," he said quietly. "From the moment I saw you."

Now she wanted to weep, because it was everything she wanted to hear, and nothing she could accept. "You don't know me."

"Neither do you."

She lifted her head, shook it fiercely. "That's exactly the point. Joking about it doesn't change the truth."

"Here's the truth, then." He sat up, took her firmly by the shoulders. "I'm in love with you. In love with the woman I'm holding right now. You're exactly what I want, what I need, and sweetheart—" he kissed her lightly "—I'm keeping you."

"You know it's not that simple."

"I'm not asking for simple." He slid his hands down, gripped hers. "I'm asking you to marry me."

"That's impossible." Panicked, she tugged on her

hands, but he gripped them calmly and held her in place. "You know that's impossible. I don't know where I come from, what I've done. I met you three days ago."

"That all makes sense, or would, except for one thing." He drew her against him and shot reason to hell with a kiss.

"Don't do this." Torn to pieces, she wrapped her arms around his neck, held tight. "Don't do this, Cade. Whatever my life was, right now it's a mess. I need to find the answers."

"We'll find the answers. I promise you that. But there's one I want from you now." He drew her head back. He'd expected the tears, knew they'd be shimmering in her eyes and turning them deep gold. "Tell me you love me, Bailey, or tell me you don't."

"I can't—"

"Just one question," he murmured. "You don't need a yesterday to answer it."

No, she needed nothing but her own heart. "I can't tell you I don't love you, because I can't lie to you." She shook her head, pressed her fingers to his lips before he could speak. "I won't tell you I do, because it wouldn't be fair. It's an answer that has to wait until I know all the others. Until I know who the woman is who'll tell you. Give me time."

He'd give her time, he thought when her head was nestled on his shoulder again. Because nothing and no one was taking her from him, whatever they found on the other side of her past.

Cade liked to say that getting to a solution was just a matter of taking steps. Bailey wondered how many more there were left to climb. She felt she'd rushed up a very long staircase that day, and when reaching the landing been just as lost as ever.

Not entirely true, she told herself as she settled down at the kitchen table with a notepad and pencil. Even the urge to make a list of what she knew indicated that she was an organized person, and one who liked to review things in black and white.

Who is Bailey?

A woman who habitually rose at the same hour daily. Did that make her tedious and predictable, or responsible? She liked coffee black and strong, scrambled eggs, and her steaks medium rare. Fairly ordinary tastes. Her body was trim, not particularly muscular, and without tan lines. So, she wasn't a fitness fanatic or a sun-worshiper. Perhaps she had a job that kept her indoors.

Which meant, she thought with some humor, she wasn't a lumberjack or a lifeguard.

She was a right-handed, brown-eyed blonde, and was reasonably sure her hair color was natural or close to what she'd been born with.

She knew a great deal about gemstones, which

could mean they were a hobby, a career, or just something she liked to wear. She had possession of a diamond worth a fortune that she'd either stolen, bought—highly unlikely, she thought—or gained through an accident of some sort.

She'd witnessed a violent attack, possibly a murder, and run away.

Because that fact made her temple start to throb again, she skipped over it.

She hummed classical music in the shower and liked to watch classic film noir on television. And she couldn't figure out what that said about her personality or her background.

She liked attractive clothes, good materials, and shied away from strong colors unless pushed.

It worried her that she might be vain and frivolous.

But she had at least two female friends who shared part of her life. Grace and M.J., M.J. and Grace. Bailey wrote the names on the pad, over and over, hoping that the simple repetition would strike a fresh spark.

They mattered to her, she could feel that. She was frightened for them and didn't know why. Her mind might be blank, but her heart told her that they were special to her, closer to her than anyone else in the world.

But she was afraid to trust her heart.

There was something else she knew that Bailey

didn't want to write down, didn't want to review in black and white.

She'd had no lover. There'd been no one she cared for enough, or who cared for her enough, for intimacy. Perhaps in the life she led she'd been too judgmental, too intolerant, too self-absorbed, to accept a man into her bed.

Or perhaps she'd been too ordinary, too boring, too undesirable, for a man to accept her into his.

In any case, she had a lover now.

Why hadn't the act of lovemaking seemed foreign to her, or frightening, as it seemed it would to the un-initiated? Instead, with Cade, it had been as natural as breathing.

Natural, exciting and perfect.

He said he loved her, but how could she believe it? He knew only one small piece of her, a fraction of the whole. When her memory surfaced, he might find her to be the very type of woman he disliked.

No, she wouldn't hold him to what he'd said to this Bailey, until she knew the whole woman.

And her feelings? With a half laugh, she set the pencil aside. She'd been drawn to him instantly, trusted him completely the moment he took her hand. And fallen in love with him while she watched him stand in this kitchen, breaking brown eggs into a white bowl.

But her heart couldn't be trusted in this case, either. The closer they came to finding the truth, the closer they came to the time when they might turn from each other and walk away.

However much she wished it, they couldn't leave the canvas bag and its contents in his safe, forget they existed and just be.

"You forgot some things."

She jolted, turned her head quickly and looked into his face. How long, she wondered, had he been standing behind her, reading her notes over her shoulder, while she was thinking of him?

"I thought it might help me to write down what I know."

"Always a good plan." He walked to the fridge, took out a beer, poured her a glass of iced tea.

She sat feeling foolish and awkward, her hands clutched in her lap. Had they really rolled naked on a sun-washed bed an hour before? How was such intimacy handled in a tidy kitchen over cold drinks and puzzles?

He didn't seem to have a problem with it. Cade sat across from her, propped his feet on an empty chair and scooted her pad over. "You're a worrier."

"I am?"

"Sure." He flipped a page, started a new list. "You're worrying right now. What should you say to this guy, now that you're lovers? Now that you know he's wildly in love with you, wants to spend the rest of his life with you?"

"Cade—"

"Just stating the facts." And if he stated them often enough, he figured she'd eventually accept them. "The sex was great, and it was easy. So you worry about that, too. Why did you let this man you've known for a weekend take you to bed, when you've never let another man get that close?" His eyes flicked up, held hers. "The answer's elementary. You're just as wildly in love with me, but you're afraid to face it."

She picked up her glass, cooled her throat. "I'm a coward?"

"No, Bailey, you're not a coward, but you're constantly worried that you are. You're a champion worrier. And a woman, I think, who gives herself very little credit for her strengths, and has very little tolerance for her weaknesses. Self-judgmental."

He wrote that down, as well, while she frowned at the words on the page. "It seems to me someone in my situation has to try to judge herself."

"Practical, logical." He continued the column. "Now, leave the judging to me a moment. You're compassionate, responsible, organized. And a creature of habit. I'd say you hold some sort of position that requires those traits, as well as a good intellect. Your work habits are disciplined and precise. You also have a fine aesthetic sense."

"How can you be so sure?"

"Bailey, forgetting who you are doesn't change who

you are. That's your big flaw in reasoning here. If you hated brussels sprouts before, it's likely you're still going to hate them. If you were allergic to cats, you're still going to sneeze if you pet a kitten. And if you had a strong, moral and caring heart, it's still beating inside you. Now let me finish up here."

She twisted her head, struggling to read upside down. "What are you putting down?"

"You're a lousy drinker. Probably a metabolism thing. And I think at this point, we could have some wine later, so I can take full advantage of that." He grinned over at her. "And you blush. It's a sweet, old-fashioned physical reaction. You're tidy. You hang up your towels after you shower, you rinse off your dishes, you make your bed every morning."

There were other details, he thought. She wiggled her foot when she was nervous, her eyes went gold when she was aroused, her voice turned chilly when she was annoyed.

"You've had a good education, probably up north, from your speech pattern and accent. I'd say you concentrated on your studies like a good girl and didn't date much. Otherwise you wouldn't have been a virgin up to a couple hours ago. There, you blushed again. I really love when you do that."

"I don't see the point in this."

"There's that cool, polite tone. Indulge me," he

added, then sipped his beer. "You've got a slim body, smooth skin. You either take care of both or you were lucky genetically. By the way, I like your unicorn."

She cleared her throat. "Thank you."

"No, thank you," he said, and chuckled. "Anyway, you have or make enough money to afford good clothes. Those classic Italian pumps you were wearing go for about two hundred and fifty at department-store prices. And you had silk underwear. I'd say the silk undies and the unicorn follow the same pattern. You like to be a little daring under the traditional front."

She was just managing to close her gaping mouth. "You went through my clothes? My underwear?"

"What there was of them, and all in the name of investigation. Great underwear," he told her. "Very sexy, simple, and pricey. I'd say peach silk ought to look terrific on you."

She made a strangled sound, fell back on silence. There was really nothing to say.

"I don't know the annual income of your average gemologist or jewelry designer—but I'll lay odds you're one or the other. I'm leaning toward the scientist as vocation, and the designer as avocation."

"That's a big leap, Cade."

"No, it's not. Just another step. The pieces are there. Wouldn't you think a diamond like the one in the safe would require the services of a gemologist? Its authenticity would have to be verified, its value assessed. Just the way you verified and assessed it yesterday."

Her hands trembled, so she put them back in her lap. "If that's true, then it ups the likelihood that I stole it."

"No, it doesn't." Impatient with her, he tapped the pencil sharply against the pad. "Look at the other facts. Why can't you see yourself? You wouldn't steal a stick of gum. Doesn't the fact that you're riddled with guilt over the very thought you might have done something illegal give you a clue?"

"The fact is, Cade, I have the stone."

"Yeah, and hasn't it occurred to you, in that logical, responsible, ordered mind of yours, that you might have been protecting it?"

"Protecting it? From—"

"From whoever killed to get their hands on it. From whoever would have killed you if he had found you. That's what plays, Bailey, that's what fits. And if there are three stones, then you might very well know where the others are, as well. You may be protecting all of them."

"How?"

He had some ideas on that, as well, but didn't think she was ready to hear them. "We'll work on that. Meanwhile, I've made a few calls. We've got a busy day ahead of us tomorrow. The police artist will come over in the morning, see if she can help you put images together. And I managed to snag one of the undercurators, or whatever they're called, at the Smithsonian. We have a one-o'clock appointment tomorrow."

"You got an appointment on a holiday?"

"That's where the Parris name and fortune come in handy. Hint at funding, and it opens a lot of musty old doors. And we'll see if that boutique opens for the holiday sale hunters, and find out if anyone remembers selling a green suit."

"It doesn't seem like we're doing enough."

"Sweetheart, we've come a long way in a short time."

"You're right." She rose, walked to the window. There was a wood thrush in the maple tree, singing its heart out. "I can't begin to tell you how grateful I am."

"I'll bill you for the professional services," he said shortly. "And I don't want gratitude for the rest of it."

"I have to give it, whether or not you take it. You made this bearable, more than that. I don't know how many times you made me smile or laugh or just forget it all for little spaces of time. I think I'd have gone crazy without you, Cade."

"I'm going to be there for you, Bailey. You're not going to be able to shake me loose."

"You're used to getting what you want," she murmured. "I wonder if I am. It doesn't feel as if that's true."

"That's something you can change."

He was right. That was a matter of patience, perseverance, control. And perhaps wanting the right things. She wanted him, wanted to think that one day she could stand here, listening to the wood thrush sing of summer while Cade drowsed in the hammock. It could be their house instead of his. Their life. Their family.

If it was the right thing, and she could persevere.

"I'm going to make you a promise." She followed the impulse and turned, letting her heart be reckless. He was so much what she needed, sitting there with his jeans torn at the knee, his hair too long, his feet bare. "If, when this is over, when all the steps have been taken, all the pieces are in place to make the whole…if I can and you still want me, I'll marry you."

His heart stuttered in his chest. Emotion rose up to fill his throat. Very carefully, he set the bottle aside, rose. "Tell me you love me."

It was there, in her heart, begging to be said. But she shook her head. "When it's all over, and you know everything. If you still want me."

"That's not the kind of promise that suits me. No qualifications, Bailey. No whens, no ifs. Just you."

"It's all I can give you. It's all I have."

"We can go into Maryland on Tuesday, get a license. Be married in a matter of days."

He could see it. The two of them, giddy in love, rousing some sleepy-eyed country J.P. out of bed in the middle of the night. Holding hands in the living room while an old yellow dog slept on a braid rug, the J.P.'s wife played the piano and he and the woman he loved exchanged vows.

And sliding the ring onto her finger, feeling her slide one on his, was the link that would bind them.

"There are no blood tests in Maryland," he continued. "Just a couple of forms, and there you are."

He meant it. It staggered her to see in those deep green eyes that he meant nothing less than he said. He would take her exactly as she was. He would love her just as she stood.

How could she let him?

"And what name would I put on the form?"

"It doesn't matter. You'll have mine." He gripped her arms, drew her against him. In all his life, there had been no one he needed as much. "Take mine."

Just take, she thought when his lips covered hers. Take what was offered—the love, the safety, the promise. Let the past come as it would, let the future drift, and seize the moment.

"You know it wouldn't be right." She pressed her cheek to his. "You need to know as much as I do."

Maybe he did. However much the fantasy of a reckless elopement appealed, creating a fake identity for Bailey, it wasn't the answer either one of them needed. "Could be fun." He struggled to lighten the mood. "Like practice for the real thing." He pulled her back to arm's length, studied her face. Delicate, troubled. Lovely. "You want orange blossoms, Bailey? A white dress and organ music?"

Because her heart sighed at the image, she managed to smile. "I think I might. I seem to be a traditional soul."

"Then I should buy you a traditional diamond."

"Cade—"

"Just speculating," he murmured, and lifted her left hand. "No, however traditional your soul, your taste in jewelry is unique. We'll find something that suits. But I should probably take you to meet the family." His eyes lifted to hers, and he laughed. "God help you."

Just a game, she thought, just pretend. She smiled back at him. "I'd love to meet your family. See Camilla do pirouettes in her tutu."

"If you can get through that and still want to marry me, I'll know you're hopelessly in love with me. They'll put you through the gauntlet, sweetheart. A very sophisticated, silk-edged gauntlet. Where did you go to school, what does your father do, does your mother play bridge or tennis? And by the way, what clubs do you belong to, and did I run into you on the slopes last season at St. Moritz?"

Instead of making her unhappy, it made her laugh. "Then I'd better find out the answers."

"I like making them up. I took a cop to Muffy's

tenth-anniversary bash. Couldn't get out of it. We told everyone she was the niece of the Italian prime minister, educated in a Swiss boarding school and interested in acquiring a pied-à-terre in D.C."

Her brows drew together. "Oh, really?"

"They all but drooled on her. Not nearly the reaction we'd have gotten with the truth."

"Which was?"

"She was a uniformed cop who grew up in New York's Little Italy and transferred to Washington after her divorce from a guy who ran a pasta place off Broadway."

"Was she pretty?"

"Sure." His grin flashed. "Gorgeous. Then there was the lounge singer in Chevy Chase who—"

"I don't think I want to know." She turned away, picked up her empty glass and made a business out of rinsing it out. "You've dated a lot of women, I suppose."

"That depends on your definition of 'a lot.' I could probably run a list of names, ages, physical descriptions and last known addresses. Want to type it up for me?"

"No."

Delighted, he nuzzled the back of her neck. "I've only asked one woman to marry me."

"Two," she corrected, and set the now sparkling glass on the counter with a snap.

"One. I didn't ask Carla. That just sort of evolved.

And now she's happily married—as far as I can tell—to a corporate lawyer and the proud mama of a bouncing baby girl named Eugenia. So it hardly counts, anyway."

She bit her lip. "You didn't want children?"

"Yes, I did. I do." He turned her around, kissed her gently. "But we're not naming any kid of ours Eugenia. Now what do you say we think about going out for dinner, someplace quiet, where we can neck at the table? Then we can watch the fireworks."

"It's too early for dinner."

"That's why I said we should think about it." He scooped her up. "First we have to go upstairs and make love again."

Her pulse gave a pleasant little jump as she curled her arms around his neck. "We have to?"

"It'll pass the time. Unless you'd rather play gin rummy?"

Chuckling, she traced a line of kisses up his neck. "Well, if those are my only choices…"

"Tell you what, we can play strip gin rummy. We can both cheat and that way— Hell." He was halfway up the stairs with her, and nicely aroused, when the doorbell sounded. "Hold that thought, okay?" He set her down, and went to answer.

One peek through the side panel of wavy glass framing the door had him groaning. "Perfect timing, as always." With a hand on the knob, he turned, looked at Bailey. "Sweetheart, the woman on the other side of this door is my mother. I realize you expressed a mild interest in meeting my family, but I'm giving you this chance, because I love you. I really do. So I'm advising you to run, hide, and don't look back."

Nerves fluttered, but she straightened her shoulders. "Stop being silly and open the door."

"Okay, but I warned you." Bracing himself, he pulled the door open and fixed a bright, welcoming smile on his face. "Mother." As was expected, he kissed her smooth, polished cheek. "What a nice surprise."

"I wouldn't have to surprise you if you'd ever return my calls." Leona Parris stepped into the foyer.

She was, Bailey realized with a stunned first glance, a striking woman. Surely, with three grown children and several grandchildren, she had to be at least fifty. She could have passed for a sleek thirty-five.

Her hair was a lush sable brown with hints of golden highlights and fashioned in a perfect and elegant French twist that complemented a face of ivory and cream, with cool green eyes, straight nose and sulky mouth. She wore an elegant tailored bronze-toned suit that nipped at her narrow waist.

The topaz stones at her ears were square-cut and big as a woman's thumb and earned Bailey's instant admiration.

"I've been busy," Cade began. "A couple of cases, and some personal business."

"I certainly don't want to hear about your cases, as you call them." Leona set her leather bag on the foyer table. "And whatever your personal business is, it's no excuse for neglecting your family duties. You put me in a very awkward position with Pamela. I had to make your pathetic excuses."

"You wouldn't have had to make excuses if you hadn't set it up in the first place." He could feel the old arguments bubbling inside him, and he struggled not to fall into the familiar, too-predictable traps. "I'm sorry it put you in an awkward position. Do you want some coffee?"

"What I want, Cade, is an explanation. At Muffy's garden party yesterday—which you also failed to attend—Ronald told me some wild tale about you being engaged to some woman I've never heard of with a connection to the Princess of Wales."

"Bailey." Because he'd all but forgotten her, Cade turned, offered an apologetic smile and held out a hand. "Bailey, come meet my mother."

Oh, good God, was all that came into Bailey's head as she descended the stairs.

"Leona Parris, meet Bailey, my fiancée."

"Mrs. Parris." Bailey's voice trembled a bit as she offered a hand. "How wonderful to meet you. Cade has told me so much about you."

"Really?" Attractive, certainly, Leona mused. Well-groomed, if a bit understated. "He's told me virtually nothing about you, I'm afraid. I don't believe I caught your full name."

"Bailey's only been in the States for a few months." Cade barreled in, all cheer and delight. "I've been keeping her to myself." He slipped an arm around Bailey's shoulders, squeezed possessively. "We've had a whirlwind courtship, haven't we, sweetheart?"

"Yes," Bailey said faintly. "A whirlwind. You could say that."

"And you're a jewelry designer." Lovely rings, Leona noted. Unique and attractive. "A distant cousin of the Princess of Wales."

"Bailey doesn't like to drop names," Cade said quickly. "Sweetheart, maybe you ought to make those calls. Remember the time difference in London."

"Where did you meet?" Leona demanded.

Bailey opened her mouth, struggling to remember if they'd spun this part of the lie for Ronald. "Actually—"

"At the Smithsonian," Cade said smoothly. "In front of the Hope Diamond. I was researching a case, and Bailey was sketching designs. She looked so intent and artistic. It took me twenty minutes of fast talking and following her around—remember how you threatened to call the security guard, sweetheart? But I finally charmed her into having a cup of coffee with me. And speaking of coffee—"

"This is just ridiculous," Bailey said, interrupting him. "Absolutely ridiculous. Cade, this is your mother, and I'm just not having it." She turned, faced Leona directly. "We did not meet in the Smithsonian, and the Princess of Wales is not my cousin. At least I seriously doubt it. I met Cade on Friday morning, when I went to his office to hire him. I needed a private investigator because I have amnesia, a blue diamond and over a million dollars in cash."

Leona waited ten humming seconds while her foot tapped. Then her lips firmed. "Well, I can see neither of you intends to tell the simple truth. As you prefer to make up outrageous fabrications, I can only presume that you're perfectly suited to one another."

She snatched up her bag and marched to the door with outraged dignity in every step. "Cade, I'll wait to hear from you when you decide to grant me the courtesy of the simple truth."

While Bailey simply stared, Cade grinned like a fool at the door his mother had closed with a snap.

"I don't understand. I did tell her the truth."

"And now I know what they mean by 'the truth shall set you free.'" He let out a whooping laugh, swung her back up into his arms. "She's so ticked off now she'll leave me alone for a week. Maybe two." He gave

Bailey an enthusiastic kiss as he headed for the stairs. "I'm crazy about you. Who would have thought telling her the real story would have gotten her off my back?"

Still laughing, he carried her into the bedroom and dropped her on the mattress. "We've got to celebrate. I've got some champagne chilled. I'm going to get you drunk again."

Pushing her hair out of her face, she sat up. "Cade, she's your mother. This is shameful."

"No, it's survival." He leaned over, gave her a smacking kiss this time. "And, sweetheart, we're both black sheep now. I can't tell you how much more fun that's going to be for me."

"I don't think I want to be a black sheep," she called as he headed out again.

"Too late." His laughter echoed back to her.

Chapter 9

They did make it out to dinner. But they settled for grilled burgers and potatoes fried in peanut oil at a country fair in rural Maryland. He'd thought about a romantic little restaurant, then a fight through the teeming crowds downtown for the huge fireworks display.

Then inspiration had struck. Ferris wheels and shooting galleries. Live music, whirling lights, the flash of fireflies in a nearby field, with fireworks to top it off.

It was, he thought, the perfect first date.

When he told her just that, while she clung to him with screams locked in her throat on the whizzing car of the Tilt-A-Whirl, she laughed, shut her eyes tight and hung on for her life.

He wanted to ride everything, and he pulled her along from line to line, as eager as any of the children tugging on an indulgent parent's hand. She was spun, shaken, twirled and zoomed until her head revolved and her stomach flopped.

Then he tilted her face upward for inspection, declared that since she wasn't turning green yet they could do it all again.

So they did.

"Now, you need a prize," he decided as she staggered off the Octopus.

"No more cotton candy. I'm begging you."

"I was thinking more of an elephant." He hooked an arm around her waist and headed toward the shooting gallery. "That big purple one up there."

It was three feet tall, with a turned-up trunk and toenails painted a bright pink. An elephant. The thought of elephants made her smile bloom brilliantly.

"Oh, it's wonderful." She grinned, fluttered her lashes at Cade. "I want it."

"Then it's my job to get it for you. Just stand back, little lady." He plunked down bills, chose his weapon. Cheery-faced rabbits and ducks rolled by, with the occasional wolf or bear rearing up at odd moments to threaten. Cade sighted the air gun and fired.

Bailey grinned, then applauded, then gaped as wildlife died in droves. "You didn't miss once." She goggled at him. "Not once."

Her wide-eyed admiration made him feel like a teenager showing off for the prom queen. "She wants the elephant," he told the attendant, then laughed when she launched herself into his arms.

"Thank you. You're wonderful. You're amazing."

Since each statement was punctuated by eager kisses, he thought she might like the floppy-eared brown dog, as well. "Want another?"

"Man, you're killing me here," the attendant muttered, then sighed as Cade pulled out more bills.

"Want to give it a try?" Cade offered the rifle to Bailey.

"Maybe." She bit her lip and studied her prey. It had looked simple enough when Cade did it. "All right."

"Just sight through the little V at the end of the barrel," he began, stepping behind her to adjust her stance.

"I see it." She held her breath and pulled the trigger. The little pop had her jolting, but the ducks swam on, and the rabbits continued to hop. "Did I miss?"

"Only by a mile or so." And he was dead certain the woman had never held a gun in her life. "Try again."

She tried again, and again. By the time she'd managed to nip a few feathers and ruffle some fur, Cade had put twenty dollars back in the attendant's grateful hands.

"It looked so easy when you did it."

"That's okay, sweetheart, you were getting the hang of it. What'd she win?"

The attendant perused his lowest row of prizes, generally reserved for children under twelve, and came up with a small plastic duck.

"I'll take it." Delighted, she tucked it in the pocket of her slacks. "My first trophy."

With hands linked, they strolled the midway, listening to the screams, the distant music of a bluegrass band, the windy whirl of rides. She loved the lights, the carnival colors, bright as jewels in the balmy night. And the smells of frying oil, of spun sugar and spiced sauces.

It seemed so easy, as if there couldn't be any trouble in the world—only lights and music and laughter.

"I don't know if I've ever been to a country carnival before," she told him. "But if I have, this one is the best."

"I still owe you a candlelight dinner."

She turned her head to smile at him. "I'll settle for another ride on the Ferris wheel."

"Sure you're up to it?"

"I want to go around again. With you."

She stood in line, flirted with a toddler who kept his head on his father's shoulder and peeked at her with huge blue eyes. She wondered if she was good with children, if she'd ever had a chance to be. And, laying her head on Cade's shoulder, dreamed a little.

If this was just a normal night in normal lives, they could be here together like this. His hand would be in hers, just like this, and they wouldn't have a care in the world. She'd be afraid of nothing. Her life would be as full and rich and bright as a carnival.

What was wrong with pretending it was, and could be, for just one night?

She climbed into the rocking car beside him, snuggled close. And rose into the sky. Beneath, people swarmed across the grass. Teenagers strutted, older couples strolled, children raced. The scents rose up on the wind, an evocative mix she could have breathed in forever.

The downward rush was fast and exciting, making her hair fly out and her stomach race to catch up. Tilting her head upward, she closed her eyes and prepared for the upward swing.

Of course, he kissed her. She'd wanted that, too, that sweet, innocent meeting of lips as they circled over the high summer grass, with the lights around them a rainbow gleam.

They circled again as the first fireworks spewed gold across a black sky.

"It's beautiful." She settled her head on his shoulder. "Like jewels tossed in the sea. Emeralds, rubies, sapphires."

The colors shot upward, fountained and faded on a

booming crash. Below, people applauded and whistled, filled the air with noise. Somewhere a baby wailed.

"He's frightened," she murmured. "It sounds like gunshots, or thunder."

"My father used to have an English setter who'd hide under his bed every Fourth." Cade toyed with her fingers as he watched the show. "Trembled for hours once the fireworks got going."

"It's so loud, scary if you don't know what it is." A brilliant flash of gold and sparkling diamonds erupted as they topped the wheel in a rush. Her heart began to race, her head to throb. It was the noise, that was all. The noise, and the sickening way the car rocked as the Ferris wheel jerked to a halt to unload passengers.

"Bailey?" He drew her closer, watching her face. She was trembling now, her cheeks white, her eyes dark.

"I'm all right. Just a little queasy."

"We'll be off soon. Just a couple more cars."

"I'm all right." But the lights flashed again, shattering the sky. And the image rolled into her head like thunder.

"He threw up his hands." She managed a whisper. She couldn't see the lights now, the colored diamonds scattered across the sky. The memory blinded her to everything else. "Threw them up to try to grab the knife. I couldn't scream. I couldn't scream. I couldn't move. There was only the desk light. Just that one beam of light. They're like shadows, and they're screaming, but I can't. Then the lightning flashed. It's so bright, just that one instant, so bright the room's alight with it. And he… Oh, God, his throat. He slashed his throat."

She turned her face into Cade's shoulder. "I don't want to see that. I can't bear to see that."

"Let it go. Just hold on to me and let it go. We're getting off now." He lifted her out of the car, all but carried her across the grass. She was shuddering as if the air had turned icy, and he could hear sobs choking her. "It can't hurt you now, Bailey. You're not alone now."

He wound his way through the field where cars were parked, swore each time a boom of gunpowder made her jerk. She curled up in the seat, rocking herself for comfort while he skirted the hood and got quickly behind the wheel.

"Cry it out," he told her, and turned the key. "Scream if you want to. Just don't let it eat at you like this."

Because he didn't make her feel ashamed, she wept a little, then rested her throbbing head against the seat as he drove down the winding road and back toward the city.

"I keep seeing jewels," she said at length. Her voice was raw, but steady. "Beautiful gemstones. Floods of them. Lapis and opals, malachite and topaz. All different shapes, cut and uncut. I can pick out each one. I know what they are, how they feel in my hand. There's a long piece of chalcedony, smooth to the touch and sword-shaped. It sits on a desk like a paperweight. And this lovely rutilated quartz with silvery threads running through it like shooting stars. I can see them. They're so familiar."

"They make you happy, comfortable."

"Yes, I think they do. When I think of them, when they drift back into my head, it's pleasant. Soothing. There's an elephant. Not this one." She hugged the plush toy against her for comfort. "Soapstone, carved with a jeweled blanket over its back and bright blue eyes. He's so regal and foolish."

She paused a moment, tried to think past the headache pounding in her temples. "There are other stones, all manner of others, but they don't belong to me. Still, they soothe. It doesn't frighten me at all to think of them. Even the blue diamond. It's such a beautiful thing. Such a miracle of nature. It's amazing, really, that just the right elements, the right minerals, the right pressure and the right amount of time can join together to create something so special.

"They're arguing about them. About it," she continued, squeezing her eyes shut to try to bring it back. "I can hear them, and I'm angry and feeling righteous. I can almost see myself marching toward that room where they're arguing, and I'm furious and satisfied. It's such an odd combination of feelings. And I'm afraid, a little. I've done something… I don't know."

She strained toward it, fisting her hands. "Something rash or impulsive, or even foolish. I go to the door. It's open, and their voices echo outside. I go to the door, and I'm trembling inside. It's not all fear, I don't think it's just fear. Some of it's temper. I close my hand over the stone. It's in my pocket, and I feel better with my hand on it. The canvas bag's there, on the table by the door. It's open, too, and I can see the money inside. I pick it up while they shout at each other."

The lights as they slipped from suburb to city made her eyes water. She closed them again. "They don't know I'm there. They're so intent on each other, they don't notice me. Then I see the knife in his hand, the curved blade gleaming. And the other one throws up his hands to grab it. They struggle over it, and they're out of the light now, struggling. But I see blood, and one of the shadows staggers. The other moves in. He doesn't stop. Just doesn't stop. I'm frozen there, clutching the bag, watching. The lights go off, all at once, and it's totally dark. Then the lightning flashes, fills the sky. It's suddenly so bright. When he slices the knife again, over his throat, he sees me. He sees me, and I run."

"Okay, try to relax." The traffic was murder, choked

and impatient. He couldn't take her hand, draw her close, comfort her. "Don't push it now, Bailey. We'll deal with this at home."

"Cade, they're the same person," she murmured, and let out a sound somewhere between a moan and a laugh. "They're the same."

He cursed the clogged streets, hunted for an opening and shot around a station wagon with inches to spare. "The same as what?"

"Each other. They're the same person. But that can't be. I know that can't be, because one's dead and one isn't. I'm afraid I'm going crazy."

Symbols again, he wondered, or truth? "How are they the same?"

"They have the same face."

She carried the stuffed elephant into the house, clutching it to her as if it were a lifeline to reality. Her mind felt musty, caught between dreams, with a sly headache hovering at the corners waiting to pounce.

"I want you to lie down. I'll make you some tea."

"No, I'll make it. I'll feel better if I'm doing something. Anything. I'm sorry. It was such a wonderful evening." In the kitchen, she set the smiling elephant on the table. "Until."

"It was a wonderful evening. And whatever helps jiggle more pieces in place is worth it. It hurts you."

He took her shoulders. "And *I'm* sorry, but you have to get through the rest of it to get where we want to be."

"I know." She lifted a hand to his, squeezed briefly, then turned to put the kettle on the stove. "I'm not going to fall apart, Cade, but I'm afraid I may not be stable." Pressing her fingers to her eyes, she laughed. "Funny statement coming from someone who can't remember her own name."

"You're remembering more all the time, Bailey. And you're the most stable woman I've ever met."

"Then I'm worried about you, too, and your choice of women."

She set cups precisely on their saucers, concentrating on the simple task. Tea bags, spoons, sugar bowl.

In the maple tree, the wood thrush had given over to a whippoorwill, and the song was like liquid silver. She thought of honeysuckle burying a chain-link fence, perfuming the evening air while the night bird called for his mate.

And a young girl weeping under a willow tree.

She shook herself. A childhood memory, perhaps, bittersweet. She thought those vignettes of the past would be coming more quickly now. And she was afraid.

"You have questions." She set the tea on the table, steadied herself and looked at him. "You're not asking them because you're afraid I'll crumble. But I won't. I wish you'd ask them, Cade. It's easier when you do."

"Let's sit down." He pulled out a chair for her, took his time stirring sugar into his tea. "The room has gray carpet, a window, a table by the door. There's a desk lamp. What does the desk look like?"

"It's a satinwood library desk, George III." She set her cup back down with a rattle. "Oh, that was clever. I never expected you to ask about the desk, so I didn't think, and it was just there."

"Concentrate on the desk, Bailey. Describe it for me."

"It's a beautiful piece. The top is crossbanded with rosewood that's inlaid with boxwood lines. The sides, even the kneehole, are inlaid with ovals. One side has a long drawer paneled with false fronts. It opens to shelves. It's so clever. The handles are brass, and they're kept well polished."

Baffled, she stared into her tea. "Now I sound like an antique dealer."

No, he thought, just someone who loves beautiful things. And knows that desk very well.

"What's on the desk?"

"The lamp. It's brass, too, with a green glass shade and an old-fashioned chain pull. And there are papers, a neat stack of papers aligned with the corner of the desk. A leather blotter is in the center, and a *briefke* sits there."

"A what?"

"A *briefke,* a little cup of paper for carrying loose stones. They're emeralds, grass green, of varying cuts and carats. There's a jeweler's loupe and a small brass scale. A glass, Baccarat crystal, with ice melting in the whiskey. And…and the knife…" Her breath was strangling, but she forced it free. "The knife is there, carved bone handle, curved blade. It's old, it's beautiful."

"Is someone at the desk?"

"No, the chair's empty." Easier to look away from the knife, to look somewhere else. "It's a dark, pewter-gray leather. Its back is to the window. There's a storm." Her voice hitched. "There's a storm. Lightning, lashing rain. They're shouting over the thunder."

"Where are they?"

"In front of the desk, facing each other."

He pushed her cup aside so that he could take her hand. "What are they saying, Bailey?"

"I don't know. Something about a deposit. Take the deposit, leave the country. It's a bad deal. Too dangerous. His mind's made up."

She could hear the voices. The words were bouncing out of the static of sound, harsh angry phrases.

Double-crossing son of a bitch.

You want to deal with him, you go ahead. I'm out of it.

Both of us. Together. No backing out.

You take the stones, deal with him. Bailey's suspicious. Not as stupid as you think.

You're not walking out with the money and leaving me twisting in the wind.

"He shoves him back. They're fighting, pushing, shoving, punching. It frightens me how much they hate each other. I don't know how they can despise each other so much, because they're the same."

He didn't want to take her through what had happened next. He had the scene now, the steps. "How are they the same?"

"The same face. Same eyes, dark eyes, dark hair. Everything. Mirror images. Even their voices, the same pitch. They're the same man, Cade. How can they be the same man, unless it didn't happen that way at all—and I've lost not only my memory, but my mind?"

"You're not looking at the simple, Bailey. At the simple and the obvious." His smile was grim, his eyes glowed. "Twins."

"Twins? Brothers?" Everything in her, every part of her being, was repelled. She could only shake her head, and continued to shake it until the movement was frantic. "No, no, no." She couldn't accept that. Wouldn't. "That's not it. That can't be it."

She pushed back from the table abruptly, her chair scraping harshly on the tile. "I don't know what I saw." Desperate now to block it out, she grabbed her cup, slopping tea on the table before she carried it to the sink and dumped it down the drain. "It was dark. I don't know what I saw."

Didn't want to know what she'd seen, Cade concluded. Wasn't ready to know. And he wasn't willing to risk playing analyst until she'd regrouped.

"Put it away for now. It's been a rough day, you need some rest."

"Yes." Her mind was screaming for peace, for oblivion. But she was terrified of sleep, and the dreams that would come with it. She turned, pressed herself against him. "Make love with me. I don't want to think. I just want you to love me."

"I do." He met her seeking mouth with his. "I will."

He led her out of the kitchen, stopping on the way to kiss, to touch. At the base of the stairs, he unbuttoned her blouse, skimmed his hands up her narrow rib cage, then cupped her breasts.

On a broken gasp, she clutched her hands in his hair and dragged his mouth down to hers.

He'd wanted to be gentle, tender. But her lips were wild and desperate. He understood that it was the wild and desperate she needed. And let himself go.

He tore the bra aside, watched the shock and arousal flare in her eyes. When his hands possessed this time, they were greedy and rough.

"There's a lot I haven't shown you." He sought the delicate curve between neck and shoulder. Bit. A lot no one had shown her, he thought with a wild spurt of sheer lust. "You may not be ready."

"Show me." Her head fell back, and her pulse scrambled like frightened birds. And fear was suddenly liberating. "I want you to."

He dragged her slacks down her hips, and plunged his fingers inside her. Her nails bit into his shoulders as she rocked on that swift, stunning peak. The whimper in her throat became a cry that was both fear and joy.

His breath hissed out as he watched her fly up, fly over. The dazed shock in her eyes brought him a dark thrill. She was helpless now, if he wanted her helpless.

And he did.

He peeled away layers of clothes, his hands quick and sure. When she was naked and quivering, his lips curved. He traced his thumbs over her nipples until her eyes fluttered closed.

"You belong to me." His voice was thick, rough, compelling. "I need to hear you say it. For now, you belong to me."

"Yes." She would have told him anything. Promised her soul, if that was what he asked of her. This was no lazy river now, but a flood of heaving sensations. She wanted to drown in them. "More."

He gave more. His mouth raced down her body, then fixed greedily on the core of heat.

She swayed, quaked, exploded. Colors burst in her

head—carnival lights and jewels, stars and rainbows. Her back pressed into the railing, and her hands gripped at it for balance while her world spun like a carousel gone mad.

Then pleasure, the sharp edge of it tipped toward pain. At that point, between glory and devastation, her body simply shattered.

He pulled her into his arms, darkly pleased that she was limp. Leaving her clothes where they lay, cradling her, he mounted the steps. His bed this time, he thought with a restless, lustful need to claim her there.

He fell to the bed with her, let the fire inside him rage.

It was unbearable. Glorious. His hands, his mouth, destroyed her, rebuilt her. Sweat dewed her skin, slickening it. And, when he'd dragged his clothes away, slickening his. Her body arched and bucked, straining for more, moving eagerly against each new demand.

When he yanked her to her knees, she wrapped herself around him eagerly, bowing back when his head lowered once more to suckle her breast. And when her head touched the mattress, her body bridged, he buried himself deep inside her.

Her moan was low and throaty, a mindless sound as he gripped her hips, braced them. With his own heart screaming in his chest, he drove them both hard and fast. No thoughts, no doubts, nothing but the hot, frenzied joining.

There was moonlight on her face, glinting in her hair, glowing on her damp skin. Even as his vision grayed, he fixed the picture of her in his mind. Locked it there, as the dark pleasure peaked and he emptied himself into her.

He waited until he was sure she slept. For a time, he simply watched her, bewitched by her and what they'd brought to each other. No woman he'd touched, no woman who had touched him, had ever reached so deep inside him, held his heart so close and fast.

He'd demanded that she tell him she belonged to him. It was no less true that he belonged to her. The miracle of it humbled him.

He touched his lips to her temple. When he left her, she was sprawled on her stomach, one arm flung out where he had lain beside her. He hoped exhaustion would tranquilize her dreams. He left the door open so that he could hear if she cried out in sleep, or called for him.

He took time to brew a pot of coffee and carried it with him into the library. He gave his computer one grim sneer before booting it up. The clock in the corner chimed midnight, then bonged the half hour before he found his rhythm.

In hardly twice the time it would have taken a ten-year-old hacker, the information he was searching for flashed up on the screen.

Gem experts. The greater metropolitan area.

He scrolled through, keeping his senses alert with caffeine, fumbled for a moment in engaging the printer for hard copy.

Boone and Son.

Kleigmore Diamond Consultants.

Landis Jewelry Creations.

His computer provided him with more detailed information than the phone book. For once he blessed technology. He scanned the data, names, dates, then continued to scroll.

Salvini.

Salvini. His eyes narrowed as he skimmed the data. Appraisers and gemologists. Estate jewelry and antiquities a specialty. Established in 1952 by Charles Salvini, now deceased.

Certified and bonded. Consultants to museums and private collectors. Personalized designs, repairs and remounting. All work done on premises.

A Chevy Chase address, he mused. The location was close enough. The firm was respected, had earned a triple-A rating. Owners Thomas and Timothy Salvini.

T.S., he thought on a quick spurt of excitement. Brothers.

Bingo.

Chapter 10

"Just take your time."

Bailey took a deep breath and struggled to be as calm and precise as Cade wanted. "Her nose is sharper than that. I think."

The police artist's name was Sara, and she was young and patient. Skilled, Bailey had no doubt, or Cade wouldn't have called on her. She sat at the kitchen table with her sketch pad and pencils, a cup of steaming coffee at her elbow.

"More like this?" With a few quick strokes, Sara honed down the nose.

"Yes, I think so. Her eyes are bigger, sort of tilted up."

"Almond-shaped?" Sara whisked the gum eraser over the pencil strokes, adjusted for size and shape.

"I suppose. It's hard to see it all in my head."

"Just give me impressions." Sara's smile was easy and relaxed. "We'll go from there."

"It seems the mouth is wide, softer than the rest of the face. Everything else is angles."

"Quite a face," Cade commented as Sara sketched. "Interesting. Sexy."

As Bailey continued to instruct, he studied the image. Angular face, carelessly short hair with long, spiky bangs, with dark, dramatically arched eyebrows peeking through. Exotic and tough, he decided, and tried to hook a personality with the features.

"That's very close to what I remember." Bailey took the sketch Sara offered. She knew this face, she thought, and looking at it brought competing urges to smile and to weep.

M.J. Who was M.J., and what had they shared?

"You want to take a break?" Cade asked and lowered his hands to Bailey's shoulders to rub away the tension.

"No, I'd like to keep at it. If you don't mind," she said to Sara.

"Hey, I can do this all day. Long as you keep the coffee coming." She held her empty mug up to Cade, with a quick smile that told Bailey they knew each other well.

"You— Ah, it's interesting work," Bailey began.

Sara tossed a long ginger-colored braid behind her back. Her outfit was both cool and casual, denim cutoffs and a plain white tank, the combination straight-up sexy.

"It's a living," she told Bailey. "Computers are slowly putting me out of business. It's amazing what they can do with imaging. But a lot of cops and P.I.'s still prefer sketches." She took her refilled mug back from Cade. "Parris here, he'll do most anything to avoid a computer."

"Hey, I'm getting the hang of it."

Sara snickered. "When you do, I'll be making my living doing caricatures in bars." She shrugged, sipped, then picked up a fresh pencil. "Want to try for the other?"

"Yes, all right." Telling herself not to focus on just how well Cade and Sara knew each other, Bailey closed her eyes and concentrated.

Grace. She let the name cruise through her mind, bring up the image.

"Soft," she began. "There's a softness to her face. It's very beautiful, almost unbelievably so. It's an oval face, very classic. Her hair's ink black, very long. It sort of spills down her back in loose waves. No bangs, just a flow of dark, thick silk. Her eyes are wide, heavy-lidded and thickly lashed. Laser-blue eyes. The nose is short and straight. Think perfect."

"I'm starting to hate her," Sara said lightly, and made Bailey smile.

"It must be hard to be wildly beautiful, don't you think? People only look at the surface."

"I think I could live with it. How about the mouth?"

"Lush. Full."

"Natch."

"Yes, that's good." Excitement began to drum. The sketch was coming together quickly. "The eyebrows are a little fuller, and there's a mole beside the left one. Just here," Bailey said, pointing to her own face.

"Now I really hate her," Sara muttered. "I don't want to know if she's got the body to match this face. Tell me she's got Dumbo ears."

"No, I'm afraid not." Bailey smiled at the sketch and felt warm and weepy again. "She's just beautiful. It startles the eye."

"She looks familiar."

At Sara's careless comment, Bailey tensed. "Does she? Really?"

"I'd swear I've seen this face before." Pursing her lips, Sara tapped her pencil against the sketch. "In a magazine, maybe. She looks like someone who'd model—pricey perfume or face cream. You got a million-dollar face, you'd be crazy not to use it."

"A model." Bailey bit her lip, fought to remember. "I just don't know."

Sara tore off the sheet, handed it to Cade. "What do you think?"

"A heart-stopper," he said after a moment. "The gene fairy was in one hell of a good mood when she was born. I can't place it, though, and that's a face no man with a pulse would forget."

Her name is Grace, Bailey told herself. And she's more than beautiful. She's not just a face.

"Good work, Sara." Cade laid the two sketches together on the counter. "Got time for one more?"

Sara took a quick look at her watch. "I've got about a half hour to spare."

"The man, Bailey." Cade crouched down until they were eye to eye. "You know what he looks like now."

"I don't—"

"You do." He said it firmly, though his hands were gentle on her arms. "It's important. Just tell Sara how you see him."

It would hurt, Bailey realized. Her stomach muscles were already clenched at the thought of letting that face back into her head. "I don't want to see him again."

"You want the answers. You want it over. This is a step. You've got to take the steps."

She closed her eyes, shifted. Her head began to throb as she put herself back in that room with the gray carpet and the storm-lashed window.

"He's dark," she said quietly. "His face is long, narrow. It's tight with anger. His mouth is grim with temper. It's thin and strong and stubborn. His nose is slightly hooked.

Not unattractive, but strong again. It's a very strong face. His eyes are deep-set. Dark. Dark eyes."

Flashing with fury. There was murder in them. She shuddered, hugged her elbows and fought to concentrate.

"Hollowed cheeks and high forehead. His eyebrows are dark and straight. So's his hair. It's well cut, full at the top, very precisely trimmed around the ears. It's a very handsome face. The jaw spoils it a little, it's soft, slightly weak."

"Is that him, Bailey?" Cade put a hand on her shoulder again, squeezed lightly in support.

Braced, she opened her eyes and looked at the sketch. It wasn't precise. It wasn't perfect. The eyes should be a bit farther apart, the mouth slightly fuller. But it was enough to have her trembling.

"Yes, it's very like him." Mustering all her control, she rose slowly. "Excuse me," she murmured, and walked out of the room.

"The lady's terrified," Sara commented, sliding her pencils back in their case.

"I know."

"Are you going to tell me what kind of trouble she's in?"

"I'm not sure." Cade dipped his hands in his pockets. "But I'm close to finding out. You did good work, Sara. I owe you."

"I'll bill you." She gathered her tools and rose.

She kissed him lightly, studied his face. "I don't think you're going to be calling me up for a night on the town anymore."

"I'm in love with her," he said simply.

"Yeah, I got that." She shouldered her bag, then touched his cheek. "I'm going to miss you."

"I'll be around."

"You'll be around," she agreed. "But those wild and wacky days are over for you, Parris. I like her. Hope you work it out." With a last wistful smile, she turned. "I know the way out."

He walked her out anyway, and closing the door, realized he was indeed shutting off a part of his life. The freedom of coming and going as he pleased, with whom he pleased. Late nights in a club, with the prospect of friendly, unfettered sex to follow. Responsible to no one but himself.

He glanced up the stairs. She was up there. Responsibility, stability, commitment. One woman from now throughout the rest of his life—a troubled woman, one who had yet to say the words he needed to hear, to make the promises he needed made.

He could still walk away, and she wouldn't blame him. In fact, he was sure that was exactly what she'd expected. It made him wonder who had left her before.

With a shake of his head, he climbed the stairs to her without the slightest regret.

She was standing in the bedroom, looking out the window. Her hands were clasped in front of her, her back was to the door.

"Are you all right?"

"Yes. I'm sorry, I was rude to your friend. I didn't even thank her."

"Sara understands."

"You've known her a long time."

"A few years, yeah."

Bailey swallowed. "You've been together."

Cade lifted a brow, decided against moving to her. "Yeah, we've been together. I've been with other women, Bailey. Women I've liked, cared for."

"Knew." She turned on the word, and her eyes were fierce.

"Knew," he agreed with a nod.

"This is out of sync." She dragged her hands through her hair. "You and me, Cade, it's out of sync with the rest of it. It should never have happened."

"It did happen." He stuck his hands in his pockets, because they'd tensed, wanted to fist. "Are you going to stand there and tell me you're upset because you've met a woman I've slept with? Because I didn't come to you the same way you came to me?"

"Blank." The word shot out of her like a bullet. "You didn't come to me blank. You have family, friends, lovers. A life. I have nothing but pieces that don't fit. I don't care if you've slept with a hundred women." Her voice snapped on that, then whispered fiercely on the rest. "It's that you remember them. Can remember them."

"You want me to tell you they don't matter?" His temper began to inch up, nudged by panic. She was pulling back, pulling away. "Of course they mattered. I can't blank out my past for you, Bailey."

"I wouldn't want you to." She covered her face with her hands for a moment as she fought for even a slippery grip on control. She'd made up her mind. Now she just had to be strong enough to follow through. "I'm sorry. Your private life before I came into it isn't my business, or even the point. The point is, you had one, Cade."

"So did you."

"So did I." She nodded, thinking that was precisely what frightened her. "I never would have gotten this close to finding it without you. But I realize I should have gone to the police straightaway. I've only complicated things by not doing so. But that's what I'm going to do now."

"You don't trust me to finish this?"

"That's not the issue—"

"Damn right it's not," he told her. "This isn't about going to the cops. It's about you and me. You think you can walk out of here and away from what's between us." His hands shot out of his pockets, grabbed her arms. "Think again."

"Someone's dead. I'm involved." Her teeth threatened to chatter as she fought to keep her eyes level with his. "And I shouldn't have involved you."

"It's too late for that now. It was too late the minute you walked into my office. You're not shaking me off." When his mouth crushed down on hers, the kiss tasted of frustration and fury. He held her close, blocking any choice, ravaging her mouth until her hands went limp on his shoulders.

"Don't," she managed when he lifted her off her feet. But that, too, was too late. She was pressed beneath him on the bed, every sense scrambling and screaming as his hands streaked over her.

"I don't give a damn what you forget." Eyes dark and reckless, he dragged at her clothes. "You'll remember this."

He spun her out of control, out of time, out of place. There was a wildness and willfulness here that she'd never experienced and couldn't resist. His mouth closed over her breast, stabbing pleasure through her. Even as she sucked in air to moan, his fingers pierced her and drove her ruthlessly to peak.

She cried out, not in alarm, not in protest, but with the staggered thrill of being plunged beyond reason. Her nails bit into his back, her body moved like lightning under his. She opened herself to him recklessly. The only thought in her head was, *Now, now, now.*

He drove himself into her hard and deep, felt her clutch convulsively around him as she flew over the new crest. It was mindless, desperate. It was wrong. It was irresistible.

He gripped her hands in his, watched pleasure chase shock across her face. The animal inside him had broken free, and it clawed at both of them. So his mouth was rough as it savaged hers. And he pistoned himself inside her until she wept out his name and what was left of his mind shattered.

Empty, hollowed out, he collapsed on her. Her body shuddered under his as a catchy whimper sounded in her throat. Her hands lay, palm out and limp, on the rumpled spread. His mind began to clear enough for shame.

He'd never taken a woman so roughly. Never given a woman so little choice. He rolled away from her, stared at the ceiling, appalled by what he'd found inside himself.

"I'm sorry." It was pathetic, that phrase. The uselessness of it scraped at him as he sat up, rubbed his hands over his face. "I hurt you. I'm sorry. There's no excuse for it." And, finding none, he rose and left her alone.

She managed to sit up, one hand pressed to her speeding heart. Her body felt weak, tingly and still pulsingly hot. Her mind remained fuzzy around the edges, even as she patiently waited for it to clear. The only thing she was certain of was that she had just been savaged. Overwhelmed by sensation, by emotion, by him.

It had been wonderful.

Cade gave her time to compose herself. And used the time to formulate his next steps. It was so difficult to think around fury. He'd been angry before. Hurt before. Ashamed before. But when she came down the stairs, looking tidy and nervous, those three emotions threatened to swamp him. "Are you all right?"

"Yes. Cade, I—"

"You'll do what you want." He interrupted her in a voice that was both cool and clipped. "And so will I. I apologize again for treating you that way."

She felt her stomach sink to her knees. "You're angry with me."

"With both of us. I can deal with myself, but first I have to deal with you. You want to walk out."

"It's not what I want." There was a plea for understanding in her voice. "It's what's right. I've made you an accessory to God knows what."

"You hired me."

She let out an impatient breath. How could he be so blind and stubborn? "It hasn't been a professional relationship, Cade. It barely started as one."

"That's right. It's personal, and you're not walking

out on me out of some misguided sense of guilt. You want to walk for other reasons, we'll get into them after this is done. I love you." There was chilly fury over the words that only deepened the emotion behind them. "If you don't, can't or won't love me, I'll have to live with it. But walking out at this point's just not an option."

"I only want—"

"You want to go to the cops." He paused a moment, hooked his thumbs in his front pockets to keep his hands from reaching for her. "That's fine, it's your choice. But meanwhile, you hired me to do a job, and I'm not finished. Whatever your personal feelings, or mine, I intend to finish. Get your purse."

She wasn't sure how to handle him now. Then again, she realized, had she ever known? Still, this cold, angry man standing in front of her was much more of a stranger than the one she had first seen in a cluttered, messy office only days before.

"The appointment at the Smithsonian," she began.

"I've postponed it. We have somewhere else to go first."

"Where?"

"Get your purse," he repeated. "We're taking this next step my way."

He didn't speak on the drive. She recognized some of the buildings. They'd ridden past them before. But when he drove out of D.C. and into Maryland, her nerves began to jump.

"I wish you'd tell me where we're going." The trees were too close to the road, she thought, panicky. Too green, too big.

"Back," he said. "Sometimes you've just got to open the door and look at what's on the other side."

"We need to talk to the curator at the museum." Her throat was closing. She'd have bartered her soul for a glass of water. "We should turn around and go back to the city."

"You know where we're going?"

"No." The denial was sharp, desperate. "No, I don't."

He only flicked a glance at her out of sharp green eyes. "The pieces are there, Bailey."

He turned left, off the main drag, listening to her breathing coming short and labored. Ruthlessly he repressed his instinct to soothe. She was stronger than he'd pretended she was. He could admit that. And she would get through this. He'd help her get through it.

If the place was being watched, he was bringing her out in the open. He had to weigh the possibility of that against doing his job. She'd hired him to solve the puzzle, he reminded himself. And this, he was sure, was the last piece.

She couldn't continue to live in the safe little world

he'd provided for her. It was time, for both of them, to move forward.

Setting his jaw, he pulled into the lot at Salvini.

"You know where we are."

Her skin was clammy. In long, restless strokes, she rubbed her damp palms over the knees of her slacks. "No, I don't."

The building was brick, two stories. Old, rather lovely, with tall display windows flanked by well established azaleas that would bloom beautifully in the spring. There was an elegance to the place that shouldn't have made her shudder.

There was a single car in the lot. A BMW sedan, dark blue. Its finish gleamed in the sunlight.

The building stood alone, taking up the corner, while behind it, across a vast parking lot, a trendy strip mall seemed to be doing a brisk holiday business.

"I don't want to be here." Bailey turned her head, refusing to look at the sign that topped the building in large, clear letters.

SALVINI

"They're closed," she continued. "There's no one here. We should go."

"There's a car in the lot," Cade pointed out. "It won't hurt to see."

"No." She snatched her hand away from his, tried to bury herself in the corner of the seat. "I'm not going in there. I'm not."

"What's in there, Bailey?"

"I don't know." Terror. Just terror. "I'm not going in."

He would rather have cut out his heart than force her to do what he intended. But, thinking of her, he got out of the car, came around to her side, opened the door. "I'll be with you. Let's go."

"I said I'm not going in there."

"Coward." He said it with a sneer in his voice. "Do you want to hide the rest of your life?"

Fury sparkled off the tears in her eyes as she ripped the seat belt free. "I hate you for this."

"I know," he murmured, but took her arm firmly and led her to the building's front entrance.

It was dark inside. Through the window he could see little but thick carpet and glass displays where gold and stones gleamed dully. It was a small showroom, again elegant, with a few upholstered stools and countertop mirrors where customers might sit and admire their choices.

Beside him, Bailey was shaking like a leaf.

"Let's try the back."

The rear faced the strip mall, and boasted delivery and employee entrances. Cade studied the lock on the employee door and decided he could handle it. From his pocket he took out a leather roll of tools.

"What are you doing?" Bailey stepped back as he chose a pick and bent to his work. "Are you breaking in? You can't do that."

"I think I can manage it. I practice picking locks at least four hours a week. Quiet a minute."

It took concentration, a good touch, and several sweaty minutes. If the alarm was set, he figured, it would go off when he disengaged the first lock. It didn't, and he changed tools and started on the second.

A silent alarm wasn't out of the question, he mused as he jiggled tumblers. If the cops came, he was going to have a lot of explaining to do.

"This is insane." Bailey took another step in retreat. "You're breaking into a store in broad daylight. You can't do this, Cade."

"Did it," he said with some satisfaction as the last tumbler fell. Fastidiously he replaced his tools in the roll, pocketed them. "An outfit like this ought to have a motion alarm in place, as well."

He stepped through the door. In the dim light, he saw the alarm box beside the doorway. Disengaged.

He could almost hear another piece fall into place.

"Careless of them," he murmured. "With the way crime pays."

He took Bailey's hand and pulled her inside.

"Nobody's going to hurt you while I'm around. Not even me."

"I can't do this."

"You're doing it." Keeping her hand firm in his, he hit the lights.

It was a narrow room, more of an entranceway with a worn wooden floor and plain white walls. Against the left wall were a watercooler and a brass coatrack. A woman's gray raincoat hung on one of the hooks.

It had called for thunderstorms the previous Thursday, he thought. A practical woman such as Bailey wouldn't have gone to work without her raincoat. "It's yours, isn't it?"

"I don't know."

"Coat's your style. Quality, expensive, subtle." He checked the pockets, found a roll of breath mints, a short grocery list, a pack of tissues. "It's your handwriting," he said, offering her the list.

"I don't know." She refused to look at it. "I don't remember."

He pocketed the list himself, and led her into the next room.

It was a workroom, a smaller version of the one at Westlake. He recognized the equipment now, and deduced that if he took the time to pick the locks on the drawers of a tall wooden cabinet, he would find loose stones. The flood of gems Bailey had described from her dreams. Stones that made her happy, challenged her creativity, soothed her soul.

The worktable was wiped spotlessly clean. Nothing, not the thinnest chain of gold links, was out of place.

It was, he thought, just like her.

"Someone keeps their area clean," he said mildly. Her hand was icy in his as he turned. There were stairs leading up. "Let's see what's behind door number two."

She didn't protest this time. She was too locked in terror to form the words. She winced as he flooded the stairway with light and drew her up with him.

On the second level, the floors were carpeted in pewter gray. Nausea swam in her stomach. The hallway was wide enough for them to walk abreast, and there were gleaming antique tables set at well-arranged spots. Red roses were fading in a silver vase. And the scent of their dying sickened her.

He opened a door, nudged it wider. And knew at first glance that it was her office.

Nothing was out of place. The desk, a pretty, feminine Queen Anne gleamed with polish and care under the light coating of weekend dust. On it was a long, milky crystal, jagged at one end, like a broken blade of a sword. She'd called it chalcedony, he remembered. And the smooth multiangled rock nearby must be the rutilated quartz.

On the walls were dreamy watercolors in thin wooden frames. There was a small table beside a love seat that was thickly upholstered in rose-toned fabric and set off with pale green pillows. On the table stood a small glass vase with drooping violets and pictures framed in polished silver.

He picked up the first. She was about ten, he judged, a little gangly and unformed, but there was no mistaking those eyes. And she'd grown to closely resemble the woman who sat beside her in a porch glider, smiling into the camera.

"It's your past, Bailey." He picked up another photo. Three woman, arms linked, laughing. "You, M.J. and Grace. Your present." He set the picture down, picked up another. The man was golden, handsome, his smile assured and warm.

Her future? he wondered.

"He's dead." The words choked out of her, slicing her heart on the journey. "My father. He's dead. The plane went down in Dorset. He's dead."

"I'm sorry." Cade set the photo down.

"He never came home." She was leaning against the desk, her legs trembling, her heart reeling as too many images crowded their way inside. "He left on a buying trip and never came back. We used to eat ice cream on the porch. He'd show me all the treasures. I wanted to learn. Lovely old things. He smelled of pine soap and beeswax. He liked to polish the pieces himself sometimes."

"He had antiques," Cade said quietly.

"It was a legacy. His father to him, my father to me. Time and Again. The shop. Time and Again. It was so full of beautiful things. He died, he died in England, thousands of miles away. My mother had to sell the business. She had to sell it when…"

"Take it slow, and easy. Just let it come."

"She got married again. I was fourteen. She was still young, she was lonely. She didn't know how to run a business. That's what he said. She didn't know how. He'd take care of things. Not to worry."

She staggered, caught herself. Then her gaze landed on the soapstone elephant with the jeweled blanket on her desk. "M.J. She gave it to me for my birthday. I like foolish things. I collect elephants. Isn't that odd? You picked an elephant for me at the carnival, and I collect them."

She passed a hand over her eyes, tried to hang on. "We laughed when I opened it. Just the three of us. M.J. and Grace and I, just a few weeks ago. My birthday's in June. June nineteenth. I'm twenty-five."

Her head spun as she struggled to focus on Cade.

"I'm twenty-five. I'm Bailey James. My name's Bailey Anne James."

Gently Cade eased her into a chair, laid his hand on hers. "Nice to meet you."

Chapter 11

"It's mixed up in my head." Bailey pressed her fingers to her eyes. Visions were rocketing in, zooming through, overlapping and fading before she could gain a firm hold.

"Tell me about your father."

"My father. He's dead."

"I know, sweetheart. Tell me about him."

"He—he bought and sold antiques. It was a family business. Family was everything. We lived in Connecticut. The business started there. Our house was there. He—he expanded. Another branch in New York, one in D.C. His father had established the first one, then my father had expanded. His name was Matthew."

Now she pressed her hand to her heart as it swelled and broke. "It's like losing him all over again. He was the center of the world to me, he and my mother. She couldn't have any more children. I suppose they spoiled me. I loved them so much. We had a willow tree in the backyard. That's where I went when my mother told me about the crash. I went out and sat under the willow tree and tried to make him come back."

"Your mother came and found you?" He was guessing now, prompting her gently through her grief.

"Yes, she came out, and we sat there together for a long time. The sun went down, and we just sat there together. We were lost without him, Cade. She tried, she tried so hard to hold the business together, to take care of me, the house. It was just too much. She didn't know how. She met—she met Charles Salvini."

"This is his building."

"It was." She rubbed her mouth with the back of her hand. "He was a jeweler, specialized in estate and antique pieces. She consulted with him on some of our stock. That's how it started. She was lonely, and he treated her very well. He treated me very well. I admired him. I think he loved her very much, I really do. I don't know if she loved him, but she needed him. I suppose I did, too. She sold what was left of the antique business and married him."

"Was he good to you?"

"Yes, he was. He was a kind man. And like my father, he was scrupulously honest. Honesty in business, in personal matters, was vital. It was my mother he wanted, but I came with the package, and he was always good to me."

"You loved him."

"Yes, it was easy to love him, to be grateful for what he did for me and my mother. He was very proud of the business he'd built up. When I developed an interest in gems, he encouraged it. I apprenticed here, in the summers, and after school. He sent me to college to study. My mother died while I was away in college. I wasn't here. I was away when she died."

"Honey." He gathered her close, tried to soothe. "I'm sorry."

"It was an accident. It happened very fast. A drunk driver, crossed the center line. Hit her head on. That was it." Grief was fresh again, raw and fresh. "Charles was devastated. He never really recovered. He was older than she by about fifteen years, and when she died, he lost interest in everything. He retired, went into seclusion. He died less than a year later."

"And you were all alone?"

"I had my brothers." She shuddered, gripped Cade's hands. "Timothy and Thomas. Charles's sons. My stepbrothers." She let out a broken sob. "Twins." Her hands jerked in his. "I want to go now. I want to leave here."

"Tell me about your brothers," he said calmly. "They're older than you."

"I want to go. I have to get out."

"They worked here," Cade continued. "They took over the business from your stepfather. You worked here with them."

"Yes, yes. They took over the business. I came to work here when I graduated from Radcliffe. We're family. They're my brothers. They were twenty when their father married my mother. We lived in the same house, we're family."

"One of them tried to kill you."

"No. No." She covered her face again, refused to see it. "It's a mistake. I told you, they're my brothers. My family. We lived together. We work together. Our parents are dead, and we're all that's left. They're impatient or brusque sometimes, but they'd never hurt me. They'd never hurt one another. They couldn't."

"They have offices here? In this building, on this floor?" She shook her head, but her gaze shifted to the left. "I want you to sit right here. Stay right here, Bailey."

"Where are you going?"

"I need to look." He cupped her face, kept his eyes level with hers. "You know I have to look. Stay here."

She let her head fall back against the cushion, closed her eyes. She would stay. There was nothing she needed to see. Nothing she needed to know. She knew her name now, her family. Wasn't that enough?

But it played back in her head, with an echoing crack of lightning that made her moan.

She hadn't moved when Cade came back into the room, but she opened her eyes. And when she did, she saw it on his face.

"It's Thomas," she said hollowly. "It's Thomas who's dead in his office down the hall."

He didn't wonder that she had blocked out what she'd seen. The attack had been vicious and violent. To witness the cause of the effect in the room he'd just left would have been horrifying. But to watch, from a few feet away, knowing it was one brother savagely slaying another, would have been unspeakable.

"Thomas," she repeated, and let tears fall. "Poor Thomas. He wanted to be the best in everything. He often was. They were never unkind to me. They ignored me a great deal of the time, as older brothers would, I suppose. I know they resented that Charles left me a part of the business, but they tolerated it. And me."

She paused, looked down at her hands. "There's nothing we can do for him, is there?"

"No. I'll get you out of here." He took her hand, helped her to her feet. "We'll call this in."

"They planned to steal the Three Stars of Mithra."

She stood her ground. She could bear it, she promised

herself, and she needed to say it all. "We'd been commissioned to verify and assess the three diamonds. Or I had, actually, since that's my field. I often do consults with the Smithsonian. The stars were going to be part of their gem display. They're originally from Persia. They're very old and were once set in a triangle of gold, held in the open hands of a statue of Mithra."

She cleared her throat, spoke calmly now, focused practical. "He was the ancient Persian god of light and wisdom. Mithraism became one of the major religions of the Roman Empire. He was supposed to have slain the divine bull, and from the bull's dying body sprang all the plants and animals."

"You can tell me in the car."

He urged her to the door, but she simply couldn't move until she'd said it all. "The religion wasn't brought to Rome until 68 B.C., and it spread rapidly. It's similar to Christianity in many respects. The ideals of brotherly love." Her voice broke, forced her to swallow. "The Three Stars were thought to be a myth, a legend spawned by the Trinity, though some scholars believed firmly in their existence, and described them as symbols of love, knowledge and generosity. It's said if one possesses all three, the combination of these elements will bring power and immortality."

"You don't believe that."

"I believe they're powerful enough to bring about

great love, great hate, great greed. I found out what my brothers were doing. I realized Timothy was creating duplicates in the lab." She scrubbed at her eyes. "Maybe he could have hidden something like that from me if he'd been more methodical, more careful, but he was always the more impatient of the two, the more reckless." Now her shoulders slumped as she remembered. "He's been in trouble a few times, for assault. His temper is very quick."

"He never hurt you?"

"No, never. He may have hurt my feelings from time to time." She tried a smile, but it faded quickly. "He seemed to feel that my mother had only married his father so that the two of us could be taken care of. It was partially true, I suppose. So it was always important to me to prove myself."

"You proved yourself here," Cade said.

"Not to him. Timothy was never one to praise. But he was never overly harsh, not really. And I never thought he or Thomas would be dishonest. Until we were commissioned to assess the Stars."

"And that was more than they could resist."

"Apparently. The fakes wouldn't fool anyone for very long, but by the time the stones were found out, my brothers would have the money and be gone. I don't know who was paying them, but they were working for someone."

She stopped on the stairs, stared down. "He chased me down here. I was running. It was pitch-dark. I nearly fell down these stairs. I could hear him coming after me. And I knew he'd kill me. We'd shared Christmas dinner every year of my life since I was fourteen. And he would kill me, the same horrible way he'd killed Thomas. For money."

She clutched the railing as she slowly walked down to the lower level. "I loved him, Cade. I loved both of them." At the base of the steps, she turned, gestured to a narrow door. "There's a basement down there. It's very small and cramped. There's where I ran. There's a little nook under the steps, with a lattice door. I used to explore the building when I was young, and I liked sitting in that nook, where it was quiet. I'd study the gem books Charles gave me. I don't suppose Timothy knew it was there. If he'd known, I'd be dead."

She walked into the sunlight.

"I honestly don't remember how long I stayed in there, in the dark, waiting for him to find me and kill me. I don't know how I got to the hotel. I must have walked part of the way, at least. I don't drive to work. I live only a few blocks from here."

He wanted to tell her it was done now, but it wasn't. He wanted to let her rest her head on his shoulder and put it behind her. But he couldn't. Instead, he took her hands, turned her to face him.

"Bailey. Where are the other two stars?"

"The—" She went dead pale, so quickly he grabbed her certain she would faint. But her eyes stayed open, wide and shocked.

"Oh, my God. Oh, my God, Cade, what have I done? He knows where they live. He knows."

"You gave them to M.J. and Grace." Moving fast, he wrenched open the car door. The cops would have to wait. "Tell me where."

"I was so angry," she told him as they sped through afternoon traffic. "I realized they were using me, my name, my knowledge, my reputation, to authenticate the gems. Then they would switch them and leave me—leave the business my stepfather had built— holding the bag. Salvini would have been ruined, after all Charles had done to build it. I owed him loyalty. And, damn it, so did they."

"So you beat them to it."

"It was impulse. I was going to face them down with it, but I wanted the Stars out of reach. At least I thought they shouldn't all be in one place. As long as they were, they could be taken. So I sent one to M.J. and one to Grace, by different overnight couriers."

"Dear Lord, Bailey, you put priceless diamonds in the mail?"

She squeezed her eyes shut. "We use special

couriers regularly for delivering gems." Her voice was prim, vaguely insulted. She'd already told herself she'd been unbelievably rash. "All I could think was that there were two people in the world I could trust with anything. I didn't consider they'd be put in danger. I never realized how far it could go. I was certain that when I confronted my brothers, told them I'd separated the diamonds for safe-keeping and would be making arrangements to have the diamonds delivered to the museum, that would have to be the end of it."

She hung onto the door as his tires spun around a corner. "It's this building. We're on the third floor. M.J. and I have apartments across from each other."

She was out of the car before he'd fully stopped, and racing toward the entrance. Cursing, he snatched his keys out of the ignition and sprinted after her. He caught her on the stairs. "Stay behind me," he ordered. "I mean it."

Both the lock and the jamb on apartment 324 were broken. Police tape was slashed across it. "M.J." was all she could manage as she pushed at Cade and reached for the knob to M.J.'s apartment.

"There you are, dearie." A woman in pink stretch pants and fluffy slippers scuffed down the hall. "I was getting worried about you."

"Mrs. Weathers." Bailey's knuckles turned white on the knob as she turned. "M.J. What's happened to M.J.?"

"Such a hullabaloo." Mrs. Weathers fluffed her helmet of blond hair and gave Cade a measuring smile. "You don't expect such things in a nice neighborhood like this. The world is going to hell in a handbasket, I swear."

"Where's M.J.?"

"Last I saw, she was running off with some man. Clattering down the steps, swearing at each other. That was after all the commotion. Glass breaking, furniture smashing. Gunshots." She nodded briskly several times, like a bird bobbing for juicy worms.

"Shot? Was M.J. shot?"

"Didn't look shot to me. Mad as a wet hen, and fired up."

"My brother. Was she with my brother?"

"No, indeed. Hadn't even seen this young man before. I'da remembered, I can tell you. He was one tall drink of water, had his hair back in one of those cute little ponytails, and had eyes like steel. Dent in his chin, just like a movie star. I got a good look at him, seeing as he nearly knocked me over."

"When did this happen, Mrs. Weathers?"

She fastened her gaze on Cade's face at the question, beamed and offered a hand. "I don't believe we've been introduced."

"I'm Cade, a friend of Bailey's." He flashed a grin back at her while impatience twisted his stomach.

"We've been away for a few days and wanted to catch up with M.J."

"Well, I haven't seen hide nor hair of her since Saturday, when she went running out. Left the door of her apartment wide open—or I thought she had till I saw it was broken. So I peeked in. Her place was a wreck. I know she's not the housekeeper you are, Bailey, but it was upside down and sideways, and..." She paused dramatically. "There was a man laid out cold on the floor. Big bruiser of a man, too. So I skedaddled back to my apartment and called the police. What else could I do? I guess he'd come to and cleared out by the time they got here. Lord knows I didn't put a toe out the door until the cops came knocking, and they said he was gone."

Cade slipped an arm around Bailey's waist. She was starting to tremble. "Mrs. Weathers, I wonder if you might have an extra key to Bailey's apartment. She left it back at my place, and we need to pick up a few things."

"Oh, is that the way of it?" She smiled slyly, fluffed her hair again and admonished Bailey. "And high time, too. Holing yourself up here, night after night. Now, let's see. I just watered Mr. Hollister's begonias, so I've got my keys right here. Here you are."

"I don't remember giving you my key."

"Of course you did, dearie, last year when you and the girls went off to Arizona. I made a copy, just in case." Humming to herself, she unlocked Bailey's door. Before she could push it open and scoot in, Cade outmaneuvered her.

"Thanks a lot."

"No trouble. Can't imagine where that girl got off to," she said, craning her neck to see through the crack in the door of Bailey's apartment. "I told the police how she was running off on her own steam. Oh, and now that I think about it, Bailey, I did see your brother."

"Timothy," Bailey whispered.

"Can't say which one for sure. They look like clones to me. He came by, let's see." She tapped a finger on her front teeth, as if to jiggle the thought free. "Must have been Saturday night. I told him I hadn't seen you, that I thought you might have taken a holiday. He looked a little perturbed. Let himself right in, then closed the door in my face."

"I didn't realize he had a key, either," Bailey murmured, then realized she'd left her purse behind when she ran. She wondered how foolishly useless it would be to change her locks. "Thank you, Mrs. Weathers. If I miss M.J. again, will you tell her I'm looking for her?"

"Of course, dearie. Now, if you—" She frowned as Cade gave her a quick wink, slid Bailey inside and shut the door in her face.

It was just as well he had. One glance around told

him his tidy Bailey didn't usually leave her apartment with cushions ripped open and drawers spilled out.

Apparently Salvini hadn't been content to search the place, he'd wanted to destroy it. "Messy amateur," Cade murmured, running a hand up and down her back.

It was the same madness, she realized. The same violent loss of control she'd seen when he grabbed the antique knife Thomas used for a letter opener off the desk. When he used it.

These were only things, she reminded herself. No matter how dear and cherished, they were only things.

She'd seen for herself just what Timothy could do to people. "I have to call Grace. She'd have gone to Grace if she could."

"Did you recognize who M.J. was with from the description?"

"No. I don't know anyone like that, and I know most of M.J.'s friends." She waded through the destruction of her living room and reached the phone. Her message light was blinking, but she ignored it and hastily punched in numbers. "It's her machine," Bailey murmured, and strained while the throaty voice recited the announcement. Then: "Grace, if you're there, pick up. It's urgent. I'm in trouble. M.J.'s in trouble. I don't know where she is. I want you to go to the police, give them the package I sent you. Call me right away."

"Give her my number," Cade instructed.

"I don't know it."

He took the phone himself, recited it, then handed the receiver back to Bailey.

It was a calculated risk, revealing Bailey's whereabouts, but the diamond was going into safekeeping and he didn't want to put up any impediments to Grace being able to reach them. "It's life-and-death, Grace. Don't stay in the house alone. Get to the police. Don't talk to my brother, whatever you do. Don't let him in the house. Call me, please, please, call me."

"Where does she live?"

"In Potomac." Bailey told him when he gently took the receiver away and hung it up. "She may not be there at all. She has a place up in the country, western Maryland. That's where I sent the package. There's no phone there, and only a few people know she goes there. Other times she just gets in the car and drives until she sees someplace that suits her. She could be anywhere."

"How long does she usually stay out of touch?"

"No more than a few days. She'd call me, or M.J." With an oath, she pounced on the message machine. The first voice to flow out was Grace's.

"Bailey, what are you up to? Is this thing real? Are we giving smuggling a try? Look, you know how I hate these machines. I'll be in touch."

"Four o'clock on Saturday." Bailey hung on to that. "She was all right at four o'clock on Saturday, according to the machine."

"We don't know where she called from."

"No, but she was all right on Saturday." She punched to get the next message. This time it was M.J.

"Bailey, listen up. I don't know what the hell's going on, but we're in trouble. Don't stay there, he might come back. I'm in a phone booth outside some dive near—" There was swearing, a rattle. "Hands off, you son of a—" And a dial tone.

"Sunday, two a.m. What have I done, Cade?"

Saying nothing, he punched in the next message. It was a man's voice this time. "Little bitch, if you hear this, I'll find you. I want what's mine." There was a sob, choked off. "He cut my face. He had them slice up my face because of what you did. I'm going to do the same to you."

"It's Timothy," she murmured.

"I figured as much."

"He's lost his mind, Cade. I could see it that night. Something snapped in him."

He didn't doubt it, not after what he'd seen in Thomas Salvini's office. "Is there anything you need from here?" When she only looked around blankly, he took her hand. "We'll worry about that later. Let's go."

"Where?"

"A quiet spot where you can sit down and tell me everything else. Then we'll make a call."

The park was shady and green. Somehow, the little bench under the spreading trees seemed to block out the punch of the oppressive July heat. It hadn't rained in days, and humidity hung like a cloud of wasps in the air.

"You need to have yourself under control when we go to the cops," Cade told her. "You have to have your mind clear."

"Yes, you're right. And I need to explain everything to you."

"I'm putting the pieces together well enough. That's what I do."

"Yeah." She looked down at her hands, felt useless. "That's what you do."

"You lost your father when you were ten. Your mother did her best, but didn't have a head for business. She struggled to keep a house, raise a daughter alone and run an antique business. Then she met a man, an older man, successful, competent, financially solvent and attractive, who wanted her and was willing to accept her daughter into his family."

She let out an unsteady breath. "I suppose that's it, cutting to the bottom line."

"The child wants a family, and accepts the stepfather and stepbrothers as such. That's it, too, isn't it?"

"Yes. I missed my father. Charles didn't replace him, but he filled a need. He was good to me, Cade."

"And the stepbrothers' noses were a little out of joint at the addition of a little sister. A pretty, bright, willing-to-please little sister."

She opened her mouth to deny it, then closed it again. It was time to face what she'd tried to ignore for years. "Yes, I suppose. I stayed out of their way. I didn't want to make waves. They were both in college when our parents married, and when they came back and were living at home again, I was off. I can't say we were close, but it seemed— I always felt we were a blended family. They never teased or abused me, they never made me feel unwelcome."

"Or welcome?"

She shook her head. "There wasn't any real friction until my mother died. When Charles withdrew into himself, pulled back from life so much, they took over. It seemed only natural. The business was theirs. I felt I'd always have a job with the company, but I never expected any percentage. There was a scene when Charles announced I'd have twenty percent. He was giving them forty each, but that didn't seem to be the point to them."

"They hassled you?"

"Some." Then she sighed. "They were furious," she admitted. "With their father, with me. Thomas backed off fairly quickly though. He was more interested in the sales-and-accounting end than the creative work, and he knew that was my area of expertise. We got along well enough. Timothy was less content with the arrangement, but he claimed I'd get tired of the routine, find some rich husband and leave it all up to them anyway."

It still hurt to remember that, the way he'd sneered at her. "The money Charles left me is in trust. It dribbles out to me until I reach thirty. It's not a great deal, but more than enough. More than necessary. He put me through college, he gave me a home, he gave me a career I love.

"And when he sent me to college, he gave me M.J. and Grace. That's where I met them. We were in the same dorm the first semester. By the second, we were rooming together. It was as if we'd known each other all our lives. They're the best friends I've ever had. Oh, God, what have I done?"

"Tell me about them."

She steadied herself, and tried. "M.J.'s restless. She changed her major as often as some women change hairstyles. Took all sorts of obscure courses. She'd bomb tests or ace them, depending on her mood. She's athletic, impatient, generous, fun, toughminded. She tended bar her last year at college for a lark, claimed she was so good at it she'd have to have her own place. She bought one two years ago. M.J.'s. It's a pub off Georgia Avenue, near the District line."

"I've missed it."

"It's kind of a neighborhood bar. Regulars, some Irish music on the weekends. If things get rowdy, she takes care of it herself most of the time. If she can't intimidate or outyell someone, she can drop-kick them around the block. She's got a black belt in karate."

"Remind me not to cross her."

"She'd like you. She can take care of herself, that's what I keep telling myself. No one can take care of herself better than M. J. O'Leary."

"And Grace?"

"She's beautiful, you saw that from the sketch. That's what most people see, and they don't see anything else. She uses that when she likes—despises it, but uses it."

Watching pigeons flutter and strut, Bailey let the memories come. "She was orphaned young, younger than I, and was raised by an aunt in Virginia. She was expected to behave, to be a certain way, a certain thing. A Virginia Fontaine."

"Fontaine? Department stores."

"Yes, money, lots of old money. At least old enough to have that luster a century or so of prestige provides. Because she was beautiful, wealthy and from a fine family, it was expected that she would be properly educated, associate with the right people and marry well. Grace had other ideas."

"Didn't she pose for...?" He trailed off, cleared his throat.

Bailey simply lifted a brow. "For a centerfold, yes, while she was still in college. The Ivy League Miss April. She did it without blinking an eye, with the idea of scandalizing her family and, as she put it, exploiting the exploiters. She came into her own money when she was twenty-one, so she didn't give a damn what her proper family thought."

"I never saw the picture," Cade said, wondering if he should be feeling regret or gratitude, under the circumstances. "But it created quite a stir."

"That's just what she was after." Bailey's lips curved again. "Grace liked creating stirs. She modeled for a while, because it amused her. But it didn't satisfy her. I think she's still looking for what will satisfy her. She works very hard for charities, travels on whims. She calls herself the last of the dilettantes, but it's not true. She does amazing work for underprivileged children, but won't have it publicized. She has tremendous compassion and generosity for the wounded."

"The bartender, the socialite and the gemologist. An unlikely trio."

It made her smile. "I suppose it sounds that way. We— I don't want to sound odd, but we recognized each other. It was that simple. I don't expect you to understand."

"Who'd understand better?" he murmured. "I recognized you."

She looked up then, met his eyes. "Knowing who I am hasn't solved anything. My life is a mess. I've put my friends in terrible danger, and I don't know how to help them. I don't know how to stop what I've started."

"By taking the next step." He lifted her hand, brushed a kiss over the knuckles. "We go back to the house, get the canvas bag, and contact a pal of mine on the force. We'll find your friends, Bailey."

He glanced up at the sky as clouds rolled over the sun. "Looks like we're finally going to get that rain."

Timothy Salvini swallowed another painkiller. His face throbbed so deeply it was difficult to think. But thinking was just what he had to do. The man who had ordered his face maimed, then ordered it tended by his personal physician, had given him one last chance.

If he didn't find Bailey and at least one of the diamonds by nightfall, there was nowhere on earth he could hide.

And fear was a deeper throb than pain.

He didn't know how it could have gone so horribly wrong. He'd planned it out, hadn't he? Handled the details when Thomas buried his head in the sand. He was the one who'd been contacted, approached. Because he was the one with the brains, he reminded himself. He was the one who knew how to play the games.

And he was the one who'd made the deal.

Thomas had jumped at it at first. Half of ten million dollars would have set his twin up nicely, and would have satisfied his own craving for real wealth.

Not the dribs and drabs of their business income, however successful the business. But real money, money to dream on.

Then Thomas had gotten cold feet. He'd waited until the eleventh hour, when everything was falling into place, and he'd been planning to double-cross his own flesh and blood.

Oh, he'd been furious to see that Thomas had planned on taking the million-plus deposit and leaving the country, leaving all the risk and the responsibility of pulling everything off on him.

Because he was afraid, Salvini thought now. Because he was worried about Bailey, and what she knew. Grasping little bitch had always been in the way. But he'd have handled her, he'd have taken care of everything, if only Thomas hadn't threatened to ruin everything.

The argument had simply gotten out of control, he thought, rubbing a hand over his mouth. Everything had gotten out of control. The shouting, the rage, the flashing storm.

And somehow the knife had just been there, in his

hand. Gripped in his hand, and already slicked with blood before he realized it.

He hadn't been able to stop himself. Simply hadn't been able to stop. He'd gone a little mad for a moment, he admitted. But it had been all the stress, the sense of betrayal, the fury at being duped by his own brother.

And she'd been there. Staring at him with those huge eyes. Staring at him out of the dark.

If not for the storm, if not for the dark, he'd have found her, taken care of her. She'd been lucky, that was all, just lucky. He was the one with the brains.

It wasn't his fault. None of it was his fault.

But he was taking the blame for all of it. His life was on the line because of his brother's cowardice and the schemes of a woman he'd resented for years.

He was certain she'd shipped off at least one of the stones. He'd found the receipt for the courier in the purse she'd left in her office when she fled from him. Thought she was clever, he mused.

She'd always thought she was the clever one. Little Miss Perfect, ingratiating herself with his father, coming back from her fancy college years with honors and awards. Honors and awards meant nothing in business. Shrewdness did. Guts did. Canniness did.

And Timothy Salvini had all three.

He would have had five million dollars, too, if his

brother hadn't bumbled and alerted Bailey then lost his nerve and tried to double-cross their client.

Client, he thought, gingerly touching his bandaged cheek. It was more like master now, but that would change, too.

He would get the money, and the stone, find the others. And then he would run far, and he would run fast. Because Timothy Salvini had looked the devil in the eye. And was smart enough to know that once the stones were in the devil's hand, his minion would be of no more use.

So he was a dead man.

Unless he was smart.

He'd been smart enough to wait. To spend hours waiting outside that apartment building for Bailey to come home. He'd known she would. She was a creature of habit, predictable as the sunrise. And she hadn't disappointed him.

Who would have thought that someone so… ordinary could have ruined all his plans? Separating the stones, shipping them off in different directions. Oh, that had been unexpectedly clever of her. And extremely inconvenient for him.

But his job now was to concentrate on Bailey. Others were concentrating on the other women. He would deal with that in time, but for now his patience had paid off.

It had been so easy, really. The fancy car had pulled up, Bailey had leaped out. And the man had followed, in too much of a hurry to lock the car door. Salvini had located the registration in the glove box, noted the address.

Now he was breaking the window on the rear door of the empty house, and letting himself inside.

The knife he'd used to kill his brother was tucked securely in his belt. Much quieter than a gun, and just as effective, he knew.

Chapter 12

"Mick's a good cop," Cade told Bailey as he pulled into the drive. "He'll listen, and he'll clear away the red tape to get to the answers."

"If I'd gone straight to them—"

"You wouldn't be any farther along than you are now," Cade said, interrupting her. "Maybe not as far. You needed time. What you'd been through, Bailey." It sickened him to think about it. "Give yourself a break." He hissed through his teeth as he remembered how ruthlessly he'd pulled her through the building where it had all happened. "I'm sorry I was so hard on you."

"If you hadn't pushed me, I might have kept backing away from it. Avoiding everything. I wanted to."

"It was catching up with you. It was hurting you." He turned, cupped her face. "But if you hadn't blocked it out, you might have gone straight back to your apartment. Like a homing pigeon, calling in your friends. He would have found you. All of you."

"He'd have killed me. I didn't want to face that. Couldn't, I suppose. I've thought of him as my brother for over ten years, even defended him and Thomas to M.J. and Grace. But he would have killed me. And them."

When she shuddered, he nodded. "The best thing you did for all three of you was to get lost for a while. No one would look for you here. Why would they?"

"I hope you're right."

"I am right. Now the next step is to bring in the cops, get them to put out an APB on Salvini. He's scared, he's hurting and he's desperate. It won't take them long."

"He'll tell them who hired him." Bailey relaxed a little. "He isn't strong enough to do otherwise. If he thinks he can make some sort of deal with the authorities, he'll do it. And Grace and M.J.—"

"Will be fine. I'm looking forward to meeting them." He leaned over, opened her door. Thunder rumbled, making her look up anxiously, and he squeezed her hand. "We'll all go to the pub, toss back a few."

"It's a date." Brightening by the image, she got out, reached for his hand. "When this is over, maybe you can get to know me."

"Sweetheart, how many times do I have to tell you? I knew you the minute you walked in my door." He jingled his keys, stuck one in the lock.

It was blind instinct, and his innate need to protect, that saved his life.

The movement was a blur at the corner of his eye. Cade twisted toward it, shoving Bailey back. The quick jerk of his body had the knife glancing down his arm, instead of plunging into his back.

The pain was immediate and fierce. Blood soaked through his shirt, dripped onto his wrist, before he managed to strike out. There was only one thought in his mind—Bailey.

"Get out!" he shouted at her as he dodged the next thrust of the knife. "Run!"

But she was frozen, shocked by the blood, numbed by the horrid replay of another attack.

It all happened so quickly. She was certain she'd no more than taken a breath. But she saw her brother's face, both cheeks bandaged with gauze, a gouge over his left brow.

Murder in his eyes, again.

He lunged at Cade. Cade pivoted, gripped Timothy's knife hand at the wrist. They strained against each other, their faces close as lovers', the smell of sweat and blood and violence fouling the air.

For a moment, they were only shadows in the dim foyer, their breath coming harsh and fast as thunder bellowed.

She saw the knife inch closer to Cade's face, until the point was nearly under his chin, while they swayed together on the bloody wood of the foyer, like obscene dancers.

Her brother would kill again, and she would stand and watch.

She lunged.

It was a mindless, animal movement. She leaped onto his back, tore at his hair, sobbing, cursing him. The sudden jolt sent Cade stumbling backward, his hand slipping, his vision graying around the edges.

With a howl of pain as she dug her fingers into his wounded face, Salvini threw her off. Her head rapped hard on the banister, sent stars circling in her head, flashing like lightning. But then she was up and back at him like vengeance.

It was Cade who pulled her away, threw her back out of the path of the knife that whistled by her face. Then the force of Cade's leap sent both him and his quarry crashing into a table. They grappled on the floor, panting like dogs. The uppermost thought in Cade's mind was to live long enough to keep Bailey safe. But his hands were slippery with blood and wouldn't keep a firm hold.

Using all his strength, he managed to twist Timothy's knife hand, veering the blade away from his own heart, then pushed away.

When he rolled weakly upright, he knew it was over.

Bailey was crawling to him, sobbing his name. He saw her face, the bruise just blooming on her cheekbone. He managed to lift a hand to it.

"You're supposed to leave the heroics to me." His voice sounded thready, faraway, to his own ears.

"How bad are you hurt? Oh God, you're bleeding so much." She was doing something with the fire in his arm, but it didn't seem to matter. Turning his head, he looked into Salvini's face. The eyes were on him, dimming but still aware.

Cade coughed his throat clear. "Who hired you, you bastard?"

Salvini smiled slowly. It ended in a grimace. His face was bloody, the bandages torn aside, his breathing thin. "The devil" was all he said.

"Well, say hello to him in hell." Cade struggled to focus on Bailey again. Her brows were drawn together in concentration. "You need your glasses for close work, honey."

"Quiet. Let me stop the bleeding before I call for an ambulance."

"I'm supposed to tell you it's just a flesh wound, but the truth is, it hurts like hell."

"I'm sorry. So sorry." She wanted to lay her head on his shoulder and weep, just weep. But she continued to make a thick pad out of what she'd torn from his shirt and pressed it firmly against the long, deep gash. "I'll call for an ambulance as soon as I finish bandaging this. You're going to be fine."

"Call Detective Mick Marshall. Be sure to ask for him, use my name."

"I will. Be quiet. I will."

"What in the world is going on here?"

The voice made him wince. "Tell me I'm hallucinating," he murmured. "Tell me, and I'm begging you, tell me that's not my mother."

"Good God, Cade, what have you done? Is this blood?"

He closed his eyes. Dimly he heard Bailey, in a firm, no-nonsense voice, order his mother to call an ambulance. And, gratefully, he passed out.

He came to in the ambulance, with Bailey holding his hand, rain pattering briskly on the roof. And again in the ER, with lights shining in his eyes and people shouting. Pain was like a greedy beast biting hunks out of his arm.

"Could I have some drugs here?" he asked, as politely as possible, and went out again.

The next time he surfaced, he was in a bed. He remained still, eyes closed, until he tested the level of pain and consciousness. He gave the pain a six on a scale of ten, but he seemed to be fully awake this time.

He opened his eyes, and saw Bailey. "Hi. I was hoping you'd be the first thing I'd see."

She got up from the chair beside the bed to take his hand. "Twenty-six stitches, no muscle damage. You lost a lot of blood, but they pumped more into you." Then she sat on the edge of the bed and indulged in a good cry.

She hadn't shed a tear since she fought to stop the bleeding as he lay on the floor. Not during the ambulance ride, speeding through the wet streets while lightning and thunder strode across the sky.

Or during the time she spent pacing the hospital corridors, or during the headachy ordeal of dealing with his parents. Not even when she struggled to tell the police what had happened.

But now she let it all out.

"Sorry," she said when she'd finished.

"Rough day, huh?"

"As days go, it was one of the worst."

"Salvini?"

She looked away toward the window where the rain ran wet. "He's dead. I called the police. I asked for Detective Marshall. He's outside waiting for you to wake up, and for the doctors to clear him in." She stood, straightened the sheets. "I tried to tell him everything, to make it clear. I'm not sure how well I did, but he took notes, asked questions. He's worried about you."

"We go back some. We'll straighten it out, Bailey," he told her, and reached for her hand again. "Can you hold up a little longer?"

"Yes, as long as it takes."

"Tell Mick to get me out of here."

"That's ridiculous. You've been admitted for observation."

"I've got stitches in my arm, not a brain tumor. I'm going home, drinking a beer and dumping this on Mick."

She angled her chin. "Your mother said you'd start whining."

"I'm not whining, I'm…" He trailed off, narrowed his eyes as he sat up. "What do you mean, my mother? Wasn't I hallucinating?"

"No, she came over to give you a chance to apologize, which apparently you never do."

"Great, take her side."

"I'm not taking her side." Bailey caught herself, shook her head. Could they actually be having this conversation at such a time? "She was terrified, Cade, when she realized what had happened, that you were hurt. She and your father—"

"My father? I thought he was off fly-fishing in Montana."

"He just got home this morning. They're in the waiting room right now, worried to death about you."

"Bailey, if you have one single ounce of affection for me, make them go away."

"I certainly will not, and you should be ashamed of yourself."

"I'll be ashamed later. I've got stitches." It wasn't going to work. He could see that plainly enough. "All right, here's the deal. You can send my parents in, and I'll square things with them. Then I want to see the doctor and get sprung. We'll talk to Mick at home and square things there."

Bailey folded her arms. "She said you always expect to have your own way." With that, she turned and marched to the door.

It took a lot of charm, arguments and stubbornness, but in just over three hours, Cade was sinking onto his own sofa. It took another two, with the distraction of Bailey fussing over him, to fill Mick in on the events since Thursday night.

"You've been a busy boy, Parris."

"Hey, private work isn't eating doughnuts and drinking coffee, pal."

Mick grunted. "Speaking of coffee." He glanced toward Bailey. "I don't mean to put you out, Miss James."

"Oh." She got to her feet. "I'll make a fresh pot." She took his empty mug and hurried off.

"Smooth, Mick, very smooth."

"Listen." Mick leaned closer. "The lieutenant's not going to be happy with two corpses and two missing diamonds."

"Buchanan's never happy."

"He doesn't like play cops like you on principle, but there's a lot of bad angles on this one. Your lady friend waiting four days to report a murder's just one of them."

"She didn't remember. She'd blocked it out."

"Yeah, she says. And me, I believe her. But the lieutenant…"

"Buchanan has any trouble with it, you send him my way." Incensed, Cade pushed himself up and ignored the throbbing in his arm. "Good God, Mick, she watched one of her brothers murder the other, then turn on her. You go to the scene, look at what she looked at, then tell me you'd expect a civilian to handle it."

"Okay." Mick held up a hand. "Shipping off the diamonds."

"She was protecting them. They'd be gone now, if she hadn't done something. You've got her statement and mine. You know exactly how it went down. She's been trying to complete the circle since she came to me."

"That's how I see it," Mick said after a moment, and glanced down at the canvas bag by his chair. "She's turned everything over. There's no question here about self-defense. He broke a pane out in the back door, walked in, waited for you."

Mick threaded a hand through his wiry hair. He knew how easily it could have gone down another way. How easily he could have lost a friend. "Thought I told you to put in an alarm."

Cade shrugged. "Maybe I will, now that I've got something worth protecting."

Mick glanced toward the kitchen. "She's, ah, choice."

"She's certainly mine. We need to find M. J. O'Leary and Grace Fontaine, Mick, and fast."

"We?"

"I'm not going to sit on my butt."

Mick nodded again. "All we've got on O'Leary is there was a disturbance in her apartment, what looks like a whale of a fight, and her running off with some guy wearing a pony tail. Looks like she's gone to ground."

"Or is being held there," Cade murmured, casting a glance over his shoulder to make certain Bailey was still out of earshot. "I told you about the message on Bailey's recorder."

"Yeah. No way to trace a message, but we'll put a flag out on her. As for Fontaine, I've got men checking her house in Potomac, and we're hunting down her place up in the mountains. I should know something in a couple hours."

He rose, hefted the bag, grinned. "Meanwhile, I get to dump this on Buchanan, watch him tap dance with the brass from the Smithsonian." He had to chuckle, knowing just how much his lieutenant hated playing diplomat with suits. "How much you figure the rocks are worth?"

"So far, at least two lives," Bailey said as she carried in a tray of coffee.

Mick cleared his throat. "I'm sorry for your loss, Miss James."

"So am I." But she would live with it. "The Three Stars of Mithra don't have a price, Detective. Naturally, for insurance purposes and so forth, the Smithsonian required a professional assessment of market value. But whatever dollar value I can put on them as a gemologist is useless, really. Love, knowledge and generosity. There is no price."

Not quite sure of his moves, Mick shifted his feet. "Yes, ma'am."

She worked up a smile for him. "You're very kind and very patient. I'm ready to go whenever you are."

"Go?"

"To the station. You have to arrest me, don't you?"

Mick scratched his head, shifted his feet again. It was the first time in his twenty-year career that he'd had a woman serve him coffee, then politely ask to be arrested. "I'd have a hard time coming up with the charge. Not that I don't want you to stay available, but I figure Cade's got that handled. And I imagine the museum's going to want to have a long talk with you."

"I'm not going to jail?"

"Now she goes pale. Sit down, Bailey." To ensure that she did, Cade took her hand with his good one and tugged.

"I assumed, until the diamonds were recovered…I'm responsible."

"Your brothers were responsible," Cade corrected.

"I have to go with that," Mick agreed. "I'm going to take a rain check on the coffee..I may need to talk to you again, Miss James."

"My friends?"

"We're on it." He gave Cade a quick salute and left.

"Timothy can't hurt them now," she murmured. "But whoever hired him—"

"Only wants the diamonds, not your friends. Odds are Grace is up in her mountain hideaway, and M.J. is out busting some guy's chops."

It almost made her smile. "You're right. We'll hear from them soon. I'm sure of it. I'd know if something had happened to them. I'd feel it." She poured a cup of coffee, then left it sitting untouched. "They're the only family I have left. I suppose they're the only family I've had for a long time. I just pretended otherwise."

"You're not alone, Bailey. You know that."

No, she wasn't alone. He was there, waiting. "You should lie down, Cade."

"Come with me."

She turned, caught the fresh cockiness of his grin. "And rest."

"I'm not tired."

Her smile faded, and her eyes went dark and serious. "You saved my life."

He thought of the way she'd leaped onto Salvini's back, biting and scratching like a wildcat. "I'd say it was a toss-up as to who saved whom."

"You saved my life," she said again, slowly. "The minute I walked into yours. I'd have been lost without you. Today, you shielded me, fought for me. Risked your life to protect mine."

"I've always wanted to slay the dragon for the damsel. You gave me the chance."

"It's not white knights or Sam Spade." Her voice went rough with emotion. "It was real blood pouring out of you. My brother who turned a knife on you."

"And you," he reminded her. "You're not responsible for what he did, and you're too smart to believe you are."

"I'm trying to be." She turned away for a moment, until she had her courage in place. "If it had gone the other way, if it had been you who died, who else could I blame? I came to you. I brought this to you."

"It's my job." He rose, winced only a little. "Are you

going to have a problem with that? What I do for a living? The risks involved with it?"

"I haven't thought that far." She turned back, faced him. "What you've done for me comes first. I'll never be able to repay you for a moment of it."

In an impatient movement, he scooped the hair out of his face. "You're going to tick me off here, Bailey."

"No, I'm going to say what I have to say. You believed me, right from the first. You took me into your home. You bought me a hairbrush. Something so simple, hundreds of others would have overlooked it. You listened to me and promised to help. You kept your promise. And today it almost killed you."

His eyes went sharp. "Do you want me to tell you I'd die for you? I suppose I would. Would I kill for you? Without question. You're not a fantasy to me, Bailey. You're what made reality snap into place."

Her heart fluttered into her throat and swelled. He was angry with her again, she noted. His eyes were impatient in his bruised face. His arm was bandaged from elbow to shoulder and had to be painful.

And he was hers, without question, for the taking.

"I guess I'm trying to figure out why."

"You want to be reasonable where reason doesn't fit. It's not a piece of the puzzle, Bailey. It's the whole puzzle." Frustrated, he dragged a hand through his hair again. "Love was the first Star, wasn't it? And so is this."

That simple, she realized. That powerful. Pressing her lips together, she took a step toward him. "I'm Bailey James," she began. "I'm twenty-five and live in Washington, D.C. I'm a gemologist. I'm single."

She had to stop, pace herself before she babbled. "I'm neat. One of my closest friends says neatness is a religion to me, and I'm afraid she may be right. I like everything in its place. I like to cook, but don't often, as I live alone. I like old movies, especially film noir."

He was grinning at her now, but she shook her head. There had to be more to her than that. "Let me think," she muttered, impatient with herself. "I have a weakness for Italian shoes. I'd rather do without lunch for a month than a nice pair of pumps. I like good clothes and antiques. I prefer buying one good thing than several inferior ones. That same friend calls me a retail snob, and it's true. I'd rather go rockhounding than visit Paris, though I wouldn't mind doing both."

"I'll take you."

But she shook her head again. "I'm not finished. I have flaws, a lot of flaws. Sometimes I read very late into the night and fall asleep with the light on and the TV going."

"Well, we'll have to fix that."

He stepped toward her, but she stepped back, held up a hand. "Please. I squint without my reading glasses, and I hate wearing them because I'm vain, so I squint quite a lot. I didn't date much in college, because I was shy and studious and boring. My only sexual experience has come about recently."

"Is that so? If you'd shut up, you could have another sexual experience."

"I'm not done." She said it sharply, like a teacher chastising a rowdy student. "I'm good at my work. I designed these rings."

"I've always admired them. You're so pretty when you're serious, Bailey. I've got to get my hands on you."

"I'm not without ambition," she continued, sidestepping his grab for her. "I intend to be successful in what I do. And I like the idea of making a name for myself."

"If you're going to make me chase you around the sofa, at least give me a handicap. I've got stitches."

"I want to be important to someone. I want to know I matter. I want to have children and cook Thanksgiving dinner. I want you to understand that I've tried to be sensible about this, because that's the way I am. I'm precise and I'm practical and I can be very tedious."

"I've never spent such a boring weekend in my entire life," he said dryly. "I could barely keep my eyes open." When she chuckled, he outmaneuvered her and pulled her into his arms. And swore as pain radiated straight up to his shoulder.

"Cade, if you've opened those stitches—"

"You're so precise and practical, you can sew me

back up." He lifted her chin with his fingers, smiled. "Are you finished yet?"

"No. My life isn't going to be settled until M.J. and Grace are back and I know they're safe and the Three Stars are in the museum. I'll worry until then. I'm very good at worrying, but I believe you already know that."

"I'll write it down in case it slips my mind again. Now, why don't you take me upstairs and play doctor?"

"There's one more thing." When he rolled his eyes, she drew in a breath. "I love you very much."

He went very still, and the fingers on her chin tightened. Emotions poured through him, sweet and potent as wine. There might not be stars in her eyes, he thought. But her heart was in them. And it belonged to him.

"Took you long enough to get to it."

"I thought it was the best place to finish."

He kissed her for a long, gentle time. "It's a better place to start," he murmured.

"I love you, Cade," she repeated, and touched her lips to his again. "Life starts now."

Epilogue

One Star was out of his reach, for the time being. He'd known the moment it was placed in the hands of the authorities. He hadn't raged or cursed the gods. He was, after all, a civilized man. He had only sent his quivering messenger away with a single icy stare.

Now, he sat in his treasure room, gliding his finger over the stem of a golden goblet filled with wine. Music poured liquidly through the air, soothing him.

He adored Mozart, and gently followed the strains of the music with his hand.

The woman had caused him a great deal of trouble. Salvini had underestimated her, had claimed she was nothing more than a token, a pet of his late father's. With some brains, of course, and undeniable skill, but no courage. A quiet mouse of a woman, he'd been told, who closed herself off with her rocks and minded her own business.

The mistake had been to trust Salvini's estimation of Bailey James.

But he wouldn't make that mistake again. He chuckled to himself. He wouldn't be required to, as Ms. James and her protector had dealt so finally with Timothy Salvini.

And with that convenience, there was nothing to link him with the stones, with the deaths. And nothing to stop him from completing his plan—with some adjustments, of course. He could be flexible when it was necessary.

Two Stars were still free, still lost or wandering. He could see them if he closed his eyes, pulsing with light, waiting for him to take them, unite them with the third. Embrace their power.

He would have them soon enough. Whoever stood in his way would be removed.

It was a pity, really. There had been no need for violence. No need for a single drop of blood to be spilled. But now that it had, well…

He smiled to himself and drank deep of warm red wine. Blood, he thought, would have blood.

Three women, three stones, three Stars. It was

almost poetic. He could appreciate the irony of it. And when the golden triangle was complete, when the Three Stars of Mithra were his alone, and he could stroke them as they sat on the altar, he would think of the women who'd tried to turn his destiny aside.

He would remember them with some fondness, even admiration.

He hoped he could arrange for them all to die poetically.

* * * * *

CAPTIVE STAR

To independent women

Chapter 1

He'd have killed for a beer. A big, frosty mug filled with some dark import that would go down smoother than a woman's first kiss. A beer in some nice, dim, cool bar, with a ball game on the tube and a few other stool-sitters who had an interest in the game gathered around.

While he staked out the woman's apartment, Jack Dakota passed the time fantasizing about it.

The foamy head, the yeasty smell, the first gulping swallow to beat the heat and slake the thirst. Then the slow savoring, sip by sip, that assured a man all would be right with the world if only politicians and lawyers would debate the inevitable conflicts over a cold one at a local pub while a batter faced a count of three and two.

It was a bit early for drinking, at just past one in the afternoon, but the heat was so huge, so intense and the cooler full of canned sodas just didn't have quite the same punch as a cold, foamy beer.

His ancient Oldsmobile didn't run to amenities like air-conditioning. In fact, its amenities were pathetically few, except for the pricey, earsplitting stereo he'd installed in the peeling faux-leather dash. The stereo was worth about double the blue book on the car, but a man had to have music. When he was on the road, he enjoyed turning it up to scream and belting them out with the Beatles or the Stones.

The muscle-flexing V-8 engine under the dented gutter-gray hood was tuned as meticulously as a Swiss watch, and got Jack where he wanted to go, fast. Just now the engine was at rest, and as a concession to the quiet neighborhood in northwest Washington, D.C., he had the CD player on murmur while he hummed along with Bonnie Raitt.

She was one of his rare bows to music after 1975.

Jack often thought he'd been born out of his own time. He figured he'd have made a pretty good knight. A black one. He liked the straightforward philosophy of might for right. He'd have stood with Arthur, he mused, tapping his fingers on the steering wheel. But he'd have handled Camelot's business his own way. Rules complicated things.

He'd have enjoyed riding the West, too. Hunting down desperadoes without all the nonsense of paperwork. Just track 'em down and bring 'em in.

Dead or alive.

These days, the bad guys hired a lawyer, or the state gave them one, and the courts ended up apologizing to them for the inconvenience.

We're terribly sorry, sir. Just because you raped, robbed and murdered is no excuse for infringing on your time and civil rights.

It was a sad state of affairs.

And it was one of the reasons Jack Dakota hadn't gone into police work, though he'd toyed with the idea during his early twenties. Justice meant something to him, always had. But he didn't see much justice in rules and regulations.

Which was why, at thirty, Jack Dakota was a bounty hunter.

You still hunted down the bad guys, but you worked your own hours and got paid for a job and didn't answer to a lot of bureaucratic garbage.

There were still rules, but a smart man knew how to work around them. Jack had always been smart.

He had the papers on his current quarry in his pocket. Ralph Finkleman had called him at eight that morning with the tag. Now, Ralph was a worrier and an optimist—a combination, Jack thought, that must be a job requirement for a bail bondsman. Personally, Jack could never understand the concept of lending money to complete strangers—strangers who, since they needed bond, had already proved themselves unreliable.

But there was money in it, and money was enough motivation for most anything, he supposed.

Jack had just come back from tracing a skip to North Carolina, and had made Ralph pitifully grateful when he hauled in the dumb-as-a-post country boy who'd tried to make his fortune robbing convenience stores. Ralph had put up the bond—claimed he'd figured the kid was too stupid to run.

Jack could have told him, straight off, that the kid was too stupid *not* to run.

But he wasn't being paid to offer advice.

Jack had planned to relax for a few days, maybe take in a few games at Camden Yards, pick one of his female acquaintances to help him enjoy spending his fee. He'd nearly turned Ralph down, but the guy had been so whiny, so full of pleas, he didn't have the heart.

So he'd gone into First Stop Bail Bonds and picked up the paperwork on one M. J. O'Leary, who'd apparently decided against having her day in court to explain why she shot her married boyfriend.

Jack figured she was dumb as a post, as well. A

good-looking woman—and from her photo and description, she qualified—with a few working brain cells could manipulate a judge and jury over something as minor as plugging an adulterous accountant.

It wasn't like she'd killed the poor bastard.

It was a cream-puff job, which didn't explain why Ralph had been so jumpy. He'd stuttered more than usual, and his eyes had danced all over the cramped, dusty office.

But Jack wasn't interested in analyzing Ralph. He wanted to wrap up the job quickly, get that beer and start enjoying his fee.

The extra money from this quick one meant he could snatch up that first edition of *Don Quixote* he'd been coveting, so he'd tolerate sweating in the car for a few hours.

He didn't look like a man who hunted up rare books or enjoyed philosophical debates on the nature of man. He wore his sun-streaked brown hair pulled back in a stubby ponytail—which was more a testament to his distrust of barbers than a fashion statement, though the sleek look enhanced his long, narrow face, with its slashing cheekbones and hollows. Over the shallow dent in his chin, his mouth was full and firm, and looked poetic when it wasn't curled in a sneer.

His eyes were razor-edged gray that could soften to smoke at the sight of the yellowing pages of a first-edition Dante, or darken with pleasure at a glimpse of a pretty woman in a thin summer dress. His brows were arched, with a faintly demonic touch accented by the white scar that ran diagonally through the left and was the result of a tangle with a jackknife wielded by a murder in the second who hadn't wanted Jack to collect his fee.

Jack had collected the fee, and the skip had sported a broken arm and a nose that would never be the same unless the state sprang for rhinoplasty.

Which wouldn't have surprised Jack a bit.

There were other scars. His long, rangy body had the marks of a warrior, and there were women who liked to coo over them.

Jack didn't mind.

He stretched out his yard-long legs, cracked the tightness out of his shoulders and debated popping the top on another soft drink and pretending it was a beer.

When the MG zipped by, top down, radio blasting, he shook his head. Dumb as a post, he thought— though he admired her taste in music. The car jibed with his paperwork, and the quick glimpse of the woman as she'd flown by confirmed it. The short red hair that had been blowing in the breeze was a dead giveaway.

It was ironic, he thought as he watched her unfold herself out of the little car she'd parked in front of him, that a woman who looked like that should be so pathetically stupid.

He wouldn't have called her easy on the eyes. There didn't look to be anything easy about her. She was a tall one—and he did have a weakness for long-legged, dangerous women. Her narrow teenage-boy hips were hugged by a pair of faded jeans that were white at the stress points and ripped at the knee. The T-shirt tucked into the jeans was plain white cotton, and her small, unhampered breasts pressed nicely against the soft fabric.

She hauled a bag out of the car, and Jack received a interesting view of a firm female bottom in tight denim. Grinning to himself, he patted a hand on his heart. Small wonder some slob had cheated on his wife for this one.

She had a face as angular as her body. Though it was milkmaid-pale, to go with the flaming cap of hair, there was nothing of the maid about it. Pointed chin and pointed cheekbones combined to create a tough, sexy face tilted off center by a lush, sensual mouth.

She was wearing dark wraparound shades, but he knew her eyes were green from the paperwork. He wondered if they'd be like moss or emeralds.

With an enormous shoulder bag hitched on one shoulder, a grocery bag cocked on her hip, she started toward him and the apartment building. He let himself sigh once over her loose-limbed, ground-eating stride.

He sure did go for leggy women.

He got out of the car and strolled after her. He didn't figure she'd be much trouble. She might scratch and bite a bit, but she didn't look like the kind who'd dissolve into pleading tears.

He really hated when that happened.

His game plan was simple. He could have taken her outside, but he hated public displays when there were other choices. So he'd push himself into her apartment, explain the situation, then take her in.

She didn't look like she had a care in the world, Jack noted as he stepped into the building behind her. Did she really figure the cops wouldn't check out the homes of her friends and associates? And driving her own car to shop for groceries. It was amazing she hadn't already been picked up.

But then, the cops had enough to do without scrambling after a woman who'd had a spat with her lover.

He hoped her pal who lived in the apartment wasn't home. He'd kept the windows under surveillance for the best part of an hour, and he'd seen no movement. He'd heard no sound when he took a lazy walk under the open third-floor windows, and he'd wandered inside to listen at the door.

But you could never be too sure.

Since she turned away from the elevator, toward the stairs, so did he. She never glanced back, making him figure she was either supremely confident or had a lot on her mind.

He closed the distance between them, flashed a smile at her. "Want a hand with that?"

The dark glasses turned, leveled on his face. Her lips didn't curve in the slightest. "No. I've got it."

"Okay, but I'm going a couple flights up. Visiting my aunt. Haven't seen her in—damn—two years. Just blew into town this morning. Forgot how hot it got in D.C."

The glasses turned away again. "It's not the heat," she said, her voice dry as dust, "it's the humidity."

He chuckled at that, recognizing sarcasm and annoyance. "Yeah, that's what they say. I've been in Wisconsin the past few years. Grew up here, though, but I'd forgotten... Here let me give you a hand."

It was a smooth move, easing in as she shifted the bag to slip her key into the lock of the apartment door. Equally smooth, she blocked with her shoulder, pushed the door open. "I've got it," she repeated, and started to kick the door shut in his face.

He slid in like a snake, took a firm hold on her arm. "Ms. O'Leary—" It was all he got out before her elbow cracked into his chin. He swore, blinked his vision clear and dodged the kick to the groin. But it had been close enough to have him swiftly changing his approach.

Explanations could damn well wait.

He grabbed her, and she turned in his arms, stomped

down hard enough on his foot to have stars springing into his head. And that was before she backfisted him in the face.

Her bag of groceries had gone flying, and she delivered each blow with a quick expulsion of breath. Initially he blocked her blows, which wasn't an easy matter. She was obvious trained for combat—a little detail Ralph had omitted.

When she went into a fighting crouch, so did he.

"This isn't going to do you any good." He hated thinking he was going to have to deck her—maybe on that sexy pointed chin. "I'm going to take you in, and I'd rather do it without messing you up."

Her answer was a swift flying kick to his midsection he wished he'd been able to admire from a distance. But he was too busy crashing into a table.

Damn, she was good.

He expected her to bolt for the door, and was up on the balls of his feet quickly to block her. But she merely circled him, eyes hidden behind the dark glasses, mouth curled in a grimace.

"Come on, then," she taunted him. "Nobody tries to mug me on my own turf and walks away."

"I'm not a mugger." He kicked away a trio of firm, ripe peaches that had spilled out of her bag. "I'm a skip tracer, and you're busted." He held up a hand, signaling peace, and, hoping her gaze had flickered there, moved in fast, hooked a foot under her leg and sent her sprawling on her butt.

He tackled her, and might have appreciated the long, economical lines of her body pressed beneath him, but her knee had better aim than her initial kick. His eyes rolled, his breath hissed, as the pain only a man understands radiated in sick waves. But he hung on.

He had the advantage now, and she knew it. Vertical, she was fast, and her reach was nearly as long as his and the odds were more balanced. But in a wrestling match, he outweighed her and outmuscled her. It infuriated her enough to have her resorting to dirty tactics. She fixed her teeth in his shoulders like a bear trap, felt the adrenaline and satisfaction rush through her as he howled.

They rolled, limbs tangling, hands grappling, and crashed into the coffee table. A wide blue bowl filled with chocolate drops shattered on the floor. A shard pierced his undamaged shoulder and made him swear again. She landed a blow to the side of his head, another to his kidneys.

She was just beginning to think she could take him, after all, when he flipped her over. She landed with a jarring smack, and before she could suck in breath, he had her hands locked behind her back and was sitting on her.

The fact that his breath was coming in pants was very little satisfaction. And for the first time, she was seriously afraid.

"Don't know why the hell you shot the guy, when you could've just beat the hell out of him," Jack muttered. He reached into his back pocket for his cuffs, swore again when he came up empty. They'd popped out during the match.

He simply rode her out as she bucked, and caught his breath. He hadn't had a fight of this magnitude with a female since he hunted down Big Betsy. And she'd been two hundred pounds of sheer muscle.

"Look, it's only going to be harder on you this way. Why don't you just go quietly, before we bust up any more of your friend's apartment?"

"You're crushing me, you jerk," she said between her teeth. "And this is my apartment. You try to rape me, and I'll twist your pride clean off and hand it to you. There won't be enough left of you for the cops to scrape off their shoes."

"I don't force women, sugar. Just because some accountant couldn't keep his hands off you doesn't mean I can't. And the cops aren't interested in me. They want you."

She blew out a breath, tried to suck another in, but he was crushing her lungs. "I don't know what the hell you're talking about."

He pulled the papers out of his pocket, shoved them in front of her face. "M. J. O'Leary, assault with a deadly, malicious wounding, and blah-blah. Ralph's real disappointed in you, sugar. He's a trusting man and didn't expect a nice woman like you to try to skip out on the ten-K bond."

"This is a crock." She could see her name and some downtown address on what appeared to be some kind of arrest warrant. "You've got the wrong person. I didn't post bail for anything. I haven't been arrested, and I live here. Idiot cops," she muttered, and tried to buck him off again. "Call in to your sergeant, or whatever. Straighten this out. And when you do, I'm suing."

"Nice try. And I suppose you've never heard of George MacDonald."

"No, I haven't."

"Then it was really rude of you to shoot him." He eased up just enough to flip her face up, then caught both of her hands at the wrist. She'd lost her glasses, he noted, and her eyes were neither moss nor emerald, he decided—they were dark shady-river green. And, just now, full of fury. "Look, you want to have a hot affair with your accountant, sister, it's no skin off my nose. You want to shoot him, I don't particularly care. But you skip bond, and it ticks me off."

She could breathe slightly easier now, but his hands were like steel bands at her wrists. "My accountant's name is Holly Bergman, and we haven't had a hot affair. I haven't shot anyone, and I haven't *skipped* bond because I haven't *posted* bond. I want to see your ID, ace."

He thought it took a lot of nerve to make demands in her current position. "My name's Dakota, Jack Dakota. I'm a skip tracer."

Her eyes narrowed as they skimmed over his face. She thought he looked like something out of the gritty side of a western. A cold-eyed gunslinger, a tough-talking gambler. Or…

"A bounty hunter. Well, there's no bounty here, jerk." It wasn't rape, and it wasn't a mugging. The fear that had iced her heart thawed into fresh temper. "You son of a bitch. You break in here, tear up my things, ruin twenty bucks' worth of produce, and all because you can't follow the right trail? Your butt's in a sling, I promise you. When I'm done, you won't be able to trace your own name with a stencil. You won't—" She broke off when he stuck a photo in her face.

It was her face, and the photograph might have been taken yesterday.

"Got a twin, O'Leary? One who drives a '68 MG, license plate SLAINTE, and is currently shacked up with some guy named Bailey James."

"Bailey's a woman," she murmured, staring at her own face while new worries raced in her head. Was this about Bailey, about what Bailey had sent her? What kind of trouble could her friend be in? "And this isn't her apartment, it's mine. I don't have a twin." She looked up into his eyes again. "What's going on? Is Bailey all right? Where's Bailey?"

Under his clamped hands, her pulse had spiked. She was struggling again, with a fresh and vicious energy he knew was brought on by fear. And he was dead certain it wasn't fear for herself.

"I don't know anything about this Bailey except this address is listed under her name on the paperwork."

But he was beginning to smell something, and he didn't like it. He was no longer thinking M. J. O'Leary was dumb as a post. A woman with any brains wouldn't have left herself with so many avenues to be tracked if she was on the run.

Ralph, Jack mused, frowning down into M.J.'s face. Why were you so jumpy this morning?

"If you're being straight with me, we can confirm it quick enough. Maybe it was a clerical mix-up." But he didn't think so. No indeed. And there was an itching at the base of his spine. "Listen," he began, just as the door broke open and the giant roared in.

"You were supposed to bring her out," the giant said, and waved an impressive .357 Magnum. "You're talking too much. He's waiting."

Jack didn't have much time to decide how to play it. The big man was a stranger to him, but he recognized the type. It looked like all bulk and no brains, with the huge bullet head, small eyes and massive shoulders. The gun was big as a cannon and looked like a toy in the ham-size hands.

"Sorry." He gave M.J.'s wrist a quick squeeze, hoping she'd understand it as a sign of reassurance and remain still and quiet. "I was having a little trouble here."

"Just a woman. You were supposed to just bring the woman out."

"Yeah, I was working on it." Jack tried a friendly smile. "Ralph send you to back me up?"

"Come on, up. Up now. We're going."

"Sure. No problem. You won't need the gun now. I've got her under control." But the gun continued to point, its barrel as wide as Montana, at his head.

"Just her." And the giant smiled, floppy lips peeling back over huge teeth. "We don't need you now."

"Fine. I guess you want the paperwork." For lack of anything better, Jack snagged a can of tomato sauce on his way up and winged it. It made a satisfactory crunching sound on the big man's nose. Ducking, Jack rushed forward like a battering ram. It felt a great deal like beating his head against a brick wall, but the force took them both tumbling backward and over a ladder-back chair.

The gun went off, putting a fist-size hole in the ceiling before it flew across the room.

She thought about running. She could have been out

of the door and away before either of them untangled. But she thought about Bailey, about what she had weighing down her shoulder bag. About the mess she'd somehow stepped in. And was too mad to run.

She went for the gun and ended up falling backward as Jack flew into her. She cushioned his fall, and he was up fast, springing into the air and landing a double-footed kick in the big man's midsection.

Nice form, M.J. thought, and scrambled to her own feet. She snagged her shoulder bag, spun it over her head and cracked it hard over the sleek, bullet-shaped head.

He went down hard on the sofa, snapping the springs.

"You're wrecking my place!" she shouted, and smacked Jack in the side, simply because she could reach him.

"Sue me."

He dodged a fist the size of a steamship and went in low. Pain sang through every bone as his opponent slammed him into a wall. Pictures fell, glass shattering on the floor. Through his blurred vision he saw the woman charge, a redheaded fireball that flew up and latched like a plague of wasps on the man's enormous back. She used her fists, pounding the sides of his face as he spun wildly and struggled to grab her.

"Hold him still!" Jack shouted. "Damn it, just hold him for a minute!"

Spotting an opening, he grabbed what was left of a

table leg and rushed in. He checked his first swing as the duo spun like a mad two-headed top. If he followed through, he might have cracked the back of M.J.'s head open like a melon.

"I said hold him still!"

"You want me to paint a bull's-eye on his face while I'm at it?" With a guttural snarl, she hooked her arms around the man's throat, clamped her thighs like a vise around his wide steel beam of a torso and screamed, "Hit him, for God's sake. Stop dancing around and hit him."

Jack cocked back like a batter with two strikes already on his record and swung full out. The table leg splintered like a toothpick, blood gushed like water in a fountain. M.J. had just enough time to jump clear as the man toppled like a redwood.

She stayed on her hands and knees a minute, gasping for air. "What's going on? What the hell's going on?"

"No time to worry about it." Self-preservation on his mind, Jack grabbed her hand, hauled her to her feet. "This type doesn't usually travel alone. Let's go."

"Go?" She snagged the strap of her purse as he pulled her toward the door. "Where?"

"Away. He's going to be mean when he wakes up, and if he's got a friend, we're not going to be so lucky next time."

"Lucky, my butt." But she was running with him, driven by a pure instinct that matched Jack's. "You son of a bitch. You come busting into my place, push me around, wreck my home, nearly get me shot."

"I saved your butt."

"I saved *yours!*" She shouted it at him, cursing viciously as they thudded down the stairs. "And when I get a minute to catch my breath, I'm going to take you apart, piece by piece."

They rounded the landing and nearly ran over one of her neighbors. The woman, with helmet hair and bunny slippers, cowered back against the wall, hands pressed to her deeply rouged cheeks.

"M.J., what in the world—? Were those gunshots?"

"Mrs. Weathers—"

"No time." Jack all but jerked her off her feet as he headed down the next flight.

"Don't you shout at me, you jerk. I'm making you pay for every grape that got smashed, every lamp, every—"

"Yeah, yeah, I get the picture. Where's the back door?" When M.J. pointed down the corridor, he gave a nod and they both slid outside, then around the corner of the building. Screened by some bushes in the front, Jack darted a gaze up and down the street. There was a windowless van less than half a block down, and a small, chicken-faced man in a bad suit dancing beside it. "Stay low," Jack ordered, thankful he'd parked right out front as they ran down the walkway and he all but threw M.J. into the front seat of his car.

"My God, what the hell is this?" She shoved at the can she'd sat on, kicked at the wrappers littering the floor, then joined them when Jack put a hand behind her head and shoved.

"Low!" he repeated in a snarl, and gunned the engine. The faint ping told him the man with the chicken face was using the silenced automatic he'd pulled out.

Jack's car screamed away from the curb, and he two-wheeled it around the corner and shot down the street like a rocket. Tossed like eggs in a broken carton, M.J. rapped her head on the dash, cursed, and struggled to balance herself as Jack maneuvered the huge boat of a car down side streets.

"What the hell are you doing?"

"Saving your butt again, sugar." His eyes flicked to the rearview as he took a hard, tire-squealing right turn. A couple of kids riding bikes on the sidewalk lifted their fists and cheered the maneuver. In instant reaction, Jack flashed a grin.

"Slow this junk heap down." M.J. had to crawl back onto the seat and clutch the chicken stick for balance. "And let me out before you run over some kid walking his dog."

"I'm not going to run over anybody, and you're staying put." He spared her a quick glance. "In case you didn't notice, the guy with the van was shooting at us. And as soon as I make sure we've lost him and find someplace quiet to hole up, you're going to tell me what the hell's going on."

"I don't know what's going on."

He shot her a look. "That's bull."

Because he was sure it was, he took a chance. He swung to the curb again, reached under his seat and came up with spare cuffs. Before she could do more than blink, he had her locked by the wrist to the door handle. No way was she skipping out on him until he knew why he'd just been tossed around by a three-hundred-pound gorilla.

To block out her shouting, and her increasingly imaginative threats and curses, Jack turned up his stereo and drowned her out.

Chapter 2

At the very first opportunity, she was going to kill him. Brutally, M.J. decided. Mercilessly. Two hours before this, she'd been happy, free, wandering around the grocery store like any normal person on a Saturday, squeezing tomatoes. True, she'd been weighed down with curiosity about what she carried in the bottom of her purse, but she'd been sure Bailey had a good reason—and a logical explanation—for sending it to her.

Bailey James always had good reasons and logical explanations for everything. That was only one of the aspects about her that M.J. loved.

But now she was worried—worried that the package Bailey had shipped to her by courier the day before was not only at the bottom of her purse, but also at the bottom of her current situation.

She preferred blaming Jack Dakota.

He'd pushed his way into her apartment and attacked her. Okay, so maybe she'd attacked first, but it was a natural reaction when some jerk tried to muscle you. At least it was M.J.'s natural reaction. She was an ace student in the school of punch first, ask questions later.

It was humiliating that he'd been able to take her down. She had a lot of notches on her fifth-degree black belt, and she didn't like to lose a match.

But she'd pay him back for that later.

All she knew for certain was that he seemed to be at the root of it all. Because of him, her apartment was wrecked, her things tossed every which way. Now they'd gone, leaving the front door open, the lock broken. She didn't form close attachments to things, but that wasn't the point. They were *her* things, and thanks to him, she was going to have to waste time shopping for replacements.

Which was almost as bad as having some gun-wielding punk the size of Texas busting down her door, having to run for her life from her own home, and being shot at.

But all of that, all of it, paled next to one infuriating fact—she was handcuffed to the door handle of an Oldsmobile.

Jack Dakota had to die for that.

Who the hell was he? she asked herself. Bounty hunter, excellent hand-to-hand fighter, slob—she added as she pushed candy wrappers and paper cups around with her foot—and nerveless driver. Under different circumstances, she'd have been impressed by the way he handled the tank of a car, swinging it around curves, screaming around corners, whipping it through yellow lights and zipping onto the Washington Beltway like the leader in a Grand Prix event.

If he'd walked into her bar, she'd have looked twice, she admitted grudgingly. Running a pub in a major city meant more than being able to mix drinks and work the books. It meant being able to size people up quickly, tell the troublemakers from the lonely hearts. And know how to deal with both.

She'd have tagged him as a tough customer. It was in his face. A damn good face, all in all, hard and handsome. Yeah, she'd have looked twice, M.J. thought, teeth gritted, as she looked out the window of the speeding car. Pretty boys didn't interest her much. She preferred a man who looked as though he'd lived, crossed a few lines and would cross a few more.

Jack Dakota fit that bill. She'd gotten a good close

look into those eyes—granite gray—and knew that he wasn't one to let a few rules get in his way.

Just what would a man like him do if he knew she was carrying a king's ransom in her battered leather purse?

Damn it, Bailey. Damn it. M.J. fisted her free hand and tapped it restlessly on her knee. Why did you send me the diamond, and where are the other two?

She cursed herself, as well, for not going directly to Bailey's door after she came home from closing M.J.'s the night before. But she'd been tired, and she'd figured Bailey was sound asleep. And as her friend was the steadiest, most practical person M.J. knew, she'd simply decided to wait for what she was certain would be a very practical, sensible reason.

Stupid, she told herself now. Why had she assumed Bailey had sent the stone to her simply because she knew M.J. would be home in the middle of the day and around to receive the package? Why had she assumed the rock was a fake, a copy, even though the note that accompanied it asked M.J. to keep it with her at all times?

Because Bailey just wasn't the kind of woman to ship off a blue diamond worth more than a million with no warnings or explanations. She was a gemologist, dedicated, brilliant, and patient as Job. How else could she continue to work for the creeps who masqueraded as her family?

M.J.'s mouth tightened as she thought of Bailey's

stepbrothers. The Salvini twins had always treated Bailey as though she were an inconvenience, something they were stuck with because their father had left her a percentage of the business in his will. And, blindly loyal to family, Bailey had always found excuses for them.

Now M.J. wondered if they were part of the reason. Had they tried to pull something? She wouldn't put it past them, no indeed. But it was hard to believe Timothy and Thomas Salvini would be stupid enough to try something fancy with the Three Stars of Mithra.

That was what Bailey had called them, and she'd had a dreamy look in her eyes. Three priceless blue diamonds, in a golden triangle that had once been held in the open hands of a statue of the god Mithra, and now property of the Smithsonian. Salvini, with Bailey's reputation behind it, was to assess, verify and appraise the stones.

What if the creeps had gotten it into their heads to keep them?

No, it was too wild, M.J. decided. Better to believe this whole mess was some sort of mix-up, a mistaken identity tangle.

Much better to concentrate on how she would repay Jack Dakota for ruining her afternoon off.

"You are a dead man." She said it calmly, relishing the words.

"Yeah, well, everybody dies sooner or later." He was heading south on 95, and he was grateful she'd stopped swearing at him long enough to let him think.

"It's going to be sooner in your case, Jack. Lots sooner." The traffic was thick, thanks to the Fourth of July holiday weekend, but it was fast.

How humiliating would it be, she wondered, to stick her head out the window and scream for help? Mortifying, she supposed, but she might have tried it if she'd believed it would work. Better if they could just run into one of the inexplicable traffic snags that stopped cars dead for miles.

Where the hell were the road crews and the rubberneckers who loved them when she needed them?

Seeing nothing but clear sailing for miles, she told herself to deal with Jack "The Idiot" Dakota herself. "If you want to live to see another sunrise, pull this excuse for a car over, uncuff me and let me go."

"Go where?" He flicked his eyes from the road long enough to glance at her. "Back to your apartment?"

"That's my problem, not yours."

"Not anymore, sister. I take it personal, real personal, when someone shoots at me. Since you seem to be the reason why, I'll be keeping you for a while."

If they hadn't been doing seventy, she'd have punched him. Instead, she rattled her chain. "Take these damn things off me."

"Nope."

A muscle twitched in her jaw. "You've stepped in it now, Dakota. We're in Virginia. Kidnapping, crossing state lines. That's federal."

"You came with me," he pointed out. "Now you're staying with me until I get this figured out." The doors rattled ominously as he whipped around an eighteen-wheeler. "And you should be grateful."

"Oh, I should be grateful. You broke into my apartment, knocked me around, busted up my things and have me cuffed to a door handle."

"That's right. If I hadn't, you'd probably be lying in that apartment right now, with a bullet in your head."

"They came after you, ace, not me."

"I don't think so. My debts are paid, I'm not fooling around with anyone's wife, and I haven't pissed anyone off lately. Except for you. Nobody's got a reason to send muscle after me. You, on the other hand…" He skimmed his gaze over her face again. "Somebody wants you, sugar."

"Thousands do," she said, stretched out her long legs as she shifted toward him.

"I'll bet." He didn't give in to the impulse to look at those legs—he just thought about them. "But other than the brainless idiots you'd kick in the heart, you've got someone real interested. Interested enough to set me up, and take me out with you. Ralph, you bastard."

He shoved aside a copy of *The Grapes of Wrath* and a torn T-shirt and snagged his car phone. Steering one-handed, he punched in numbers then hooked the receiver under his chin.

"Ralph, you bastard," he repeated when the phone was answered.

"D-D-Dakota? That you? You track d-d-down that skip?"

"When I figure my way clear of this, I'm coming for you."

"What—what're you talking about? You find her? Look, it's a straight trace, Jack. I g-g-gave you a plum. Just a c-c-couple's hours' work for full f-f-fee."

"You're stuttering more than usual, Ralph. That won't be a problem after I knock your teeth down your throat. Who wants the woman?"

"Look, I—I—I got problems here. I gotta close early. It's the holiday weekend. I got p-p-personal problems."

"There's no place you can hide. Why the phony paperwork? Why'd you set me up?"

"I got p-p-problems. Big p-p-problems."

"I'm your big problem right now." He tapped the brakes, swung around a convertible and hit the fast lane. "If whoever's pushing your buttons is trying to trace this, I'm in my car, just tooling around." He thought for a moment, then added, "And I've got the woman."

"Jack, listen to me. L-l-listen. Tell me where you

are, dump her and d-d-drive away. J-j-just drive. Stay out of it. I wouldn'ta tagged you for the job, 'cept I knew you could handle yourself. Now I'm telling you, stash her somewhere, give me the l-l-location and drive away. Far away. You don't want this."

"Who wants her, Ralph?"

"You don't n-n-need to know. You d-d-don't want to know. Just d-d-do it. I'll throw in five large. A b-b-bonus."

"Five large?" Jack's brows lifted. When Ralph parted with an extra nickel, it was big. "Make it ten and tell me who wants her, and we may deal."

It pleased him that M.J. protested that with a flurry of curses and threats. It added substance to the bluff.

"T-t-ten!" Ralph squeaked it, stuttered for a full ten seconds. "Okay, okay, ten grand, but no names, and b-b-believe me, Jack, I'm saving your life here. Just t-t-tell me where you're going to stash her."

Smiling grimly, Jack made a pithy and anatomically impossible suggestion, then disconnected.

"Well, sugar, your hide's now worth ten thousand to me. We're going to find a nice, quiet spot so you can tell me why I shouldn't collect."

He zipped off an exit, did a quick turnaround and headed back north.

Her mouth was dry. She wanted to believe it was from shouting, but there was fear clawing at her throat. "Where are you going?"

"Just covering my tracks. They wouldn't get much of a trace on a cellular, but it doesn't hurt to be cautious."

"You're taking me back?"

He didn't look at her, and didn't grin. Though the waver of nerves in her voice pleased him. If she was scared enough, she'd talk. "Ten thousand's a hefty incentive, sugar. Let's see if you can convince me you're worth more alive."

He knew just what he was looking for. He trolled the secondary roads, skimming through the holiday traffic. He'd forgotten it was the Fourth of July weekend. Which was just as well, he thought, as it didn't look like there were going to be a lot of opportunities to kick back with that cold beer and watch any fireworks.

Unless they came from the woman beside him.

She was a firecracker, all right. She had to be afraid by now, but she was holding her own. He was grateful for that. There was nothing more irritating than a whiner. But scared or not, he was certain she'd try to take a chunk out of him at the first opportunity.

He didn't intend to give her one.

With any luck, once they were settled, he'd have the full story out of her within a couple hours.

Then maybe he'd help her out of her jam. For a fee, that is. It could be a small one because at this point he was ticked and figured he had a vested interest in dealing with whoever had set him on her.

Whoever it was, they'd gone to a great deal of trouble. But they hadn't picked their goons very well. He could figure the scam well enough. Once he captured his quarry and had her secured and in his car, the men in the van would have run them off the road. He'd have figured it to be the action of a competing bounty hunter, and though he wouldn't have given up his fee without a fight, he'd have been outnumbered and outgunned.

Skip tracers didn't go crying to the cops when a competitor snatched their bounty.

The goons might have let him off with a few bruises, maybe a minor concussion. But the way that mountain of a man had been waving his cannon in M.J.'s apartment, Jack thought it was far more likely that he'd have sported a brand-new hole in some vital part of his body.

Because the mountain had been an moron.

So at this point he was on the run with an angry woman, a little over three hundred in cash and a quarter tank of gas.

He intended to know why.

He spotted what he was after north of Leesburg, Virginia. The tourists and holiday travelers, unless they were very down on their luck, would give a dilapidated dump like the Kountry Klub Motel a wide berth. But the low-slung building with the paint peeling on the green doors and the pitted parking lot met Jack's requirements perfectly.

He pulled to the farthest end of the lot, away from the huddle of rusted cars near the check-in, and cut the engine.

"Is this where you bring all your dates, Dakota?"

He smiled at her, a quick flash of teeth that was unexpectedly charming. "Only first class for you, sugar."

He knew just what she was thinking. The minute he cut her loose, she'd be all over him like spandex. And if she could get out of the car, she'd be sprinting toward the check-in as fast as those mile-long legs would carry her.

"I don't expect you to believe me." He said it casually as he leaned over to unlock the cuff from the door handle. "But I'm not going to enjoy this."

She was braced. He could feel her body tense to spring. He had to be quick, and he had to be rough. She'd no more than hissed out a breath before he had her hands secured and locked behind her. She sucked in air just as he clamped a hand over her mouth.

She bucked and rolled, tried to bring up her legs to kick, but he pinned her on the seat, flipped her facedown. He was out of breath by the time he'd tied the bandanna over her mouth.

"I lied." Panting, he rubbed the fresh bruise where

her elbow had connected with his ribs. "Maybe I enjoyed that a little."

He used the torn T-shirt to tie her legs, tried not to appreciate overmuch the length and shape of them. But, hell, he was only human. Once he had her trussed up like a turkey, he looped the slack of the handcuffs around the gearshift, then wound up the windows.

"Hot as hell, isn't it?" he said conversationally. "Well, I won't be long." He locked the car and walked away whistling.

It took her a moment to regain her balance. She was scared, she realized. Really, bone-deep scared, and she couldn't remember if she'd ever felt this kind of mind-numbing panic before. She was trembling, and had to stop. It wouldn't help her out of this fix.

Once, when she'd just opened her pub, she'd been closing down late at night. She'd been alone when the man came in and demanded money. She'd been scared then, too, terrified by the wild look in his eyes that shouted drugs. So she'd handed over the till, just as the cops recommended.

Then she'd handed him the fat end of the Louisville Slugger she had behind the bar.

She'd been scared, but she'd dealt with it.

She would deal with this, too.

The gag tasted of man and infuriated her. She couldn't push or wiggle or slide it out, so she gave up on it and concentrated on freeing the loop of the cuffs. If she could free her hands from the gearshift, she could fold herself up, bend her legs through her arms and get some mobility.

She was agile, she told herself. She was strong and she was smart. Oh, God, she was scared. She moaned and whimpered in frustration. The handcuffs might as well have been cemented to the gearshift.

If she could only see, twist herself around so that she could see what she was doing. She struggled, all but dislocating her shoulder, until she managed to flip around. Sweat seemed to boil over her, dripped into her eyes as she yanked at the steel.

She stopped herself, closed her eyes and got her breath back. She used her shaking fingers to probe, to trace along the steel, slide over the smooth length of the gearshift. Keeping them closed, she visualized what she was doing, carefully, slowly, shifting her hands until she felt steel begin to slide. Her shoulders screamed as she forced them into an unnatural position, but she bit down on the gag and twisted.

She felt something give, hoped it wasn't a joint, then collapsed in an exhausted, sweaty heap as the cuffs slipped off the stick.

"Damn, you're good," Jack commented as he wrenched open the door. He dragged her out and tossed her over his shoulder. "Another five minutes, you might have pulled it off." He carried her into a room at the end of the concrete block. He'd already unlocked the door, and he'd paused for a minute to observe, and admire, her struggles before he came back to the car.

Now he dumped her on the bed. Because her adrenaline was back and she was fighting him, he simply lay flat on her back, letting her bounce until she was worn out.

And he enjoyed that, too. He wasn't proud of it, he thought, but he enjoyed it. The woman had incredible energy and staying power. If they'd met under different circumstances, he imagined they could have torn up those cheap motel sheets like maniacs and parted as friends.

As it was, he was going to have a hard time not imagining her naked.

Maybe he lay on her, smelled her, just a little longer than necessary. He wasn't a saint, was he? he asked himself grimly as he unlocked one of her hands and secured the cuff to the iron headboard.

He rose, ran a hand through his hair. "You're making this tougher than necessary for both of us," he told her, as she murdered him with a scalding look out of hot green eyes. He was out of breath and knew he couldn't blame it entirely on the last, minor skirmish. That tight little bottom of hers pressing against his crotch had left him uncomfortably aroused.

And he didn't want to be.

Turning from her, he switched on the TV, let the volume boom out. M.J. had already ripped the gag away with her free hand and was hissing like a snake. "You can scream all you want now," he told her as he took out a small knife and sliced through the phone cord. "The three rooms down from here are vacant, so nobody's going to hear you." Then he grinned. "Besides, I put it around at check-in that we're on our honeymoon, so even if they hear, they're not going to bother us. Be back in a minute."

He went out, shutting the door behind him.

M.J. closed her eyes again. Dear God, what was going on with her? For a moment, for just one insane moment, when he pressed her into the mattress with his body, she'd felt weak and hot. With lust.

It was sick, sick, sick.

But just for that one insane moment, she'd imagined being stripped and taken, being ravaged, having his mouth on her. His hands on her.

More, she'd wanted it.

She shuddered now, praying it was just some sort of weird reaction to shock.

She wasn't a woman who shied away from good, healthy, hot sex. But she didn't give herself to strangers, to men who knocked her down, tied her up and tossed her into bed in some cheap motel.

And he'd been aroused. She hadn't been so stupid, or so dazed with shock, that she was unaware of his reaction. Hell, the man had been wrapped around her, hadn't he? But he'd backed off.

She struggled to even her breathing. He wasn't going to rape her. He didn't want sex. He wanted— God only knew.

Don't feel, she ordered herself. Just think. Just clear your mind and think.

Slowly, she opened her eyes, took a survey of the room.

It was, in a word, hideous.

Obviously, some misguided soul had thought that using an eye-searing combo of orange and blue would turn the cheaply furnished, cramped little room into the exotic.

He couldn't have been more wrong.

The drapes were as thin as paper, and looked to be of about the same consistency. But he'd pulled them closed over the narrow front window, so the room was deep in shadow.

The television blared out a poorly dubbed Hercules movie on its rickety gray pedestal. The single dresser was ringed with interlinking watermarks. There was a metal box beside the bed. For a couple of bucks in quarters, she could treat herself to dancing fingers. Whoopee.

The yellow glass ashtray on the night table was

chipped, and didn't look heavy enough to make an effective weapon. Even over the din of Hercules, she could hear the roaring sputter of an air-conditioning unit that was doing absolutely nothing to cool the room.

The print near a narrow door she assumed was to the bathroom was a garish reproduction of a country landscape in autumn, complete with screaming red barn and stupid-faced cows.

Reaching over, she tested the bedside lamp. It was bright blue glass, with a dingy and yellowing shade, but it had some heft. It might come in handy.

She heard the rattle of the key and set it down again, stared at the door.

He came in with a small red-and-white cooler and dropped it on the dresser. Her heart thumped when she saw her purse slung over his shoulder, but he tossed it on the floor by the bed so casually that she relaxed again.

The diamond was still safe, she thought. And so was the can of Mace, the can opener and the roll of nickels she habitually carried as weapons.

"Nothing I like better than a really bad movie," he commented, and paused to watch Hercules battle several fierce-looking warriors sporting pelts and bad teeth. "I always wonder where they come up with the dialogue. You know, was it really that bad when it was scripted in Lithuanian or whatever, or does it just lose it in the translation?"

With a shrug, he walked over, lifted the top on the cooler and took out two soft drinks.

"I figure you're thirsty." He walked to her, offered a can. "And you're not the type to cut off your nose." His assessment was proved correct when she grabbed the can and drank deeply. "This place doesn't run to room service," he continued. "But there's a diner down the road, so we won't go hungry. You want something now?"

She eyed him over the top of the can. "No."

"Fine." He sat on the side of the bed, settled himself and smiled at her. "Let's talk."

"Kiss my butt."

He blew out a breath. "It's an attractive offer, sugar, but I've been trying not to think along those lines." He gave her thigh a friendly pat. "Now, the way I see it, we're both in a jam here, and you've got the key. Once you tell me who's after you and why, I'll deal with it."

The worst of her thirst was abated, so she sipped slowly. Her voice dripped sarcasm. "*You'll* deal with it?"

"Yeah. Consider me your champion-at-arms. Like good old Herc there." He stabbed a thumb at the set behind him. "You tell me about it, then I'll go take care of the bad guys. Then I'll bill you. And if the offer about kissing your butt's still open, I'll take you up on that, too."

"Let's see." She leaned her head back, kept her eyes level on his. "What was it you told your pal Ralph to do? Oh, yeah." She peeled her lips back in a snarl and repeated it.

He only shook his head. "Is that any way to talk to the guy who kept you from getting a bullet in the brain?"

"*I* kept *you* from getting a bullet in the brain, pal, though I have serious doubts he'd have been able to hit it, as it's clearly so small. And you pay me back by manhandling me, tying me up, gagging me, and dumping me in some cheap rent-by-the-hour motel."

"I'm assured this is a family establishment," he said dryly. God, she was a pistol, he thought. Spitting at him despite his advantage, daring him to take her on, though she didn't have a hope of winning the game. And sexy as bloody hell in tight jeans and a wrinkled shirt.

"Think about this," he said. "That brainless giant said something about me taking too long, talking too much, which leads me to believe they were listening from the van. They must have had surveillance equipment, and he got antsy. Otherwise, if you'd gone along with me like a good girl, they'd have pulled us over somewhere along the line and taken you. They didn't want direct involvement, or witnesses."

"You'd be a witness," she corrected.

"Nothing to sweat over. I'd have been ticked off about having another bounty hunter snatch my job, but people in my line of work don't go running to the cops. I'd have lost my fee, considered my day wasted, maybe bitched to Ralph. That's the way they'd figure it, anyway. And Ralph would have probably passed me some fluff job to keep me happy."

His eyes changed, went hard again. Knife-edged gray ice. "Somebody's got their foot on his throat. I want to know who."

"I couldn't say. I don't know your friend Ralph—"

"Former friend."

"I don't know the gorilla who broke my door, and I don't know you." She was pleased her voice was calm, without a single hitch or quiver. "Now, if you'll let me go, I'll report all this to the police."

His lips twitched. "That's the first time you've mentioned the cops, sugar. And you're bluffing. You don't want them in on this. That's another question."

He was right about that. She didn't want the police, not until she'd talked to Bailey and knew what was going on. But she shrugged, glanced toward the phone he'd put out of commission. "You could call my bluff if you hadn't wrecked the phone."

"You wouldn't call the cops, but whoever you called might have their phone tapped. I didn't go through all the trouble to find us these plush out-of-the-way surroundings to get traced."

He leaned over, took her chin in his hand. "Who would you call, M.J.?"

She kept her eyes steady, fighting to ignore the heat

of his fingers, the texture of his skin against hers. "My lover." She spit the words out. "He'd take you apart limb by limb. He'd rip out your heart, then show it to you while it was still beating."

He smiled, eased a little closer. He just couldn't resist. "What's his name?"

Her mind was blank, totally, completely, foolishly blank. She stared into those slate-gray eyes a moment, then shook his hand away. "Hank. He'll break you in half and toss you to the dogs when he finds out you've messed with me."

He chuckled, infuriated her. "You may have a lover, sugar. You may have a dozen. But you don't have one named Hank. Took you too long. Okay, you don't want to spill it and rely on me to work us out of this, we'll go another route."

He rose, leaned over. He heard her quickly indrawn breath when he reached down for her purse. Without a word, he dumped the contents on the bed. He'd already removed the weapons. "You ever use that can opener for more than popping a beer?" he asked her.

"How dare you! How dare you go through my things!"

"Oh, I think this is small potatoes after what we've been through together." He picked up the velvet pouch, slid the stone into his hand, where it flashed like fire, despite its lowly surroundings.

He admired it, as he had been unable to in the car,

when he searched her bag. It was deeply, brilliantly blue, big as a baby's fist and cut to shoot blue flame. He felt a tug as it lay nestled in his hand, an odd need to protect it. Almost as inexplicable, he thought, as his odd need to protect this prickly, ungrateful woman.

"So." He sat, tossing the stone up, catching it. "Tell me about this, M.J. Just where did you get your hands on a blue diamond big enough to choke a cat?"

Chapter 3

Options whirled through her mind. The simplest, and the most satisfying, she thought, was to make him feel like a fool.

"Are you crazy?" She rolled her eyes and scoffed. "Yeah, that's a diamond, all right, a big blue one. I carry a green one in my glove compartment, and a pretty red one in my other purse. I spend all the profits from my pub on diamonds. It's a weakness."

He studied her, idly tossing the stone, catching it. She looked annoyed, he decided. Amused and cocky. "So what is it?"

"A paperweight, for God's sake."

He waited a beat. "You carry a paperweight in your purse."

Hell. "It was a gift." She said it primly, her nose in the air.

"Yeah, from Hank the Hunk, no doubt." He rose, casually pushed through the rest of the contents he'd dumped out. "Let's see, other than the blackjack—"

"It was a roll of nickels," she corrected.

"Same effect. Mace, a can opener I doubt you cart around to pop Bud bottles, we've got an electronic organizer, a wallet with more photos than cash—"

"I don't appreciate you rifling my personal belongings."

"Sue me. A bottle of designer water, six pens, four pencils. Some eyeliner, matches, keys, two pair of sunglasses, a paperback copy of Sue Grafton's latest— good book, by the way, I won't tell you the ending—a candy bar…" He tossed it to her. "In case you're hungry. A flip phone." He tucked that in his back pocket. "About three dollars in loose change, a weather radio and a box of condoms." He lifted a brow. "Unopened. But then, you never know."

Heat, a combination of mortification and fury, crawled up her neck. "Pervert."

"I'd say you're a woman who believes in being prepared. So why not carry a paperweight around with you? You might run into a stack of paper that needs anchoring. Happens all the time."

He made a couple of swipes to gather and dump the items scattered on the bed back into her bag, then tossed it aside. "I won't ask what kind of fool you take me for, because I've already got that picture." Moving to the mirror over the dresser, he scraped the stone diagonally across the glass. It left a long, thin scratch.

"They just don't make motel mirrors like they used to," he commented, then came back and sat on the bed beside her. "Now, back to my original question. What are you doing with a blue diamond big enough to choke a cat?"

When she said nothing, he vised her chin in his hand, jerked her face to his. "Listen, sister, I could truss you up again, leave you here and walk away with your million-dollar paperweight. That's door number one. I can kick back, watch the movie and wait you out, because sooner or later you'll tell me what I want to know. That's door number two. Behind door number three, you tell me now why you're carrying a stone that could buy a small island in the West Indies and we start figuring out how to get us both out of this jam."

She didn't flinch, she didn't blink. He had to admire the sheer nerve. Because he did, he waited patiently while she studied him out of those deep green cat-tilted eyes.

"Why haven't you taken door number one already?"

"Because I don't like having some gorilla try to break me in half, I don't like getting shot at, and I don't like being hosed by some skinny woman with an attitude." He leaned closer, until they were nose-to-nose. "I've got debts to pay on this one, sugar. And you're the first stop."

She grabbed his wrist with her free hand, shoved. "Threats aren't going to cut it with me, Dakota."

"No?" He shifted gears smoothly. His hand came back to her face, but lightly now, a skim of knuckles along a cheekbone that had her blinking in shock before her eyes narrowed. "You want a different approach?"

His fingers trailed down her throat, down the center of her body and back, before sliding around to cup her neck. His mouth hovered, one hot breath away from hers.

"Don't even think about it," she warned.

"Too late." His lips curved, and his eyes stared straight into hers. "I've been thinking about it ever since you swaggered up the apartment steps in front of me."

No, he'd been thinking about it, he realized, since Ralph shoved her photo at him. But he'd consider that later.

He skimmed his mouth over hers, drew back fractionally. He'd expected her to cringe away or fight. God knew he was ruthlessly pushing all those female fear buttons. It was deplorable, but he'd consider that later, as well. He just wanted the pressure to work, to get her to spill before they both got killed. And if he got a little twisted pleasure out of the whole thing, well, hell, he had his flaws.

But she didn't fight and she didn't cringe. She didn't move a muscle, just kept those goddess-green eyes lasered on his. A dark, primitive thrill rippled down to his loins.

What was one more sin on his back, he thought, and, clamping his hand on her free one, he took a long, deep gulp of her.

It was all heat, primitive as tribal drums. No thought, no reason, all instinct. That surprisingly lush mouth gave under his, so he dived deeper. A rumble of pure male triumph sounded in his throat as he moved into her, plunging his tongue between those full, inviting lips, sinking into that long, tough body, fisting his hand in that cap of flame-colored hair.

His mind shut off like a shattered lamp. He forgot it was a con, a ploy to intimidate, forgot he was a civilized man. Forgot she was a job, a puzzle, a stranger. And knew only that she was his for the taking.

His hand closed greedily over her breast, his thumb and forefinger tugging at the nipple that pressed hard against the thin cotton of her shirt. She moved under him, arched to him. And the blood pounded like thunder in his brain.

She moved fast, all but twisting his ear from his

head while her teeth clamped down like a bear trap on his bottom lip.

He yelped, jerked back, and, certain she would saw off a chunk of him, pinched her chin hard until she let him loose. He pressed the back of his hand to his throbbing lip, scowled at the blood he saw on it when he took it away.

"Damn it."

"Pig." She was vibrating now, scrambling to her knees on the bed to take another swipe at him, swearing when her reach fell short. "Pervert."

He spared her one murderous look, then turned on his heel. The bathroom door slammed shut behind him. She heard water running. And, closing her eyes, she sank back and let the shudders come.

My God, dear God, she thought, pressing a hand to her face. She'd lost her mind.

Had she fought him? No. Had she been filled with outrage, with disgust? No.

She'd enjoyed it.

She rocked herself, berated herself, and damned Jack Dakota to hell.

She'd let him kiss her. There was no pretending otherwise. She'd stared into those dangerous gray eyes, felt the zip of an electric current when that cocky mouth brushed over hers.

And she'd wanted him.

Her muscles had gone lax, her breasts had tingled, and her blood had begun to swim. She'd let him kiss her without a murmur of protest. She'd kissed him back, without a thought for the consequences.

M. J. O'Leary, she thought, wincing, tough gal, who prided herself on always being in control, who could flip a two-hundred-pound man onto his back and have her foot on his throat in a heartbeat—confident, kick-butt M.J.—had melted into a puddle of mindless lust.

And he'd tied her up, he'd gagged her, he had her handcuffed to a bed in some cheap motel. Wanting him even for an instant made her as much of a pervert as he was.

Thank God she'd snapped out of it. It didn't matter that bone-deep fear of her feelings had been the motivation for stopping him. The fact was, she had stopped him—and she knew she'd been an instant away from letting him do whatever he wanted to do.

She was very much afraid that if she'd had both hands free, she would have flipped him onto his back. Then ripped off his clothes.

It was the shock, she told herself. Even a woman who prided herself on being able to handle anything that came her way was entitled to go a little loopy with shock under certain circumstances.

Now she had to put this aberration behind her and figure out what to do.

The facts were few, but they were clear. She had to

contact Bailey. Whatever her friend's purpose in sending the stone, Bailey couldn't have had any idea just how dangerous the act would be. She'd had her reasons, M.J. was sure, and she thought it was likely to have been one of Bailey's rare acts of impulse and defiance.

She didn't intend for Bailey to pay the price for it.

What had Bailey done with the other two stones? Did she have them, or… Oh God.

She dropped back weakly on the bricklike pillow. She would have sent one to Grace. It had to be. It was logical, and Bailey was nothing if not logical. There'd been three stones, and she'd sent one to M.J. So it followed that she'd kept one, and sent the other to the only other person in the world she'd trust with such a responsibility.

Grace Fontaine. The three of them had been close as sisters since college. Bailey, quiet, studious and serious. Grace, rich, stunning and wild. They'd roomed together for four years at Radcliffe and stayed close since. Bailey moving into the family business, M.J. following tradition and opening her own bar, and Grace doing whatever she could to shock her wealthy, conservative and disapproving relatives.

If one of them was in trouble, they were all in trouble. She had to warn them.

She would have to escape from Jack Dakota. Or she'd have to use him.

But how much, she asked herself, did she dare trust him?

* * *

In the bathroom, Jack studied his mutilated lip in the mirror. He'd probably have a scar. Well, he admitted, he deserved it. He *had* been a pig and a pervert.

Not that she was entirely innocent, either, lying there on the bed with that just-try-it-buster look in her eyes.

And hadn't she pressed that long, tight body to his, opened that soft, sexy mouth, arched those neat, narrow hips?

Pig. He scrubbed his hands over his face. What choice had he given her?

Dropping his hands, he looked at himself in the mirror, looked dead-on, and admitted he hadn't wanted to give her a choice.

He'd just wanted her.

Well, he wasn't an animal. He could control himself, he could think, he could reason. And that was just what he was going to do.

He'd probably have a scar, he thought again, grimly, as he touched a fingertip gingerly to his swollen lip. Just let that be a lesson to you, Dakota. He jerked his head in a nod at the reflection in the spotty mirror. If you can't trust yourself, you sure as hell can't trust her.

When he came out, she was frowning at the hideous drapes on the window. He glared at her. She glared back. Saying nothing, he sat in the single ratty chair, crossed his feet at the ankles and tuned into the movie.

Hercules was over. He'd probably triumphed. In his place was a Japanese science-fiction flick with an incredibly poorly produced monster lizard who was currently smashing a high-speed train. Hordes of extras were screaming in terror.

They watched awhile, as the military came rushing in with large guns that had virtually no effect on the giant mutant lizard. A small man in a combat helmet was devoured. His chickenhearted comrades ran for their lives.

M.J. found the candy bar from her purse that Jack had tossed her earlier, broke off a chunk and ate it contemplatively as the lizard king from outer space lumbered toward Tokyo to wreak reptilian havoc.

"Can I have my water?" she asked in scrupulously polite tones.

He got up, fetched it out of her bag, handed it over.

"Thanks." She took one long sip, waited until he'd settled again. "What's your fee?" she demanded.

He took another soda out of his cooler. Wished it was a beer. "For?"

"What you do." She shrugged. "Say I had skipped out on bail. What do you get for bringing me back?"

"Depends. Why?"

She rolled her eyes. "Depends on what?"

"On how much bail you'd skipped out on."

She was silent for a moment as she considered.

The lizard demolished a tall building with many innocent occupants. "What was it I was supposed to have done?"

"Shot your lover—the accountant. I believe his name was Hank."

"Very funny." She broke off another hunk of chocolate and, when Jack held out a hand, reluctantly shared. "How much were you going to get for me?"

"More than you're worth."

Now she sighed. "I'm going to make you a deal, Jack, but I'm a businesswoman, and I don't make them blind. What's your fee?"

Interesting, he thought, and drummed his fingers on the arm of the chair. "For you, sugar, considering what you're carrying in that suitcase you call a purse, adding in what Ralph offered me to turn you over to the goons?" He thought it over. "A hundred large."

She didn't bat an eye. "I appreciate you trying to lighten the situation with an attempt at wry humor. A hundred K for a man who can't even take out a single hired thug by himself is laughable—"

"Who said I couldn't take him out?" His pride leaped up and bit him. "I *did* take him out, sugar. Him and his cannon, and you haven't bothered to thank me for it."

"Oh, excuse me. It must have slipped my mind while I was being dragged around and handcuffed. How rude. And you didn't take him out, I did. But re-

gardless," she continued, holding up her free hand like
a traffic cop, "now that we've had our little joke, let's
try to be serious. I'll give you a thousand to work with
me on this."

"A thousand?" He flashed that quick, dangerous
grin. "Sister, there isn't enough money in the world to
tempt me to work with you. But for a hundred K, I'll
get you out of the jam you're in."

"In the first place—" she drew up her legs, sat lotus-
style "—I'm not your sister, and I'm not your sugar.
If you have to refer to me, use my name."

"You don't have a name, you have initials."

"In the second place," she said, ignoring him, "if a
man like you got his hands on a hundred thousand, he'd
just lose it in Vegas or pour it down some stripper's
cleavage. Since I don't intend for that to happen to my
money, I'm offering you a thousand." She smiled at
him. "With that, you can have yourself a nice weekend
at the beach with a keg of imported beer."

"It's considerate of you to look out for my welfare,
but you're not really in the position to negotiate terms
here. You want help, it'll cost you."

She didn't know if she wanted his help. The fact
was, she wasn't at all sure why she was wrangling
with him over a fee. Under the circumstances, she felt
she could promise him any amount without any obligation to pay up if and when the time came.

But it was the principle of the thing.

"Five thousand—and you follow orders."

"Seventy-five, and I don't ever follow orders."

"Five." She set her teeth. "Take it or leave it."

"I'll leave it." Casually he picked up the stone again, held it up, studied it. "And take this with me." He rose, patted his back pocket. "And maybe I'll call the cops on your fancy little phone after I'm clear."

She fisted her fingers, flexed them. She didn't want to involve the police, not until she'd contacted Bailey. Nor could she risk him following through on his threat to simply take the stone.

"Fifty thousand." She bit the words off like raw meat. "That's all I'll be able to come up with. Most everything I've got's tied up in my business."

He cocked a brow. "The finder's fee on this little bauble's got to be worth more than fifty."

"I didn't steal the damn thing. It doesn't belong to me. It's—" She broke off, clamped her mouth shut.

He started to sit on the edge of the bed again, remembered what had happened before, and chose the arm of the chair. "Who does it belong to, M.J.?"

"I'm not spilling my guts to you. For all I know you're as big a creep as the one who broke down my door. You could be a thief, a murderer."

He cocked that scarred eyebrow. "Which is why I've robbed and murdered you."

"The day's young."

"Let me point out the obvious. I'm the only one around."

"That doesn't inspire confidence." She brooded a moment. How far did she dare use him? she wondered. And how much did she dare tell him?

"If you want my help," he said, as if reading her mind, "then I need facts, details and names."

"I'm not giving you names." She shook her head slowly. "That's out until I talk to the other people involved. And as for facts and details, I don't have many."

"Give me what you do have."

She studied him again. No, she didn't trust him, not nearly as far as she could throw him. If she ever got the opportunity. But she had to start somewhere. "Unlock me."

He shook his head. "Let's just leave things as they are for the moment." But he rose, walked over and shut off the television. "Where'd you get the stone, M.J.?"

She hesitated another instant. Trust wasn't the issue, she decided. He might help, if in no other way than just by providing her with a sounding board. "A friend sent it to me. Overnight courier. I just got it yesterday."

"Where did it come from?"

"Originally from Asia Minor, I believe." She shrugged off his hiss of annoyance. "I'm not telling you where it was sent from, but I will tell you there had to be a good reason. My friend's too honest to steal a handshake. All I know is it was sent, with a note that said for me to keep it with me at all times, and not to tell anyone until my friend had a chance to explain."

Abruptly she pressed a hand to her stomach and the arrogance died out of her voice. "My friend's in trouble. It's got to be terrible trouble. I have to call."

"No calls."

"Look, Jack—"

"No calls," he repeated. "Whoever's after you might be after your pal. His phone could be tapped, which would lead them back to you. Which leads them to me, so no calls. Now how did your honest friend happen to get his hands on a blue diamond that makes the Hope look like a prize in a box of Cracker Jack?"

"In a perfectly legitimate manner." Stalling, she combed her fingers through her hair. He thought her friend was male—why not leave it that way?

"Look, I'm not getting into all of that. All I'm going to tell you is he was supposed to have his hands on it. Look, let me tell you about the stone. It's one of three. At one time they were part of an altar set up to an ancient Roman god. Mithraism was one of the major religions of the Roman Empire—"

"The Three Stars of Mithra," he murmured, and had her eyeing him first in shock, then with suspicion.

"How do you know about the Three Stars?"

"I read about them in the dentist's office," he murmured. Now, when he picked up the stone, it wasn't simply with admiration, it was with awe. "It was supposed to be a myth. The Three Stars, set in the golden triangle and held in the hands of the god of light."

"It's not a myth," M.J. told him. "The Smithsonian acquired the Stars through a contact in Europe just a couple months ago. My friend said the museum wanted to keep the acquisition quiet until the diamonds were verified."

"And assessed," he thought aloud. "Insured and under tight security."

"They were supposed to be under security," M.J. told him, and he answered with a soft laugh.

"Doesn't look like it worked, does it? The diamonds represent love, knowledge and generosity." His eyes narrowed as he contemplated the ancient stone. "I wonder which this one is?"

"I couldn't say." She continued to stare at him, fascinated. He'd gone from tough guy to scholar in the blink of an eye. "But apparently you know as much about it as I do."

"I know about Mithraism," he said easily. "It predates and parallels Christianity. Mankind's always looked for a kind and just god." His shoulders moved as he turned the stone in his hand. "Mankind doesn't always get what it wants. And I know the legend of the Three Stars. It was said the god held the triangle for centuries, and holding it tended the world. Then it was lost, or looted, or sank with Atlantis."

For his own pleasure, he switched on the lamp, watched the stone explode with power in the dingy light. "More likely it just ended up in the treasure room of some corrupt Roman procurer." He traced the facets with his thumbs. "It's something people would kill for. Or die for," he murmured. "Some legends have it in Cleopatra's tomb, others have Merlin casing it in crystal and holding it in trust until Arthur's return. Others say the god himself hurled them into the sky and wept at man's ignorance. But the smart money was that they'd simply been stolen and separated."

He looked up, over the stone and into her eyes. "Worth a fortune singly, and within the triangle, worth immortality."

Yes, she could admit he fascinated her, the way that deep, all-man voice had cooled into professorial tones. And the way he stroked the gleaming diamond as a man might stroke a woman's gleaming flesh.

But she shook her head over the last statement. "You don't believe that."

"No, but that's the legend, isn't it? Whoever holds the triangle, with the Stars in place, gains the power of the god, and his immortality. But not necessarily his compassion. People have killed for less. A hell of a lot less."

He set the stone on the table between them, where it glowed with quiet fire. It had all changed now, he realized. The stakes had just flown sky-high, and the odds mirrored them.

"You're in a hell of a spot, M.J. Whoever's after this won't think twice about taking your head with it." He rubbed his chin, his fingers dancing over the shallow dimple. "And my head's awfully damn close to yours just now."

He couldn't believe how poor his luck was. His own mistake, he told himself as he calmed himself with Mozart and Moët. Because he tried to keep his distance from events, he'd had to count on others to handle his business.

Incompetents, one and all, he thought, and soothed himself by stroking the pelt of a sable coat that had once graced the shoulder of Czarina Alexandra.

To think he'd enjoyed the irony of having a bounty hunter track down the annoying Ms. O'Leary. It would have been simpler to have her snatched from her apartment or place of business. But he'd preferred finesse and, again, the distance.

The bounty hunter would have been blamed for her abduction, and her death. Such men were violent by nature, unpredictable. The police would have closed the case with little thought or effort.

Now she was on the run, and most certainly had the stone in her possession.

She would turn up, he thought, taking slow, even breaths. She would certainly contact her friends before too much longer. He'd been assured they were admirably loyal to each other.

He was a man who appreciated loyalty.

And when Ms. O'Leary attempted to contact her friends—one who had vanished, the other out of reach—he would have her.

And the stone.

With her, he had no doubt he would acquire the other two stars.

After all, he thought with a pleasant smile. Bailey James was reputed to be a good friend, a compassionate and intelligent woman. Intelligent enough, he mused, to have uncovered her stepbrothers' attempt to copy the Stars, smart enough to thwart them before they had made good on delivery.

Well, that, too, would be dealt with.

He was sure Bailey would be loyal to her friend, compassionate enough to put her friend first. And her loyalty and compassion would deliver the stones to him without much more delay.

In exchange for the life of M. J. O'Leary.

He had spent many years of his life in search of the Three Stars. He had invested much of his great wealth. And had taken many lives. Now they were almost in his hands. So close, he thought, so very close, his fingers tingled with anticipation.

And when he held them, fit them into the triangle, set them on the altar he'd had built for them, he would have the ultimate power. Immortality.

Then, of course, he would kill the women.

A fitting sacrifice, he reflected, to a god.

Chapter 4

He'd left her alone. Now she had to consider the matter of trust. Should she believe he'd just go out, pick up food and come back? He hadn't trusted her to stay, M.J. mused, rattling the handcuffs.

And she had to admit he'd gauged her well. She'd have been out the door like a shot. Not because she was afraid of him. She'd considered all the facts, all her instincts, and she no longer believed he'd hurt her. He would have done so already.

She'd seen the way he dealt with the gorilla who broke in her door. True, he'd had his hands full, but he'd handled himself with speed, strength, and an admirable streak of mean.

It galled to admit it, but she knew he'd held back when he tangled with her. Not that it excused him trussing her up and tossing her in some cheap motel room, but if she was going to be fair-minded, she had to say he could have done considerable damage to her during their quick, sweaty bout if he'd wanted to.

And all he'd really bruised was her pride.

He had a brain—which had surprised her. That was, she supposed, a generalizing-from-a-first-impression mistake she'd fallen into because of his looks, and that sheer in-your-face physicality. But in addition to the street smarts she would have expected from his type, it appeared Jack Dakota had an intellect. A good one.

And she didn't believe he did his reading in the dentist's office. A guy didn't read about ancient religions while he was waiting to have his teeth cleaned. So, she had to conclude there was more to him than she'd originally assumed. All she had to do was decide whether that was an advantage, or a disadvantage.

Now that she'd calmed down a little, she was certain that he wasn't going to push himself on her sexually, either. She'd have given odds that little interlude had shaken him as much as it had shaken her. It had been, she was sure, a misstep on his part. Intimidate the woman, flex the testosterone, and she'll tell you whatever you want to know.

It hadn't worked. All it had done was make them both itchy.

Damn, the man could kiss.

But she was getting off track, she reminded herself, and scowled at the ridiculous movie he'd left blaring on the television.

No, she wasn't afraid of him, but she was afraid of the situation. Which meant she didn't want to sit here on her butt and do nothing. Action was her style. Whether the action was wise or not wasn't the point. The doing was.

Shifting to her knees, she peered at the handcuffs, turning her wrist this way and that, flexing her hand as if she were an escape artist preparing to launch into her latest trick.

She tested the rungs on the headboard and found them distressingly firm.

They didn't make cheap hotels like they used to, she thought with a sigh. And wished for a hairpin, a nail file, a hammer.

All she found in the sticky drawer of the nightstand was a torn phone book and a linty wedge of hard candy.

He'd taken her purse with him, and though she knew she wouldn't find that hairpin, nail file or hammer inside, she still resented the lack of it.

She could scream, of course. She could shout down the roof, and endure the humiliation if someone actually paid any attention to the sounds of distress.

And that wouldn't get her out of the cuffs, unless someone called a locksmith. Or the cops.

She took a deep breath, struggled for the right avenue of escape. She was sick with worry for Bailey and Grace, desperate to reassure herself that they were both well.

If she did go to the police, what kind of trouble would Bailey be in? She had, technically, taken possession of a fortune. Would the authorities be understanding, or would they slap Bailey in a cell?

That, M.J. wouldn't risk. Not yet. Not as long as she felt it was remotely possible to even the odds. And to do that, she had to know what the hell she was up against.

Which again meant getting out of the room.

She was considering gnawing at the headboard with her teeth when Jack unlocked the door. He flashed a quick smile at her, one that told her he had her thoughts pegged.

"Honey, I'm home."

"You're a laugh riot, Dakota. My sides are aching."

"You make quite a picture cuffed to that bed, M.J." He set down two white take-out bags. "A lesser man would be toying with impure notions right about now."

It was her turn to smile, wickedly. "You already did. And you'll probably have a scar on your bottom lip."

"Yeah." He rubbed his thumb gingerly over the wound. It still stung. "I'd say I deserved it, but you were cooperating initially."

That stung, too. The truth often did. "You go right on thinking that, Jack." She all but purred it. "I'm sure an ego like yours requires regular delusions."

"Sugar, I know a delusion from a lip lock. But we've got more important things to do than discuss your attraction for me." Pleased with that last sally, he reached into one of the bags. "Burgers."

The smell hit her like a fist, right in the empty stomach. Her mouth watered. "So are we going to hole up here like a couple of escaped convicts—" she rattled her chain for emphasis "—and eat greasy food?"

"You bet." He handed her a burger and took out an order of fries designed to clog the arteries and improve the mood. "I think better when I'm eating."

Companionably, he stretched out beside her, back against the headboard, legs extended, food on his lap. "We've got us a serious problem here."

"If *we've* got us a serious problem here, why am I the only one with handcuffs?"

He loved the sarcastic edge in her voice, and he wondered what was wrong with him. "Because you'd have done something stupid if I hadn't left you secured. I'm looking out for my investment." He gestured with the rest of his burger. "And that's you, sugar."

"I can look out for myself. And if I'm hiring you, then you should be taking orders. The first order is unlock these damn things."

"I'll get to it, once we set up the ground rules." He popped open a paper package of salt, dribbled it on the fries. "I've been thinking."

"Well then." She munched bitterly on an over-cooked burger between two slices of slightly stale bun. "Why am I worried? You've been thinking."

"You've got a sarcastic mouth. But I like that about you." He handed her a tiny paper napkin. "You got ketchup on your chin. Now, somebody put the pressure on Ralph—enough that Ralph falsified official paper-work and put my butt in a sling. He wouldn't have done it for money—not that Ralph doesn't like money," Jack continued. "But he wouldn't risk his license, or risk me coming after him, for a few bucks. So he was saving his skin."

"And since Ralph is a pillar of the community, no doubt, this narrows down the list?"

"It means it was somebody with punch, somebody who wasn't afraid old Ralph would tip me off or go to the cops. Somebody who wanted you taken out. Who knows you've got the rock?"

"Nobody, except the person who sent it to me." She frowned at her burger. "And possibly one other."

"If more than one person knows a secret, it isn't a

secret. How did your friend get the diamond, M.J.? You can't keep dancing around the data here."

"I'll tell you after I clear it with my friend. I have to make a phone call."

"No calls."

"You called Ralph," she pointed out.

"I took a chance, and we were mobile. You're not making any calls until I know the score. The diamond was shipped just yesterday," he mused. "They tagged you fast."

"Which means they tagged my friend." Her stomach turned over. "Jack, please. I have to call. I have to know."

The emotion choking her voice both weakened and annoyed him. He stared into her eyes. "How much does he mean to you?"

She started to correct him, then just shook her head. "Everything. No one in the world means more to me."

"Lucky guy."

It wasn't the response she'd wanted or expected. Fueled by frustration and fears, she grabbed his shirt. "What the hell's wrong with you? Someone tried to kill us. How can we just sit here?"

"That's just why we're sitting here. We let them chase their tails awhile. Your friend's on his own for now. And since I can't picture you falling for some jerk who can't handle himself, he should be fine."

"You don't understand anything." She sat back,

dragged her fingers through her hair. "God, this is a mess. I should be getting ready to go in to work now, and instead I'm stuck here with you. I'm supposed to be behind the stick tonight."

"You tend bar?" He lifted a brow. "I thought you owned the place."

"That's right, I own the place." It was a source of pride. "I like tending bar. You have a problem with that?"

"Nope." Since the topic had distracted her, he followed it. "Are you any good?"

"Nobody complains."

"How'd you get into the business?" When she eyed him owlishly, he shrugged. "Come on, a little conversation over a meal can't hurt. We got time to kill."

That wasn't all she wanted to kill, but the rest would have to wait. "I'm a fourth-generation pub owner. My great-grandfather ran his own public house in Dublin. My grandfather immigrated to New York and worked behind the stick in his own pub. He passed it to my father when he moved to Florida. I practically grew up behind the bar."

"What part of New York?"

"West Side, Seventy-ninth and Columbus."

"O'Leary's." The grin came quick and close to dreamy. "Lots of dark wood and lots of brass. Live Irish music on Saturday nights. And they build the finest Guinness this side of the Atlantic."

She eyed him again, intrigued despite herself. "You've been there?"

"I downed many a pint in O'Leary's. That would have been ten years ago, more or less." He'd been in college then, he remembered. Working his way through courses in law and literature and trying to make up his mind who the devil he was. "I was up there tracing a skip about three years ago. Stopped in. Nothing had changed, not even the scars on that old pine bar."

It made her sentimental—couldn't be helped. "Nothing changes at O'Leary's."

"I swear the same two guys were sitting on the same stools at the end of the bar—smoking cigars, reading the *Racing Form* and drinking Irish."

"Callahan and O'Neal." It made her smile. "They'll die on those stools."

"And your father. Pat O'Leary. Son of a bitch." Steeped in the haze of memory, he shut his eyes. "That big, wide Irish face and wiry shock of red hair, with a voice straight out of a Cagney movie."

"Yeah, that's Pop," she murmured, only more sentimental.

"You know, when I walked in—it had been at least six years since I'd walked out—your father grinned at me. 'How are you this evening, college boy?' he said to me, and took a pint glass and starting building my beer."

"You went to college?"

His hazy pleasure dimmed considerably at the shock in her voice. He opened one eye. "So?"

"So, you don't look like the college type." She shrugged and went back to her burger. "I build a damn good Guinness myself. Could use one now."

"Me too. Maybe later. So this friend of yours, how long have you known him?"

"My friend and I go back to our own college days. There's no one I trust more, if that's what you're getting at."

"Maybe you ought to rethink it. Just consider," he said when her eyes fired. "The Three Stars are a big temptation, for anyone. So maybe he was tempted, maybe he got in over his head."

"No, it doesn't play like that. but I think someone else might have, and if my friend found out about it…" She pressed her lips together. "If you wanted to protect those stones, to make certain they weren't stolen, didn't fall as a group into the wrong hands, what would you do?"

"It isn't a matter of what I'd do," he pointed out, "but what he'd do."

"Separate them," M.J. said. "Pass them on to people you could trust without question. People who would go to the wall for you, because you'd do the same for them. Without question."

"Absolute trust, absolute loyalty?" He balled his napkin, two-pointed it into the waste can. "I can't buy it."

"Then I'm sorry for you," she murmured. "Because you can't buy it. It just is. Don't you have anyone who'd go to the wall for you, Jack?"

"No. And there's no one I'd go to the wall for." For the first time in his life, it bothered him to realize it. He scooted down, closed his eyes. "I'm taking a nap."

"You're taking a what?"

"A nap. You'd be smart to do the same."

"How can you possibly sleep at a time like this?"

"Because I'm tired." His voice was edgy. "And because I don't think I'm going to get much sleep once we get started. We've got a couple hours before sundown."

"And what happens at sundown?"

"It gets dark," he said, and tuned her out.

She couldn't believe it. The man had shut down like a machine switched off—like a hypnotist's subject at the snap of a finger. Like a… She scowled when she ran out of analogies.

At least he didn't snore.

Well, this was just fine, she fumed. This was just dandy. What was she supposed to do while he had his little lie-me-down?

M.J. nibbled on the last of her fries, frowned at the TV screen, where the giant lizard was just meeting his violent end. The cable channel had promised more where that came from on its Marathon Monsters and Heroes Holiday Weekend Festival.

Oh, goody.

She lay in the darkened room, considering her options. And, considering, fell asleep.

And, sleeping, dreamed of monsters and heroes and a blue diamond that pulsed like a living heart.

Jack woke wrapped in female. He smelled her first, a tang, just a little sharp, of lemony soap. Clean, fresh, and simple.

He heard her—the slow, even, relaxed breathing. Felt the quiet intimacy of shared sleep. His blood began to stir even before he felt her.

Long, limber limbs. A shapely yard of leg was tossed over his own. One well-toned arm, with skin as smooth as new cream, was flung over his chest. Her head was settled companionably on his shoulder.

M.J. was a cuddler, he realized, and smiled to himself. Who'd have thought it? Before he could talk himself out of it, he lifted a hand, brushed it lightly over her tousled cap of hair. Bright silk, he mused. It was quite a contrast to all that angled toughness.

She sure had style. His kind of style, he decided, and wondered what direction they might have taken if he just walked into her pub one night and put some moves on her.

She'd have kicked him out on his butt, he thought, and grinned. What a woman.

It was too bad, too damn bad, that he didn't have time to try out those moves. Because he really wanted another taste of her.

And because he did, he slid out from under her, stood and stretched out the kinks while she shifted and tried to find comfort. She rolled onto her back and flung her free hand over her head.

The restless animal inside him stirred.

He grabbed it in a choke hold and reminded himself that he was, occasionally, a civilized man. Civilized men didn't climb onto a sleeping woman and dive in.

But they could think about it.

Since it would be safer all around to think about it at a distance, he went into the bathroom, splashed cold water on his face and considered his next move.

In dreams, she was holding the stone in her hand, wondering at it, as streams of sunlight danced through the canopy of trees. Instead of penetrating the stone, the rays bounced off, creating a flashing whirl of beauty that stung the eyes and burned the soul.

It was hers to hold, if not to keep. The answers were there, secreted inside, if only she knew where to look.

From somewhere came the growl of a beast, low and feral. She turned toward it, rather than away, the stone protected in the fist of her hand, her other raised to defend.

Something moved slyly in the brush, hidden, waiting, searching. Hunting.

Then he was there, astride a massive black horse. At his side was a sword of dull silver, its width a thick slab of violence. His gray eyes were granite-hard, and as dangerous as any beast that slunk over the ground. He held a hand down to her, and there was challenge in that slow smile.

Danger ahead. Danger behind.

She stepped forward, clasped hands with him and let him pull her up on the gleaming black horse. The horse reared high, trumpeted. When they rode, they rode fast. The blood beating in her head had nothing to do with fear, and everything to do with triumph.

She came awake with her heart pounding and her blood high. She was in the dim, cramped motel room, with Jack shaking her shoulder roughly.

"What? What?"

"Nap's over." He considered kissing her awake, risking her fist in his face. But it would be too distracting. "We've got places to go."

"Where?" She struggled to shake off sleep, and the silky remnants of the dream.

"To visit a friend." He unlocked the cuffs from the headboard, snapped them on his own wrist, linking M.J. to him.

"You have a friend?"

"Ah, she's awake now." He pulled her outside, into a misty dusk that still pulsed with heat. "Get in and slide over," he instructed when he opened the driver's side door.

She was still groggy enough that she obeyed without question. But by the time he'd started the engine, her wits were back. "Look, Jack, these handcuffs have got to go."

"I don't know, I kind of like them this way. Did you ever see that movie with Tony Curtis and Sidney Poitier? Great flick."

"We're not escaped cons running for a train here, Dakota. If we're going to have a business relationship, there has to be an element of trust."

"Sugar, you don't trust me any more than I trust you." He steered out of the pitted lot, kept to the speed limit. "Look at it this way." He lifted his hand, causing hers to jerk. "We're both in the same boat. And I could have just left you back there."

She drummed her fingers on her knee. "Why didn't you?"

"I thought about it," he admitted. "I could move faster without you along. But I'd rather keep my eye on you. And if things go wrong and I can't get back, I'd hate for you to have to explain why you're cuffed to the bed of a cheap motel."

"Damn considerate of you."

"I thought so. Though it's your fault I'm flying blind. It'd be easier if you'd fill in the blanks."

"Think of it as a challenge."

"Oh, I do. It, and you." He slanted her a look. "What's this guy got, M.J.? This *friend* of yours you'd risk so much for?"

She looked out her window, thought of Bailey. Then pushed the thought aside. Worry for Bailey only brought the fear back, and fear clouded the mind and made it sluggish.

"You wouldn't understand love, would you, Jack?" Her voice was quiet, without its usual edge, and her gaze passed over his face in a slow search. "The kind that doesn't ask questions, doesn't require favors or have limits."

"No." Inside the emptiness her words brought him curled an edgy fist of envy. "I'd say if you don't ask questions or have limits, you're a fool."

"And you're no fool."

"Under the circumstances, you should be grateful I'm not. I'll get you out of this, M.J. Then you'll owe me fifty thousand."

"You know your priorities," she said with a sneer.

"Yeah, money smooths out a lot of bumps on the road. And I say before you pay me off we end up in bed again. Only this time it won't be to take a nap."

She turned toward him fully, and ignored the quick pulse of excitement in her gut. "Dakota, the only way I'll end up in the sack with you is if you handcuff me again."

There was that smile, slow, insolent, damnably attractive. "Well, that would be interesting, wouldn't it?"

Wanting to make time, he swung onto the interstate, headed north. And he promised himself that not only would he get her into bed, but she wouldn't think of another man when he did.

"You're heading back to D.C."

"That's right. We've got some business there." In the glare of oncoming headlights, his face was grim.

He took a roundabout route, circling, cruising past his objective, winding his way back, until he was satisfied none of the cars parked on the block were occupied.

There was pedestrian traffic, as well. He'd sized it up by his second pass. Deals were being made, he mused. And that kind of business kept people moving.

"Nice neighborhood," she commented, watching a drunk stumble out of a liquor store with a brown paper sack. "Just charming. Yours?"

"Ralph's. We're only a couple blocks from the courthouse." He cruised past a prostitute who was well off the usual stroll and pulled around the corner. "He likes the location."

It was an area, she knew, that even the most fearless cabbies preferred to avoid. An area where life was often worth less than the spit on the sidewalk, and those who valued theirs locked their doors tight before sundown and waited for morning.

Here, the graffiti smeared on the crumbling buildings wasn't an art form. It was a threat.

She heard someone swearing viciously, then the sound of breaking glass. "A man of taste and refinement, your friend Ralph."

"Former friend." He took her hand, obliging her to slide across the seat when he climbed out.

"That you, Dakota? That you?" A man slipped out of the shadows of a doorway. His eyes were fire red and skittish as a whipped dog's. He ran the back of his hand over his mouth as he shambled forward in battered high-tops and an overcoat that had to be stifling in the midsummer heat.

"Yeah, Freddie. How's it going?"

"Been better. Been better, Jack, you know?" His eyes passed over M.J., then moved on. "Been better," he said again.

"Yeah, I know." Jack reached in his front pocket for the bills he'd already placed there. "You could use a hot meal."

"A hot meal." Freddie stared at the bills, moistened his lips. "Sure could do with a hot meal, all right."

"You seen Ralph?"

"Ain't." Freddie's shaky fingers reached for the money, clamped on. He blinked up when Jack continued to hold the bills. "Ain't," he repeated. "Musta closed up early. It's a holiday, the Fourth of July. Damn kids been setting off firecrackers already. Can't tell them from gunshots. Damn kids."

"When's the last time you saw Ralph?"

"I dunno. Yesterday?" He looked at Jack for approval. "Yesterday, probably. I've been here awhile, but I ain't seen him. And his place is locked up."

"Have you seen anybody else who doesn't belong here?"

"Her." Freddie pointed at M.J. and smiled. "She don't."

"Besides her."

"Nope. Nobody." The voice went whiny. "I sure been better, Jack, you know."

"Yeah." Without bothering to sigh, Jack turned the money loose. "Get lost, Freddie."

"Yeah, okay." And he hurried down the street, around the corner.

"He's not going to buy food," M.J. murmured. "You know what he's going to buy with that."

"You can't save the world. Sometimes you can't

even save a little piece of it. But maybe he won't mug anybody tonight, or get himself shot trying to." Jack shrugged. "He's been dead since the first time he picked up a needle. Nothing I can do about it."

"Then why do you feel so lousy about it?" She lifted a brow when he looked down at her. "It's all over your face, Dakota."

"He used to have a family" was all he said by way of an answer. "Let's go." He led her up the street, then ducked down the side of a building. To her surprise, he unlocked the cuffs. "You've got more sense than to take off in this neighborhood." He smiled. "And I've got your rock locked in the trunk of my car."

"On a street like this, you'll be lucky if your car's still there when you get back around."

"They know my car. Nobody'll mess with it." Then he turned—whirled, really—and made her jolt as he slammed two vicious kicks into a dull gray door.

She heard wood splinter, and pursed her lips in appreciation as the door gave way on the third try. "Nice job."

"Thanks. And if Ralph didn't get cute and change the code, we're in business." He stepped inside, scanned an alarm box beside the broken door. With quick fingers he stabbed numbers.

"How do you know his code?"

"I make it my business to know things. Move aside." With a strength she had to admire, he hauled the broken door up, muscled it back into place. "Ralph should have gone for steel. Too cheap."

He flicked on the lights, scanned the tiny space that was crammed with file boxes and smelled of must. M.J. watched a mouse scamper out of sight.

"Charming. I'm very impressed with your associates so far, Dakota. Would this be his secretary's year off?"

"Ralph doesn't have a secretary, either. He's a big believer in low overhead. Office is through here."

"I can't wait." Wary of rodents and anything else with more than two legs, she watched her step as she followed him. "This is what they call nighttime breaking and entering, isn't it?"

"Cops have a name for everything." He paused with his hand on a doorknob, glanced over his shoulder. "If you wanted someone who'd knock politely on the front door, you wouldn't be with me."

She lifted her arm, rattled the dangling handcuffs. "Remember these?"

He only shook his head. "You wouldn't be with me," he repeated, and opened the door.

She sucked in her breath, but it was the only sound she made. Later, he would remember that and appreciate her grit and her control. The backwash of light from the anteroom spilled into the closet-size office.

Gunmetal-gray file cabinets, scarred and dented, lined two walls. Papers spilled out of the open drawers, littered the floor, fluttered on the desk under the breeze of a whining electric fan.

Blood was everywhere.

The smell of it roiled in her stomach, had her clamping her teeth and swallowing hard. But her voice was steady enough when she spoke.

"That would be Ralph?"

Chapter 5

It had been a messy job, Jack thought. If it had been pros, they hadn't bothered to be quick or neat. But then, there'd been no reason for either. Ralph was still tied to the chair.

Or what was left of him was.

"You can wait in the back," Jack told her.

"I don't think so." She wasn't a stranger to violence. A girl didn't grow up in a bar and not see blood spilled from time to time.

But she'd never seen anything like this. As realistic as she considered herself, she hadn't really believed it was possible for one human being to inflict this kind of horror on another.

She kept her eyes on the wall, but stepped in beside him. "What do you think they were after?"

"The same thing I am. Anything that leads back to whoever used Ralph to set us up. Stupid son of a bitch." His voice softened all at once, with what could only have been termed regret. "Why didn't he run?"

"Maybe he didn't have the chance." Her stomach was settling, but she continued to take small, shallow breaths. "We have to call the police."

"Sure, we'll call 911, then we'll wait and explain ourselves. From the inside of a cell." Crouching down, he began shuffling through papers.

"Jack, for God's sake, the man's been murdered."

"He won't be any less dead if we call the cops, will he? Never could figure out Ralph's filing system."

"Haven't you got any feelings at all? You knew him."

"I haven't got time for feelings." And since they were trying to surface, his voice was rough as sand. "Think about it, sugar. Whoever did this to him would love to play the same game with you. Take a good look, and ask yourself if that's how you want to end up."

He waited a moment, then accepted her silence as understanding. "Now you can go in the back room and save your sensibilities, or you can help me sort through this mess."

When she turned, he assumed she'd walk away.

That she might keep on walking, no matter the neighborhood. But she stopped at a file cabinet, grabbed a handful of papers. "What am I looking for?"

"Anything."

"That narrows it down. And why should there be anything left? They've already been here."

"He'd keep a backup somewhere." Jack hissed at the snowfall of papers. "Why the hell didn't he use a computer like a normal person?"

Rising, he went to the desk, wrenched out a drawer. He searched it, turning it over, checking the underside, the back, then tossing it aside and yanking out another. On the third try, he found a false back.

His quick grunt of approval had M.J. turning, watching him take out a penknife and pry at wood. Giving up her own search, she walked to him. By tacit agreement with him, she gripped the loosened edge and tugged while he worked the knife around. Wood splintered from wood.

"It's practically cemented on," Jack muttered. "And recently."

"How do you know it's recent?"

"It's clean. No dust, no grime. Watch your fingers. Here, you take the knife. Let me…" They switched jobs. He skinned his knuckles, swore, and continued to peel the wood back. All at once it popped free.

Jack took the knife again, cut through the tape affixing a key to the back of the drawer. "Storage locker," he muttered. "I wonder what Ralph has tucked away."

"Bus station? Train station? Airport?" M.J. leaned closer to study the key. "It doesn't have a name, just a number."

"I'd go with one of the first two. Ralph didn't like to fly, and the airport's a trek from here."

"That still leaves a lot of locks on a lot of boxes," she reminded him.

"We'll track it down."

"Do you know how many storage lockers there must be in the metropolitan area?"

He turned the key between his fingers and smiled thinly. "We only need one." He took her hand, and before she realized his intent, he'd cuffed them together again.

"Oh, for God's sake, Jack."

"Just covering my bases. Come on, we've got work to do."

At the first bus station, he'd grudgingly removed the cuffs before dragging M.J. into a phone booth, and making an anonymous call to the police to report the murder. Then he carefully wiped down the phone. "If they've got caller ID," he told her, "they'll track down where the call was made."

"And I take it your prints are on file."

He flashed a grin. "Just a little disagreement over pool in my misspent youth. Fifty dollars and time served."

Because he'd shifted, she was backed into the corner of the booth, pressed to the wall by his body. "It's a little crowded in here."

"I noticed." He lifted a hand, skimmed back the hair at her temple. "You did all right back there. A lot of women would have gotten hysterical."

"I don't get hysterical."

"No, you don't. So give me a break here, will you?" He tipped her face up, lowered his head. "Just for a minute." And he closed his mouth over hers.

She could have resisted. She meant to. But it was an easy kiss, with need just a whispering note. It was almost friendly, could have been friendly, if not for the press of his body to hers, and the heat rising from it.

And an easy, almost friendly kiss shouldn't have made her want to cling, to hold on and hold tight. She compromised by fisting a hand on his back, not holding but not protesting.

If her lips softened under his, warmed and parted, it was only for a moment. It meant nothing. Could mean nothing.

"I want you." He murmured the words against her mouth, then again when his lips pressed to her throat. "This is a hell of a time for it, a hell of a place. But I want you, M.J. I'm having a hard time getting past that."

"I don't go to bed with strangers."

"Who's asking you to?" He lifted his head, met her eyes. "We've got each other figured, don't we? And you're not the kind of woman who needs fussy dates or fancy words."

"Maybe not." The fire he'd kindled inside her was still smoldering. "Maybe I haven't figured out what I need."

"Then think about it." He backed off, then took her hand and pulled her out of the booth. "We'll check the lockers. Maybe we'll get lucky."

They didn't. Not in that terminal or in the next two. It was nearly one in the morning before he pocketed the key.

"I want a drink."

She let out a breath, rolled her shoulders. After twelve hours in a waking nightmare, she could see his point. "I wouldn't turn one down. You buying?"

"Why not?"

He steered clear of any of the places where he might be recognized and chose instead a dingy little dive not far from Union Station.

"Good thing I've had my shots." M.J. wrinkled her nose at the sticky, stamp-size table and checked the chair before she sat.

"It was either this or a fern bar. We can check out

Union Station when we've had a break. Two of what you've got on tap," he told the waitress, and cracked a peanut.

"I don't know how places like this stay in business." With a critical eye, M.J. studied the atmosphere. Smoke-choked air, a generally stale smell, sticky floor littered with peanut shells, cigarette butts and worse. "A few gallons of disinfectant, some decent lighting, and this joint would turn up one full notch."

"I don't think the clientele cares." He glanced toward the surly-faced man at the bar, and the weary-eyed working girl who was casing him. "Some people just come into a bar to engage in the serious business of drinking until they're drunk enough to forget why they came into the bar to begin with."

She acknowledged his comment with a nod. "That's the type I don't want in my place. You get them from time to time, but they rarely come back. They're not looking for conversation and music or a companionable drink with a pal. That's what I serve at my place."

"Like father, like daughter."

"You could say that." M.J.'s eyes narrowed in disapproval as the waitress slammed down their mugs. Beer sloshed over the tops. "She wouldn't last five minutes at M.J.'s."

"Rude barmaids have their own charm." Jack picked up his beer and sipped gratefully. "I meant what I said earlier." He grinned when her gaze narrowed on his. "About that, too, but I meant how you handled yourself. It was a tough room, M.J., for anybody."

"It was a first for me." She cleared her throat, drank. "You?"

"Yeah, and I don't mind saying I hope it's my last. Ralph was a jerk, but he didn't deserve that. I'd have to say whoever did that to him enjoyed his work. You've got some real bad people interested in you."

"It looks that way." And those same people, she thought, would be interested in Bailey and Grace. "How long do you figure it'll take to find the lock that fits that key?"

"No telling. Knowing Ralph, he wouldn't go too far afield. He hid the key in his office, not his apartment, so odds are the box is close."

But if it wasn't, it could be hours, even days, before they found it. She wasn't willing to wait that long. She took another gulp of beer. "I need the rest room." When he narrowed his eyes, she smirked. "Want to come with me?"

He studied her a moment, then moved his shoulders. "Make it fast."

She didn't rush toward the back, but her mind was racing. Ten minutes, she calculated. That was all she needed, to get out, get to the phone booth she'd seen outside and get through to Bailey.

She closed the door of the ladies' room at her back, scanned the woman in black spandex primping in the mirror, then grinned at the small casement window set high in the wall.

"Hey, give me a leg up."

The woman perfected a second coat of bloodred lipstick. "A what?"

"Come on, be a pal." M.J. hooked a hand on the narrow sill. "Give me a boost, will you?"

Taking her maddening time, the woman slid the top back on her tube of lipstick. "Bad date?"

"The worst."

"I know the feeling." She tottered over on ice-pick heels. "Do you really think you can squeeze through that? You're skinny, but it'll be a tight fit."

"I'll make it."

The woman shrugged, exuded a puff of too-sweet designer-knockoff perfume and cupped her hands. "Whatever you say."

M.J. bounced a foot in the makeshift stirrup, then boosted herself up until she had her arms hooked on the sill. A quick wriggle and she was chest-high. "Just another little push."

"No problem." Getting into the spirit, the woman set both hands on M.J.'s bottom and shoved. "Sorry," she said when M.J. cracked her head on the window and swore.

"It's okay. Thanks." She wiggled, grunted, twisted and forced herself through the opening. Head, then shoulders. Taking a quick breath, trying not to imagine herself remaining corked in the window, she muscled her way through with only a quick rip of denim.

"Good for you, honey."

M.J. stayed on her hands and knees long enough to shoot her assistant a quick grin. Then she was off and running. She dug in her pocket as she went for the quarter habitually carried there.

She could hear her mother's voice. *Never leave the house without money for a phone call in your pocket. You never know when you'll need it.*

"Thanks, Ma," she murmured, and reached the phone booth at a dead run. "Be there, be there," she whispered, plugging in the coin, stabbing numbers.

She heard Bailey's calm, cool voice answer on the second ring and swore as she recognized the recorded message.

"Where are you, where are you?" She clamped down on panic, took a breath. "Bailey, listen up," she began, the instant after the beep. "I don't know what the hell's going on, but we're in trouble. Don't stay there, he may come back. I'm in a phone booth outside some dive near—"

"Damn idiot." Jack reached in, grabbed her arm.

"Hands off, you son of a bitch. Bailey—" But he'd

already disconnected her. Using the confines of the booth to his advantage, he twisted her around and clamped the cuffs on so that her arms were secured. Then he simply lifted her up and tossed her over his shoulder.

He let her rant, let her kick, and had her dumped back into the car before a single Good Samaritan could take interest. Her threats and promises bounced off him as he peeled away from the curb and shot down side streets.

"So much for trust." And where there wasn't trust, he thought, there had to be proof. Cautious, he doubled back, scouting the area until he found a narrow alley half a block from the phone booth. He backed in, shut off the lights and engine.

Reaching over, he vised a hand around the back of her neck, pulled her face close. "You want to see where your phone call would have gotten us? Just sit tight."

"Take your hands off me."

"At the moment, having my hands on you is the least of my concerns. Just be quiet. And wait for it."

When his grip loosened, she jerked back. "Wait for what?"

"It shouldn't take much longer." And, brooding into the dark, he watched the street.

It took less than five minutes. By his count, a little more than fifteen since her call. The van crept up to the curb. Two men got out.

"Recognize them?"

Of course she did. She'd seen them only that morning. One of them had broken in her door. The other had shot at her. With a quick tremor of reaction, she shut her eyes. They'd traced the call from Bailey's line, she realized. Traced it quickly and efficiently.

And if Jack hadn't moved fast, they might very well have snapped her up just as quickly, just as efficiently.

The smaller of the two went into the bar while the other stood by the phone booth, scanning the street, one hand resting under his suit jacket.

"He'll pass the bartender a couple of bucks to see if you were in there, if you were alone, how long ago you left. They won't hang around long. They'll find out you're still with me, so they'll be looking for the car. We won't be able to use it anymore around here tonight."

She said nothing as the second man came back out, joined the first. They appeared to discuss something, argue briefly, and then they climbed back in the van. This time it didn't creep down the street, it rocketed.

She remained silent for another moment, continued to stare straight ahead. "You were right," she said at length. "I'm sorry."

"Excuse me? I'm not sure I heard that."

"You were right." She had to swallow when she found herself distressingly close to tears. "I'm sorry."

Hearing the tears in her voice only heightened his

temper. "Save it," he snapped, and started the engine. "Next time you want to commit suicide, just make sure I'm out of range."

"I needed to try. I couldn't not try. I thought you were overreacting, or just pushing my buttons. I was wrong. How many times do you want me to say it?"

"I haven't decided. If you start sniveling, I'm really going to get ticked."

"I don't snivel." But she wanted to. The tears were burning her throat. It cost nearly as much to swallow them as it would have to let them free.

She worked on calming herself as he drove out of the city and headed down a deserted back road in Virginia. The city lights giving way to comforting dark.

"No one's following us," she said.

"That's because I'm good, not because you're not stupid."

"Get off my back."

"If I'd sat in there another five minutes waiting for you, I could be as dead as Ralph right now. So consider yourself lucky I don't just dump you on the side of the road and take myself off to Mexico."

"Why don't you?"

"I've got an investment." He caught the look, the glimmer of wet eyes, and ground his teeth. "Don't look at me like that. It really makes me mad."

Swearing, he swerved to the shoulder. Yanking the

key from his pocket, he unlocked her hands, then slammed out of the car to pace.

Why the hell was he tangled up with this woman? he asked himself. Why hadn't he cut himself loose? Why wasn't he cutting loose right now? Mexico wasn't such a bad place. He could get himself a nice spot on the beach, soak up the sun and wait for all this to blow over.

Nothing was stopping him.

Then she got out of the car, spoke quietly. "My friend's in trouble."

"I don't give a damn about your friend." He whirled toward her. "I give a damn about me. And maybe I give one about you, though God knows why, because you've been nothing but grief ever since I watched you swagger up those apartment steps."

"I'll sleep with you."

That cut his minor tirade off in midstream. "What?"

She squared her shoulders. "I'll sleep with you. I'll do whatever you want, if you help me."

He stared at her, at the way the moonlight showered over her hair, at the way her eyes continued to glisten. And wanted her mindlessly.

But not in a barter.

"Oh, that's nice." Bitterness spewed through his voice. "That's great. I don't even have to tie you to the damn railroad tracks." He stepped toward her, grabbed her by the arms and shook. "What the hell do you take me for?"

"I don't know."

"I don't use women," he said between his teeth. "And when I take one to bed, it's a two-way street. So thanks for the offer, but I'm not interested in the supreme sacrifice."

He let her go, started back to the car. Fury had him turning back. "Do you think your friend would appreciate the gesture if he found out you'd slept with me to help him?"

She took a deep, steadying breath. The depth of his sense of insult had gone farther toward gaining her trust than any promise or oath could have. "No. It wouldn't stop me, but no."

She stepped toward him, stopping only when they were within an armspan. "My friend's name is Bailey James. She's a gemologist."

He recognized the name from the doctored paperwork. But the pronoun was the most vital piece of information to him. "She?"

"Yes, she. We went to college together, we roomed together. One of the reasons I located in D.C. was because of Bailey, and Grace. She was our other roommate. They're the closest friends I have, ever have had. I'm afraid for them, and I need your help."

"Bailey's the one who sent you the stone?"

"Yes, and she wouldn't have done it without good reason. I think she may have sent the third one to

Grace. It would be Bailey's kind of logic. She does a lot of consulting work for the Smithsonian."

Suddenly tired, M.J. rubbed her gritty eyes. "I haven't seen her since Wednesday evening. We were supposed to get together tonight at the pub. I put a note under her door to check the time with her. I work a lot of nights, she works days, so even though we live right across the hall from each other, we pass a lot of notes under the door. And lately, since she got the job working on the Three Stars for the Smithsonian, she's been putting in a lot of overtime. I didn't think anything of it when I didn't see her for a couple days."

"And Friday you got the package."

"Yes. I called her at work right away, but I only got the service. They'd closed until Tuesday. I'd forgotten she'd told me they were closing down for the long weekend, but that she'd probably work through it. I went by, but the place was locked up. I called Grace, got her machine. By that time, I was annoyed with both of them. I figured I just was going to have to assume Bailey had her reasons and would let me know. So I went to work. I just went on to work."

"There's no use beating yourself up about that. You didn't have much choice."

"I have a key to her place. I could have used it. We've got this privacy arrangement, which is why we pass notes. I didn't use the key out of habit." She shuddered out a breath. "But she didn't answer the phone now, when I called from outside that bar, and it was two o'clock in the morning. Bailey's arrow-straight, she's not out at 2:00 a.m., but she didn't answer the phone. And I'm afraid... What they did to that man... I'm afraid for her."

He put his hands on her shoulders, and this time they were gentle. "There's only one thing to do." Because he thought she might need it, he pressed a kiss to her brow. "We'll check it out."

She let out her breath on a shuddering sigh. "Thanks."

"But this time you have to trust me."

"This time I will."

He opened the door, waited for her to get in. "The other friend you were talking about, the he?"

She pushed her hair back, looked up. "There is no he."

So he leaned down, captured her mouth with his in one long, searing kiss. "There's going to be."

He took a chance, went back to Union Station first. They'd be looking for his car, true enough, but he was banking on the moldy gray of the Olds, with its scarred vinyl top, blending in.

And he intended to be quick.

Bus and train stations were all very much the same in the middle of the night, he thought. The people curled in chairs or stretched out in blankets weren't all waiting for transportation. Some of them just had nowhere else to go.

"Keep moving," he told M.J. "And keep sharp. I don't want to get cornered in here."

She wondered, as she matched her pace to his, why such places smelled of despair in the early hours. There was none of the excitement, the bustle, the anticipation of goings and comings, so evident during the daylight hours. Those who traveled at night, or looked for a dry corner to sleep, were usually running low on hope.

"You said we were going to check on Bailey."

"Soon as I'm done with this." He headed straight for the storage lockers, did a quick scan. "Sometimes you just get lucky," he murmured, and, matching numbers, slid the key into a lock.

M.J. leaned over his shoulders. "What's in there?"

"Stop breathing down my neck and I'll see. Backup copies of your paperwork," he said, and handed them to her. "Souvenir for you."

"Gee, thanks. I'm really going to want a memento of our little vacation jaunt." But she stuffed them in her bag after a cursory glance. Her interest perked up when Jack drew out a small notebook covered in fake black leather. "That looks more promising."

"Where's his running money?" Jack wondered, deeply disappointed not to find any cash when he swiped his hand around the locker a last time. "He'd have kept some ready in here if he had to catch a train fast."

"Maybe he'd already taken it out."

He opened his mouth to disagree, then shut it again. "Yeah, you've got a point. Could be he wanted to have it on him if he wanted to make a fast exit." Brows knit, he flipped through the book. "Names, numbers."

"Addresses? Phone numbers?" she asked, craning her neck to try to see.

"No. Amounts, dates. Payoffs," he decided. "Looks to me like Ralph was running a little blackmail racket on the side."

"Salt of the earth, your friend Ralph."

"Former friend," Jack said automatically, before he remembered it was literally true. "Very former," he murmured. "If this got out, he'd have lost more than his business. He'd have been doing time in a cell."

"Do you think someone decided to blackmail the blackmailer?"

"Follows. And not everybody puts the arm on for money." He shook his head. According to the figures, Ralph had made more than a decent income with his sideline. "Sometimes they go for blood."

"What good does this do us?" M.J. demanded.

"Not a hell of a lot." He tucked the book into his back pocket, scanned the terminal again. "But some-one Ralph was squeezing squeezed back. Or, more likely, someone who knew about Ralph's little moonlighting project saved the information until it became useful."

"Then killed him," M.J. added as her stomach tightened. "Whoever did isn't just connected with that little book, or Ralph. They're connected to Bailey through the stones. I have to find her."

"Next stop," he said, and took her hand in his.

Chapter 6

M.J. understood the risk, and prepared herself to make no arguments whatever about Jack's instructions. She'd ask no questions. This was his area of expertise, after all, and she needed a pro.

That vow lasted less than thirty minutes.

"Why are you just driving around?" she demanded. "You should have turned left back at the corner. Did you forget how to get there?"

"No, I didn't forget how to get there. I don't forget how to get anywhere."

She rolled her eyes in his direction. "Well, if you've got a map in your head, you've just taken a wrong turn."

"No, I didn't."

Men, she thought on a huff of breath. "I'm telling you—I live here. The apartment's three blocks that way."

He'd told himself he'd be patient with her. She was under a lot of stress, they'd both put in a long, rough day.

His good intentions fled to the place M.J.'s vow had gone.

"I know where you live," he snapped. "I had your place staked out for two hours while you were out shopping."

"I wasn't shopping. I was buying, and that's entirely different. And you still haven't answered my very simple question."

"Do you ever shut up?"

"Are you ever anything but rude?"

He braked at a light, drummed his fingers on the wheel. "You want to know why I'm driving around, I'll tell you why I'm driving around. Because there are two guys with guns in a van looking for us, specifically in this car, and if they happen to be in the area, I'd just as soon see them before they see us. And the reason for that is, I'd prefer not being shot tonight. Is that clear enough?"

She folded her arms over her chest. "Why didn't you just say so in the first place?"

His answer was a mutter as he turned again. He drove sedately for a half block, then pulled over to the curb, shut off the engine.

"Why are you stopping here? We're still blocks away. Look, Jack, if your testosterone's low and you're lost, I won't hold it against you. I can—"

"I'm not lost." He put both hands in his hair, and was tempted to pull. "I never get lost. I know what I'm doing." He reached over, popped open the glove box.

"Well, then, why—"

"We're going on foot," he told her, and grabbed a pencil-beam flashlight and a .38. He made sure she saw the gun and took his time checking the clip. She barely blinked at it.

"That doesn't make any sense. If we have to—"

"We're doing this my way."

"Oh, big surprise. I'm simply asking—"

"I'm tired of answering, *really* tired of answering." But he sighed out a breath. "We're going to cut down this street, then between those two yards, around the building on the next block, then through to the back of the apartment. We're going on foot because we'll be tougher to spot if they've got your building staked out."

She thought it over, considered the angles, then nodded. "Well, that makes sense."

"Thanks, thanks a lot." He grabbed her purse and, while she stuttered out a shocked protest, emptied her wallet of cash.

"Just what the hell do you think you're doing? That's my money." She snatched back her empty wallet as he stuffed bills in his pocket, then goggled as he plucked out the diamond and pushed it in after the bills. "Give me that. Are you out of your mind?"

She made a grab for him. Jack simply shoved her back against the seat, held her in place and, risking another bloody lip, crushed his mouth to hers. She wriggled, muttered what he assumed were oaths, popped her fist against his ribs. Then she decided to cooperate.

And her cooperation, hot, avid, was a great deal more difficult to resist than her protests. He lost himself in her for a moment, experienced the shock of being helpless to do otherwise.

It was like the first time. Consuming. The thought circled in his mind that he'd been waiting all his life to find his mouth pressed to hers.

Just that simple. Just that terrifying.

The fist she'd struck him with relaxed, and her open fingers slid around, up his back, hooked possessively over his shoulder. Mine, she thought.

Just that easy. Just that staggering.

When he shifted back, they stared at each other in the dim light, two strong-minded people who'd just had their worlds tilt under them. Her hand was still gripped on his shoulder, and his on hers.

"Why'd you do that?" she managed.

"It was mostly to shut you up." His hand skimmed up her shoulder, into her hair. "It changed."

Very slowly, she nodded. "Yes, it did."

He had a strong urge to drag her into the back seat and play teenager. The idea nearly made him smile. "I can't think about this now."

"No, me either."

The hand in her hair moved and, in a surprisingly sweet gesture took hers, laced fingers with hers. "We're going to do more than think about it later."

"Yeah." Her lips curved a little. "I guess we are."

"Let's go. No, don't take the purse." When she opened her mouth to argue, he simply tugged it away from her, tossed it into the back. "M.J., that thing weighs a ton. We may have to move fast. I'm taking the cash, and the stone, because they might make the car, or we may not get back to it."

"All right." She got out, waited for him on the sidewalk. Glanced briefly at the gun he secured in a shoulder holster. "I know this is risky. I have to do it, Jack."

He took her hand again. "Then let's do it."

They followed the route he'd mapped out, slipped between yards, a dog barking halfheartedly at them. The moon was out, a bright beacon that both guided their path and spotlighted them.

He had a moment to intensely wish he'd had her change out of the white T-shirt. It glowed in the dark like a lit-up flag. But she moved well, with quiet, long strides. He already knew she could run if necessary. He had to be satisfied with that.

"You have to do what I tell you," he began, keeping his voice low as he surveyed the back of her building. "I know that goes against the grain for you, but you'll have to swallow it. If I tell you to move, you move. If I tell you to run, you run. No questions, no arguments."

"I'm not stupid. I just like to know the reasons."

"This time you just do what you're told, and we'll discuss my reasoning later."

She struggled to fall into step. "Her car's here," she told him quietly. "The little white compact."

"Okay, so maybe she's home." Or, he thought, she hasn't been able to drive. But he didn't think that was what M.J. needed to hear. "We'll go in the side, through the fire door, work our way around to the stairs. No noise, M.J., no conversation."

"Okay."

Her eyes were already on Bailey's windows as they hurried toward the side door. The windows were dark, the curtains drawn. Bailey left her curtains open, was all she could think. Bailey liked to look out the windows and rarely shut out her view.

They slipped inside like shadows and, with Jack a half step in the lead, walked quietly to the steps. The security light beamed, lighting the hall and stairs. Jack glanced out the front door, keeping well to the side. If anyone was watching, he mused, they'd be spotted easily going into the light.

It was a chance they'd have to take.

As they moved up the stairs, he listened for any sound, any movement. It was so late it was early. The building slept. There wasn't even the murmur of a late-night TV behind any of the doors they passed on the second floor.

When they reached the third, M.J. made her first sound, just a quickly indrawn breath, instantly muffled. There was police tape over her door.

"Your neighbor with the bunny slippers called the cops," Jack murmured. "Odds are they're looking for you, too." He held out a hand. "Key?"

She turned, kept her eyes on Bailey's door as she dug into her pocket, handed it to him. He gestured her back toward the steps to give her room to run away, unsheathed his gun, then unlocked the door.

Keeping low, he used his light to scan, saw no movement. Holding a hand up to keep M.J. in place, he stepped inside. What he'd seen had already decided him that no one was there, but he wanted to check the bedroom, the kitchen, before M.J. joined him.

He'd taken the first steps when her gasp, unmuffled this time, had him turning. "Stay back," he ordered. "Stay quiet."

"Oh, God. Bailey." She shot toward the bedroom,

leaping over ripped cushions, overturned chairs like a hurdler coming off the mark.

He reached the door a step ahead, shoved her roughly out of the way. "Hold it together, damn it," He hissed, then opened the door. "She's not here," he said a moment later. "Go close the front door, lock it."

On legs that trembled, she crossed back, taking a winding path through the destruction of the living room. She closed the door, locked it, then leaned back weakly.

"What have they done to her, Jack? Oh, God, what have they done to her?"

"Sit down. Let me look."

She squeezed her eyes tight, fought for control. Images flitted through her head. Her and Grace sitting in the shade of a boulder while Bailey gleefully hunted rocks. The three of them giggling like fools late at night over jug wine. Bailey, a wave of blond hair falling into her face soberly contemplating a pair of Italian shoes in a store display.

"I'll help," she said, and let out a whoosh of breath. "I can help."

Yeah, he thought, watching the way her spine stiffened, her shoulders squared, she probably could. "Okay, you've got to keep it quiet, and keep it quick. We can't risk the lights, or much time."

He skimmed the beam over the room. Contents of drawers and closets had been tossed and scattered. A few breakables smashed. The cushions, the mattress, even the back of chairs, had been slashed so that stuffing poured out in an avalanche of destruction.

"You're not going to be able to tell if anything's missing in all this mess." He surveyed the surface damage and calculated that the woman had gone in for tchotchkes in a big way. "But I can tell you, I don't think your friend was here when this went on."

M.J. pressed a hand to her heart, as though to hold in hope. "Why?"

"This wasn't a struggle, M.J. It was a search, a quick, messy and mostly quiet one. I'd say we have a pretty good idea what they were looking for. Whether they found it or not—"

"She'd have it with her," M.J. said quickly. "Her note was very clear that I should keep the stone with me. She'd have kept it with her."

"If that's true, then odds are she still has it. She wasn't here," he repeated, scanning the light into the living room. "She didn't put up a fight here, she wasn't hurt here. There's no blood."

Her knees wobbled again. "No blood." And she pressed a hand to her mouth to cut off the little sob of relief. "Okay. She's okay. She went underground, the same way we did."

"If she's as smart as you say she is, that's just what she'd do."

"She's smart enough to run if she had to run." It helped to look at the tumbled room with a more careful eye. "She doesn't have her car, so she's on foot or using public transportation." And M.J.'s heart sank at the thought of it. "She doesn't know the streets, Jack. She doesn't know the ropes. Bailey's brilliant, but she's naive. She trusts too easily, likes to believe the best in people. She's sweet," M.J. added, on a little shudder.

"She must have picked up something from you." He appreciated the fact that she could smile at that, even a little. "Let's just take a quick look through this stuff, see if anything pops out. Check her clothes—you could probably tell if she'd packed things."

"She has a travel kit, fully stocked. She'd never go anywhere without it." Buffered by that simple, everyday fact, M.J. headed into the bath to check the narrow linen closet.

Even there, items had been pulled out, the shelves stripped, bottles opened and emptied. But she found the kit itself, opened and empty on the floor, recognized several of its contents—the travel toothbrush, the fold-up hair brush, the travel-size shampoos and soaps.

"It's here." She stepped into the bedroom, did her best to inventory clothes. "I don't think she took anything. There's a suit missing. It's fairly new, so I remember. A neat little blue silk. She might be wearing it. Hell, shoes and bags, I don't know. She collects them like stamps."

"She keep a stash anywhere?"

Insulted, she jerked up her head. "Bailey doesn't do drugs."

"Not drugs." Patience, he told himself, and cast his eyes at the ceiling. "You sure have an opinion of me, sugar. Money, cash."

"Oh." She rose from her crouch. "Sorry. Yeah, she keeps some cash." It bothered her a little, but she led him into the kitchen. "Boy, is she going to hate seeing this. She really likes things ordered. It's kind of an obsession with her. And her kitchen." She kicked some cans, coated with the flour and sugar and coffee that had been dumped out of canisters. "You'd be hardpressed to find a crumb in the toaster."

"I'd say we've all got bigger problems than housekeeping."

"Right." She bent down, retrieved a soup can. "It's one of those fake safe things," she explained, and twisted off the top. "She didn't take her emergency money, either." And there was relief in that. "She probably hasn't even been back here since— Hey!" She jerked the can back, but he'd already scooped out the cash. "Put that back."

"Listen, we can't risk using plastic, so we need money. Cash money." He stuck a comfortingly thick wad of it in his pocket. "You can pay her back."

"I can? You took it."

"Details," he muttered, grabbing her hand. "Let's go. There's nothing here, and we're pushing our luck."

"I could leave her a note, in case she comes back. Stop dragging me."

"She may not be the only one who comes back." He yanked her through the door and kept tugging until they were heading down the stairs.

"I've got to see about Grace."

"One friend at a time, M.J. We're getting out of Dodge for a while."

"I could call her, on my phone, or your cellular. Jack, if Bailey and I are in the middle of this, Grace is, too."

"Travel as a pack, do you?"

"So?" She hurried toward the side door with him, fueled by fresh worry. "I have to contact her. She has a place in Potomac. I don't think she's there. I think she's up at her country place, but—"

"Quiet." He eased open the door, scanned the quiet side lot, the sleeping neighborhood. It had been smooth and easy so far. Smooth and easy made him edgy. "Keep it down until we're clear, will you? God, you've got a mouth."

She snarled with it as he pulled her outside and started eating up the ground. "I don't see what the problem is. Whoever was looking for Bailey and the diamond have been and gone."

"Doesn't mean they won't come back." He caught the glint of moonlight off the chrome of the van just as it squealed into the lot. "Sometimes I hate being right. Go!" he shouted, shoving her ahead of him.

He whirled to protect her back, tried a quick prayer that they hadn't been spotted. And decided God was busy at the moment, when the van doors burst open. The gun was in his hand, the first shot fired, before he spun around and sprinted after her.

He hoped the single shot would give his pursuers something to consider. "I said go!" he snapped out when he all but mowed her down.

"I heard a shot. I thought—"

"Don't think. Run." He grabbed her hand to be certain she did, and was grateful she had no problem keeping pace.

They stormed between the yards, and this time the dog took a keener interest, sending up a wild din that carried for blocks. Moonlight flowed in front of them. Though he heard no footsteps pounding in pursuit, Jack didn't break stride as they whipped around the side of a building, turned the corner.

He took time to scan the street, then hit the ground running. "In" was all he said as he sprinted to the driver's side.

He needn't have bothered with the order. M.J. was already wrenching open the door and diving onto the seat. "They didn't come after us," she panted. "That's bad. They should have come after us."

"You catch on." He flicked the key, hit the gas and shot out from the curb just as the van screamed around the corner. "Grab on to something."

Though she wouldn't have believed it possible, he spun the big car into a fast U-turn, riding two wheels over the opposing curb. His bumper kissed lightly off the fender of a sedan, and then he was screaming down the quiet suburban street at sixty.

He took the first turn with the van three lengths behind. "You know how to use a gun?"

M.J. picked it up off the seat. "Yeah."

"Let's hope you don't have to. Get your seat belt on, if you can manage it," he suggested as he jerked the Olds around another corner. M.J.'s elbow rapped against the dash. "And don't point that thing in this direction."

"I know how to handle a gun." Teeth set, she braced herself and watched through the rear window. "Just drive. They're closing in."

Jack flicked his gaze into the rear view, measured the distance from the oncoming headlights. "Not this time," he promised.

He wound through the streets like a snake, tapping the brake, flooring the gas, whipping the wheel so that his tires whined. The challenge of it, the speed, the insanity, had him grinning.

"I like to do this to music." And he switched the radio up to blare.

"You're crazy." But she found herself grinning madly back at him. "They want to kill us."

"People in hell want snow cones." He hit a four-lane and pushed the car to eighty. "This tank might not look like much, but she moves."

"So does that van. You're not shaking them."

"I haven't gotten started." He skimmed his gaze fast, left, right, then plowed recklessly through a red light. Traffic was sparse, even as they zipped toward downtown. "That's the trouble with D.C.," he commented. "No nightlife. Politicians and ambassadors."

"It has dignity."

"Yeah, right." He wrestled the car around a curve at fifty, and began to travel the rabbit warren of narrow back streets and circles. He heard the ping of metal against metal as a bullet hit his rear fender.

"Now they're getting nasty."

"I think they're trying to shoot out the tires."

"I just bought these babies."

Old or new, she thought, if a bullet hit rubber, the game was over. M.J. took a deep breath, held it, then popped out the window to her waist and fired.

"Are you crazy?" His heart jumped into his throat and nearly had him crashing into a lamppost. "Get your head back in here before you get it blown off."

Grim-eyed, too wired to be afraid, she fired again. "Two can play." With the third shot, she hit a headlight. The shattering glass pumped her adrenaline. It hardly mattered that she'd been aiming at the windshield. "I hit them."

With a mindless snarl, Jack grabbed the seat of her jeans and dragged her in. For the first time in his life, his hands trembled on the wheel of his car. "Who do you think you are, Bonnie Parker?"

"They backed off."

"No, they didn't. I'm outrunning them. Just let me handle this, will you?"

He twisted his way back to the four-lane, careened straight across, shooting over the median with a bone-rattling series of bumps. Sparks spewed out like stars as steel skidded on concrete. With a skill M.J. admired, he wrestled the car into a wide arc, then headed north.

"They're trying it." She twisted in the seat, poked her head out the window again, despite Jack's steady swearing. "I don't think they're gonna—" She hooted at the sound of crunching metal. "They're backing up, heading north on the southbound."

"I can see. I don't need a damn play-by-play. Get back in here. Strap in this time."

He hit the on-ramp for the Beltway at sixty. And had gained just enough time, he calculated, to make it work. He barreled off at the first exit and headed into Maryland.

"You lost them." She crawled over and gave him an enthusiastic smack on the cheek. "You're good, Dakota."

"Damn right." He was also shaky. The moment he felt he could afford it, he pulled to the shoulder and wiped her grin away by grabbing her shoulders and giving her a hard, teeth-rattling shake. "Don't you ever do anything so stupid again. You're lucky you didn't fall out of the window, or get your head shot off."

"Cut it out, Jack." Her hand was already fisting. "I mean it." Then she went limp as he hauled her against him and held tight. His face was buried in her hair, his heart was pounding. "Hey." Baffled, moved, she patted his back. "I was just pulling my weight."

"Don't." His mouth found hers in a desperate kiss. "Just don't." And as abruptly as he'd grabbed her, he shoved her away. "You've gotten to me," he muttered, furious at the emotions storming through him. "Just shut up." His head whipped around when she opened her mouth. "Just shut up. I don't want to talk about it."

"Fine." Her own stomach was trembling. As if the fate of the world depended on it, she meticulously buckled her seat belt as he pulled back onto the road. "I'd really like to call my friend Grace."

His hands were tensed on the wheel, but he kept his voice even. "We can't risk it now. We don't know what kind of equipment they've got in that van, and they're too close yet. We'll see what we can manage tomorrow."

Knowing she'd have to settle for that, she rubbed her restless hands on her knees. "Jack, I know what you risked going to Bailey's to try to ease my mind. I appreciate it."

"Just part of the service."

"Is it?"

He glanced over, met her eyes. "Hell, no. I said I don't want to talk about it."

"I'm not talking about it." She wasn't sure she knew how, or what to do about these unexpected feelings swimming through her. "I'm thanking you."

"Then you're welcome. Look, I'm heading back to the Bates Motel. Which are you more—hungry or tired?"

That, at least, didn't take any thought. "Hungry."

"Good, so am I."

She had a lot of considering to do, M.J. decided. Her friend was missing, she had a priceless blue diamond in her possession—or in Jack's pocket—and she'd been chased, shot at and handcuffed.

Added to that, she was very much afraid she was falling for some tough-eyed, swaggering bounty hunter who drove like a maniac and kissed like a dream.

A hot, sweaty dream.

And she knew barely more of him than his name.

It made no sense, and though she enjoyed being reckless in some areas, her heart wasn't one of them. She'd always kept a firm hand there, and it was frightening to feel that grip slipping over a man she'd literally rammed into only the day before.

She wasn't a romantic woman, or a fanciful one. But she was an honest woman. Honest enough to admit that whatever danger she was facing from the outside, she was facing danger just as great, just as real, from her own heart.

He was trembling with fury. Incompetence. It was unacceptable to find himself surrounded by utter incompetence. It was true he'd had to hire the men quickly, and with only the thinnest of recommendations, but their failure to execute one small task, to deal with one woman, was simply outrageous.

He had no doubt he could have dealt with her handily himself, if he could have risked the exposure.

Now, with the moon set and the stars fading, he stood on the terrace, calming his soul with a glass of wine the color of new blood.

It was partly his fault, he conceded. Certainly, he should have checked more carefully into the matter of Jack Dakota. But time had been of the essence, and he had assumed the fool of a bail bondsman was capable of following the orders to assign someone just competent enough to take her, and wise enough to turn her over.

Apparently, Jack Dakota wasn't a wise man, but a stubborn one. And the woman was infuriatingly lucky.

M. J. O'Leary. Well, perhaps she had the luck of the Irish, but luck could change.

He would see to that.

Just as he would see to Bailey James. She would have to surface eventually. He'd be ready. And Grace Fontaine... Pity.

Well, he would find the third stone, as well.

He would have all of them. And a heavy price would be paid by all who had tried to stop him.

His fingers snapped the fragile stem. Glass tinkled on the stone. Wine splattered and pooled. Grimly he smiled down, watched the red liquid seek the cracks.

More than blood would be spilled, he promised himself.

And soon.

Chapter 7

They settled in the little all-night diner just down from the motel. Coffee, strong enough to walk on, came first, served by a sleepy-eyed waitress wearing a cotton-candy-pink uniform and a plastic name tag that declared her Midge.

M.J. shifted in the booth, catching her jeans on the torn vinyl of the seat, perused the hand-typed menu under its plastic coating, then propped an elbow on the scarred surface of the coffee-stained linoleum that covered their table.

A very ancient country-and-western tune was

twanging away on the juke, and the air was redolent of the thick odor of frying grease.

Aesthetics weren't served there, but breakfast was. Twenty-four hours a day.

"That's almost too perfect," M.J. commented after she ordered a whopping breakfast, including a short stack, eggs over and a rasher of bacon. "She even looks like a Midge—hardworking, competent and friendly. I always wondered if people grew into their names or vice versa. Like Bailey—cool, studious, smart. Or Grace, elegant, feminine and generous."

Jack rubbed a hand over the stubble on his chin. "So what's M.J. stand for?"

"Nothing."

He cocked a brow. "Sure it does. Mary Jo, Melissa Jane, Margaret Joan, what?"

She sipped her coffee. "It's just initials. And that's been made legal, too."

His lips curved. "I'll get you drunk and you'll spill it."

"Dakota, I come from a long line of Irish pub owners. Getting me drunk is beyond your capabilities."

"We'll have to check that out—maybe in your place. Dark wood?" he asked with a half smile. "Lots of brass. Irish music, live on weekends?"

"Yep. And not a fern in sight."

"Now we're talking. And seeing as you own it, you can buy the first round as soon as we're clear."

"It's a date." She picked up her cup again. "And, boy, am I looking forward to it."

"What, we're not having fun yet?"

She eased back as the waitress set their heaping plates on the table. "Thanks." Then picked up a fork and dug in. "It's had its moments," she told him. "Can I see Ralph's book?"

"What for?"

"So I can admire its handsome plastic binding," she said sweetly.

"Sure, why not?" He lifted his hips, drew it out and tossed it on the table. As she flipped through the pages, he sampled his eggs. "See anyone you know?"

It was the cocky tone of his voice that made her delighted to be able to glance up at him, smile and say, "Actually, I do."

"What?" He would have snatched the book back if she hadn't held it out of reach. "Who?"

"T. Salvini. That's got to be one of Bailey's stepbrothers."

"No kidding?"

"No kidding. There's a five and three zeros after his name. Just think. Tim or Tom did business with Ralph. You did business with Ralph, now I'm—in a loose manner of speaking—doing business with you." Those dark-river-green eyes shifted up, met his. "Small world, right, Jack?"

"From where I'm sitting," he agreed.

"Here's another payment, about five K. Looks like the bill came in on the eighteenth of the month—goes four, no, five months back." Thoughtfully she tapped the book on the edge of the table. "Now I wonder what one, or both, of the creeps did that was worth twenty-five thousand to keep Ralph quiet about it."

"People do things all the time they want kept quiet—and they pay for it, one way or another."

She angled her head. "You're a real student of human nature, aren't you, Dakota? And a cynic, as well."

"Life's a cynical journey. Well, we've got one solid connection back to Ralph. Maybe we'll pay the creeps a visit soon."

"They're businessmen," she pointed out. "Slimy, from my viewpoint, but murder's a big jump. I can't see it."

"Sometimes it's a much smaller step than you'd think." He took the book back, pocketed it again. "On that cynical journey."

"I can see them cooking the books," she said speculatively. "Timothy has a gambling problem—meaning he likes to play and tends to lose."

"Is that so? Well, Ralph had a lot of connections when it came to, let's say, games of chance. That's a link that slides neat onto the chain."

"So Ralph finds out the creep's playing deep, maybe

skimming the till to keep from getting his legs broken, and he puts the pressure on."

"It might work. And Salvini whines to somebody who's got more muscle—somebody who wants the Stars." He moved his shoulders and decided to give it a chance to brew. "In any case, that wasn't bad work, sugar."

"It was great work," she corrected.

"I'll cop to good. And you looked pretty natural with your hips hanging out the car window, shooting at a speeding van." He drowned his pancakes in syrup. "Even if it did stop my heart. If you ever decide to change careers, you'd make a passable skip tracer."

"Really?" She wasn't sure if she should be complimented or worried by the assessment. She decided to be flattered. "I don't think I could spend my life on the hunt—or being hunted." She shook enough salt on her eggs to make Jack—a sodium fan—wince. "How do you? Why do you?"

"How's your blood pressure?"

"Hmm?"

"Never mind. I figure you go with your strengths. I'm good at tracking, backtracking, then figuring out the steps people are planning to take. And I like the hunt." He grinned wolfishly. "I love the hunt. Doesn't matter what size the prey is, as long as you bring them down."

"Crime's crime?"

"Not exactly. That's a cop attitude. But if you've got the right point of view, it's just as satisfying to snag some deadbeat father running from back child support as it is to bag a guy who shot his business partner. You can bring down both if you get to know your quarry. Mostly they're stupid—they've got habits they don't break."

"Such as?"

"A guy dips into the till where he works. He gets caught, charged, then he jumps bail. Odds are he's got friends, relatives, a lover. It won't take long before he asks somebody for help. Most people aren't loners. They think they are, but they're not. Something always pulls them back. They'll make a call, a visit. Leave a paper trail. Take you."

Surprised, she frowned. "I hadn't done anything."

"That's not the issue. You're a smart woman, a self-starter, but you wouldn't have gone far, you wouldn't have gone long without calling your friends." He scooped up eggs, smiled at her. "In fact, that's just what you did."

"And what about you? Who would you call?"

"Nobody." His smile faded. He continued to eat as the waitress topped off their coffee.

"No family?"

"No." He picked up a slice of bacon, snapped it in two. "My father took off when I was twelve. My mother handled it by hating the world. I had an older brother, signed with the army the day he hit eighteen. He decided not to come back. I haven't heard from him in ten, twelve years. Once I got into college, my mother figured her job was done and hit the road. You could say we don't keep in touch."

"I'm sorry."

He jerked his shoulder against the sympathy, irritated with himself for telling her. He didn't talk family. Ever. With anyone.

"You haven't seen your family in all these years," she continued, unable to prevent herself from probing just a bit. "You don't know where they are—they don't know where you are?"

"We weren't what you'd call close, and we didn't spend enough time together to be considered dysfunctional."

"But still—"

"I always figured it was in the blood," he said, cutting her off. "Some people just don't stay put."

All right, she thought, his family was out of the conversation. It was a tender spot, even if he didn't realize it. "What about you, Jack? How long have you stayed put?"

"That's part of the appeal of the job. You never know where it's going to take you."

"That's not what I meant." She searched his face. "But you knew that."

"I never had any reason to stay." Her hand rested on the table, an inch from his. He was tempted to take it, just hold it. That worried him. "I know people, a lot of people. But I don't have friends—not the way you do with Bailey and Grace. A lot of us go through life without that, M.J."

"I know. But do you want to?"

"I never gave it a hell of a lot of thought." He rubbed both hands over his face. "God, I must be tired. Philosophizing over breakfast in the Twilight Diner at five in the morning."

She glanced out the window at the lightening sky to the east, the all-but-empty road. "'And down the long and silent street, the dawn—'"

"'With silver-sandaled feet, crept like a frightened girl.'" Finishing the quote, he shrugged. She was goggling at him.

"How do you know that? Just what did you take in college?"

"Whatever appealed to me."

Now she grinned, propped her elbows on the table. "Me too. I drove my counselors crazy. I can't tell you how many times I was told I had no focus."

"But you can quote Oscar Wilde at 5:00 a.m. You can shoot a .38, drop-kick your average man, you eat like a trucker, understand ancient Roman gods, and I bet you mix a hell of a boilermaker."

"The best in town. So here we are, Jack, a couple of people most would say are overeducated for their career choices, drinking coffee at an ungodly hour of the morning, while a couple of guys in a van with one headlight hunt for us and the pretty rock you've got in your pocket. It's the Fourth of July, we've known each other less than twenty-four hours under very possibly the worst of circumstances, and the person who brought us together is dead as Moses."

She pushed her plate aside. "What do we do now?"

He took bills out of his pocket, tossed them on the table. "We go to bed."

The motel room was still tacky, cramped and dim. The thin flowered spread was still mussed where they had stretched out on it hours before.

Only hours, she thought. It felt like days. A lifetime. More than a lifetime. It felt as if she'd known him forever, she realized as she watched him empty his pocket onto the dresser, that he'd been a vital part of her forever.

If that wasn't enough, maybe the wanting was. Maybe wanting like this was the best thing to hold on to when your world had gone insane. There was nothing and no one left to trust but him.

Why should she say no? Why should she turn away from comfort, from passion? From life?

Why should she turn away from him, when every instinct told her he needed those things as much as she did?

He turned, and waited. He could have seduced her. He had no doubt of it. She was running on sheer nerves now, whether she knew it or not. So she was vulnerable, and needy, and he was there.

Sometimes that alone was enough.

He could have seduced her, would have, if it hadn't been important. If she hadn't been so inexplicably and vitally important. Sex would have been a relief, a release, a basic physical act between two free-willed adults.

And that should have been all he wanted.

But he wanted more.

He stayed where he was, beside the dresser, as she stood at the foot of the bed.

"I've got something to say," he began.

"Okay."

"I'm in this with you until it's over because that's the way I want it. I finish what I start. So I don't want anything that comes from gratitude or obligation."

If her heart hadn't been jumping, she might have smiled. "I see. So if I suggested you sleep in the bathtub, that wouldn't be a problem?"

He eased a hip onto the dresser. "It'd be your problem. If that's what you want, you can sleep in the bathtub."

"Well, you never claimed to be a gentleman."

"No, but I'll keep my hands off you."

She angled her head, studied him. He looked dangerous, plenty dangerous, she decided as her pulse quickened. The dark stubble, the wild mane of hair, those hard gray eyes so intense in that tough, rawboned face.

He thought he was giving her a choice.

She wondered if either of them was fool enough to believe she had one.

So her smile was slow, arrogant. She kept her eyes on his as she reached down, tugged her T-shirt out of her jeans. She watched his gaze flick down to her hands, follow them up as she pulled the shirt over her head, tossed it aside.

"I'd like to see you try," she murmured, and unsnapped her jeans. He straightened on legs gone watery when she began to lower the zipper.

"I want to do that."

With heat already tingling in her fingertips, she let her hands fall to her sides. "Help yourself."

Her shoulders were long, fascinating curves. Her breasts were pale and small and would cup easily in a man's palm. But for now, he looked only at her face.

He took his time, tried to, crossing to her, catching the metal tab between his thumb and finger, drawing it slowly down. And his eyes were on hers when he slid his hand past the parted denim and cupped her.

Felt her, hot, naked. Felt her tremble, quick, deep.

"I had a feeling."

She let out a careful breath, drew in another through lungs that had become stuffed with cotton. "I didn't get to my laundry this week."

"Good." He eased the denim down another inch, slid his hands around her bottom. "You're built for speed, M.J. That's good, because this isn't going to be slow. I don't think I could manage slow right now." He yanked her against him, arousal to arousal. "You're just going to have to keep up."

Her eyes glinted into his, her chin angled in a dare. "I haven't had any trouble keeping up with you so far."

"So far," he agreed, and ripped a gasp from her when he lifted her off her feet and clamped his hungry mouth to her breast.

The shock was stunning, glorious, an electric sizzle that snapped through her blood and slapped her heartbeat into overdrive. She let her head fall back and wrapped her legs tight around his waist to let him feed. The scrape of his beard against her skin, the nip of teeth, the slide of his tongue—each a separate, staggering thrill.

And each separate, staggering thrill tore through her system and left her quivering for more.

The fall to the bed—a reckless dive from a cliff. The grip of his hands on hers—another link in the chain. His mouth, desperate on hers—a demand with only one answer.

She pulled at his shirt, rolled with him until he was free of it and they were both bare to the waist. And found the muscles and bones and scars of a warrior's body. The heat of flesh on flesh raged through her like a firestorm.

Her hands and mouth were no less impatient than his. Her needs no less brutal.

With something between an oath and a prayer, he flipped her over, dragging at her jeans. His mouth busily scorched a path down her body as he worked the snug denim off. Desire was blinding him with hammer blows that stole the breath and battered the senses. No hunger had ever been so acute, so edgy and keen, as this for her. He only knew if he didn't have her, all of her, he'd die from the wanting.

Those long naked limbs, the energy pulsing in every pore, those harsh, panting gasps of her breath, had the blood searing through his veins to burn his heart. Wild for her, he yanked her hips high and used his mouth on her.

The climax screamed through her, one long, hot wave with jagged edges that had her sobbing out in shock and delight. Her nails scraped heedlessly down his back, then up again until they were buried in his thick mane of gold-tipped hair. She let him destroy her, welcomed it. And, with her body still shuddering from the onslaught, wrestled him onto his back to tear at the rest of his clothes.

She felt his heart thud, could all but hear it. Their flesh, slick with sweat, slid smoothly as they grappled. His fingers found her, pierced her, drove her past desperation. If speech had been possible, she would have begged.

Rather than beg, she clamped her thighs around him, and took him inside, fast and deep.

His fingers dug hard into her hips when she closed over him. His breath was gone; his heart stopped. For an instant, with her raised above him, her head thrown back, his hands sliding sinuously up her body, he was helpless.

Hers.

Then she began to move, piston-quick, riding him ruthlessly in a wild race. Her breath was sobbing, her hands were clutched in her hair. In some part of his brain he realized that she, too, was helpless.

His.

He reared up, his mouth greedy on her breast, on her throat, wherever he could draw in the taste of her while they moved together in a merciless, driving rhythm.

Then he wrapped his arms around her, pressed his lips to her heart, groaning out her name as they shattered each other.

They stayed clutched, joined, shuddering. Time was lost to him. He felt her grip slacken, her hands slide weakly down his back, and brushed a kiss over her shoulder. He lay back, drawing her with him so that she was sprawled over his chest.

He stroked a hand over her hair and murmured, "It's been an interesting day."

She managed a weak chuckle. "All in all." They were sticky, exhausted, and quite possibly insane, she thought. Certainly, it was insane to feel this happy, this perfect, when everything around you was wrecked.

She could have told him she'd never been intimate with a man so quickly. Or that she'd never felt so in tune, so close to anyone, as with him.

But there didn't seem to be a point. What was happening to them was simply happening. Opening her eyes, she studied the stone resting atop the scarred dresser. Did it glow? she wondered. Or was it simply a trick of the light of the room?

What power did it have, really, beyond material wealth? It was just carbon, after all, with some elements mixed in to give it that rare, rich color. It grew in the earth, was of the earth, and had once been taken, by human hands, from it.

And had once been held in the hands of a god.

The second stone was knowledge, she thought, and closed her eyes. Perhaps some things were known only to the heart.

"You need to sleep," Jack said quietly. The tone of his voice made her wonder where his mind had wandered.

"Maybe." She rolled off him, stretched out on her stomach across the width of the bed. "My body's tired, but I can't shut off my head." She chuckled again. "Or I can't now that I'm able to think again. Making love with you is a regular brain drain."

"That's a hell of a compliment." He sat up, running a hand over her shoulder, down her back, then stopping short at the subtle curve of her bottom. Intrigued, he narrowed his eyes, leaned closer. Then grinned. "Nice tattoo, sugar."

She smiled into the hot, rumpled bedspread. "Thanks. I like it." She winced when he switched on the bedside lamp. "Hey! Lights out."

"Just want a clear look." Amused, he rubbed his thumb over the colorful figure on her butt. "A griffin."

"Good eye."

"Symbol of strength—and vigilance."

She turned her head, cocked it so that she could see his face. "You know the oddest things, Jack. But yeah, that's why I chose it. Grace got this inspiration about the three of us getting tattoos to celebrate graduation. We took a weekend in New York and each got our little butt picture."

Her smile slid away as thoughts of her friends weighed on her heart. "It was a hell of a weekend. We made Bailey go first, so she wouldn't chicken out. She picked a unicorn. That's so like her. Oh, God."

"Come on, turn it off." He was mortally afraid she might weep. "As far as we know, she's fine. No use borrowing trouble," he continued, kneading the muscles of her back. "We've got plenty of our own. In a couple hours, we'll clean up, go out and cruise around, try to call Grace."

"Okay." She pulled in the emotion, tucked it into a corner. "Maybe—"

"Did you run track in college?"

"Huh?"

The sudden change of subject accomplished just what he'd wanted it to. It distracted her from worry. "Did you run track? You've got the build for it, and the speed."

"Yeah, actually, I was a miler. I never liked relays. I'm not much of a team player."

"A miler, huh?" He rolled her over and, smiling, traced a fingertip over the curve of her breast. "You gotta have endurance."

Her brows lifted into her choppy bangs. "That's true."

"Stamina." He straddled her.

"Absolutely."

He lowered his head, toyed with her lips. "And you have to know how to pace yourself, so you've got wind for that final kick."

"You bet."

"That's handy." He bit her earlobe. "Because I'm planning on pacing myself this time. You know the saying, M.J.? The one about slow and steady winning the race?"

"I think I've heard of it."

"Why don't we test it out?" he suggested, and captured her mouth with his.

This time she slept, as he'd hoped she would. Facedown again, he mused, studying her, crossways over the bed. He stroked her hair. He couldn't seem to touch her enough, and couldn't remember ever having this need to touch before. Just a brush on the shoulder, the link of fingers.

He was afraid it was ridiculously sentimental, and was grateful she was asleep.

A man with a reputation for being tough and cynical didn't care to be observed mooning like a puppy over a sleeping woman.

He wanted to make love with her again. That, at least, was understandable. To lose himself in sex—the hot, sweaty kind, or the slow and sweet kind.

She'd turn to him, he knew, if he asked. He could wake her now, arouse her before her mind cleared. She'd open for him, take him in, ride with him.

But she needed to sleep.

There were shadows under her eyes—those dark, witchy green eyes. And when the flush of passion faded from her skin, her cheeks had been pale with fatigue. Sharp-boned cheeks, defined by a curve of silky skin.

He pressed his fingers to his eyes. Listen to him, he thought. The next thing he knew, he'd be composing odes or something equally mortifying.

So he nudged her over, made himself comfortable. He'd sleep for an hour, he thought, setting his internal clock. Then they would step back into reality.

He closed his eyes, shut down.

M.J. woke to the sound of rain. It reminded her of lazy mornings, summer showers. Snuggling into the pillow, shifting from dream to dream.

She did so now, sliding back into sleep.

The horse leaped over the narrow stream, where shallow water flashed blue. Her heart leaped with it, and she clutched the man tighter. Smelled leather and sweat.

Around them, buttes rose like pale soldiers into a sky fired by a huge white sun. The heat was immense.

He was in black, but it wasn't her knight. The face was the same—Jack's face—but it was shadowed under a wide-brimmed black hat. A gun belt rode low on his hips, instead of a silver sword.

The empty land stretched before them, wide as the sea, with waves of rocks, sharp-edged as honed knives. One misstep, and the ground would be stained with their blood.

But he rode fearlessly on, and she felt nothing but the power and excitement of the speed.

When he reined in, turned in the saddle, she poured herself into his arms, met those hard, demanding lips eagerly with her own.

She offered him the stone that beat with light and a fire as blue as the hottest flame.

"It belongs with the others. Love needs knowledge, and both need generosity."

He took it from her, secured it in the pocket over his heart. "One finds the other. Both find the third." His eyes lit. "And you belong to me."

In the shadow of a rock, the snake uncoiled, hissed out its warning. Struck.

M.J. shot up in bed, a scream strangled in her throat. Both hands pressed to her racing heart. She swayed, still caught in the dream fall.

The snake, she thought with a shudder. A snake with the eyes of a man.

Lord. She concentrated on steadying her breathing, controlling the tremors, and wondered why her dreams were suddenly so clear, so real and so odd.

Rather than stretch out again, she found a T-shirt—Jack's—and slipped it on. Her mind was still fuzzy, so it took her a moment to realize it wasn't rain she was hearing, but the shower.

And that alone—knowing he was just on the other side of the door—chased away the last remnants of fear.

She might be a woman whose pride was based on

being able to handle herself in any situation. But she'd never faced one quite like this. It helped to know there was someone who would stand with her.

And he would. She smiled and rubbed the sleep out of her eyes. He wouldn't back down, he wouldn't turn away. He would stick. And he would face with her whatever beasts were in the brush, whatever snakes there were in the shadows.

She rose, raking both hands through her hair, just as the bathroom door opened.

He stepped out, a billow of steam following. A dingy white towel was hooked at his waist, and his body still gleamed with droplets of water. His hair was slick and wet to his shoulders, gold glinting through rich brown.

He had yet to shave.

She stood, heavy-eyed, tousled from sleep, wearing nothing but his wrinkled T-shirt, tattered at the hem that skimmed her thighs.

For a moment, neither of them could do more than stare.

It was there, as real and alive in the tatty little room as the two of them. And it gleamed as bright, as vital, as the stone that had brought them to this point.

Jack shook his head as if coming out of a dream— perhaps one as vivid and unnerving as the one M.J. had awakened from. His eyes went dark with annoyance.

"This is stupid."

If she'd had pockets, her hands would have been in them. Instead, she folded her arms and frowned back at him. "Yeah, it is."

"I wasn't looking for this."

"You think I was?"

He might have smiled at the insulted tone of her voice, but he was too busy scowling, and trying desperately to backpedal from what had just hit him square in the heart. "It was just a damn job."

"Nobody's asking you to make it any different."

Eyes narrowed, he took a step forward, challenge in every movement. "Well, it is different."

"Yeah." She lowered her hands to her sides, lifted her chin. "So what are you going to do about it?"

"I'll figure it out." He paced to the dresser, picked up the stone, set it down again. "I thought it was just the circumstances, but it's not." He turned, studied her face. "It would have happened anyway."

Her heartbeat was slowing, thickening. "Feels like that to me."

"Okay." He nodded, planted his feet. "You say it first."

"Uh-uh." For the first time since he'd opened the door, her lips twitched. "You."

"Damn it." He dragged a hand through his dripping hair, felt a hundred times a fool. "Okay, okay," he muttered, though she was waiting silently, patiently.

Nerves drummed under his skin, his muscles coiled like wires, but he looked her dead in the eye.

"I love you."

Her response was a burst of laughter that had him clamping his teeth until a muscle jerked in his jaw. "If you think you're going to play me for a sucker on this, sugar, think again."

"Sorry." She snorted back another laugh. "You just looked so pained and ticked off. The romance of it's still pittering around in my heart."

"What, do you want me to sing it?"

"Maybe later." She laughed again, the delighted sound rolling out of her and filling the room. "Right now I'll let you off the hook. I love you right back. Is that better?"

The ice in his stomach thawed, then heated into a warm glow. "You could try to be more serious about it. I don't think it's a laughing matter."

"Look at us." She pressed a hand to her mouth and sat down on the foot of the bed. "If this isn't a laughing matter, I don't know what is."

She had him there. In fact, he realized, she had him, period. Now his lips curved, with determination. "Okay, sugar, I'm just going to have to wipe that smirk off your face."

"Let's see if a big tough guy like you can manage it."

She was grinning like a fool when he shoved her back on the bed and rolled on top of her.

Chapter 8

She had to learn to defer to him on certain matters, M.J. told herself. That was compromise, that was relationship. The fact was, he had more experience in situations like the one they were in than she did. She was a reasonable person, she thought, one who could take instruction and advice.

Like hell she was.

"Come on, Jack, do I have to wait till you drive to Outer Mongolia to make one stupid phone call?"

He flipped her a look. He'd been driving for exactly ten minutes. He was surprised she'd waited that long to complain. She was worried, he reminded himself.

The past twenty-four hours had been rough on her. He was going to be reasonable.

In a pig's eye.

"You use that phone before I say, and I'll toss it out the window."

She drummed her fingers on the little pocket phone in her hand. "Just answer me this. How is anybody going to trace us through this portable? We're out in the middle of nowhere."

"We're less than an hour outside of D.C., city girl. And you'd be surprised what can be traced."

Okay, maybe he wasn't exactly sure himself if it could be done. But he thought it was possible. If her friend's phone was tapped, and whoever was after them had the technology, it seemed possible that the frequency of her flip phone could be a trail of sorts.

He didn't want to leave a trail.

"How?"

He'd been afraid she'd ask. "Look, that thing's essentially a radio, right?"

"Yeah, so?"

"Radios have frequencies. You tune in on a frequency, don't you?" It was the best he could do, and it was a relief to see her purse her lips and consider it. "Plus, I want to put some distance between where we are and where we're staying. If it was the FBI on our tails, I'd want them chasing in circles."

"What would the FBI want with us?"

"It's an example." He didn't beat his head on the steering wheel, but he wanted to. "Just deal with it, M.J. Just deal with it."

She was trying to, trying to remind herself that it had only been a day, after all. One single day.

But her life had changed in that single day.

"At least you could tell me where we're going."

"I'm taking 15, north toward Pennsylvania."

"Pennsylvania?"

"Then you can make your call. After, we'll head southeast, toward Baltimore." He flicked her another glance. "If the Os are in town, we can take in a game."

"You want to go to a ball game?"

"Hey, it's the Fourth of July. Ball games, beer, parades and fireworks. Some things are sacred."

"I'm a Yankee fan."

"You would be. But the point is, a ballpark's a good place to lose ourselves for a couple hours—and a good place for a meet if you're able to contact Grace."

"Grace at a baseball game?" She snorted. "Right."

"It's a good cover," he began, then frowned. "Your friend has something against the national pastime?"

"Sports aren't exactly Grace's milieu. Now, a nice, rousing fashion show, or maybe a thrilling opera."

It was his turn to snort. "And you're friends?"

"Hey, I've been known to go to the opera."

"In chains?"

She had to laugh. "Practically. Yeah, we're friends." She let out a sigh. "I guess it's hard, surface-wise, to see why. The scholar, the Mick and the princess. But we just clicked."

"Tell me about them. Start with Bailey, since this starts with Bailey."

"All right." She drew a deep breath, watched the scenery roll by. Little snatches of country, thick with trees and hills that rolled. "She's lovely, has this fragile look about her. Blond, brown-eyed, with rose-petal skin. She has a weakness for pretty things, silly, pretty things, like elephants. She collects them. I gave her one carved out of soapstone for her birthday last month."

Remembering how normal it had all been, how simple, had her pressing her lips together. "She likes old movies, especially the film noir type, and she can be a little dreamy at times. But she's very focused. Of the three of us back in college, she was the only one who knew exactly what she wanted and worked toward it."

He liked the sound of Bailey, Jack thought. "And what did she want?"

"Gemology. She's fascinated by rocks, stones. Not just jewel types. We keep talking about the three of us going to Paris for a couple weeks, but last year we ended up in Arizona, rockhounding. She was happy as a pig in slop. And she's had a lot of unhappiness in her life. Her father died when she was a kid. He was an antique dealer—so that's another of her weaknesses, beautiful old things. Anyway, she adored her dad. Her mother tried to hold the business together, but it must have been rough. They lived up in Connecticut. You can still hear New England in her voice. It's classy."

She lapsed into silence a moment, struggling to push back the worry. "Her mother married again a few years later, sold the business, relocated in D.C. Bailey was fond of the guy. He treated her well, got her interested in gems—that was his area—sent her to college. Her mother died when she was in college—a car accident. It was a rough time for Bailey. Her stepfather died a couple years later."

"It's tough, losing people right and left."

"Yeah." She glanced at Jack, thought of him losing father, brother, mother. Perhaps never really having them to lose. "I've really never lost anyone."

He understood where her mind had gone, and he shrugged. "You get through. You go on. Didn't Bailey?"

"Yeah, but it scarred her. It's got to scar a person, Jack."

"People live with scars."

He wouldn't discuss it, she realized, and turned back to the scenery. "Her stepfather left her a percentage of the business. Which didn't sit well with the creeps."

"Ah, yeah, the creeps."

"Thomas and Timothy Salvini—they're twins, by the way, mirror images. Slick-looking characters in expensive suits, with hundred-dollar haircuts."

"That's one reason to dislike them," Jack noted. "But it's not your main one."

"Nope. I never liked their attitudes—toward Bailey, and women in general. It's easiest to say Bailey considered them family from the get-go, and the sentiment wasn't returned. Timothy was particularly rough on her. I get the impression they mostly ignored her before their old man died, and then went ballistic when she inherited part of Salvini in the will."

"And what's Salvini?"

"That's their name, and the name of the gem business. They design, buy, sell gems and jewelry out of a fancy place in Chevy Chase."

"Salvini... Can't say I've heard of it, but then I don't buy a lot of baubles."

"They sell some awesome glitters—especially the ones Bailey designs. And they do consultant work for estates, museums. That's primarily Bailey's forte, too. Though she loves design work."

"If Bailey does design work and consulting, what do the creeps do?"

"Thomas handles the business end—accounts, sales, takes a lot of trips to check out sources for gems.

Timothy works in the lab when it suits him, and likes to stride around the showroom looking important."

Restless, she reached out to fiddle with the buttons of his stereo and had her fingers slapped. "Hands off."

"Touchy about your toys, aren't you?" she muttered. "Well, anyway, it's a pretty posh little firm, old established rep. It was her contacts at the Smithsonian that copped them the job with the Three Stars. She was dancing on the ceiling when it came through, couldn't wait to get her hands on them, put them under one of those machines she uses. The somethingmeters, and whattayascopes she uses in their lab."

"So she was verifying authenticity, assessing value."

"You got it. She was dying for us to see them, so Grace and I went in last week. That was the first time I'd laid eyes on them—but they seemed almost familiar. Spectacular, almost unreal, yet familiar. I suppose it's because Bailey'd described them to us." She rolled her shoulders to toss off the sensation, and the memory of the dreams. "You've seen the one, touched it. It's magnificent. But to see the three of them, together, it just stops your heart."

"Sounds to me as though they stopped someone's conscience. If Bailey's as honest as you say—"

M.J. interrupted him. "She is."

"Then we'll have to check out the stepbrothers."

Her brows shot up. "Would they actually have the

nerve to try to steal the Three Stars?" she wondered. "Could that be why Ralph was blackmailing one of them, rather than the gambling?"

"No."

"Well, why not?" Then she shook her head, answering her own question. "Couldn't be—the payments started months ago, and they'd just recently got the contract."

"There you go."

She brooded over it a moment longer. "But maybe they were planning to steal the Stars. If they were trying to pull a fast one, got away with it, it would destroy their business…the business their father slaved a lifetime to build," she added slowly. "And that would destroy Bailey. Even the thought of it. She'd do almost anything to prevent that from happening."

"Like ship off the stones to the two people in the world she felt she could trust without question."

"Yeah—and face down her stepbrothers. Alone." Fear was a claw in her throat. "Jack."

"Stay logical." His voice snapped to combat the waver in hers. "If they're involved in this—and I'd say it fits—it means they've got a client, a buyer. And they need all three Stars. She's safe as long as they don't. She's safe as long as we're out of reach."

"They'd be desperate. They could be holding her somewhere. They might have hurt her."

"Hurt's a long way from dead. They'd need her alive, M.J., until they round up all three. And from the rundown you've just given me, your pal may have a fragile side, and she may be naive, but she's not a chump."

"No, she's not." Steadying herself, M.J. looked at the phone in her lap. The call, she realized, wasn't just a risk for herself, but a risk for all of them. "If you want to drive to New York before I use this, it's okay with me."

He reached out, squeezed a hand over hers. "We're not going to Yankee Stadium, no matter how much you beg."

"I don't just owe you for me now. I should have realized it before. I owe you for Bailey, and for Grace. I've put them in your hands, Jack."

He drew his away, clamped it on the wheel. "Don't get sloppy on me, sugar. It pisses me off."

"I love you."

His heart did a long, slow circle in his chest, made him sigh. "Hell. I guess you want me to say it again, now."

"I guess I do."

"I love you. What's the M.J. stand for?"

It made her smile, as he'd hoped it would. "Look, Jack, wild sex and declarations of love are one thing. But I haven't known you long enough for that one."

"Martha Jane. I really think it's Martha Jane."

She made a rude buzzing sound. "Wrong. And that puts you out of this round, sir, better luck next time."

There'd be a birth certificate somewhere, he mused. He knew how to hunt. "Okay, tell me about Grace."

"Grace is a complicated woman. She's utterly, unbelievably beautiful. That's not an exaggeration. I've seen grown men turn into stuttering fools after one flash of her baby blues."

"I'm looking forward to meeting her."

"You'll probably swallow your tongue, but that's all right, I'm not the jealous sort. And it's kind of a kick to watch guys go into instant meltdown around Grace. You flipped through the pictures in my wallet when you searched my purse, didn't you?"

"Yeah, I took a look."

"There's a couple of me with Grace and Bailey in there."

He skimmed his mind back, focused in. And didn't want to tell her he'd barely noted the blonde or the brunette. The redhead had taken most of his attention. "The brunette—wearing a big silly hat in one of them."

"Yeah, that was on our rockhounding trip last year. We had a tourist snap it. Anyway, she's gorgeous, and she grew up privileged. And orphaned. She lost her folks young and lived with an aunt. The Fontaines are filthy rich."

"Fontaine…Fontaine…" His mind circled. "As in Fontaine Department Stores?"

"Right the first time. They're rich, stuffy, snotty

snobs. Grace enjoys shocking them. She was expected to do her stint at Radcliffe, do the obligatory tour of Europe, and land the appropriate rich, stuffy, snotty snob husband. She's done everything but cooperate, and since she's got mountains of money of her own, she doesn't really give two damns what her family thinks."

She paused, considered. "I don't think she'd give two damns if she was flat broke, either. Money doesn't drive Grace. She enjoys it, spends it lavishly, but she doesn't respect it."

"People who work for their money respect it."

"She's not a do-nothing trust-funder." M.J. said, immediately defensive. "She just doesn't care if people see her that way. She does a lot of charity work—quietly. That's private. She's one of the most generous people I know. And she's loyal. She's also contrary and moody. She'll take off for days at a time when the whim strikes her. Just go. It might be Rome—or it might be Duluth. She just has to go. She has a place up in western Maryland—I guess you'd call it a country home, but it's small and sweet. Lots of land, very isolated. No phone, no neighbors. I think she was going there this weekend."

She shut her eyes, tried to image. "I don't know if I could find the place. I've only been up there once, and Bailey did the driving. Once I get out of the city, all those country roads look the same. It's in the mountains, near some state forest."

"It might be worth checking out. We'll see. Would she go to her family if there was trouble?"

"The last place."

"How about a man?"

"Why would you depend on something you could twist into knots with a smile? No, there's no man she'd go to."

He thought about that one awhile, then blinked, remembered and grinned. "Grace Fontaine—the Ivy League Miss April. It was the hat in the wallet shot that threw me off. I'd never forget that… face."

"Really?" Voice dry as dirt, she shifted to look at him over the top of her sunglasses. "Do you spend a lot of your time drooling over centerfolds, Dakota?"

"I did over Miss April," he admitted cheerfully, and rubbed a hand over his heart. "My God, you're pals with Miss April."

"Her name's Grace, and she posed for that years ago, when we were in college. She did it to needle her family."

"Thank the Lord. I think I still have that issue somewhere. I'm going to have to take a much closer look now. What a body," he remembered, fondly. "Women built like that are a gift to mankind."

"Perhaps you'd like to pull over, and we'll have a moment of silence."

He looked over, kept right on grinning. "Gee, M.J.,

your eyes are greener. And you said you weren't the jealous sort."

"I'm not." Normally. "It's a matter of dignity. You're having some revolting, prurient fantasy about my best friend."

"It's not revolting, I promise. Prurient, maybe, but not revolting." He took the punch on the arm without complaint. "But it's you I love, sugar."

"Shut up."

"Do you think she'll sign the picture for me? Maybe right across the—"

"I'm warning you."

Fun was fun, he thought, but a man could push his luck. In more ways than one. He turned off 15, headed east.

"Wait, I thought we were going up to P.A. to call."

"You just said Grace had a place in western Maryland. It wouldn't be smart to head in that general direction just now. Change of plans. We head in toward Baltimore first. Go ahead and make the call. I think we've said our last goodbye to our little motel paradise." He smiled patted her hand. "Don't worry, sugar, we'll find another."

"It couldn't possibly be the same. I hope," she added, and dialed hurriedly. "It's ringing."

"Keep it short, don't say where you are. Just tell her to go to a public phone, public place, and call you back."

"I—" She swore. "It's her machine. I was afraid of

this." She tapped her fist impatiently against her knees as Grace's recorded voice flowed through the receiver. "Grace, pick up, damn it. It's urgent. If you check in for messages, don't go home. Don't go to the house. Get to a public phone and call my portable. We're in trouble, serious trouble."

"Wrap it up, M.J."

"Oh, God. Grace, be careful. Call me." She disconnected with a little catch of breath. "She's up in the mountains—or she got a wild hair and decided to fly to London for the Fourth. Or she's on the beach in the West Indies. Or…they've already found her."

"Doesn't sound like a lady who's easy to track. I'm leaning toward your first choice." He cut off on the interstate, headed north. "We're going to circle around a little, then stop and fill up the tank. And buy a map. Let's see if we can jog some of your memory and find Grace's mountain hideaway."

The prospect settled her nerves. "Thanks."

"Isolated, huh?"

"It's stuck in the middle of the woods, and the woods are stuck in the middle of nowhere."

"Hmm. I don't suppose she walks around naked up there." He chuckled when she hit him. "Just a thought."

They found a gas station, and a map. In a truck stop just off the interstate, they stopped for lunch.

With the map spread out over the table, they got down to business.

"Well, there's only, like, a half a dozen state forests in western Maryland," Jack commented, and forked up some of his meat-loaf special. "Any one of them ring a bell?"

"What's the difference? They're all trees."

"A real urbanite, aren't you?"

She shrugged, bit into her ham sandwich. "Aren't you?"

"Guess so. I never could understand why people want to live in the woods, or in the hills. I mean, where do they eat?"

"At home."

They looked at each other, shook their heads. "Most every night, too," he agreed. "And where do they go for fun, for a little after-work relaxation? On the patio. That's a scary thought."

"No people, no traffic, no restaurants or movie theaters. No life."

"I'm with you. Obviously our pal Grace isn't."

"*My* pal," she said with an arched brow. "She likes solitude. She gardens."

"What, like tomatoes?"

"Yeah, and flowers. The time we went up, she'd been grubbing in the dirt, planting—I don't know, petunias or something. I like flowers, but all you have to do is buy them. Nobody says you have to grow them. There were deer in the woods. That was pretty cool," she remembered. "Bailey got into the whole business. It was okay for a couple days, but she doesn't even have a television up there."

"That's barbaric."

"You bet. She just listens to CDs and communes with nature or whatever. There's a little store—had to be at least four miles away. You can get bread and milk or sixpenny nails. It looked like something out of Mayberry, except that's in the South. There was a bank, I think, and a post office."

"What was the name of the town?"

"I don't know. Dogpatch?"

"Funny. Try to imagine the route, just more or less. You'd have headed up 270."

"Yeah, and then onto 70 near, what is it? Frederick. I zoned out some. Think I even slept. It's an endless drive."

"You had pit stops," he prompted her. "Girls don't take road trips without plenty of pit stops."

"Is that a slam?"

"No, it's a fact. Where'd you stop—what did you do?"

"Somewhere off 70. I was hungry. I wanted fast food."

She shut her eyes, tried to bring it back.

You're still eating like a teenager, M.J.

So?

Why don't we try a salad for a change?

Because a day without fries is a sad and wasted day.

It made her smile, remembering now how Bailey had rolled her eyes, laughed, then given in.

"Oh, wait. We grabbed a quick lunch, but then she saw this sign for antiques. Big antique barnlike place. She went orgasmic, had to check it out. It was off the interstate, had a silly country-type name. Ah…" She strained for it. "Rabbit Hutch, Chicken Coop. No, no, with water. Trout Stream. Beaver Creek!" she remembered. "We stopped to antique at this huge flea market or whatever it's called at Beaver Creek. She'd have spent the weekend there if I hadn't dragged her out. She bought this old bowl and pitcher for Grace—like a housewarming gift. I bought her a rocking chair for her porch. We had a hell of a time loading it in Bailey's car."

"Okay." With a nod, he folded the map. "We'll finish eating, then head toward Beaver Creek. Take it from there."

Later, when they stood in the parking lot of the antique mart, M.J. sipped a soft drink out of a can. She'd done the same on the trip with Bailey, and she hoped it would somehow jog her memory.

"I know we got back on 70. Bailey was chattering away about some glassware—Depression glass. She was going to come back and buy the place out. There was some table she wanted, too, and she was irritated she hadn't snapped it up and had it shipped. I won the tune toss."

"The what?"

"The tune toss. Bailey likes classical. You know, Beethoven. Whenever we drive, we flip a coin to see who gets to pick the tunes. I won, so we went for Aerosmith—my version of longhair."

"I think we're made for each other. It's getting scary." He leaned down, nipped her mouth with his. "What was she wearing?"

"What is this sudden obsession with how my friends dress?"

"Just bring it all back. Complete the picture. The more details, the clearer it should be."

"Oh, I get it." Mollified, she pursed her lips and studied the sky. "Slacks, sort of beige. Bailey shies away from bold colors. Grace is always giving her grief about it. A silk blouse, tailored, sort of pink and pale. She had on these great earrings. She'd made them. Big chunks of rose quartz. I tried them on while she was driving. They didn't suit me."

"Pink wouldn't, not with that hair."

"That's a myth. Redheads can wear pink. We got off the interstate onto a western route. I can't remember the number, Jack. Bailey had it in her head. It was written down, but she didn't need me to navigate."

He consulted the map. "68 heads west out of Hagerstown. Let's see if it looks familiar."

"I know it was another couple hours from here," she said as she climbed back in. "I could drive for a while."

"No, you couldn't."

She skimmed her gaze over the car, noting that the back door was hooked shut with wire. "This heap is hardly something to be proprietary about, Jack."

His jaw set. The heap had, until recently, been his one true love. "There's more chance of you remembering if we stick with the plan."

"Fine." She stretched out her legs as he turned out of the parking lot. "Do you ever think about a paint job?"

"The car has character just the way it is. And it's what's under the hood that counts, not a shiny surface."

"What's under the hood," she said, then glanced at the stereo system. "And in the dash. I bet that toy set you back four grand."

"I like music. What about that Tinkertoy you drive?"

"My MG is a classic."

"It's a kiddie car. You must have to fold up your legs just to get behind the wheel."

"At least when I parallel-park, it's not like docking a steamship in port."

"Pay attention to the road, will you?"

"I am." She offered him the rest of her soft drink.

"I know it looks like it, but you don't actually live in this car, do you?"

"When I have to. Otherwise, I've got a place on Mass Avenue. A couple of rooms."

Dusty furniture, he thought now. Mountains of books, but no real soul. No roots, nothing he couldn't leave behind without a second thought.

Just like his life had been, up to the day before.

What the hell was he doing with her? he thought abruptly. There was nothing behind him that could remotely be called a foundation. Nothing to build on. Nothing to offer.

She had family, friends, a business she'd forged herself. What did they have in common, other than the situation they were in, similar tastes in music and a preference for city life?

And the fact that he was in love with her.

He glanced over at her. She was concentrating now, he noted. Leaning forward in the seat, frowning out the window as she tried to pick out landmarks.

She wasn't beautiful, he thought. He might have been blind in love, but he would never have termed her by so simple a term. That odd, foxy face caught the eye—certainly the male eye. It was sexy, unique, with the contrast of planes and angles and the curve of that overlush mouth.

Her body was built for speed and movement, rather than for fantasy. Yet he'd lost himself in it, in her.

He knew he'd turned a corner when he met her, but hadn't a clue where the road would lead either of them.

"This is the road." She turned, beamed at him, and stopped his heart. "I'm sure of it."

He bumped up the speed to sixty-five. As long as one of them was sure, he thought.

Chapter 9

The road cut straight through the mountain. M.J. supposed it was some sort of nifty feat of engineering, but it made her uneasy. Particularly all the signs warning of falling rock and those high, jagged walls of cliffs on either side of them.

Muggers she could understand, anticipate, but who, she wondered, could anticipate Mother Nature? What was to stop her from having a minor tantrum and perhaps heaving down a couple of boulders at the car? And since it was big enough to sleep eight, it was a dandy target.

M.J. kept a wary eye out of the side window, willing the rocks to stay put until they were through the pass.

Ahead, mountains rose and rolled, lushly green with summer. Heat and humidity merged to make the air thick as syrup. Tires hummed along the highway.

Occasionally she would see houses behind the roadside trees, glimpses only, as if they were hiding from prying eyes. She wondered about them, those tucked-away houses, undoubtedly with neat yards guarded by yapping dogs, decorated with gardens and swing sets, accented with decks and patios for grills and redwood chairs.

It was one way to live, she supposed. But you had to tend that garden, mow that lawn.

She'd never lived in a house. Apartments had always suited her lifestyle. To some, she supposed, an apartment would seem like a box tucked with other boxes within a box. But she'd always been satisfied with her own space, with the camaraderie of being part of the hive.

Why would you need a lawn and a swing set unless you had kids?

She felt a quick little jitter in her stomach at the idea. Had she actually ever thought about having children before? Rocking a baby, watching it grow, tying shoes and wiping noses.

It was Grace who was soft on children, she thought. Not that she herself didn't like them. She had a platoon of cousins who seemed bent on populating the world, and M.J. had spent many an hour on a visit home cooing over a new baby, playing on the floor with a toddler or pitching a ball to a fledgling Little Leaguer.

She didn't imagine it was quite the same when the child was yours. What did it feel like, she mused, to have your own baby rest its head on your shoulder and yawn, or to have a shaky-legged toddler lift its arms up to you to be held?

And what in God's name was she doing thinking about children at a time like this? Weary, she slipped her fingers under her shaded glasses, pressed them to her eyes.

Then slid a considering glance at Jack's profile. What, she wondered, did he think about kids?

Incredibly, she felt heat rising to her cheeks, and turned her face back to the window quickly. Idiot, she told herself. You've known the guy an instant, and you're starting to think of diapers and booties.

That, she thought grimly, was just what happened to a woman when she got herself tied up over some man. She went soft all over, particularly in the head.

Then she let out a shout that surprised them both. "There! That's the exit! That's where we got off. I'm sure of it."

"Next time just shoot me," Jack suggested as he swung the car into the right lane. "It's bound to be less of a shock than a heart attack."

"Sorry."

He eased off the exit, giving her time to orient herself as they came to a two-lane road.

"Left," she said after a moment. "I'm almost sure we went left."

"Okay, I need to gas up this hog, anyway." He headed for the closest service station and pulled up next to the pumps. "What was on your mind back there, M.J.?"

"On my mind?"

"You went away for a while."

The fact that he'd been able to tell disconcerted her. She shifted in the seat, shrugged her shoulders. "I was just concentrating, that's all."

"No, you weren't." He cupped a hand under her chin, turned her face to his. "That's exactly what you weren't doing." He rubbed his thumb over her lips. "Don't worry. We'll find your friends. They're going to be all right."

She nodded, felt a wash of shame. Grace and Bailey should have been on her mind, and instead she'd been daydreaming over babies like some lovesick idiot. "Grace will be at the house. All we have to do is find it."

"Hold that thought." He leaned forward, touched his lips to hers. "And go buy me a candy bar."

"You've got all the dough."

"Oh, yeah." He got out, reached into his front pocket

and pulled out a handful of bills. "Splurge," he suggested, "and buy yourself one, too."

"Gee, thanks, Daddy."

He grinned as she walked away, long legs striding, narrow hips twitching under snug denim. Hell of a package, he mused as he slipped the nozzle into the gas tank. He wasn't going to question the twist of fate that had dropped her into his life, and into his heart.

But he wondered how long it would be before she did. People didn't stay in his life for long—they came and went. It had been that way for so long, he'd stopped expecting it to be different. Maybe he'd stopped wanting it to be.

Still, he knew that if she decided to take a walk, he'd never get over it. So he'd have to make sure she didn't take a walk.

Feeding the greedy tank of the Olds, he watched her come back out, cross to the soft-drink machine. And he wasn't the only one watching, Jack noted. The teenager fueling the rusting pickup at the next pump had an eye on her, too.

Can't blame you, buddy, Jack thought. She's a picture, all right. Maybe you'll grow up lucky and find yourself a woman half as perfect for you.

And blessing his luck, Jack screwed the cap back on his tank, then strolled over to her. She had her hands full of candy and soft drinks when he yanked her against him and covered her mouth in a long, smolder-ing, brain-draining kiss.

Her breath whooshed out when he released her. "What was that for?"

"Because I can," he said simply, and all but swag-gered in to pay his tab.

M.J. shook her head, noted that the teenager was gawking and had overfilled his tank. "I wouldn't light a match, pal," she said as she passed him and climbed into the car.

When Jack joined her, she went with impulse, plunging her hands into his hair and pulling him against her to kiss him in kind.

"That's because I can, too."

"Yeah." He was pretty sure he felt smoke coming out of his ears. "We're a hell of a pair." It took him a moment to clear the lust from his mind and remember how to turn the key.

Both thrilled and amused by his reaction, she held out a chocolate bar. "Candy?"

He grunted, took it, bit in. "Watch the road," he told her. "Try to find something familiar."

"I know we weren't on this road very long," she began. "We turned off and did a lot of snaking around on back roads. Like I said, Bailey had it all in her head. Bailey!" As the idea slammed into her, she pressed her hands to her mouth.

"What is it?"

"I kept asking myself where she would go. If she was in trouble, if she was running, where would she go?" Eyes alight, she whirled to face him. "And the answer is right there. She knows how to get to Grace's place. She loved it there. She'd feel safe there."

"It's a possibility," he agreed.

"No, no, she'd go to one of us for sure." She shook her head fiercely, desperately. "And she couldn't get to me. That means she headed up here, maybe took a bus or a train as far as she could, rented a car." Her heart lightened at the certainty of it. "Yes, it's logical, and just like her. They're both there, up in the woods, sitting there figuring out what to do next and worrying about me."

And so was he worrying about her. She was putting all her hope into a long shot, but he didn't have the heart to say it. "If they are," he said cautiously, "we still have to find them. Think back, try to remember."

"Okay." With new enthusiasm, she scanned the scenery. "It was spring," she mused. "It was pretty. Stuff was blooming—dogwoods, I guess, and that yellow bush that's almost a neon color. And something Bailey called redbuds. There was a garden place," she remembered suddenly. "A whatchamacallit, nursery. Bailey wanted to stop and buy Grace a bush or something. And I said we should get there first and see what she already had."

"So we look for a nursery."

"It had a dopey name." She closed her eyes a moment, struggled to bring it back. "Corny. It was right on the road, and it was packed. That's one of the reasons I didn't want to stop. It would have taken forever. Buds 'N' Blooms." She smacked her hands together as she remembered. "We made a right a mile or so beyond it."

"There you go." He took her hand, lifted it to his mouth to kiss. And had them both frowning at the gesture. He'd never kissed a woman's hand before in his entire life.

Inside M.J.'s stomach, butterflies sprang to life. Clearing her throat, she laid her hand on her lap. "Well, ah… Anyway, Grace and Bailey went back to the plant place. I stayed at her house. Those two get a big bang out of shopping. For anything. I figured they'd buy out the store—which they almost did. They came back loaded with those plastic trays of flowers, and flowers in pots, and a couple of bushes. Grace keeps a pickup at her place. I can imagine what they'd write in the *Post*'s style section about Grace Fontaine driving a pickup truck."

"Would she care?"

"She'd laugh. But she keeps this place to herself. The relatives—that's what she calls her family, the relatives—don't even know about it."

"I'd say that's to our favor. The less people who know about it, the better." His lips curved as he noted a sign. "There's your garden spot, sugar. Business is pretty good, even this late in the year."

Delight zinged through her as she spotted the line of cars and trucks pulled to the side of the road, the crowds of people wandering around tables covered with flowers. "I bet they're having a holiday sale. Ten percent off any red, white or blue posies."

"God bless America. About a mile, you said?"

"Yeah, and it was a right. I'm sure of that."

"Don't you like flowers?"

"Huh?" Distracted, she glanced at him. "Sure, they're okay. I like ones that smell. You know, like those things, those carnations. They don't smell like sissies, and they don't wimp out on you after a couple days, either."

He chuckled. "Muscle flowers. Is this the turn?"

"No...I don't think so. A little farther." Leaning forward, she tapped her fingers on the dash. "This is it, coming up. I'm almost sure."

He downshifted, bore right. The road rose and curved. Beside it fences were being slowly smothered by honeysuckle, and behind them cows grazed.

"I think this is right." She gnawed on her lip. "All the damn roads back here look the same. Fields and rocks and trees. How do people find where they're going?"

"Did you stay on this road?"

"No, she turned again." Right or left? M.J. asked herself. Right or left? "We kept heading deeper into the boonies, and climbing. Maybe here."

He slowed, let her consider. The crossroads was narrow, cornered on one side by a stone house. A dog napped in the yard under the shade of a dying maple. Concrete ducks paddled over the grass.

"This could be it, to the left. I'm sorry, Jack, it's hazy."

"Look, we've got a full tank of gas and plenty of daylight. Don't sweat it."

He took the left, cruised along the curving road that climbed and dipped. The houses were spread out now, and the fields were crammed with corn high as a man's waist. Where fields stopped, woods took over, growing thick and green, arching their limbs over the road so that it was a shady tunnel for the car to thread through.

They came to the rise of a hill, and the world opened up. A dramatic and sudden spread of green mountains, and land that rolled beneath them.

"Yes. Bailey almost wrecked the car when we topped this hill. If it is this hill," she added. "I think that's part of the state forest. She was dazzled by it. But we turned off again. One of these little roads that winds through the trees."

"You're doing fine. Tell me which one you want to try."

"At this point, your guess is as good as mine." She felt helpless, stupid. "It just looks different now. The trees are all thick. They just had that green haze on them when we came through."

"We'll give this one a shot," he decided, and, flipping a mental coin, turned right.

It took only ten minutes for them to admit they were lost, and another ten to find their way out and onto a main road. They drove through a small town M.J. had no recollection of, then backtracked.

After an hour of wandering, M.J. felt her patience fraying. "How can you stay so calm?" she asked him. "I swear we've fumbled along every excuse for a road within fifty miles. Every street, lane and cow path. I'm going crazy."

"My line of work takes patience. I ever tell you about tracking down Big Bill Bristol?"

She shifted in her seat, certain she'd never feel sensation in her bottom again. "No, you never told me about tracking down Big Bill Bristol. Are you going to make this up?"

"Don't have to." To give them both a breather, he swung off the road. There was a small pulloff beside what he supposed could be called a swimming hole. Trees overhung dark water and let little splashes of sun hit the surface and bounce back. "Big Bill was up on assault. Lost his temper over a hand of seven-card stud and tried to feed the pot to his opponent. That was after he broke his nose and knocked the guy out. Big Bill is about six-five, two-eighty, and has hands the size of Minneapolis. He doesn't like to lose. I know this for a fact, as I have spent the occasional evening playing games of chance with Big Bill."

M.J. smiled winningly. "Gosh, Jack, I just can't wait to meet your friends."

Recognizing sarcasm when it was aimed at him, he merely slanted her a look. "In any case, Ralph fronted his bond, but Big Bill found out about a floating game in Jersey and didn't want to miss out. The law frowns, not only on floating games, but on bail-jumping, and his bail was revoked. Bill was on the skip list."

"And you went after him."

"Well, I did." Jack rubbed his chin, thought fleetingly about shaving. "It should have been cut-and-dried. Find the game, remind Bill he had to have his day in court, bring him back. But it seemed Bill had won large quantities of money in Jersey, and had moved on to another game. I should add that Bill is big, but not in the brain department. And he was on a hot streak, moving from game to game, state to state."

"With Jack Dakota, bounty hunter, hot on his trail."

"On his trail, anyway. A lot of it his back trail. If the jerk had planned to lose me, he couldn't have done a better job. I crisscrossed the Northeast, hit every game."

"How much did you lose?"

"Not enough to talk about." He answered her grin. "I got into Pittsburgh about midnight. I knew there was a game, but I couldn't bribe or threaten the location out of anyone. I'd been on Bill's trail for four days, living out of my car and playing poker with guys named Bats and Fast Charlie. I was tired, dirty, down to my last hundred in cash. I walked into a bar."

"Of course you did."

"I'm telling the story," he said, tugging her hair. "Picked it at random, no thought, no plan. And guess who was in the back room, holding a pair of bullets and bumping the pot?"

"Let's see…. Could it have been…Big Bill Bristol?"

"In the flesh. Patience and logic had gotten me to Pittsburgh, but it was instinct that had me walking into that game."

"How'd you get him to go back with you?"

"There I had a choice. I considered hitting him over the head with a chair. But more than likely that would have just annoyed him. I thought about appealing to his good nature, reminding him he owed Ralph. But he was still on that hot streak, and wouldn't have given a damn. So I had a drink, joined the game. After a couple of hours, I explained the situation to Bill, and appealed to him on his own level. One cut of the cards. I draw high, he comes back with me, no hassle. He draws high, I walk away."

"And you drew high?"

"Yeah, I did." He scratched his chin again. "Of course, I'd palmed an ace, but like I said, brains weren't Big Bill's strong suit."

"You cheated?"

"Sure. It was the clearest route through the situation, and everybody ended up happy."

"Except Big Bill."

"No, him, too. He'd had a nice run, had enough of the ready to pay off the guy whose skull he'd cracked. Charges dropped. No sweat."

She cocked her head. "And what would you have done if he'd decided to welsh and not go back with you peacefully?"

"I'd have broken the chair over his head, and hoped to live through it."

"Quite a life you lead, Jack."

"I like it. And the moral of the story is, you just keep looking, follow logic. And when logic peters out, you go with instinct." So saying, he reached into his pocket, drew out the stone. "The second stone is knowledge." His eyes met hers. "What do you know, M.J.?"

"I don't understand."

"You know your friends. You know them better than I know Big Bill, or anyone else, for that matter." He could come to envy her that, he realized. And would think on it more closely later. "They're part of what you were, who you are, and, I guess, who you will be."

Her chest went tight. "You're getting philosophical on me, Dakota."

"Sometimes that works, too. Trust your instincts, M.J." He took her hand, closed it over the stone. "Trust what you know."

Her nerves were suddenly on the surface of her skin, chilling it. "You expect me to use this thing like some sort of compass? Divining rod?"

"You feel that, don't you?" It was a shock to him, as well, but his hands stayed steady, his eyes remained on hers. "It's all but breathing. You know the thing about myths? If you reach down deep enough inside them, you pull out truth. The second stone is knowledge." He shifted back, put his hands on the wheel. "Which way do you want to go?"

She was cold, shudderingly cold. Yet the stone was like a sun burning in her hand. "West." She heard herself say it, knew it was odd for a city woman to use the direction, rather than simply right or left. "This is crazy."

"We left sanity behind yesterday. No use trying to find that back trail. Just tell me which way you want to go. Which way feels right."

So she held the stone gripped in her hand and directed him through the winding roads sided with trees and outcroppings of rock. Along a meandering stream that trickled low from lack of rain, past a little brown house so close that its door all but opened into the road.

"On the right," M.J. said, through a throat dust-dry and tight as a drum. "You have to watch for it. We passed it, had to double back. Her lane's narrow, just a cut through the woods. You can barely see it. She doesn't have a mailbox. She goes into town and picks it up when she's here. There." her hand trembled a bit as she pointed. "Just there."

He turned in. The lane was indeed narrow. Branches skimmed and scraped along the sides of the car as he drove slowly up, over gravel, around a curve that was sheltered by more trees.

And there, in the center of the lane, still as a stone statue, stood a deer with a pelt that glowed dark gold in the flash of sun.

It should be a white hind, Jack thought foolishly. A white hind is the symbol of a quest.

The doe watched the lumbering approach, her head up, her eyes wide and fixed. Then, with a flick of the tail, a quick spin of that gorgeous body, she leaped into the trees on thin, graceful legs. And was gone with barely a rustle.

The house was exactly as M.J. remembered. Tucked back on the hill, above a small, bubbling creek, it was a neat two stories that blended into the backdrop of woods. It was wood and glass, simple lines, with a long front porch painted a bold blue. Two white rockers sat on it, along with copper pots overflowing with trailing flowers.

"She's been busy," M.J. murmured, scanning the gardens. Flowers bloomed everywhere, wildly, as if unplanned. The flow of colors and shapes tumbled down the hill like a river. Wide wooden steps cut through the color, meandered to the left, then marched down to the lane.

"At the house in Potomac she hired a professional landscaper. She knew just what she wanted, but she had someone else do it. Here, she wanted to do everything herself."

"It looks like a fairy tale." He shifted, uncomfortable with his own impressions. He wasn't exactly up on his fairy tales. "You know what I mean."

"Yeah."

A shiny blue pickup truck was parked at the end of the lane. But there was no sign of the car Grace would have driven to her country home. No dusty rental car announcing Bailey's presence.

They've just gone to the store, M.J. told herself. They'll be back any minute.

She wouldn't believe they'd come this far, found the house, and not found Grace and Bailey.

The minute Jack pulled up beside the truck, she was out and dashing toward the house.

"Hold it." He gripped her arm, skidded her to a halt. "Let's get the lay of the land here." Gently he uncurled her fingers, took the stone. When it was tucked back in his pocket, he took her hand. "You said she leaves the truck here?"

"Yes. She drives a Mercedes convertible, or a little Beemer."

"Your pal has three rides?"

"Grace rarely owns one of anything. She claims she doesn't know what she's going to be in the mood for."

"There's a back door?"

"Yeah, one out the kitchen, and another on the side." She gestured to the right, fought to ignore the weight pressing against her chest. "It leads onto a little patio and into the woods."

"Let's look around first."

There was a gardening shed, neatly filled with tools, a lawn mower, rakes and shovels. Where the lawn gave way, stepping-stones had been set, with springy moss growing between. More flowers—a raised bed with blooms and greenery spilling over the dark wall, and the cliff behind growing with ivy.

A hummingbird hovered at a bright red feeder, its iridescent wings blurred with speed. It darted off like a bullet at their approach, its whirl the only sound.

He spotted no broken windows or other signs of forced entry as they circled around the back, passed an herb garden fragrant with scents of rosemary and mint. Brass wind chimes hung silently near the rear door. Not a leaf stirred.

"It's creepy." She rubbed her arm. "Skulking around like this."

"Let's just skulk another minute."

They came around the far side with the little patio. There, a glass table, a padded chaise, more flowers in concrete troughs and clay pots. Just beyond was a small pond with young ornamental grasses.

"That's new." M.J. paused to study. "She didn't have that before. She talked about it, though. It looks fresh."

"I'd say your pal's done some planting this week. You think there's a plant or flower in existence she's missed?"

"Probably not." But M.J.'s smile was weak as they came back around to the front. "I want to go in, Jack. I have to go in."

"Let's take a look." He climbed the porch steps, found the front door locked. "She got a hidey-hole for a key?"

"No." Despite the miserable heat, she rubbed her hands over her chilled arms. Too quiet, was all she could think. It was much too quiet. "She used to keep an extra for the Potomac house, in this flowerpot outside the door, but her cousin Melissa found it and made herself at home while Grace was in Milan. Really ticked her off."

He crouched, examined the locks. "She's got good ones. Simpler to break a window."

"You're not breaking one of her windows."

He sighed, rose. "I was afraid you'd say that. Okay, we do it the hard way."

While she frowned, he went back to his car, popped the trunk. Inside, it was loaded with tools, clothes, books, water jugs and paperwork. He pushed around, selected what he needed.

"Does she have an alarm system?"

"No. Not that I know of, anyway." M.J. studied the leather pouch. "What are you going to do?"

"Pop the locks. It may take a while, I'm rusty." But he rubbed his hands together, anticipating the challenge. "You could go around, check the other doors and windows, just in case she left something unlocked."

"If she locked one, she locked them all. But okay."

She circled around again, pausing at each window, tugging, then peering in. By the time she'd made a complete circuit, Jack was on the second lock.

Intrigued, she watched him finesse it. It was cooler here than in the city, but the heat was still nasty. Sweat dampened his shirt, gleamed on his throat.

"Can you teach me to do that?" she asked him.

"Ssh!" He wiped his hands on his jeans, took a firmer hold on his pick. "Got it." He stood, swiped an arm over his brow. "Cold shower," he murmured. "Cold beer. I'll kiss your pal's feet if she's got both."

"Grace doesn't drink beer." But M.J. was pushing in the door ahead of him.

The living area was homey, tidy but still lived-in, with its wide striped sofa, the deep chairs that picked up the rich blue tones. In the brick fireplace, a lush green fern rose out of a brass spittoon.

M.J. moved quickly through the rooms, over wide-planked chestnut floors and Berber rugs, into the sunny kitchen, with its forest green counters and white tiles, through to the cozy parlor Grace had turned into a library.

The house seemed to echo around her, as she raced upstairs, looked in the bedrooms, the baths.

Grace's gleaming brass bed was tidily made, the handmade lace spread she'd purchased in Ireland accented with rich dots of colorful pillows. A book on gardening lay on the nightstand.

The bathroom was empty, the ivory shell of the sink scrubbed clean and shining in its powder blue counter. Towels were neatly folded on the shelves on a tall wicker stand.

Knowing it was useless, she looked in the bedroom closet. It was ridiculously full and ruthlessly organized.

"They're not here, M.J." Jack touched her shoulder, but she jerked away.

"I can see that, can't I?" Her voice snapped out, broke like a rigid twig. "But Grace was here. She was just here. I can still smell her." She closed her eyes, drew in the air. "Her perfume. It hasn't faded yet. That's her scent. Some fragrance tycoon who fell for her had it designed for her. I can smell her in here."

"Okay." He caught the scent himself, classy sex with wild undertones. "Maybe she ran into town for supplies, or took a drive."

"No." She walked away from him, toward the window as she spoke. "She wouldn't have locked the house up for that. She always says how lovely it is not to worry about locking up out here. She only does when she closes the place up and heads somewhere else. Bailey isn't here. Grace isn't here, and she's not planning on coming back for a while. We've missed her."

"Back to Potomac?"

She shook her head. The tightness in her chest was unbearable, as if greedy hands were squeezing her heart and lungs. "Not likely. She'd avoid the city on the Fourth. Too much traffic, too many tourists. That's why I was sure she'd stay through until tomorrow at least. She could be anywhere."

"Which means she'll surface somewhere." He started toward her, caught the gleam on her cheek and stopped dead, like a man who'd run facefirst into a glass wall. "What are you doing? Are you crying?" It was an accusation, delivered in a voice edged with abject terror.

M.J. merely wrapped her arms over her chest and

hugged her elbows. All the excitement, the tension, the frustration, of the search fell away into sheer despair.

The house was empty.

"I want you to stop that. Right now. I mean it. Sniveling isn't going to do you any good." And it certainly wasn't going to do him any good. It terrified him, left him feeling stupid, clumsy and annoyed.

"Just leave me alone," she said, and her voice broke on a muffled sob. "Just go away."

"That's just what I'm going to do. You keep that up, and I'm walking. I mean it. I'm not standing around and watching you blubber. Get a grip on yourself. Haven't you got any pride?"

At the moment, pride was low on her list. Giving up, she pressed her brow to the window glass and let the tears fall.

"I'm walking, M.J." He snarled at her and turned for the door. "I'm getting a drink and a shower. So when you've got yourself in order, we'll figure out what to do next."

"Then go. Just go."

He made it as far as the threshold, then, swearing ripely, whirled back. "I don't need this," he muttered.

He hadn't a clue how to handle a woman's tears, particularly those from a strong woman who was obviously at the end of her endurance. He cursed her again as he turned her into his arms, folded her into them. He continued to swear at her as he picked her up, sat with her in a wide-backed chair.

He rocked and cursed and stroked.

"Get it over with, then." Kissed her temple. "Please. You're killing me."

"I'm afraid." Her breath hitched as she turned her face into his shoulder. His strong, broad shoulder. "I'm so tired and afraid."

"I know." He kissed her hair, held her closer. "I know."

"I couldn't stand for anything to happen to them. I just can't bear it."

"Don't." He tightened his grip, as if he could strangle off those hot, terrifying tears. But his mouth skimmed up her cheek, found hers, and was tender. "It's going to be all right. Everything's going to be all right." He brushed at her tears clumsily with his thumbs. "I promise."

Eyes brimming, she stared into his. "I was just so sure they'd be here."

"I know." He brushed the hair back from her face. "You've got a right to break down. I don't know anyone else who'd have made it this far without a blowout. But don't cry anymore, M.J. It rips me up."

"I hate to cry." She sniffled, knuckled tears away.

"I'm glad to hear it." He took her hands, kissed them both this time, without that moment of surprise. "Think about this. She was here today, maybe as little as an hour ago. She's tidied up, locked up. Which means she was just fine when she left."

She let out an unsteady breath, drew in another. "You're right. I'm not thinking straight."

"That's because you need a break. A decent meal, a little rest."

"Yeah." But she laid her head against his shoulder again. "Can we just sit here for a little while. Just sit like this?"

"Sure." It was easy to wrap his arms around her, hold her close. And just sit.

Chapter 10

He told her it didn't make sense to drive back to the city, fight the traffic generated by fireworks fans. Not when they had a perfectly good place to stay the night.

The fact was, he thought, if she'd broken down once, she could easily do so again. And a decent meal, along with a decent night's sleep, might shore up some holes in her composure.

In any case, they'd been in the car for more than five hours that day already, after little more than an hour's sleep. Driving straight back was bound to make them both feel as though the effort to find Grace's house had been wasted.

And he wanted time to work on a plan that was beginning to form in his mind.

"Take a shower," he told her. "Borrow a shirt or something from your pal. You'll feel better."

"It couldn't hurt." She managed a smile. "I thought you wanted a shower? Don't you want to conserve water?"

"Well…" It was tempting. He could envision himself getting under a cool spray with her, lathering up—lathering her up—and letting nature take its very interesting course.

And it also occurred to him that she hadn't had five full minutes of privacy in hours. It was about all he had the power to give her at the moment.

"I'm going to hunt up a drink. See if your friend has some cans around here I can open." He kissed the tip of her nose affectionately. "Go ahead and get started without me."

"Okay, you can hunt me up a drink while you're at it, but you're not going to find any beer in the fridge. And God knows what she's got in cans around here."

M.J. headed for the bath, stopped, turned. "Jack? Thanks for letting me get it out."

He tucked his hands in his pockets. Her eyes, those exotically tilted cat's eyes, were still swollen from weeping, and her cheeks were pale with fatigue. "I guess you needed to."

"I did, and you didn't make me feel like too much of a jerk. So thanks," she said again, and stepped into the bath.

She stripped gratefully, all put peeling cotton and denim away from her clammy, overheated skin. The simple style Grace had chosen for the rest of the house didn't follow through to the master bath. This was pure self-indulgence.

The tiles were soft blue and misty green, so that it was like stepping into a cool seaside glade. The tub was an oversize lake of white, fueled with water jets and framed by a wide lip where more ferns grew lushly in biscuit-toned pots.

The acre of counter boasted a cutout for a vanity stool and held a brass makeup mirror. Overhead was a garden of tulip-shaped lights of frosted glass. Doors holding linens and sheet-size towels were mirrored, tossing the room back and giving the illusion of enormous, luxurious space.

Though M.J. briefly considered the tub, and the bubbling jets, she stepped instead toward the wavy glass block of the shower enclosure. Her showerheads were set in three sides at varying levels. With a need for pampering, M.J. turned them all on full, then, after one enormous sigh, helped herself to some of Grace's pricey soap and shampoo.

And the fragrance made her weepy again. It was so Grace.

But she refused to cry, already regretted her earlier tears. They helped nothing. Practicalities did, she reminded herself. A shower, a meal, a respite from activity for a brief time, would all serve to clear the brain. Undoubtedly, she needed a few hours' sleep to recharge. It wasn't just the crying jag that made her feel woozy and weak, she imagined.

Something had to be done, some move had to be made, and quickly. To make it, she needed to be sharp and to be ready.

It hardly mattered that it hadn't been much more than a day that had passed. Every hour she lived through without being able to contact either Bailey or Grace was one short, tense lifetime.

Things had to be settled, her world had to be set right again. And then she would have to face whatever was happening, and whatever would happen, between her and Jack.

She was in love with him, there was no doubt of that. The speed with which she'd fallen only increased the intensity of the emotion. She'd never felt for any man what she felt for him—this emotion that cut clean through the bone. And melded with the feeling of passion, which she could have dismissed, was a sense of absolute trust, an odd and deep affection, a prideful respect, and the certainty that she could pass the years of her life with him—if not in harmony, in contentment.

She understood him, she realized as she held her face under the highest spray. She doubted he knew that, but it was absolutely true. She understood his loneliness, his scarred-over pain, and his pride in his own skills.

He had kindness and cynicism, patience and impulse. He had a questing intellect, a touch of the poet— and more than a touch of the nonconformist. He lived his own way, making his own rules and breaking them when he chose.

She would have wanted no less in a life partner.

And that was what worried her. Finding herself thinking of marriage, permanence and making a family with a man who so obviously ran from all three, and had run from them most of his life.

But perhaps, since those concepts had bloomed so recently in her, she could nip them in the bud. She had a business of her own, a life of her own. Wanting Jack to be a part of that didn't have to change the basic order of things.

She hoped.

She switched off the showerheads, toweled off and, because it was there, slathered on some of Grace's silky body cream. And felt nearly human again. Rubbing a towel over her hair, she padded naked into the bedroom to raid the closet.

At least in the country Grace's choice of attire ran toward the simple. M.J. slipped on a short-sleeved shirt of minute white-and-blue checks and found a pair of cotton shorts in the bureau. They bagged a little. Grace was still built like the centerfold she'd once been, and M.J. had no hips to speak of. They also ran short, as M.J. had several inches more leg than her friend.

But they were cool, and when she slid them on she stopped feeling like a woman who'd been living in her clothes for two days.

She started to toss the towel aside, then rolled her eyes when she thought of how Grace would react to that. Fastidiously she went back to the bath and draped it over the shower. Then, in bare feet, her hair still damp and curling around her face, she went in search of Jack.

"I not only started without you," she said when she found him in the kitchen, "I finished without you. You're slow, Dakota."

Still frowning at the small jar in his hand, he turned. "All I found was…" And trailed off, staggered.

He'd told himself she wasn't beautiful, and that was true. But she was striking. The impact of her slammed into him anew, those sharp, sexy looks, the long, long legs set off by tiny blue shorts. She had her thumbs tucked in the front pockets of them, a half-cocked grin on her face, and her hair was dark and damp and curling foolishly over her ears.

His mouth simply watered.

"You clean up good, sugar."

"It's hard not to, in that fancy shower of Grace's. Wait till you get a load of it." She angled her head as a nice flush of heat began to work up from her toes. "I don't know why you're looking at me like that, Jack. You've seen me naked."

"Yeah. Maybe I've got a weakness for long women in little shorts." He lifted a brow. "Did you borrow any of her underwear?"

"No. Some things even close friends don't share. Men and underwear being the top two."

He set the jar down. "In that case—"

She shot a hand up, slapped in on his chest. "I don't think so, pal. You don't exactly smell like roses at the moment. And besides, I'm hungry."

"The woman gets cleaned up, she gets picky." But he ran a hand over his chin again, reminded himself to get his shaving kit out of the trunk this time. "There's not a hell of a lot to choose from around here. She's got fancy French bubbly in the fridge, more fancy French wine in a rack in the closet over there. Some crackers in tins, some pasta in glass jars. I found some tomato paste, which I guess is embryonic spaghetti sauce."

"Does that mean one of us has to cook?"

"I'm afraid it does."

They considered each other for ten full seconds.

"Okay," he decided. "We flip for it."

"Fair enough. Heads, you cook," she said as he dug out a quarter. "Tails, I cook. Either way, I have a feeling we'll be looking for her antacid."

She hissed when the quarter turned up tails. "Isn't there anything else? Something we can just eat out of a can or jar?"

"You cook," he said, but held out a jar. "And there's fish eggs."

She blew out a breath as she studied the jar of beluga. "You don't like caviar?"

"Give me a trout, fry it up, and that's dandy. What the hell do I want to eat eggs that some fish has laid?" But he tossed her the jar. "Help yourself. I'll go clean up while you do something with that tomato paste."

"You probably won't like it," she said darkly, but dug out a pan as he wandered off.

Thirty minutes later, he wandered in again. His hair was slicked back, his face clean-shaven. The smells coming from the simmering pan weren't half-bad, he decided. The kitchen door was open, and there was M.J., sitting out on the patio, cramming a caviar-loaded cracker in her mouth.

"Not too bad," she said over it when she saw him. "You just pretend it's something else, then wash it down with this." She sipped champagne, shrugged. "Grace goes for this stuff. Always did. It was the way she was raised."

"Environment can twist a person," he agreed, then opened his mouth and let M.J. ram a cracker in. He grimaced, snagged her glass and downed it. "A hot dog and a nice dark beer."

She sighed, perfectly in tune with him. "Yeah, well, beggars can't be choosers, pal. It's nice out here. Cooled off some. But you know the trouble? You just can't hear anything. No traffic, no voices, no movement. It kind of creeps me out."

"People that live in places like this don't really like being around other people." He was hungry enough to load up a cracker for himself. "You and me, M.J., we're social animals. We're at our best in a crowded room."

"Yeah, that's why I work the pub most nights. I like the busy hours." She brooded, looking off to where the sun was sinking fast behind the trees. "Tonight would be slow. Sunday, holiday. Everybody'll be wondering where I am. I've got a good head waitress, though. She'll handle it."

She shifted restlessly, reached for her glass. "I guess the cops have gone by, talked to her and my bartenders, some of the regulars. They'll be worried."

"It won't take much longer." He'd been working on

refining his plan, looking for the pitfalls. "Your pub'll run a few days without you. You take vacations, right?"

"A couple weeks here and there."

"It's supposed to be Paris next."

She was surprised he remembered. "That's the plan. Have you ever been there?"

"No, have you?

"Nope. We went to Ireland when I was a kid, and my father got all misty-eyed and sentimental. He grew up on the West Side of Manhattan, but you'd have thought he'd been born and bred in Dublin and had been wrenched away by Gypsies. Other than that, I've never been out of the States."

"I've been up to Canada, down to Mexico, but I've never flown over the ocean." He smiled and took the glass from her again. "I think your sauce is burning, sugar."

She swore, shot up and scrambled inside. While she muttered, he eyed the level of the bottle. Normally he wouldn't have recommended alcohol as a tranquilizer, but these were desperate times. He'd seen that misery come into her eyes when he mentioned Paris—and reminded her of her friends.

For a few hours, for this one night, he was going to make her forget.

"I caught it in time," she told him, dragging her hair back as she stepped out again. "And I put on the water for the pasta. I don't know how long that sauce is supposed to cook—probably for three days, but we're eating it rare."

He grinned, handed her the glass he'd just topped off. "Fine with me. There was another bottle of this chilling, right?"

"Yeah, I get it for her by the case. My distributor just loves it." She knocked some back, chuckled into the exquisite bubbles. "I can imagine what my customers would say if I put Brother Dom on the menu."

"I'm getting used to it." He rose, skimmed a hand over her hair. "I'm going to put some music on. Too damn quiet around here."

"Good idea." With a considering look, she glanced over her shoulder. "You know, I think Grace said they have, like, bears and things up here."

He looked dubiously into the woods. "Guess I'll get my gun, too."

He got more than that. To her surprise, he brought candles into the kitchen, turned the stereo on low and found a station that played blues. He stuck a pink flower that more or less resembled a carnation to him behind her ear.

"Yeah, I guess redheads can wear pink," he decided after a smiling study. "You look cute."

Blowing her hair out of her eyes, she drained the pasta. "What's this? A romantic streak?"

"I've got one I keep in reserve." And while her hands were full, he leaned in and nuzzled the back of her neck. "Does that bother you?"

"No." She angled her head, enjoying the leaping thrill up her spine. "But to complete the mood, you're going to have to eat this and pretend it's good." She frowned a little when he retrieved another bottle of champagne from the refrigerator. "Do you know what that costs a bottle, ace? Even wholesale?"

"Beggars can't be choosers," he reminded her, and popped the cork.

As meals went, they'd both had better—and worse. The pasta was only slightly overdone, the sauce was bland but inoffensive. And, being ravenous, they dipped into second helpings without complaint.

He made certain he steered the conversation away from anything that worried her.

"Probably should have used some of those herbs she's got growing out there," M.J. considered. "But I don't know what's what."

"It's fine." He took her hand, pressed a kiss to the palm, and made her blink. "How are you feeling?"

"Better." She picked up her glass. "Full."

Nerves? Funny, he thought, she hadn't shown nerves when he handcuffed her, or when he drove like a madman through the streets of Washington with potential killers on their tail.

But nuzzle her hand and she looked edgy as a virgin bride on her wedding night. He wondered just how much more nervous he could make her.

"I like looking at you," he murmured.

She sipped hastily, set the glass down, picked it up again. "You've been looking at me for two days."

"Not in candlelight." He filled her glass again. "It puts fire in your hair. In your eyes. Star fire." He smiled slowly, held the glass out to her. "What's that line? 'Fair as a star, when only one is shining in the sky.'"

"Yeah." She gulped wine, felt it fizz in her throat. "I think that's it."

"You're the only one, M.J." He pushed the plates aside so that he could nibble on her fingers. "Your hand's trembling."

"It is not." Her heart was, but she tugged her hand free, just in case he was right. She drank again, then narrowed her eyes. "Are you trying to get me drunk, Dakota?"

His smile was slow, confident. "Relaxed. And you were relaxed, M.J. Before I started to seduce you."

A hot ball of need lodged in the pit of her stomach. "Is that what you call it?"

"You're ripe for seducing." He turned her hand over, grazed his teeth over the inside of her wrist. "Your head's swimming with wine, your pulse is unsteady. If you were to stand right now, your legs would be weak."

She didn't have to stand for them to be weak. Even

sitting, her knees were shaking. "I don't need to be seduced. You know that."

"What I know is that I'm going to enjoy it. I want you trembling, and weak, and mine."

She was afraid she already was, and pulled back, unnerved. "This is silly. If you want to go to bed—"

"We'll get there. Eventually." He rose, drew her to her feet, then slid his hands in one long, possessive stroke down the sides of her body. Then back up. "You're worried about what I can do to you."

"You don't worry me."

"Yes, I do." He eased her against him, kept his mouth hovering over hers a moment, then lowered it to nip lightly at her jaw. "Just now I worry you a lot."

Her breath was thick, unsteady. "Cook a man one meal and he gets delusions of grandeur." And when he chuckled, his breath warm on her cheek, she shivered. "Kiss me, Jack." Her mouth turned, seeking his. "Just kiss me."

"You're not afraid of the fire." He evaded her lips, heard her moan as his mouth skimmed her throat. "But the warmth unnerves you. You can have both." His lips brushed hers, retreated. "Tonight, we'll have both. There won't be any choice."

The wine was swimming in her head, just as he'd said. In sparkling circles. She was trembling, just as he'd said. In quick, helpless quivers.

And she was weak, just as he'd said.

Even as she strained for the fire, the flash danced out of her reach. There was only the warmth, enervating, sweet, drugging. Her breath caught, then released in a rush when he lifted her.

"Why are you doing this?"

"Because you need it," he murmured. "And so do I."

He heated her skin with nibbling kisses as he carried her from the room. Filled his head with the scent that was foreign to both of them and only added to the mystery.

The house was dark, empty, with the silvery shower of moonlight guiding his path up the steps. He laid her on the bed, covered her with his body. And finally, finally, lowered his mouth to hers.

Her limbs went weak as the kiss drained her, sent her floating. She struggled once, tried to find level ground. But he deepened the kiss so slowly, so cleverly, so tenderly, she simply slid into the velvet trap he'd already laid for her.

She murmured his name, heard the echo of it whisper through her head. And surrendered.

He felt the change, that soft and complete yielding. The gift of it was powerfully arousing, sent dark ripples of delight dancing through his blood. Even as his desire quickened, his mouth slipped down to gently explore the pulse that beat so hard and thick in the hollow of her throat.

"Let go," he said quietly. "Just let go of everything, and let me take you."

His hands were gentle on her, skimming and tracing those curves and angles. This, he thought, makes her sigh. And that makes her moan. As if their time were endless, he tutored himself in the pleasures of her. The strong curve of her shoulder, the long muscles of her thigh, the surprisingly fragile line of her throat.

He undressed her slowly, pressing his lips to the hands that reached for him until they went limp again.

He left her nothing to hold on to but trust. Gave her nothing to experience but pleasure. Tenderness destroyed her, until her world was whittled down to the slowly rising storm inside her own body.

The fire was there, that flash of lightning and outrageous heat, the whip of wind and roll of power. But he held it off with clever hands and patient mouth, easing her along the path he'd chosen for them.

He turned her over, and those hands stroked the muscles in her shoulders and turned them to liquid. That mouth traced kisses down her spine and made her quake even as her mind went misty.

She could hear the rustle of the sheets as he moved over her, hear the whisper of his promises, feel the warm glow of promises kept.

And from outside, in the deepening night, came the long haunting call of an owl.

No part of her body was ignored. No aspect of seduction forgotten. She lay helpless beneath him, open to any demand. And when demand finally came, her moan was long, throaty, the response of her body instant and full.

He buried his face between her breasts, fighting back the urge to rush, now that he'd brought her so luxuriously to the peak.

"I want more of you," he murmured. "I want all of you. I want everything."

He closed his mouth over her breast until she moved under him again, until her breath was nothing but feverish little pants. When her voice broke on his name, he slipped inside her, filled her slowly.

Teetering on a new brink, she arched toward him. Her eyes locked on his as they linked hands. There was only his face in the moonlight, dark eyes, firm mouth, the rich flow of hair threaded with gold.

Swept by a rushing tide of love, she smiled up at him. "Take more of me." She felt his fingers tremble in hers. "Take all of me." Saw the flash that was both triumph and need in his eyes. "Take everything."

The fire reached out for both of them.

While she slept, he held her close against him and worked out the final points of his plan. It had as much chance of working, he'd decided, as it did of blowing up in his face.

Even odds weren't such a bad deal.

He'd have risked much worse for her, much more to prevent those tears from slipping down her cheeks again. He'd waited thirty years to fall, which, he concluded, was why he'd fallen so hard, and so fast.

Unless he wanted to take the more mystical route and believe it was all simply fated—the timing, the stone, M.J. Either way, he'd come to the same place. She was the first and only person he'd ever loved, and there was nothing he wouldn't do to protect her.

Even if it meant breaking her trust.

If this was the last time he'd lie beside her, he could hardly complain. She'd given him more in two days than he'd had in his entire life.

She loved him, and that answered all the questions.

As Jack lay in the deep country dark, contemplating his life, wondering about his future, another sat in a room washed with light. His day had been full, and now he was weary. But his mind wouldn't shut off, and he couldn't afford the fatigue.

He had watched fireworks streak across the sky. He had smiled, conversed, sipped fine wine. But all the while the rage had eaten at him, like a cancer.

Now, he was blessedly alone, in the room that soothed his soul. He feasted his eyes on the Renoir. Such lovely, subtle colors, he mused. Such exquisite brush strokes. And only he would ever look upon its magnificence.

There, the puzzle box of a Chinese emperor. Glossy with lacquer, a red dragon streaking over it and into a black sky. Priceless, full of secrets. And only he had the key.

Here, a ruby ring that had once graced the royal finger of Louis XIV. He slipped it on his pinkie, turned the stone toward the light and watched it shoot fire. From the king's hand to his, he thought. With a few detours along the way, but it was where it belonged now.

Usually such things brought him a deep, exquisite pleasure.

But not tonight.

Some had been punished, he thought. Some were beyond punishment. Yet it wasn't enough.

His treasure room was filled with the stunning, the unique, the ancient. Yet it wasn't enough.

The Three Stars were the only thing that would satisfy him. He would trade every treasure he owned for them. For with them, he would need nothing else.

The fools believed they understood them. Believed they could control them. And elude him. They were meant for him, of course. Their power was always meant for him.

And the loss of them was like ground glass in his throat.

He rose, ripping the ruby from his finger and flinging it across the room like a child tossing a broken toy. He would have them back. He was sure of it. But a sacrifice must be made. To the god, he thought with a slow smile. Of course, a sacrifice to the god.

In blood.

He left the room, leaving the lights burning. And most of his sanity behind.

Chapter 11

Jack considered leaving a note. When she woke, she'd be alone. At first, she'd probably assume he'd gone out to find that little store she'd spoken of, to buy some food.

She'd be impatient, a little annoyed. After an hour or so, she might worry that he'd gotten himself lost on the back roads.

But it wouldn't take her long to realize he was gone.

As he walked quietly down the stairs, just as dawn broke, he imagined her first reaction would be anger. She'd storm through the house, cursing him, threatening him. She'd probably kick something.

He was almost sorry to miss it.

She might even hate him for a while, he thought. But she'd be safe here. That was what mattered most.

He stepped outside, into the quiet mist of morning that shrouded the trees and hazed the sky. A few birds were up with him, stretching their vocal cords. Grace's flowers perfumed the air like a fantasy, and there was dew on the grass. He saw a deer, likely the same doe that had been on the lane the day before, standing at the edge of the woods.

They studied each other a moment, each both interested in and wary of the alien species. Then, dismissing him, she moved with hardly a sound along the verge of the trees, until she was slowly swallowed by them.

He glanced back at the house where he'd left M.J. sleeping. If everything went as he hoped, he'd be back for her by nightfall. It would take some doing, he knew, but he had to believe he'd convince her—eventually— that he'd acted for the best. And if her feelings were hurt, well, hurt feelings weren't terminal.

Again, he considered leaving a note—something short and to the point. But he decided against it. She'd figure it out for herself quickly enough. She was a sharp woman.

His woman, he thought as he slipped behind the wheel of the car. Whatever happened to him in the course of this day, she would be safe.

A soldier prepared for battle, a knight armed for the

charge, he steeled himself to leave his lady and ride off into the mist. Such was his mood when he turned the key and the engine responded with a dull click.

His mood deflated like a sail emptied of wind.

Terrific, great, just what he needed. He swung out of the car, resisted slamming the door, and rounded the hood. Muttering oaths, he popped it, stuck his head under.

"Lose something, ace?"

Slowly he withdrew his head from under the hood. She was standing on the porch, legs spread, hands fisted on her hips, venom in her eyes. It had taken only a glance to see that his distributor cap was missing. He didn't even need to look at her to conclude that she'd nailed him.

But he was cool. He'd faced down worse than one angry woman in his checkered career. "Looks that way. You're up early, M.J."

"So are you, Jack."

"I was hungry." He flashed a smile—and kept his distance. "I thought I'd hunt up some breakfast."

She cocked a brow. "Got your club in the car?"

"My club?"

"That's what Neanderthals do, don't they? Get their club and go off into the woods to bash a bear for meat."

As she came down the steps toward him, he kept the smile plastered to his face, leaned back on the fender. "I had something a little more civilized in mind. Something like bacon and eggs."

"Oh? And where are you going to find bacon and eggs around here at dawn?"

She had him there. "Ah…I thought I could, you know, find a farmer and—" The breath whooshed out of his lungs as her fist plunged into his belly.

"Don't you lie to me. Do I look stupid?"

He coughed, got his breath back and managed to straighten. "No. Listen—"

"Did you think I couldn't tell what was going on last night? The way you made love to me? Did you think you'd soften me up so I wouldn't know that was a big goodbye scene? You bastard!" She swung again, but this time he ducked, so she missed his jaw by inches.

Now his own temper began to climb. He'd never treated a woman with such care as he'd treated her with in the night, and now she was tossing it back in his face. "What did you do, sneak down here in the middle of the night and sabotage my ride?"

He saw the answer to that in the thin, satisfied smile that spread on her face. "Oh, that's nice. Real nice. Trusting."

"How dare you talk about trust! You were going to leave me here."

"Yeah, that's right. Now where's the distributor cap?" He took her by the arms, firmly, before she could take another shot at him. "Where is it?"

"Where do you think you're going? What sort of

idiotic plan have you mapped out in that tiny, feeble brain of yours?"

"I'm going to take care of business," he said grimly. "I'll come back for you when I'm done."

"Come back for me? What am I, a pet?" She jerked, but didn't manage to free herself until she'd hammered her heel onto his instep. "You're going back to the city, aren't you? You're going looking for trouble."

His fury was such that he wondered only briefly how many bones in his foot she might have broken. "I know what I'm doing. It's what I do. And what you're going to do is give me the cap, then you're going to wait."

"The hell I am. We started this together, and we finish it together."

"No." He swung her around until her back was pressed into the car. "I'm not taking any chances with you."

"Since when are you in charge? I take my own chances. Get your hands off me."

"No." He leaned in, cuffing her hands with his. "For once in your life, you're going to do what you're told. You're going to stay here. I can move faster without you, and I'll be damned if I'm going to be distracted worrying about you."

"Nobody's asking you to worry about me. Just what are you planning to do?"

"I've wasted enough time letting them chase me. It's time to flush them out, on my turf, my terms."

"You're going after those two maniacs in the van?" Her heart lodged in her throat and was ruthlessly swallowed. "Fine. Good idea. I'm going with you."

"You're staying here. They haven't found this place, and it doesn't look like they're going to. You'll be safe." He lifted her to her toes, shook her. "M.J., I can't risk you. You're everything that matters to me. I love you."

"And I'm supposed to sit here, like some helpless female, and risk you?"

"Exactly."

"You arrogant jerk. What am I supposed to do if you get yourself killed? In case you've forgotten, this is my problem, my deal. You're the one who's along for the ride, and you're not going anywhere without me."

"You'll be in my way."

"That's bull. I've held my own through this thing. I'm going, Jack, and unless you want to ride your thumb back to D.C., that's the deal."

He jerked away, snarling. Then whirled to pace. He considered cuffing her inside the house. It would be an ugly struggle—he could almost have looked forward to that aspect of it—and he'd win. But if things went wrong, he couldn't know how long it would be before someone found her.

No, he couldn't leave her alone and handcuffed in some isolated house in the boondocks.

He could lie. Agree to her terms, then ditch her. She wouldn't be easy to shake, but it was an option. Or he could try a different tack altogether.

He turned, smiled winningly. "Okay, sugar, I'll come clean. I've had enough."

"Have you?"

"It was fun. It was educational. But it's getting tedious. Even the fifty thousand you promised me just isn't worth risking my neck for. So I figured I'd cruise up north for a few weeks, wait for things to blow over." He gave a careless shrug as she stared at him. "Things were getting a little heavy between you and me. That's not my style. So I figured I'd take off, avoid the obligatory scene. If I were you, I'd call the cops, turn over the stone, and chalk it all up to one of your more interesting holiday weekends."

"You're dumping me," she said, in a small voice that made him feel like sludge.

"Let's say I'm just moving on. A guy's got to look out for number one."

"All the things you said to me…"

"Hey, sugar, we're both free agents. We both know the score. Tell you what. I'll drop you off at the nearest town, give you a few bucks for transpo."

In answer, she staggered toward the porch, every step a slice through his heart. When she collapsed, buried her face in her hands, he wished himself in hell.

She'll be safe, he reminded himself. All that mattered was that she'd be—

Laughing her guts out. He gaped as she threw back her head and roared with laughter. Her arms were clutched around her stomach, not in defense against heartbreak, but to keep herself from shaking apart with mirth.

"Oh, you idiot," she managed. "Did you really think I was going to fall for that?" She could hardly get the words out between great gusts of laughter. The darker his expression, the wilder her glee. "Now, I guess, I'm supposed to tearfully hand over the distributor cap and let you leave me off somewhere to nurse my shattered heart." She wiped her streaming eyes. "You're so in love with me, Dakota, you can't think straight."

He was thinking straight enough, he determined. He wondered how she'd like it if he closed his hands over that throat of hers and gave it a nice, loving squeeze.

"I could get over it," he muttered.

"No, you couldn't. It's hit you right between the eyes, and I know the feeling. We're stuck with each other, Jack. There's no getting past it for either of us." She breathed deep, rubbed a hand over her aching ribs. "I ought to kick your butt for trying this, but it was too stupid. And too sweet."

He jammed his hands in his pockets. It was the "sweet" that made him feel most foolish. Outmaneuvering her hadn't worked, he considered. Temper and threats hadn't made a dent, and lies had only amused her.

So he would try the truth, he decided. Simple, unvarnished. And he would plead with it.

"Okay, you got me." He walked over, sat beside her, took her hand. "I've never told anyone I loved them before," he began. "I never loved anyone. Not a woman, not family, not a friend."

"Jack." Swamped with emotion, she brushed the hair from his brow. "You just never had a chance to."

"Doesn't matter." He said it fiercely, his fingers tightening on hers. "I meant what I said last night. There's only you, M.J."

He pressed the back of her hand to his lips, held it there a moment. "You wouldn't understand that, not really. You've had other people in your life, important people."

"Yes." Touched, she leaned over, kissed his cheek. "There are people I love. Maybe there's not only you, Jack. But there is you. And what I feel for you is different than anything I've felt before, for anyone."

He stared down at their hands a moment. They fit so well, didn't they? he noticed. Just slid together, as if they'd been waiting for the match. "I've done things my own way for a long time," he continued. "I've avoided complications that I wasn't interested in. It's been easy to evade attachments. Until you."

He looked into her eyes as he touched a hand to her

cheek. "You cried yesterday, over those other people you love. It cut me off at the knees. And when I was holding you, and you were crying, I knew I'd do anything for you. Let me do this."

"You planned to leave me here because I cried?"

"Because when you did I finally realized just what your friends mean to you, and how much you'd been holding it in. I need to help you. And them."

She looked away from him for a moment. It wouldn't do either of them any good if she wept again. And his words, and the quiet and deep emotion that flowed behind them, had touched her in a new part of her heart. "I already love you, Jack." She let out a long sigh. "Now, I'm close to adoring you."

"Then you'll stay."

"No." She cupped his face as irritation raced over it. "But I'm not mad at you anymore."

"Great." He pushed off the steps to pace again. "Haven't you heard anything I've said? I can't risk you. I couldn't handle it if anything happened to you."

"But I'm supposed to handle it if something happens to you? It doesn't work that way, Jack." She rose and faced him. "Not for me. What you feel for me, I feel for you. We're in this together. Equal ground." She held up a hand before he could speak. "And you're not going to say something lame about you being a man and me being a woman."

Actually, it had been very close to coming out of his mouth. "A lot of good it would do me."

"Then it's settled." She angled her head. "And let me add something here, just in case you've got a bright idea about ditching me along the way. If you try it, I'll go to the nearest phone and call the cops. I'll tell them you kidnapped me, molested me. I'll give them your description, a description of what you call a car, and your tag number. You'll be trying to explain yourself to Sheriff Bubba and his team before you get twenty miles."

His eyes kindled. "You would, wouldn't you?"

"Damn straight. And I'll make it good, so good they'll probably mess up your pretty face before they toss you in a cell. Now, do we know where we stand?"

"Yeah." He pushed impotently against the corner she'd boxed him into. "We know where we stand. You cover your angles, sugar."

"You can count on that." She walked toward him, laid her hands on his tensed shoulders. "And you can count on me, Jack. I'm sticking with you." Expecting no response, she touched her lips to his. And got none. "I won't walk out on you," she murmured, and saw the flicker of understanding in his eyes. "And I won't let you down." She brushed her lips over his again. "I won't go away and leave you."

She saw too much, he realized. More, perhaps, than he'd seen himself. "This isn't about me."

"Yes, it is. No one's stuck with you, but I will. No one loved you enough, but I do." She skimmed her hands up his shoulders until they framed his face. "That makes all this about us. I'm going to be there for you, even when you try to play hero and shake me loose."

He was losing, and knew it. "You could start being there tomorrow."

"I'm already there. Now, are you going to kiss me, or not?"

"Maybe."

Her lips curved as they met his. Then they softened, and opened, and gave. He felt himself slide into her— a homecoming that was both sweet and exciting. The kiss heated even before she slipped her hands under his shirt, ran them up his back, then down again with nails scraping lightly.

"I want you," she murmured, moving sinuously against him. "Now, before we go—" she turned her head, nipped her teeth into his throat "—for luck."

His head swam as she reached between their bodies and found him. "I can always use a little extra luck."

She laughed, tugged him away from the car. They fell on the ground together and rolled over grass still damp with dew.

It was fast, and a little desperate. As the sun grew stronger, burning through the morning mist, they tugged at clothes, pawed each other.

"Let me…" He panted and dragged at denim. "I can't—"

"Here." Her hands fumbled with his, dragged material aside. "Hurry. God."

She rolled again, reared up and raced her mouth over his bare chest. She wanted to feast on him, needed to feast of those flavors, those textures. Sate herself with them. She would have sworn she felt the ground tremble as he turned her, hooked his teeth into her shoulder, one hand taking her breast, and the other…

"What are you… How can you…" Her head fell back as he ripped her viciously over the edge. Breath sobbing, she reached up, locked her arms around his neck and let the animal free.

She was with him, beat for beat, her body strong and agile. Her need was as greedy and as primal as his. Perhaps his hands bruised her in his rush, but hers were no less bold, no less rough. She turned her head, took his mouth with a wild avidity that tasted of the dark and the secret.

It was she who twisted, who dragged him down to her. "Now," she demanded, and her eyes gleamed like those of a cat on the hunt. "Right now." And wrapping herself around him, took him in.

He drove hard, burying himself in her. She met each rough, wild stroke, those tilted cat's eyes wide and focused on his. The heat of her fueled him, and through that edgy violence of need he felt his heart simply shatter with an emotion just as brutal.

"I love you." His mouth clamped on hers, drank from it. "God, I love you."

"I know." And when he pressed his face into her hair, shuddering as he poured himself into her, she needed to know nothing else.

"Jack." She stroked his hair. The sun was in her eyes, his weight was on her, and the grass was damp against her back. She thought it one of the finest moments of her life. "Jack," she said again, and sighed.

He nearly had his wind back. "Maybe there's something to country living after all." With a little groan, he propped up on his elbows. And felt his stomach sink. "What are you crying for? Are you trying to kill me?"

"I'm not. The sun's in my eyes." Then, feeling foolish, she flicked the single tear away. "It's not that kind of crying, anyway. Don't worry, I'm not going to blubber."

"Did I hurt you? Look, I'm sorry, I—"

"Jack." She heaved another sigh. "It's not that kind of crying, okay? And I'm done now, anyway."

Wary, he studied those gleaming eyes. "Are you sure?"

"Yes." Then she smiled. "You coward."

"Guilty." And he wasn't ashamed to admit it. He kissed her nose. "Now that we've got all this extra luck, we'd better get going."

"You're not going to try to pull a fast one, are you?"

He thought of the way she'd taken his face in her hands and told him she was sticking. There had never been anyone in his life who ever made him that one simple promise.

"No. I guess we're a team."

"Good guess."

M.J. waited until they were back on the highway, heading toward civilization, before she asked. "Okay, Jack, what's the plan?"

"Nothing fancy. Simplicity has fewer pitfalls. The way I see it, we've got to get to whoever's pulling the strings. Our only link with him, or her, is the guys in the van and maybe the Salvinis."

"So far, I'm with you."

"I need to have a little chat with them. To do that, I have to lure them out, maintain the advantage and convince them it's in their best interest to pass on some information."

"Okay, there are two guys with guns, one of whom is the approximate size of the Washington Monument. And you're going to convince them to chat with you." She beamed at him. "I admire your optimism."

"It's all a matter of leverage," he said, and explained how he planned to accomplish it.

Thunder was rumbling in a darkened sky when he pulled up in the lot at Salvini. It was a dignified building, separated from a strip mall by a large parking lot. And it was locked tight for the Monday holiday.

In the smaller, well-tended Salvini lot sat a lone Mercedes sedan.

"Know who owns that?"

"One of the creeps—Bailey's stepbrothers. Thomas, I think. Bailey said they were closing down for an extended weekend. If he's inside, I don't know why."

"Let's poke around." Jack got out, wandered to the sedan. It was locked tight, its security light blinking. He checked the front doors of the building first, scanned the darkened showroom, saw no signs of life.

"Offices upstairs?" he asked M.J.

"Yeah. Bailey's, Thomas's, Timothy's." Her heart began to race. "Maybe she's in there, Jack. She rarely drives to work. We live so close."

"Uh-huh." And though it wasn't part of his plan, the worry in her voice had him going with impulse and pressing the buzzer beside the door. "Let's check the rear," he said a moment later.

"They could be holding her inside. She could be hurt. I should have thought of it before." Toward the west, lightning forked down like jagged blades. "She could be in there, hurt and—"

He turned. "Listen, if we're going to get through this, you've got to hold it together. We don't have time for a lot of hand-wringing and speculation."

Her head jerked back, then she squared her shoulders. "All right. Sorry."

After a short study of her face, he nodded, then continued to the back, where he took a long look at the steel security door. "Someone's been at the locks."

"What do you mean, 'at'?" She leaned over his shoulder as he crouched down. "Do you mean someone picked the locks?"

"Fairly recently, no rust, no dust in the scrapes. Wonder if he got in." He rose, examined the sides, the jambs. "He didn't try to jimmy it or hammer against it. I'd say he knew what he was doing. Under different circumstances, I'd say it was just your average break-in, but that's stretching it."

"Can you get in?"

That wasn't part of the immediate plan, either, but he considered. "Probably. Do you know what kind of alarm system they've got?"

"There's a box inside the door. It's coded. I don't know the code. You punch some numbers." She caught herself before she could indeed wring her hands. "Jack." She struggled to keep her voice calm. "She could be in there. She could be hurt. If we don't check, and something goes wrong…"

"Okay. But if I can't deal with the alarm, and fast, we're going to get busted." Still, he got his tools out of the trunk and went to work.

"Watch my back, will you?" he told her. "Make sure none of those holiday shoppers next door take an interest over here."

She turned, scanned the lot and the strip mall beyond. People came and went, obviously too involved in the bargains they'd bagged or those they were hunting to take notice of a man crouched at a security door of a locked building.

Thunder walked closer, and rain, long awaited, began to flood out of the sky. She didn't mind getting wet, considered the storm only a better cover. But she shuddered with relief when he gave her the all-clear.

"Once I open this, I've probably got a minute to ninety seconds before the alarm. If I can't disengage it, we'll have to go, and fast."

"But—"

"No arguments here, M.J. If, by any chance, Bailey's in there, the cops'll be along in minutes, and they'll find her. We'll take our show on the road elsewhere. Agreed?"

What choice was there? "Agreed."

"Fine." He swiped dripping hair out of his eyes. "You stay right here. If I say go, you head for the car." Taking her silence for assent, he stepped inside. He saw the alarm box immediately, lifted a brow. "Interesting," he murmured, then signaled M.J. inside. "It's off."

"I don't understand that. It's always set."

"Just our lucky day." He winked, took her hand,

then flipped on his flashlight with the other. "We'll try upstairs first, see if we get lucky again."

"Up these stairs," she told him. "Bailey's office is right down the hall."

"Nice digs," he commented, scanning the expensive carpeting, the tasteful colors, while keeping his ears tuned for any sound. There was nothing but drumming rain. He blocked M.J. with an outstretched arm, and swept the light into the office.

Quiet, organized, elegant and empty. He heard M.J. let out a rusty breath.

"No sign of struggle," he pointed out. "We'll check the rest of the floor, then downstairs before we go into phase one of plan A."

He moved down the hall and, a full yard before the next door, stopped. "Go back in her office, wait for me."

"Why? What is it?" Then she caught the heaviness in the air, recognized it for what it was. "Bailey! Oh, my God."

Jack rapped her back against the wall, pinned her until her struggles ceased. "You do what I tell you," he said between his teeth. "You stay here."

She closed her eyes, admitted there were some things she wasn't strong enough to face. Nodded.

Satisfied, he eased back. He moved down the hall quietly, eased the door open.

It was as bad as he'd ever seen, and death was rarely pretty. But this, he thought, trailing the light over the wreckage caused by a life-and-death struggle, had been madness.

Life had lost.

He turned away from it, went back to M.J. She was pale as wax, leaning against the wall. "It's not Bailey," he said immediately. "It's a man."

"Not Bailey?"

"No." He put a hand to her cheek, found it icy, but her eyes were losing their glazed look. "I'm going to check the other rooms. I don't want you to go in there, M.J."

She let out the breath that had been hot and trapped in her lungs. Not Bailey. "Was it like Ralph?"

"No." His voice was flat and hard. "It was a hell of a lot worse. Stay here."

He went through each room, checked corners and closets, careful not to touch anything or to wipe a surface when he had no choice but to touch. Saying nothing, he led M.J. downstairs and did a quick, thorough search of the lower level.

"Someone's been in here," he murmured, hunkering down to shine the light into a tiny alcove under the stairs. "The dust's disturbed." Considering, he stroked his chin. "I'd say if somebody was smart and needed a bolt hole, this would be a good choice."

Her clothes were clinging wet against her skin. But that wasn't why she was shivering. "Bailey's smart."

He nodded, rose. "Keep that in mind. Let's do what we came for."

"Okay." She cast one last look over her shoulder, imagined Bailey hiding in the dark. From what? she wondered. From whom? And where was she now?

Outside, Jack secured the door, wiped the knob. "I figure if you need to, you can get over to that mall on those legs of yours in about thirty seconds at a sprint."

"I'm not running away."

"You will if I tell you." He pocketed the flashlight. "You're going to do exactly what I tell you. No questions, no arguments, no hesitation." His eyes flared into hers, made her shiver again. "Whoever did what I found upstairs is an animal. You remember that."

"I will." She clamped down ruthlessly on the next tremor. "And you remember we're in this together."

"The idea is for me to take these guys down, one at a time. If you can get to the van while I'm distracting them and disable it, fine. But don't take any chances."

"I've already told you I wouldn't."

"Once I have them secured," he continued, ignoring the impatience in her voice, "we can use their van. I can have a nice chat with them. I think I can get a name out of them." He examined his fist, then smiled craftily over it into her eyes. "Some basic information."

"Oooh…" She fluttered her wet lashes. "So macho."

"Shut up. Depending on the name and information we get, and the situation, we either go to the cops—which would be my second choice—or we follow the next lead."

"Agreed."

He opened the door of his car, waited until she slid over the seat, then picked up her phone. "Make the call. Stretch it out for about a minute, just in case."

She dialed, then began to ramble to Grace's answering machine in Potomac. She kept her eyes on Jack's, and when he nodded, she pushed disconnect. "Phase two?" she said, struggling for calm.

"Now we wait."

Within fifteen minutes, the van turned into the lot at Salvini. The rain had slowed now, but continued to fall in a steady stream. In his position beside an aging station wagon, Jack hunched his shoulders against the wet and watched the routine.

The two men got out, separated and did a slow circle of the building.

The big one was his target.

Using parked cars as cover, Jack made his way over, watching as the man bent, picked up M.J.'s phone from the ground. It was a decent plant, Jack mused, gave him something to consider in that pea-size brain of his. As the big man pondered over the phone, Jack sprang and hit him at a dead run, bashing into his kidneys like a cannonball.

He took his quarry to his knees, and had the cuffs snapped over one steel-beam wrist before he was flicked off like a fly.

He felt the searing burn as his flesh scraped over wet, grainy asphalt, and rolled before a size-sixteen shoe could bash into his face. He made the grab, snagged the sledgehammer of a foot and heaved.

From her post, M.J. watched the struggle, wincing as Jack hit the ground, praying as he rolled. Hissing as fists crunched against bone. She started quietly toward the van, glancing back to see the progress of the bout.

He was outmatched, she thought desperately. Was going to get his neck broken, at the very least. Braced to spring to his aid, she saw the second man rounding the far corner of the building.

He'd be on them in moments, she thought. And Jack's plan to take them both quickly and separately was in tatters. She sucked in the breath to call out a warning, then narrowed her eyes. Maybe there was still a way to make it work.

She dashed out from behind cover, took a short run toward Salvini, away from Jack. She skidded to a halt when she saw the second man spot her, made her eyes widen with shock and fear. His hand went inside his jacket, but she held fast, waiting until he began closing in.

Then she ran, into the curtaining rain, drawing him away from Jack.

Both Jack and his sparring partner heard the shout. Both looked over instinctively and saw the woman with the bright cap of red hair racing away, and the man pursuing her.

Never listens, Jack thought with a bright spear of terror. Then he looked back, saw the big man grinning at him.

Jack grinned back, and his swollen left eye gleamed bright with malice. "Gotta take you down, and fast," he said conversationally as he rammed a fist into the man's mouth. "That's my woman your pal's chasing."

The giant swiped blood from his face. "You're meat."

"Yeah?" There wasn't any time to dally. Praying M.J.'s legs and his neck would hold out, he lowered his head and charged like a mad bull. The force of the attack shot the man back, rapping his head smartly on the steel door. Bloodied, battered and exhausted, Jack drove his knee up, hard and high, and heard the satisfactory sound of air gushing out of a deflated blimp.

Blinking stinging sweat and warm rain out of his

eyes, Jack wrenched the man's arms back, snapped on the second cuff.

"I'll be back for you," he promised, as he retrieved the phone and tore off in search of M.J.

Chapter 12

Jack had told her, if anything went wrong, to head for the shops, to lose herself in the crowds. Scream bloody murder if necessary.

With that on her mind, M.J. veered that way, her priority to lure the second gunman away from Jack and give him an even chance.

But as she raced toward the stores, with their bright On Sale signs, she saw couples, families, children being led by the hand, babies in strollers. And thought of the way the man chasing her had slipped a hand under his jacket.

She thought of what a gun fired at her in the midst of a crowd would do.

And she pivoted, changed direction on a dime and ran toward the far end of the lot.

Pumping her arms, she tossed a quick look over her shoulder. She'd left her pursuer in the dust. He was still coming, but lagging now, overheated, she imagined, in his bagging suit coat and leather shoes. Slippery shoes on wet pavement. Just how far would he chase her, she wondered, before giving up and turning back to pick up his friend?

And stumble over Jack.

Deliberately she slowed her pace, let him close some of the distance, in order to keep his interest keen. Part of her worried that he would simply use that gun, slam a bullet into her leg. Or her back. With the image of that running riot in her head, she streaked into a line of parked cars.

She could hear her own breath whistling now. She'd run the equivalent of a fifty-yard touchdown dash in the blistering heat of a midsummer storm. Crouching behind a minivan, she swiped sweat from her eyes and tried to think.

Could she circle back, find a way to help Jack? Had the gorilla already pounded him into dust and set off to help his buddy? How long would her luck last before some innocent family of four, their bargain-hunting complete, ran through the downpour and into the line of fire?

Concentrating on silence more than speed, she duckwalked around the van, slid her way around a compact. She needed to catch her breath, needed to think. Needed to see what was happening behind the Salvini building.

Bracing herself, she put one trembling hand on the fender of the compact and risked a quick look.

He was closer than she'd anticipated. Four cars to the left, and taking his time. She ducked down fast, pressed her back into the bumper. If she stayed where she was, would he pass by, or would he spot her?

Better to die on the run, she thought, or with your fists raised, than to be picked off cowering behind an economy import.

She sucked in a breath, said another quick prayer for Jack, and headed for new ground. It was the ping on the asphalt beside her that stopped her heart. She felt the sharp edge of rock bounce off her jeans.

He was shooting at her. Her heart bounced from throat to stomach and back like a Ping-Pong ball, and she skidded around a parked car. Another inch, two at the most, and that bullet would have met flesh.

He'd tagged her, she realized. And now it would only be a matter of running her down, cornering her like a rabbit. Well, she would see about that.

Gritting her teeth, she bellied under the car, ignored the wet grit, the smell of gas and oil, and slid like a snake beneath the undercarriage, held her breath as she pulled herself through the narrow space and under the next vehicle.

She could hear him now. He was breathing hard, a wheeze on each inhale, a whistle on the exhale. She saw his shoes. Little feet, she thought irreverently, decked out in glossy black wing tips and argyle socks.

She closed her eyes for one brief moment, trying to get a picture of him planted in her mind. Five-eight, tops, maybe a hundred and sixty. Mid-thirties. Sharp eyes, a well-defined nose. Wiry but not buff. And out of breath.

Hell, she thought, going giddy. She could take him.

She scooted another inch, was just preparing to make her move when she saw those shiny wing tips leave the ground.

There in front of her eyes were a pair of scuffed boots. Jack's boots. Jack's voice was muttering panting curses. Her vision blurred with relief and the terror as she heard the muffled thump that was the silenced gun firing again.

Skinning elbows and knees, she was out from under the car in time to see the gunman running for cover and Jack starting off in pursuit.

"Jack."

He skidded to a halt, whirled, sheer relief covering

his battered face. And it was then that she saw the blood staining his shirt.

"Oh, God. Oh, God. You're shot." Her legs went weak, so that she stumbled toward him as he glanced down absently, pressing a hand to his side.

"Hell." The pain registered, but only dimly, as his arms filled with woman. "The car," he managed. "Get to the car. He's heading back."

His hand, wet with blood and rain, locked on hers.

Later, she would remember running. But none of it seemed real as it happened. Feet pounding on pavement, skidding, the jittery thud of her heart, the rising sense of fear and fury, the wide, shocked eyes of a woman carrying shopping bags who was nearly mowed down in their rush.

And Jack cursing her, steadily, for not doing as she was told.

The van screamed out of the lot as they skidded down the incline. "Damn it all to hell and back again." His lungs were burning, his side shot fire. Desperately he dug the keys out of his pocket. "In the car. Now!"

She all but dived through the window, barely maintaining her balance as he burned rubber in reverse. "You're hurt. Let me see—"

He batted her worried hands away and whipped the wheel around. "He got his three-ton friend, too. After all that trouble, they're not getting away." The car shimmied, fishtailed, then the tires bit the road as he swung into the chase. "Get the gun out of the glove box. Give it to me."

"Jack, you're bleeding. For God's sake."

"Didn't I tell you to run?" He punched the gas, screaming on the van's rear bumper as they rocketed toward the main drag. "I told you to head for people, to get lost. He could have killed you. Give me the damn gun."

"All right, all right." She beat a fist on the glove compartment until the sticky door popped open. "He's heading for the Beltway."

"I see where he's going."

"You're not going to shoot at him. You could hit some poor schmuck's car."

Jack snatched the gun out of her hand, swerved to make the exit, skidded on the damp roadway. "I hit what I aim at. Now strap in and be quiet. I'll deal with you later."

Her fear for him was such that she didn't blink an eye at his words. He zipped through traffic like a madman, hugging the bumper of the van like a lover. And when they hit ninety, a cold numbness settled over her, as if her system had been shot full of novocaine.

"You're going to kill someone," she said calmly. "It might not even be us."

"I can handle the car." That, at least, was perfect

truth. He threaded through traffic, staying on target like a heat-seeking missile, his fat new tires gripping true on the slick roadway. He was close enough that he could see the big man hunched in the passenger seat turn around and snarl.

"Yeah, I'm coming for you, you son of a bitch," Jack muttered. "You've got my spare cuffs."

"You're bleeding on the seat." M.J. heard herself speak, but the words seemed to come from outside her mind.

"I've got more." And with the gun on his lap, he whipped the wheel, gained inches on the side. He'd cut them off, he calculated, drive them to the shoulder. The big man was cuffed, and he could handle the other.

And then, they would see.

His eyes narrowed as he saw the driver of the van twist his head around, heard the wheels screech. The van shimmied, shuddered, then swerved wildly toward the oncoming exit.

"He can't make it." Jack pumped his brakes, fell back a foot and prepared to make the quick, sharp turn. "He can't make that turn. He'll lose it."

He swore when the van rocked, lost control on the rain-slicked road and hit the guardrail at eighty. The crash was huge, and sent the van flying up like a drunken high diver. It rolled once in the air. And amid the squeal of brakes of other horrified drivers, it landed twelve feet below, on the incline.

He had time to swing to the side, to push out of the car, before the explosion shoved him back like a huge, hot hand. M.J.'s hand gripped his shoulder as the flames spewed up. The air stank with gas.

"Not a chance," he murmured. "Lost them."

"Get in the car, Jack." It amazed her how cool, how composed, her voice sounded. Cars were emptying of drivers and passengers. People were rushing toward the wreck. "In the passenger side. I'm driving now."

"After all that," he said, dazed with smoke and pain. "Lost them anyway."

"In the car." She led him around, ignoring the high, excited voices. Someone, surely, would have already called 911 on his car phone. There was nothing left to do. "We need to get out of here."

She drove on instinct back to her apartment. Safe or not, it was home, and he needed tending. Driving Jack's car was like manning a yacht, she thought, concentrating on her speed and direction as the rain petered out to a fine drizzle. A very old, very big boat. With a vague sense of surprise, she pulled in beside her MG.

Nothing much had changed, she realized. Her car was still there, the building still stood. A couple of kids who didn't mind getting wet were tossing a

Frisbee in the side yard, as if it was an ordinary day in ordinary lives.

"Wait for me to come around." She dragged up her purse from the floor, found her keys. Of course, he didn't listen, and was standing on the sidewalk when she came around the hood. "You can lean on me," she murmured, sliding an arm around his waist. "Just lean on me, Jack."

"It should be all right to be here," he decided. "At least for a little while. We may have to move again soon." He realized he was limping, favoring an ache in his right leg that he hadn't noticed before.

Her heart had stopped stuttering and was numb. "We'll just get you cleaned up."

"Yeah. I could use a beer."

"I'll get you one," she promised as she led him inside. Though she habitually took the stairs, she steered him to the elevator. "Let's just get you inside." And then to a hospital, she thought. She had to see how bad it was first. Once she'd done what she could, she was dumping it all and going official. Cops, doctors, FBI, whatever it took.

She sent up a small prayer of thanksgiving when she saw that the corridor was empty. No nosy neighbors, she thought, ignoring the police tape and unlocking her door. No awkward questions.

She kicked a broken lamp out of her way, walked him around the overturned couch and into the bath. "Sit," she

ordered, and flicked on the lights. "Let's have a look."
And her trembling hands belied her steady voice as she
gently lifted his bloody shirt over his head.

"God, Jack, that guy beat the hell out of you."

"I left him with his face in the dirt and his hands
cuffed behind his back."

"Yeah." She made herself look away from the
blooming purple bruises over his torso and wet a cloth.
"Have you been shot before?"

"Once, in Abilene. Caught me in the leg. Slowed me
down awhile."

Ridiculous as it was, it helped that this wasn't the
first time. She pressed the cloth to his side, low along
the ribs. Her eyes stung with hot tears that she wouldn't
shed. "I know it hurts."

"You were going to get me a beer." Didn't she look
pretty, he thought, playing nurse, with her cheeks pale,
her eyes dark, and her hands cool as silk.

"In a minute. Just be still now." She knelt beside
him, steeling herself for the worst. Then sat back on her
heels and hissed. "Damn it, Jack, it's only a scratch."

He grinned at her, feeling every bump and bruise as
if in a personal carnival of pain. "That's supposed to
be my line."

"I was ready for some big gaping hole in your side.
It just grazed you."

He looked down, considered. "Bled pretty good,

though." He took the cloth himself, pressed it against the long, shallow wound. "About that beer…"

"I'll get you a beer. I ought to hit you over the head with it."

"We'll talk about who conks who after I eat a bottle of aspirin." He got up, wincing, and pawed through the mirrored cabinet over the sink. "Maybe you could get me a shirt out of the car, sugar. I don't think I'm going to be wearing the other one again."

"You scared me." Anger, tears and desperate relief brewed a messy stew in her stomach. "Do you have any idea how much you scared me?"

He found the aspirin, closed the cabinet and met her eyes in the mirror. "I've got an idea, seeing how I felt when I saw you trying to draw that puss-for-brain's fire. You promised to head for the mall."

"Well, I didn't. Sue me." Out of patience, she shoved him down again, ignoring his muffled yelp of pain. "Oh, be quiet and let me finish up here. I must have some antiseptic here somewhere."

"Maybe just a leather strap to bite on while you pour salt in my wounds."

"Don't tempt me." She dampened another cloth, then knelt down and began to clean his face. "You've got a black eye blooming, your lip's swollen, and you've got a nice big knot right here." He yelped again when she pressed the cloth to his temple. "Baby."

"If you're going to play Nurse Nancy, at least give me some anesthesia first." Since she didn't seem inclined to give him any water, he swallowed the aspirin dry.

He continued to complain as she swabbed him with antiseptic, slapped on bandages. Out of patience, she pressed her lips to his, which caused him equal amounts of pain and pleasure. "Are you going to kiss everywhere it hurts?" he asked.

"You should be so lucky." Then she laid her head in his lap and let out a long, long sigh. "I don't care how mad you are. I didn't know what else to do. He was coming. He'd have had you. I only knew I had to draw him away from you."

He weakened, stroked her hair. "Okay, we'll get into all that later." He noticed for the first time the raw skin on her elbow. "Hey, you've got a few scrapes yourself."

"Burns some," she murmured.

"Aw. Come on, sugar, I'll be the doctor." He reversed their positions, grinned. "This may sting a little."

"You'd love that, wouldn't— Ouch! Damn it, Jack."

"Baby." But he kissed the abraded skin, then bandaged it gently. "You ever scare me like that again, and I'll keep you cuffed to the bed for a month."

"Promises, promises." She leaned forward, wrapped her arms around him. "They're dead, aren't they? They couldn't have lived through that."

"Chances are slim. I'm sorry, M.J., I never got anything out of them. Not a clue."

"*We* never got anything out of them," she corrected. "And we did our best." She struggled to bury the worry, straighten her shoulders. "There's still the creeps," she began, then went pale again, remembering. Odds were at least one of the Salvini brothers was dead.

But it hadn't been Bailey in there, she reminded herself, and took two deep breaths. "Well, at least now I can get myself some fresh clothes and some cash. And I'm calling into the pub." This was a dare. "I'll wait until we're ready to head out again, but I'm checking in, letting them know I'm okay, giving them the schedule for the rest of the week."

"Fine, be a businesswoman." He stood up, held her still. "We'll find your friends, M.J. I promise you that. And as much as it goes against the grain, it's time to call in the cops."

She let out a wavering sigh of relief. "Yeah. Three days of this is enough."

"There'll be a lot of questions."

"Then we'll give them the answers."

"I should tell you that a man in my line of work isn't real popular with straight cops. I've got a couple of contacts, but when you start moving up the ranks, the tolerance level shoots way down."

"We'll handle it. Should we call from here, or just go in?"

"Here. Cop shops make me itchy."

"I'm not giving them the stone." She planted her feet, prepared for an argument. "It's Bailey's—or it's her decision. I'm not turning it over to anyone but her."

"Okay," he said easily, and made her blink. "We'll work around it. She and Grace come first, with both of us now."

Her smile spread. And the jangling ring made them both jolt. "What?" She stared down at her purse as if it had suddenly come alive and snapped at her. "It's my phone. My phone's ringing."

He touched a hand to his pocket, reassured when he felt the gun. "Answer it."

Barely breathing, she dug into the purse she'd dropped on the floor, hit the switch. "O'Leary." The tears simply rushed into her eyes as she sank down on the floor. "Bailey. Oh, my God, Bailey. Are you all right? Where are you? Are you hurt? What— What? Yes, yes, I'm fine. In my apartment, but where—"

Her hand reached up, gripped Jack's. "Bailey, stop asking me that and tell me where the hell you are. Yeah, I've got it. We'll be there in ten minutes. Stay."

She clicked off. "I'm sorry," she told Jack. "I've got to." Then burst into tears. "She's all right," she managed as he rolled his eyes and picked her up. "She's okay."

* * *

It was a quiet, established neighborhood with lovely old trees. M.J. gripped her hands together on her lap and scanned house numbers. "Twenty-two, twenty-four, twenty-six. There! That one." Even as Jack turned into the driveway of a tidy Federal-style home, she was reaching for the door handle. He merely hooked a hand in the waist of her jeans and hauled her back.

"Hold on, wait until I stop."

Even as he did, he saw the woman, a pretty blonde of fragile build, come racing out of the front door and across the wet grass. M.J. shoved herself out of the car and streaked into her arms.

It made a nice picture, Jack decided as he climbed out, gingerly. The two of them standing in the watery sunlight, holding on as if they could swallow each other whole. They swayed together on the lush grass, weeping, talking over each other and just clinging.

And as touching and attractive a scene as it was, there was nothing he wanted to avoid more than two sobbing women. He spotted the man standing just outside the door, noted the smile in his eyes, the fresh bandage on his arm. Without hesitation, Jack gave the women a wide berth and headed for the front door.

"Cade Parris."

Jack took the extended hand, measured his man.

About six-two, trim, brown hair, eyes of a dreamier green than M.J.'s. A strong grip that Jack felt balanced out the glossy good looks.

"Jack Dakota."

Cade scanned the bruises, shook his head. "You look like a man who could use a drink."

Despite his sore mouth, Jack's lips spread in a grateful smile. "Brother, you just became my best friend."

"Come on in," Cade invited, with a last glance toward M.J. and Bailey. "They'll need some time, and we can fill each other in."

It took a while, but Jack was feeling considerably more relaxed, with his feet propped up on a coffee table, a beer in his hand.

"Amnesia," he murmured. "Must have been tough on her."

"She's had a rough few days. Seeing one slimy excuse for a stepbrother kill her other slimy excuse for a stepbrother, then come for her."

"We dropped in on Salvini's. I saw the results."

Cade nodded. "Then you know how bad it was. If she hadn't gotten away... Well, she did. She still doesn't remember all of it, but she'd already sent one of the diamonds to M.J. and one to Grace. I've been working the case since Friday morning, when she came to my office. You?"

"Saturday afternoon," Jack told him and cooled his throat with beer.

"It's been fast work all around." But Cade frowned as he looked toward the window. "Bailey was scared, confused, but she wanted answers and figured a private investigator could get them for her. We had a major breakthrough today."

Jack lifted a brow, gesturing toward the bandage. "That part of it?"

"The remaining Salvini," Cade said, his eyes level and cold. "He's dead."

Which meant one more dead end, Jack mused. "You figure they set the whole thing up?"

"No. They had a client. I haven't tracked him yet." Cade rose, wandered to the window. M.J. and Bailey were still standing in the yard, talking fast. "Cops are on it too, now. I've got a friend. Mick Marshall."

"Yeah, I know him. He's a rare one. A cop with a brain and a heart."

"That's Mick. Buchanan's over him, though. He doesn't much like P.I.'s."

"Buchanan doesn't much like anybody. But he's good."

"He's going to want to talk to you, and M.J."

The prospect had Jack sighing. "I think I could use another beer."

With a laugh, Cade turned from the window. "I'll

get us both another. And you can tell me how you spent your weekend." His eyes roamed over Jack's face. "And how the other guy looks."

"Timothy," M.J. said with surprise. "I never liked him, but I never pictured him as a murderer."

"It was as if he'd lost his mind." Bailey kept her hand linked with M.J.'s, as if afraid her friend would vanish without the connection. "I blanked it all, just shut it out. Everything. Little pieces started to come back, but I couldn't get a grip on them. I wouldn't have made it through without Cade."

"I can't wait to meet him." She looked into Bailey's eyes, and her own narrowed in speculation. "It looks as though he works fast."

"It shows?" Bailey asked, and flushed.

"Like a big neon sign."

"Just days ago," Bailey said, half to herself. "It all happened fast. It doesn't seem like just a few days. It feels as if I've known him forever." Her lips curved, warmed her honey-brown eyes. "He loves me, M.J. Just like that. I know it sounds crazy."

"You'd be surprised what doesn't sound crazy to me these days. He makes you happy?" M.J. tucked Bailey's wave of hair behind her ear. "That's what counts."

"I couldn't remember you. Or Grace." A tear

squeezed through as Bailey shut her eyes. "I know it was only a couple of days, but it was so lonely without you. Then, when I started to remember, it wasn't specifics, more just a feeling. A loss of something important. Then, when I did remember, and we went to your apartment, you were gone. There'd been the break-in, and I couldn't find you. Everything happened so fast after that. It was only hours ago. Then I remembered that phone you cart around in your purse. I remembered and I called. And there you were."

"It was the best call I ever got."

"The best I ever made." Her lips trembled once. "M.J., I can't find Grace."

"I know." Drawing together, M.J. draped an arm around Bailey's shoulders. "We have to believe she's all right. Jack and I were just up at her country place this morning. She'd been there, Bailey. I could still smell her. And we found each other. We'll find her."

"Yes, we will." They walked toward the house together. "This Jack? Does he make you happy?"

"Yeah. When he's not ticking me off."

With a chuckle, Bailey opened the door. "Then I can't wait to meet him, either."

"I like your friend." Jack stood out on Cade's patio, contemplating after-the-rain in suburbia.

"She likes you, too."

"She's classy. And she's come through a rough time holding her own. Parris seems pretty sharp."

"He helped get her through, so he's aces with me."

"We filled in most of the blanks for each other. He's got a cool head, a quick mind. And he's crazy about your friend."

"I think I noticed that."

Jack took her hand, studied it. Not delicate like Bailey's, he mused, but narrow, competent. Strong. "He's got a lot to offer. Class again, money, fancy house. I guess you'd call it security."

Intrigued, she watched his face. "I guess you would."

He hadn't meant to get started on this, he realized. But however fast certain things could move, he'd decided life was too short to waste time.

"My old man was a bum," he said abruptly. "My mother served drinks to drunks when she felt like working. I worked my way thorough college hauling bricks and mixing mortar for a mason, which led me to a useless degree in English lit with a minor in anthropology. Don't ask me why, it seemed like the thing to do at the time. I've got a few thousand socked away for dry spells. You get dry spells in my line of work. I rent a couple of rooms by the month." He waited a beat, but she said nothing. "Not what you'd call security."

"Nope."

"Is that what you want? Security?"

She thought about it. "Nope."

He dragged his hand through his hair. "You know how those two stones looked when you and Bailey put them together? They looked spectacular, sure, all that fire and power in one spot. But mostly, they just looked right." He met her eyes, tried to see inside her. "Sometimes, it's just right."

"And when it is, you don't have to look for the reasons."

"Maybe not. I don't know what I'm doing here. I don't know why this is. I've lived my life alone, and liked it that way. Do you understand that?"

She enjoyed the irritation in his voice, and smirked. "Yeah, I understand that. The lone wolf. You want to howl at the moon tonight, or what?"

"Don't get smart with me when I'm trying to explain myself."

He took a quick circle around the patio. There was a hammock swinging between two big trees, and somewhere in those dripping green leaves a bird was singing its heart out.

His life, Jack mused, had never been that simple, that calm, or that pretty. He didn't have anything to offer but what he was, and what he had inside himself for her.

She'd have to decide if that was enough to build on.

"The point is, I don't want to keep living my life

alone." His head snapped up, and his bruised eye glared out from under the arched, scarred brow. "Do you understand that?"

"Why wouldn't I?" Her smirk remained firmly in place. "You're sloppy in love with me, pal."

"Keep it up, just keep it up." He hissed out a breath, eased a hand onto his aching side. "My feelings aren't the issue, and maybe yours aren't, either. Things happen to people's emotions under intense circumstances."

"Now he's being philosophical again. Must be that minor in anthropology."

He closed his eyes, prayed for patience. "I'm trying to lay out my cards here. You come from a different place than I do, and maybe you don't want to head where I'm heading. Maybe you want to slow down some now, take it in more careful steps. More traditional."

Now she snorted. "Is that how I strike you? The traditional type?"

His frown only deepened. "Maybe not, but it doesn't change the fact that a week ago you were cruising along in your own lane just fine. You've got a right to ask questions, look for reasons. A couple of days with me—"

"I'm not asking questions or looking for reasons, Jack," she said, interrupting him. "I stopped cruising in my own lane the day I met you, and I'm glad of it."

Oh, hell, she thought, and braced. "It stands for Magdalen Juliette."

A cough of laughter escaped him. It was the last thing he'd expected. "You're kidding."

"It stands for Magdalen Juliette," she repeated between clenched teeth. "And the only people who know that are my family, Bailey and Grace. In other words, only people I love and trust, which now includes you."

"Magdalen Juliette," he repeated, rolling it around on his tongue. "Quite a handle, sugar."

"It's M.J. Legally M.J., because that's what I wanted. And if you ever call me any form of Magdalen Juliette other than M.J., I will personally and with great pleasure skin you alive."

She would, too, he thought with a quick, crooked grin. "If you don't want me using it, why did you tell me?"

She took a step toward him. "I told you that, and I'm telling you this, because my name is M. J. O'Leary, and I know what I want."

His eyes flared and burned away the grin. "You're sure of that?"

"The second stone's knowledge. And I know. Do you?"

"Yeah." His breathing took a hitch. "It's a big step."

"The biggest."

"Okay." His palms were sweaty in his pockets, so he pulled them free. "You go first."

Her grin flashed. "No, you."

"No way. I said it first last time. Fair's fair."

She supposed it was. Angling her head, she took a good long look at him. Yes, she thought. She knew. "Okay. Let's get married."

Relishing the swift kick of joy, he tucked his thumbs in his pockets. "Aren't you supposed to ask? You know, propose? A guy's entitled to a little romance at big moments."

"You're pushing your luck." Then she laughed and locked her arms around his neck. "But what the hell—will you marry me, Jack?"

"Sure, why not?"

And when she laughed again, he caught her against his sore and battered body.

Perfect fit.

* * * * *

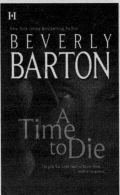

REQUEST YOUR FREE BOOKS!
2 FREE NOVELS PLUS 2 FREE GIFTS!

SPECIAL EDITION®
Life, Love and Family!

YES! Please send me 2 FREE Silhouette Special Edition® novels and my 2 FREE gifts. After receiving them, if I don't wish to receive any more books, I can return the shipping statement marked "cancel." If I don't cancel, I will receive 6 brand-new novels every month and be billed just $4.24 per book in the U.S., or $4.99 per book in Canada, plus 25¢ shipping and handling per book and applicable taxes, if any*. That's a savings of at least 15% off the cover price! I understand that accepting the 2 free books and gifts places me under no obligation to buy anything. I can always return a shipment and cancel at any time. Even if I never buy another book from Silhouette, the two free books and gifts are mine to keep forever.

235 SDN EEYU 335 SDN EEY6

Name	(PLEASE PRINT)	
Address		Apt.
City	State/Prov.	Zip/Postal Code

Signature (if under 18, a parent or guardian must sign)

Mail to the Silhouette Reader Service™:
IN U.S.A.: P.O. Box 1867, Buffalo, NY 14240-1867
IN CANADA: P.O. Box 609, Fort Erie, Ontario L2A 5X3

Not valid to current Silhouette Special Edition subscribers.

Want to try two free books from another line?
Call 1-800-873-8635 or visit www.morefreebooks.com.

* Terms and prices subject to change without notice. NY residents add applicable sales tax. Canadian residents will be charged applicable provincial taxes and GST. This offer is limited to one order per household. All orders subject to approval. Credit or debit balances in a customer's account(s) may be offset by any other outstanding balance owed by or to the customer. Please allow 4 to 6 weeks for delivery.

Your Privacy: Silhouette is committed to protecting your privacy. Our Privacy Policy is available online at www.eHarlequin.com or upon request from the Reader Service. From time to time we make our lists of customers available to reputable firms who may have a product or service of interest to you. If you would prefer we not share your name and address, please check here. ☐

SSE07

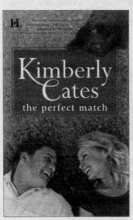

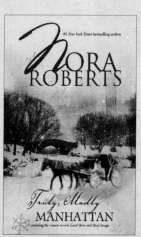

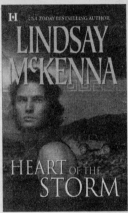

NORA ROBERTS

28561	THE GIFT	___ $7.99 U.S.	___ $9.50 CAN.
28560	THE MacGREGOR BRIDES	___ $7.99 U.S.	___ $9.50 CAN.
28559	THE MacGREGORS:		
	ROBERT & CYBIL	___ $7.99 U.S.	___ $9.50 CAN.
28545	THE MacGREGORS:		
	DANIEL & IAN	___ $7.99 U.S.	___ $9.50 CAN.
28541	IRISH DREAMS	___ $7.99 U.S.	___ $9.50 CAN.
28533	TIME AND AGAIN	___ $7.99 U.S.	___ $9.50 CAN.
28529	DANGEROUS	___ $7.99 U.S.	___ $9.50 CAN.
28503	GOING HOME	___ $7.99 U.S.	___ $9.50 CAN.
28505	REUNION	___ $7.99 U.S.	___ $9.50 CAN.
21892	WINNER TAKES ALL	___ $7.99 U.S.	___ $9.50 CAN.
28504	WITH OPEN ARMS	___ $7.99 U.S.	___ $9.50 CAN.

(limited quantities available)

TOTAL AMOUNT	$ _____
POSTAGE & HANDLING	$ _____
($1.00 FOR 1 BOOK, 50¢ for each additional)	
APPLICABLE TAXES*	$ _____
TOTAL PAYABLE	$ _____

(check or money order—please do not send cash)

To order, complete this form and send it, along with a check or money order for the total above, payable to Harlequin Books, to: **In the U.S.:** 3010 Walden Avenue, P.O. Box 9077, Buffalo, NY 14269-9077; **In Canada:** P.O. Box 636, Fort Erie, Ontario, L2A 5X3.

Name: _____

Address: _____ City: _____

State/Prov.: _____ Zip/Postal Code: _____

Account Number (if applicable): _____

075 CSAS

*New York residents remit applicable sales taxes.
*Canadian residents remit applicable GST and provincial taxes.

Silhouette®
Where love comes alive™

Visit Silhouette Books at www.eHarlequin.com   PSNR1207BL